EMMA AND THE BOX OF WONDER

TALES OF WIDOWSWOOD
BOOK SIX

MATTHEW S. COX

DIVISION ZERO PRESS

ISBN (ebook): 978-1-950738-58-8

ISBN (paperback): 978-1-950738-59-5

CONTENTS

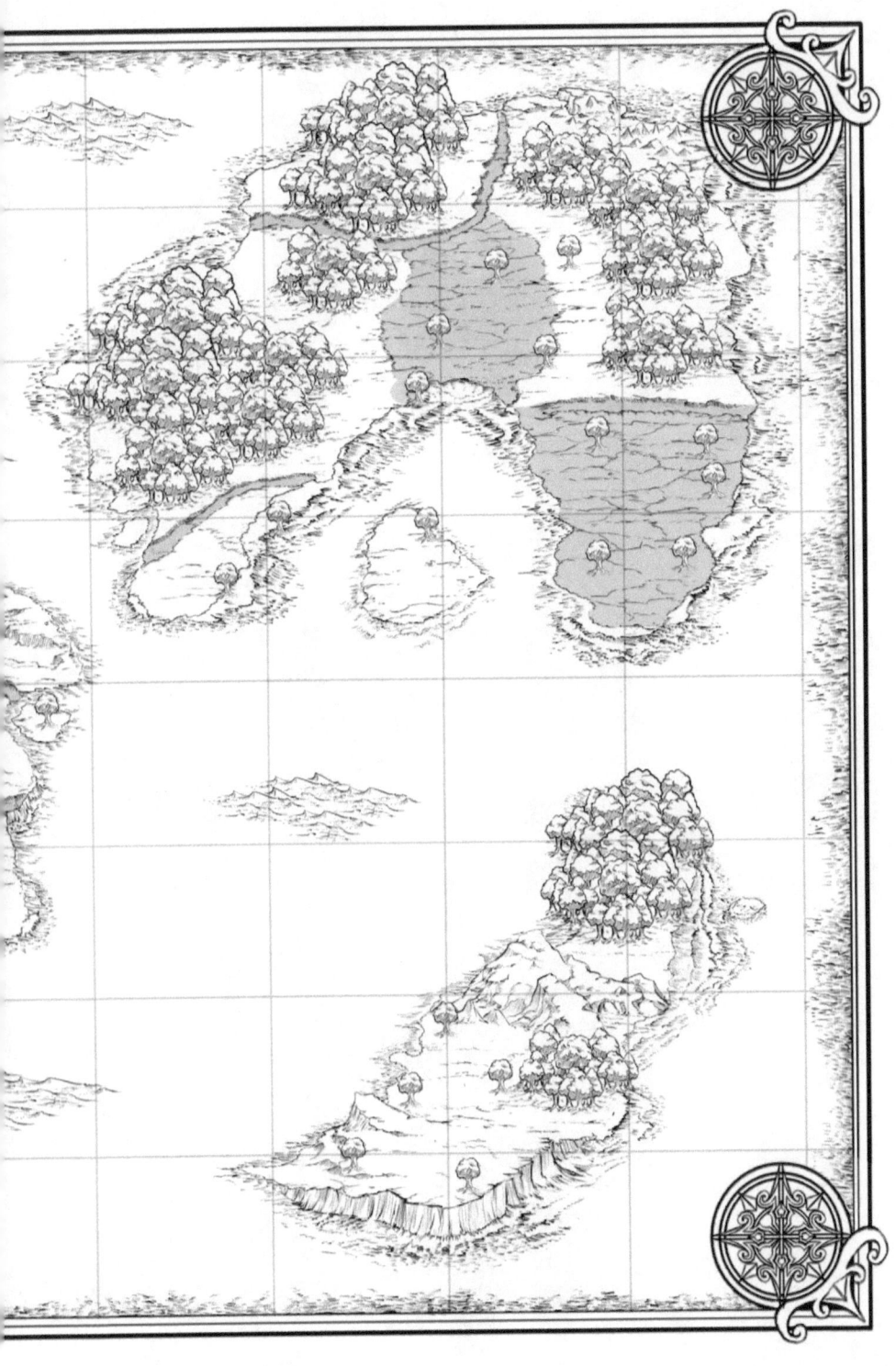

A FOREVER HOME

*F*amily discussions didn't often feel serious, though they usually didn't involve death.

Emma sat on the back porch steps beside Kimber, who did not at all appear to be serious enough for the occasion. Her little sister couldn't stop smiling, or bouncing, or radiating pure joy. They could've been twins insofar as both of them happened to be human, both happened to be girls, both had long hair, and both wore dresses without any shoes. Alas, their similarities ended there. Emma looked much like a younger version of Mama, slim and willowy to the point some people thought they might be sickly, or worse, faerie-touched. While also on the scrawny side thanks to her horrible father and years of not being fed properly, no one ever wondered none-too-quietly about Kimber being part elf. She had green eyes to Emma's blue, fluffy red hair to Emma's straight raven black, and a perfectly ordinary human lifespan.

But none of that mattered to Emma. Kimber belonged to the family as much as if she'd been born to it.

Well, a little bit of it mattered: Kimber's ordinary lifespan.

A thin layer of bright orange ran across the top of Widowswood, the last traces of the day's sunlight. Above the fiery strip, the sky progressed from blue, to darker blue, then indigo. Tiny specks of white flittered across the meadow in the clearing behind the house, spiraling, dipping, and weaving in the wind. They might have been moths or puffweed seeds. A soft, continuous rustle came from the forest, the song of the breeze swaying the outermost branches and all the meadow grass. Here and there, a bird chirped or squawked.

Emma dug her toes into the dirt past the bottom porch step, savoring the sense of being connected to the earth and the life within. She couldn't imagine ever wanting to be anywhere else.

It hadn't been too long ago she learned some secrets about Mama, Nan, and even herself. It's not as though her family never meant for her to find out. They would have told her at some point. The secrets had been secret for an acceptable reason: to let her be a child, be happy, and not have to worry. Of course, now that she'd turned ten and started to notice how other children the same age tended to be bigger than her, Mama decided it time for her to know things.

The people who dwelled near Widowswood long told stories of the Witch of the Wood. They varied from scary to cautionary. Most claimed that in the deepest parts of Widowswood Forest there lived an old woman who took young girls away from their families and kept them forever. Some of the tales said the witch didn't take anyone's daughters; rather, the various sightings of an old crone, a young woman, or a little girl had all been the same person because the Witch of the Wood could appear as any age she cared to.

The truth, as it turned out, hadn't been in any of the stories.

Nan, Emma's beloved grandmother, came from the deep woods. It remained something of a mystery exactly what Nan happened to be… some manner of forest spirit, dryad, ancient elven energy, or perhaps even a dragon—though Emma doubted that one. Nan didn't hoard enough treasure to be a dragon. Simple stories of the Witch had been around for a long time. The ones about her whisking little girls off into the woods only started when people ran into Mama years and years ago. She'd been a child much longer than anyone would imagine normal. Villagers who spotted Mama through the years believed her to be different little girls, since a child who appeared to be nine or ten should not *still* appear to be nine or ten after two decades.

Mama looked around twenty years of age, despite being much older. Exactly *how* old, Mama refused to say, though she did give Emma a hint by saying her true age would be considered exceptionally old for a normal person, though not so old as to be impossible with good luck.

Emma, too, would grow up much slower compared to normal human children. Mama believed it started already. Everyone thought her small for ten. She—as well as her brother, Tam, would take the span of many human childhoods to grow up. Mama told her not to worry about it. She would not feel or think differently from an ordinary child, merely take her sweet old time getting bigger. However, Mama didn't grow up in a village. She'd spent her entire childhood with Nan, the two of them by themselves way off in the forest. Mama didn't have other children around to watch turning into adults while she remained the same. She wouldn't have thought herself strange at all.

Fortunately, or unfortunately as it may be, Emma did not have many close friends. She knew, and sometimes played with, other kids in the village, though never formed an inseparable friendship with them. There had always been something different around her, something the other children picked up on. She couldn't say they'd been afraid of her, or even tried to avoid her. Except for a few mean boys who gave her trouble, the village liked her and its children seemed to as well. Mama did her best to protect and take care of everyone here, and the goodwill she spread extended to her entire family.

Yet, Emma hadn't made any dear friends. She spent most of her time at home watching her little brother and now Kimber, doing chores, all while being way too serious and mature for her age. Knowing she would remain more or less the same while the other children who lived here grew into adults felt strange, but not bad. Mostly, it meant she had a lot more time to have fun before she grew up and had to be responsible *all* the time.

It *did* bother her that Kimber would turn into an old woman before Emma looked even as old as Hannah, the sixteen-year-old who'd come wandering out of the forest some time ago after the Banderwigh released her. Thankfully, Nan could help Kimber. For some reason, Nan, Mama, and Da thought it a highly serious undertaking that required Kimber knowing everything about what would happen if she accepted.

Nan would call upon the magic of Widowswood to infuse Kimber with life energy. It ended up as a sort of bargain with nature. The forest spirits would allow her to live much longer than she ought to otherwise. In exchange, she would be forever bound to Widowswood. If she spent too much time away from the forest, the separation from the spirits would make her progressively weaker. At first, this didn't present a significant problem, but the older she became, the more dangerous distance could be. When the day came where Kimber had lived longer than humans normally do, if she went too far away from Widowswood for even a single month, she could die.

Kimber didn't think it a problem. The look she'd given Da as if he'd said something stupid even made Nan laugh. When the girl told him she'd be dead anyway in a hundred years, so what difference would it make if going too far away could kill her, he relented.

The effect of the weakening could be partially managed with a magical link to someone who already had a deep connection to Widowswood. Emma figured out right away Nan meant her. That way, if Kimber ever wound up too far away from home and got sick, being near Emma would make her feel better and keep her alive, hopefully long enough to get back home. So what if keeping Kimber alive would take so much of Emma's power she wouldn't be able to call upon druidic magic at the same time. They'd both get better after enough time spent home. Even before she knew about being a druid, when she didn't even believe in magic, she'd been ready to get into a fistfight with a grown man—Kimber's awful father—to protect the girl once. This felt like an easy choice.

So, the girls agreed.

Nan explained it as a sort of deal they made with the spirits of the forest. They protect Widowswood and the forest gives them life. Emma didn't mind, as she had no plans to ever go anywhere away from home. She didn't even want to visit other places. Neither did Kimber.

Emma smoothed the fabric of the blue dress Nan made for her over her leg, unable to stop fidgeting in her excitement. This did not sound like a bad idea, despite how grim Da acted about the whole thing. Some people, according to Da, couldn't tolerate living in the same little village forever and experienced something he called wanderlust, which meant they wanted to keep traveling to new places without staying anywhere for long. After everything Kimber had been through in her meager eight years of life, finding a real family who loved and protected her so thrilled her she had no desire to go anywhere else. She didn't want to grow up too fast while Emma and Tam remained children. If she did, she could no longer have fun playing with them... and worse, would have to watch her siblings get sad when she turned old and eventually had to go away to the realm of the dead.

She'd not hesitated at all when Da kept asking her if she was sure she wanted the magic.

Nan appeared to believe Kimber did truly understand and prepared to go ahead with the ritual tonight. Mama acted pleased as well, though she didn't bounce around like Kimber or Emma.

"You really understand it?" whispered Emma.

"Aye. Why ya fink I donnae?" Kimber made a silly face. "An' I fought it was yer idea, roight? Ya keep askin' me if I's sure. I'm sure. I kinna be 'appier, 'avin a real mama, da, sister, and bruvvah."

Emma laughed. Kimber's accent—from the not so nice parts of Calebrin City—always shone through in her voice whenever her emotions ran high. It proved her sister couldn't be more thrilled.

"I mean..." Emma glanced over at her. "How we'll be connected. What Nan said about the magic needs to go through our fey blood."

"Aye. Es loike 'ow Mama and Da are togevvah fer a long time." Kimber swished her feet back and forth over the weeds growing near the bottom step. "Oi know Oi donnae got the fey blood loike you an' Tam. But donnae care none."

"Almost. We wouldn't be like Mama and Da. We're sisters."

Kimber lifted her head, grinning at her past a fluff of wild red hair draped half over her face. "I kinnae wait."

The fiery stripe of fading sunlight shimmered behind the treetops, no longer above them. Night would be there soon, and with it, the moon.

"You understand what it means?" asked Nan, behind them.

Emma twisted to peer up at her grandmother. She'd donned her cloak and carried her walking stick, a sure sign the time had come to go into the forest. Mama, Da, and Tam stood behind her.

"Aye." Kimber stood and turned to face everyone. "If I go tae far off'n the woods, I'ma get sick and moight die."

The wrinkles on Nans' face deepened as she smiled. She reached out and patted Kimber on the head, then caressed her cheek. "Not for a long time, my dear. But, eventually, yes."

Kimber leapt into a hug, almost taking the old one off her feet. "I donnae wan' evah leave me family er me home."

"What about me?" whispered Tam.

Wonder and worry made her six-year-old brother's deep brown eyes large. His fluffy orb of light brown hair surrounded a face of total innocence. Emma couldn't help but think he looked an awful lot like a giant faerie who didn't have wings... or pointy ears. His smallish size and hints of fey in his features occasionally got him teased by bigger boys. But it also made him irresistible to every auntie and grandmother in the town proper.

"Tam..." Emma stood, stepped up onto the porch, and squeezed him. "You don't need it. You're already part forest spirit. It's why you're so adorable."

The boy held up his wooden sword and tried to puff up his chest. "I'm not adorable. I'm a knight."

Mama rested her face against Da's shoulder and shook as if trying to laugh without making a sound.

"Well then, it's almost time." Nan squinted at the darkening sky. "Are you ready, child?"

Kimber bounced on her toes. "Yes."

"Are you absolutely certain?" Da took a knee in front of her and held both the girl's hands in his. "This is what you want?"

"Aye. Why wouldn' I? I don' wan' 'o ge' big befaw Emma. Then we cannae play an' she'd be choked."

Emma put a hand to her neck. "Choked? What?"

Kimber exhaled hard out her nose. "Choked. Like when ya be so sad, ya cannae speak."

"Liam..." Mama leaned close to Da and whispered, "It's not as grim as you're making it out to be. Yes, she will be bound to the woods, but by the time it's dangerous, she'd already be old if not dead."

Da rose from his knee and looked at Mama. "It can't be so simple. There has to be some great price she will regret."

"Why do you say that?" Nan ambled closer, raising an eyebrow. "The child makes a bargain with me and with the spirits of the wood, not with foul demons." She headed down the steps. "And it's less of a bargain than me granting a boon to my granddaughter."

Kimber squealed in delight, again bouncing.

Emma and Kimber hurried to follow Nan as she headed toward the forest edge.

"So, you can simply make anyone you care to immortal?" Da rushed up along Nan's right side.

"Liam, it is not immortality. None of you, not Bethany, not Emma, Tam, or Kimber are or will be immortal." Nan clucked. "You are not elves. This is merely additional time."

Da stared at her in silent contemplation for a moment. "You didn't include yourself in that."

"I did not," said Nan matter-of-factly, stepping over a root and balancing on her walking stick.

Emma covered her mouth to hold back a giggle.

"You are immortal?" Da leaned back, both eyebrows up.

"Perhaps. I still haven't quite figured that out." Nan winked at him. "I shall know eventually, I suppose."

Emma closed her eyes as they entered the forest and called out to the spirit of plants and trees. "Linganthas, please guide my step."

A tingle of magic radiated outward from her chest, tingling down her arms and legs. Thorny vines, weeds, and the undergrowth receded, curling out of her way as she neared until she passed, then going back as it had been before. Emma extended the spell to Kimber and Tam by holding their hands. Mama did the same for Da. Thinking about all the people who tried to find Nan or Mama out in the woods before she decided to live in Widowswood Village almost made Emma laugh. Linganthas allowed them to walk through the thickest of brambles and not leave a trace. No ordinary farmer could follow them—or even tell where they'd been.

Kimber swished her free arm around, looking around at the trees, ever in search of the next chance to spot a faerie. The girl didn't appear to be the least bit afraid of the dark or anything else. Emma could barely contain her joy as well. She practically skipped along.

Soon, Nan decided they'd reached a spot perfect for the ritual. This particular patch of forest didn't look terribly important. No grand stones, no huge tree, no lifespring bubbling up with pure water. They'd merely found a space among the trees with a nice area of flat open space.

Emma glanced around. Her grandmother hadn't been too forthcoming with information about what the ritual would involve. They might need to lay down and be painted head to toe in glyphs drawn from mud or perhaps sit in a pool of water together. Yet, Nan didn't bring a big satchel of supplies, nor had they gone to a spring, creek, or other source of water. Allowing Kimber to stay alive for so much longer than humans usually lived had to be a big deal. Shouldn't the ritual be a big deal, too? Complicated?

"All right." Nan pointed at the ground. "Kimber, you stand there." She moved her finger a little to the side. "Emma, there."

Kimber dutifully marched over to the spot and stood, arms clamped to her sides, trying not to laugh.

Emma moved to stand in front of Kimber, facing her about an arm's length away. She couldn't make eye contact without smiling. Her smile made Kimber giggle, which got Emma laughing. This all seemed so serious and huge. It shouldn't be funny, but they couldn't stop giggling.

Nan smiled, as did Mama. Da stood there with his head titled somewhat to the side, seeming baffled. Tam wandered in circles, not particularly interested in anything more than his pretend guard duty to stop any goblins from bothering them.

A few minutes later, the laughter subsided. Emma and Kimber managed to stand there looking at each other without snickering, merely grinning. Nan walked over to stand on their right, arms out to either side. Mama stood opposite her. Neither spoke or did much more than close their eyes.

Emma took a deep breath and tried to be serious. This moment would make Kimber even more a part of the family. Nan acted as if the magic she prepared to infuse them with happened all the time, no great task. Emma knew better. She recognized Nan's way. Perhaps the actual doing it part would be easy for her. But… she wouldn't simply do it for anyone. That she'd agreed to do the ritual for Kimber—because Emma asked her to—proved Nan considered the girl part of their family, too.

Small orbs of green light appeared out of nowhere, flying in circles around the four of them. Every few seconds, another one appeared. Even more light orbs emerged from nearby trees, gliding over to join the swirling mass. The air took on a charge; Emma's skin tingled. Kimber's hair fluffed up, as did Emma's.

The giggly expression on Kimber's face turned awestruck as she floated up off the ground. Her eyes fluttered and her head tilted forward as if she'd become too drowsy to stay awake.

Emma, whispered a distant feminine voice. *You wish to serve as a conduit for this young one?*

She had no idea what 'conduit' meant, but Emma knew two things. One: Nan already explained how she would be like a bridge, allowing energy to move between Widowswood and Kimber. Two: the voice whispering in her mind sounded like Mythandriel herself.

"Yes," whispered Emma. "I would like very much for my sister to be able to stay with us and I want to help her any way I can."

This boon, I do not grant lightly, child. A sense of a smile washed over her. *I feel the depth of your love and your desire to protect this one. So shall it be done. Your souls are entwined.*

The forest disappeared.

Emma found herself in a dingy shack, cowering away from Old Man Drinn—Kimber's horrible father. He raised a hand and swung it down at her face. The image changed before the strike made contact. She lay curled up on cobblestones in the rain, tucked against the side of a bleak grey building. A small barred window at ground level beside her looked in on a prison cell holding her father. She had nowhere else to go, so she slept in the alley outside his cell. Again, the image shifted. She saw through Kimber's eyes as the girl half climbed, half got thrown through a window into a rich person's house. Even though her father treated her horribly, she would help him break into the place to steal. She didn't care about money. Kimber believed if she did this, he might start to love her.

Emma fumed. If the man hadn't already died, she'd have thumped him.

Again, the image shifted. Kimber sat on the floor in the loft at Emma's home, looking at her and Tam. Tiny ghostly lights danced around Emma. She remembered using the Wildkin Whisper to make the magical lights appear for a few seconds while she officially declared Kimber part of the family. Kimber believed it worked and clung to this memory as the happiest moment of her life. Emma felt a little guilty for deceiving her. The spell had nothing to do with making the girl part of the family. She'd cast the spell because it created some tiny dancing lights, hoping her sister would see 'magic' happen and think she'd *really* become family. Guilt didn't last long before Emma dismissed it. The 'officialness' of being part of a family didn't require magic, merely acceptance. Emma wholly embraced Kimber as a sister, so the magic—even though it only let her talk to animals—served as a way to show her feelings.

Emma opened her eyes. A stream of blue-white energy connected upward from her chest to Kimber's. The girl's long, fluffy red hair swirled around in the air above her like she'd been caught in a tornado, despite Emma not feeling any wind. After a few seconds, the energy stream disappeared, though Emma still felt something tickling her heart.

Dozens of floating green light orbs swirled around them, spinning faster and faster until they became rings of light. The dazzling display of druidic magic collapsed inward on Kimber and disappeared. For an instant, her emerald-green eyes glowed bright, then faded back to normal. The magical energy holding her up in the air ebbed, allowing her to float back down to her feet.

"It is done," said Nan.

Tam faced Da and saluted with his wooden sword. "No goblins in sight."

"I don' feel any diffren'," whispered Kimber.

Nan smiled. "That is good."

"Did it work?" asked Emma.

Nan playfully scoffed, rolling her eyes. "Did it work, she says. Of course, it worked." She tugged at her shawl. "Do you think me an apprentice druid?"

Emma grinned.

"Come then, girls." Nan made a goofy face at Emma, then urged them to start walking with a hand to their backs. "It's well past your bedtime."

2

A PLAY DATE GONE WRONG

*L*ittle about Kimber appeared different.

In the following few days after the ritual, life continued as it had before. The most noticeable change as far as Emma could tell happened to her: she no longer felt sad worrying about Kimber growing up way too fast. Nan's ritual gave her more time, but *only* time. It didn't grant her any strange faerie powers, magic, or protection. They still had to be careful. Anything that might harm an ordinary human child could still hurt Kimber. Such things could still harm Emma, too. She didn't worry so much about being hurt herself as she did protecting her younger siblings.

They also had to prepare for the other children in the town of Widowswood growing up while they remained small. Obviously, Nan couldn't do the ritual for everyone, not that Emma wanted her to. She wouldn't be heartbroken if the other kids couldn't play with her anymore because they'd become adults. Not like she often played with them, anyway.

However, she and Kimber did have something of a friend in Ambril Starling. Daughter to a wealthy gem and jewelry merchant, the girl spent most of her time alone at home. Her mother didn't want her associating with 'peasants' if at all possible, fearing it would make

Ambril 'too common' in sensibility. The few other girls in town wealthy enough to earn her mother's approval didn't really make 'friends' as much as they tolerated each other's company, because it happened to be the socially acceptable thing to do. Rich girls spent their time with rich girls, and so on.

Alas, the town of Widowswood didn't have too many wealthy families. What counted as 'wealthy' here wouldn't even be close to wealthy in a big city like Calebrin, where the Starlings—and Da— came from. Only three other girls near in age to Ambril, with enough money for her mother to approve of, lived here. Neither Emma nor Ambril much cared for them, considering them quite shallow, self-absorbed, and petty. Since Mrs. Starling demanded her daughter spend social time with these girls, Ambril pretended to smile but honestly dreaded every minute in their company.

In Emma and Kimber, she found two friends who didn't care about how much money her parents had or how many fancy toys they could play with if they pretended to like her. At first, Mrs. Starling disapproved of her daughter even speaking to a pair of dirt-covered barefoot 'commoners' and would not normally have allowed them to play together *outside,* much less invite Emma and Kimber into the house.

A magical mishap caused by an addled old alchemist carelessly disposing of failed potions fooled everyone into thinking Ambril had been abducted. Emma found her, and Nan succeeded in reversing the magic responsible for shrinking the girl to the size of a mouse. As such, Mrs. Starling managed to set aside her opinions and allowed Ambril to befriend Emma and Kimber. The woman still looked down her nose somewhat at them for running around without shoes and in the simplest of dresses, but didn't complain out loud. It seemed she realized her daughter truly enjoyed having genuine friends rather than self-absorbed pretend princesses.

Emma liked Ambril, though thought her a bit strange for her preoccupation with fancy dresses, fancier shoes, fear of dirt, fear of bugs, and so on. She did not, however, believe it necessary to change the girl's opinion on anything and simply accepted her oddities as they were. If Ambril preferred to be stuck in a burdensome, heavy gown, it didn't have any effect on Emma at all, so no need to quibble about it. Likewise, Ambril didn't try to 'civilize' Emma or Kimber by insisting that they dress properly.

Of course, they did play dress-up on occasion. Emma didn't mind putting on the fancy things for a few minutes to laugh at herself. Ambril had a closet full of gowns, after all.

Today, Emma and Kimber went into Widowswood Town to spend a while at Ambril's house. She'd invited them over for an event she called a 'play date.' Evidently, once a family had a certain amount of money, they needed to schedule the times their children could have fun. Emma thought it horribly stuffy and perhaps a bit cruel. Ambril didn't seem to mind. At least Mrs. Starling no longer watched her and Kimber like a town guard keeping an eye on thieves.

It helped that the Starlings knew Da came from Calebrin and his family had money. Despite Emma's fondness for the plain life she'd always known, thanks to her father, she technically counted as 'wealthy enough' to be an approved friend. It baffled Mrs. Starling how Da 'allowed' Emma to prance about like a peasant child, though she confined her complaining to her husband, speaking in low whispers when she didn't think the girls could hear them.

Emma didn't consider Mrs. Starling to be a bad person, merely confused and perhaps a bit preoccupied with money and status. The woman thought the wrong things in life were important. Money, prestige, social standing, and a strange set of silly, arbitrary rules she called 'etiquette.' The woman would gasp in shock if Emma or Kimber used the wrong spoon or fork at the wrong time during lunch. Quite hilarious to watch her reactions, though Emma didn't do it wrong on purpose. A fork was a fork. Silly and wasteful to have four of them for one person at one meal.

Tam decided he did not fancy spending late morning into afternoon in a wealthy girl's bedroom watching three older girls play with dolls and do girl things. So, he accompanied Mama on her rounds throughout Widowswood. Emma felt a little bad for not minding him, but Mama told her not to worry and to enjoy the time she had to be a child. She didn't need to be a mama yet, especially not to her little brother.

Ambril greeted them at the door when they arrived, as thrilled to see them as if they'd been family separated for months. The gemcutter's daughter was also ten years old, like Emma, though a little taller and not as willowy. She somewhat resembled her mother in that they both had long, straight blonde hair, blue eyes, and presently wore the same style of peach-colored fancy dress, and the same emerald teardrop earrings. A silver pendant hung from Ambril's neck in the shape of a five-pointed hollow star with a little sapphire trapped inside.

Though the accessories looked pretty, Emma thought it strange for a girl so young to wear such expensive jewelry. It probably explained why she wasn't allowed to go play outside, since she'd be likely to lose them if she did anything even remotely fun.

Ambril let out a delighted squeal and hugged Emma into Kimber.

Mrs. Starling made a face, not approving of the undignified greeting. She said nothing, instead shifting her attention to Mama, who'd walked the girls there, engaging in pleasant conversation. Emma took no small degree of humor in how Mrs. Starling didn't dare make faces at Mama for wearing common clothing. Surprisingly, Ambril's mother did genuinely appear to respect her.

While Mama and Mrs. Starling spoke in the foyer, Ambril practically dragged Emma and Kimber to her second-floor bedroom. Despite the exquisite plush carpet, the rich girl bafflingly insisted on wearing shoes inside. Emma couldn't help herself and rolled around on the thick carpet.

"It's so soft, like a bed." Emma swished her arms back and forth as if playing in snow.

"You're acting like a little puppy." Ambril knelt by the big dollhouse, grinning at her.

Emma rolled over and rubbed her cheek across the plush material, then made a soft yip like a wolf pup. She'd spent hours watching actual wolf pups at the grove with Greyfang and Moonsong and could imitate them perfectly.

Kimber and Ambril burst into giggles.

Sprawled on the floor, Emma, Kimber, and Ambril played with dolls and the giant dollhouse taller than them. In the midst of a truly happy moment, Emma suffered a pang of guilt.

"Ambril?" she whispered rather than say a line in the character of her doll. "I'd like to tell you something."

"What?" Ambril spun her head to stare at her. "Please say it isn't that you have to go already? You've only just arrived."

Emma smiled. "No. We don't have to leave yet."

"You are having fun?" Ambril bit her lower lip.

"Yes. Quite." Emma exhaled. "It's not that. I want to tell you something about us, so you know the truth and aren't confused."

"All right." Ambril set her doll down. "Is it a secret?"

Emma thought it over. "Umm. Not really. I mean, you shouldn't go about telling everyone all at once, but you don't have to keep it to yourself."

Ambril nodded. "What is it then?"

"You know Nan is..."

"People made up stories about her." Ambril lowered her voice to a whisper. "The Witch of the Wood. It's not real, it's just things they made up about her because they didn't know."

Kimber put on a toy tiara studded in false diamonds, then flashed a cheesy smile.

"Mostly." Emma fidgeted at the doll in her hands. "There's some fey blood in my family. Not elves. Some sort of fey spirits."

"Of course, silly." Ambril smiled. "You look somewhat like a half-elf."

"Wot's a half elf?" Kimber tilted her head; the tiara fell off.

"It's a person whose mum and papa are an elf and a human. I've met one or two when we go to the big city sometimes." Ambril reached over to touch Emma's ear. "But you're not, 'cause your ears aren't pointy. I thought you might've had a half-elf grandparent."

Emma shrugged. "Close. What I want to tell you is... we're growing up really slow. People thought the Witch of the Wood stole little girls away from their families because they saw my Mama when she was small. She stayed small for a long time, so people thought they kept seeing different girls wandering in the forest."

"Oh, wow. How lovely." Ambril hugged her doll.

"You're not sad?" Emma blinked.

"Why would I be sad?" Ambril resumed making the dolls have a tea party.

"Because you're gonna grow up and we'll still be this size." Emma added her doll to the party.

"It will be fine. Even if I'm bigger than you, we can still play and have tea parties. If you'd care to." Ambril let out a small sigh. "And if Father doesn't send me away to be married. I don't think he will, though. He's not like those other girls' fathers. If I don't want to do something, he won't insist."

Emma played in silence for a moment, then peered over at her. "We'll still be children and you'll be grown."

"You don't act much like a child already." Ambril poured imaginary tea for the dolls. "Always so serious... except when you are here and we play. I think you should keep visiting, even if I am all grown up."

"Okay." Kimber laughed.

"I suppose. If you're sure it's all right." Emma scratched her head, confused at how this girl could have such little reaction to the news.

"Of course it is." Ambril made a silly face. "You already ignore the rules of society, traipsing about in common rags without even shoes on, not knowing which fork belongs to the appetizer and which to the entrée. Why should it surprise anyone you ignore the rules of time, too?"

The girl's utter lack of seriousness made Emma crack up into giggles all over again.

"I treasure having you as friends." Ambril looked back and forth between Emma and Kimber. "I may grow up and have to move away or I may stay here my entire life. Right now, I'm ten years old and don't know what the future will bring. I do know that I am grateful we met and hope that you continue to be my friend no matter how far apart we may be, either in time or place."

"You go' that from ae book?" asked Kimber. "Soun' like the way Da talks."

"No, I just said it." Ambril lightly poked Kimber on the tip of the nose. "Though, I do read a rather lot of books. Perhaps I remembered words from different stories and put them together. Truly, it is how I feel."

"She's not talking like Da." Emma tickled Kimber. "She's smart... and educated."

Ambril laughed. "Are you saying your father is not smart?"

Emma blinked. "No. I mean, you are smart, too. You're not trying to talk like Da."

"Wha's educated?" Kimber scrunched her nose.

"She has a tutor." Emma made her doll sip tea.

"Does it 'urt?" Kimber winced.

Ambril laughed. "Only when I fall asleep while reading the most boring, dreadful things and my head hits the table."

They kept playing for a while, talking a little about everything, from how Emma and Kimber would take a long time to grow up to what it meant to have a tutor. Once they'd had enough of dolls for now, they proceeded to play with Ambril's vast collection of toys, mostly puzzle boxes, wooden horses, or games. Emma lost herself in the fun of it, enjoying the time not having to worry about taking care of Tam or being responsible.

Eventually, a servant called the girls downstairs for lunch.

After a nice meal of bread, cheese, sliced meat, and fruit, they went out to sit in the garden. Ambril's father hired workmen years ago to dig a small stream along the house's rear wall. It ran off through a hole in the backyard wall to rejoin the larger natural creek the water diverted from on the north. It made the garden prettier, but Emma had no temptation to go wading in it. The little waterway served the same purpose as a privy, thanks to a garderobe on the second story hanging over it. Ambril's parents had so much money, they had an outhouse put into their house. The water carried the foulness away. Of course, constantly flowing water would be reasonably clean. Still, she didn't want to be in the water at the wrong time.

Sitting in the grass—Ambril on a bench, of course, so as not to ruin her dress—and talking about this, that, and nothing offered a most bizarre combination of boring and interesting. She suspected Ambril had to suffer through many insincere conversations with the other wealthy girls, where they each tried to brag about their fathers or families. Now, with Emma and Kimber to talk to, the conversation involved fanciful topics like faeries, dragons, and magic, as well as the usual prattle about notable goings-on in town. Naturally, Ambril couldn't resist asking Emma about her aunt's wedding. Da's younger sister Jamie recently married in Calebrin.

Emma got to dishing on the affair, telling Ambril all about the ceremony and the following party… then going into detail about how insufferable some of Da's family was. She softened that part by pointing out the blame for most of it rested on a long-dead necromancer haunting the mansion.

Ambril stared at her, clutching a small folding fan to her chest. "You are being serious about all that?"

"Yes." Emma exhaled. "It was really scary."

"A big 'airy spoider leap' from the chamber pot an' tried ta nip Emma on the butt!" Kimber squirmed. "I screamed so loud!"

"Eek." Ambril shivered. "That sounds so horrible."

"It was." Emma squirmed. "I don't like undead things."

"Who does?" Ambril fanned herself. "Why would you even say that?"

Emma held her arms out to either side. "I mean, they're *extra* icky to me. Death magic is the direct opposite to mine."

"Oh. I see." Ambril exhaled. "Can we talk of something else? Oh, Papa recently returned from Sondaren with a bunch of treasures."

"Wot's a Sondaren?" asked Kimber.

"I don't know." Emma swished her feet back and forth in the grass.

Ambril chuckled. "It's another kingdom, south of us. If you go all the way to the bottom end, there's a harbor city where boats come in from all over. Papa goes there once or twice a year to buy fancy things from other places."

"Ooh," said Kimber.

Ambril leaned forward, flashing a mischievous grin. "Want to go see the treasure room?"

"Treasure room?" Kimber looked up from a fuzzy green caterpillar crawling over her toes. "Wot's 'at?"

Before she could say a word, Ambril noticed the bug and froze, staring at it in horror as if a monster that could devour all three of them had already begun to eat Kimber.

"Wot?" asked Kimber. "Why ya lookin' at me like 'at? A fink ya gonna faint."

"There's a creature on your foot." Ambril pointed her shaking fan at it.

"Is a 'pillar." Kimber held her foot up higher. "He won' 'urt nobody. Wanna 'old him?"

Ambril leaned back. "No, thank you. He's all yours."

"What's a treasure room?" Emma leaned against Kimber, watching the caterpillar crawl over the girl's foot and start up her leg toward her knee.

"It's where Papa puts things he's collected while traveling that he wants to sell but hasn't gotten around to taking to the shop yet." Ambril looked away from the fuzzy creature and fanned herself. "He also makes rings and necklaces there when he's home and doesn't want to walk all the way to the shop."

All the way? Emma stopped herself from laughing. After visiting Calebrin City, the whole of Widowswood Town seemed tiny. Going to the jewelry shop from here would take less than two minutes. Though, perhaps if it rained, he wouldn't want to get wet, or maybe he preferred to be here with his family than at the store with only a few hired guards for company.

"Can we see it?" Kimber plucked the caterpillar off her shin and set it on the ground.

Emma twirled a strand of her hair around her finger. "If we won't get you in trouble."

"You won't get me in trouble." Ambril stood up from the stone bench. "But you have to promise not to touch anything. Some of the music boxes are delicate. I'm not even allowed to touch them unless Papa is there."

"Okay." Emma took Kimber's hand. "We won't."

"Promise." Kimber tucked her other hand behind her back. "Won't touch nothin'."

Ambril smiled, then led the way back into the house. They entered through the backdoor after crossing a tiny stone bridge over the 'moat', then proceeded past a few servants in the hall to the stairs. On the third floor, Ambril went left, hurrying past multiple closed doors on both sides.

The size of the Starling house used to leave Emma staring in disbelief. Now that she'd been to Calebrin and seen the enormous manor Da grew up in, this place didn't feel so overwhelming. It might not even be the biggest house in Widowswood Town. A handful of other wealthy families built homes here as well. Some lived here, some only lived here for part of the year in the warmer months.

Ambril stopped at a large set of double doors, opened the one on the left, and went inside. Emma followed, making sure to hold Kimber's hand. It's not that she didn't trust Kimber to keep her promise not to touch things. More that she knew her little sister could easily be overwhelmed with emotion and might be so fascinated at the sight of a pretty thing she'd reach out to touch it before thinking.

Unlike most of the rooms in the house, this one did not have carpeting. Dark, polished hardwood covered a space a little smaller than the average ballroom. Various tables held display cases showing off everything from strange helmets to decorated animal horns to jewelry boxes, little vases, and all manner of stuff. Most of it didn't appear to be valuable. At least, the items looked to be made of common materials. Any value they might have possessed would've come from their exotic nature or perhaps great age. Three tall, narrow windows in the opposite wall allowed daylight in past massive teal-blue curtains. A single heavy wooden door with a rounded top appeared to be the only other way out of the room.

Ambril knew what some of the items were, thanks to her father teaching her. She told them about a damaged helmet made of iron and leather with a pointy spike on top. It had evidently come from a far-off land named Ondremmar, worn by someone important several hundred years ago who died in a battle. The horn once belonged to something called a clansman from the Bannoc. Sensing confusion, Ambril went on to explain the Bannoc was like a kingdom, but they didn't have a king or queen. Instead, multiple separate clans lived there and each one ruled a little piece of the land. If an outside nation made war, the clans would often come together as one to defend their homes. This horn had something to do with their god of war, perhaps used to sound a call to battle or maybe as part of their rituals honoring their gods.

The girls spent a while wandering around admiring artifacts.

"He jes' leaves all this sittin' out 'ere?" Kimber whistled. "The room nae even locked."

"None of this is worth much gold." Ambril gestured around. "Only a collector or a historian would pay a lot of money for these things. Thieves wouldn't think anything here was worth stealing."

Kimber scratched her head. "'Ow can somefin' cost a lo' a money but no' look et?"

"Well…" Ambril pointed at an old iron dagger in a case. It didn't appear sharp anymore, rusted in spots, even cracked. "It doesn't appear to be worth much, right?"

"No." Kimber shook her head. "Looks broke."

"Right." Ambril lowered her voice to almost a whisper. "A really long time ago, someone tried to kill the king of Andorath. The old king used to be a warrior and still knew how to fight. Even though he only carried this dagger, he beat the assassin."

"Eep." Emma fidgeted. "That knife killed someone?"

"So Papa says." Ambril shrugged. "It's got some value to scholars because it belonged to a king, not because of what it is."

Kimber furrowed her brows. "I donnae see 'ow a dagger is worth more 'cause a king 'ad it. Tis nae gold er magic."

Emma and Ambril laughed.

"Let's look at nicer things." Ambril pointed at some music boxes.

Since she wasn't allowed to touch anything without her father present, Ambril settled for whistling or singing the tunes each one made in between telling Emma and Kimber where each one came from. In fairness, her father hadn't been to all those other kingdoms. He obtained the music boxes from traders who took boats or from other merchants who'd been across the ocean.

Right before Ambril started humming another tune, she froze, staring at the door.

Murmuring voices out in the hallway drew closer.

"Eep!" whispered Ambril. "Quick. Hide!"

She ran to the leftmost window, closest to the round-topped door, and ducked behind the curtain. Emma and Kimber raced after her, squishing together to hide. The curtain barely stopped moving when the outer door to the 'treasure room' opened.

Emma held her breath, feeling conflicted. Ambril's reaction made it seem like she would get in trouble for being in this room, perhaps more so for bringing two other children with her. Almost everything there looked breakable. Still, it didn't seem right for Ambril to run and hide. Her father tended to be lenient, especially if she made sad eyes at him. Da once made a remark about the man being lucky Ambril wasn't like most high society daughters and kept demanding he buy her fancy things.

The girls hadn't touched a thing, so the worst punishment they'd likely face would be a sternly worded 'don't do that again.' Yet, Ambril ran for the curtain like a girl terrified of a severe beating for slight misbehavior. As far as Emma knew, Mr. Starling never raised a hand to her. He barely raised his voice.

"Well, this is a bit of a mess, ain't it," whispered a man who did not sound like Mr. Starling.

"Just a small one. We can manage," replied a second man.

Multiple footsteps on the hardwood floor drew closer, almost as if they walked straight at the curtain. Emma braced herself to be caught. Ambril squeezed her hand a bit too tight for simple worry over getting scolded for going in here without her father present. She appeared pale and tried to hold her breath to stay as quiet as possible. The fear in her friend's eyes set off Emma's protective inner wolf spirit.

Something was wrong.

3

THE WORKSHOP

*S*omeone moved close to the curtain—but went past it.

A doorknob rattled as if locked.

"Figures," muttered a man with a bit of a scratch in his voice.

"Go on then. Make it quick," said the other, his voice smooth and refined like a minstrel's.

"Hurry it along already," whisper-shouted a third man who sounded farther away.

Soft scratching and rattling noises came from the door.

"Are you certain this is where he keeps the good stuff?" whispered the minstrel.

"Of course I am certain." grumbled the scratchy-throated man. "Been watching the place for months."

The click of a man in hard-soled shoes pacing came from the middle of the room. "That's one thing, but we aren't finished yet. Where's the princess?"

Ambril nearly crushed Emma's hand.

"Saw her go upstairs wit' them other two kids," said the gruff man, who seemed to be the one near the curtain by the door.

"She's not in her room," replied the minstrel. "We can't leave here without her, or the rest of the plan falls apart."

Ambril closed her eyes and mouthed, "Not again..."

A click came from the right.

"Got it. Door's open," whispered the man with the gruff voice.

"Worry not." The more distant man stopped pacing. "I don't think we'll have to go too far to find our princess. Look there. Bunch o' toes and two fancy little shoes peeking out from under that curtain."

Before anyone could pounce or grab them, Emma burst out from behind the curtain and cut loose with her best attempt at a war cry. Two men close by on her right near the door yelped and scrambled backward so abruptly they almost tripped over each other. The third man, about fifteen feet away in the middle of the room, shook his head and appeared to be fighting the urge to laugh.

All three wore simple shirts, pants, and shoes, the same type of attire worn by the male servants Mr. Starling hired to help maintain the grounds and house.

The two who jumped collected themselves and glared at her.

Emma raised her hand, making a hint of lightning dance between her fingers. "I'll not let you hurt Ambril."

The men took another step back, evidently concerned at the display of magic, but not frightened enough to run away as she'd hoped. She narrowed her eyes at them one at a time. The shortest man had a square face darkened by going too long without a shave. The second man appeared well groomed and relatively handsome. He had to be the 'minstrel.' Man three, who kept his distance, appeared unremarkable in every respect. Neither tall, nor short, handsome, nor ugly.

Ambril darted forward to the nearest table and swiped a fancy letter opener, which she brandished in the manner of a dagger at the men.

Emma made tiny arcs of lightning dance across her hands again. "Go away while you still can."

Alas, the men didn't seem terribly afraid of a girl her age. Emma truly didn't want to harm anyone, but she wouldn't simply let them hurt Ambril.

"I don't have magic." Ambril raised the letter opener higher. "But what I do have is a particular set of skills."

The men exchanged glances, then stared at her in confusion.

Ambril held her chin high. "I know which utensils to use for which course of a grand meal. I can say hello and introduce myself in nine different languages. I am familiar with the twelve proper types of gowns and on what occasions to wear each one... and I can walk across an entire ballroom without dislodging a stack of books balanced upon my head. I am also quite capable of delivering a rather scathing critique of one's shoddy wardrobe or manners."

"Oy," muttered Kimber. "That sounds roight 'andy. I'm sure this lot'll be quite cross wif yas fer tellin' 'em 'eir clothes are dodgy an' cheap."

The farthest man waved dismissively at the girls. "Get them already."

"Run!" yelled Kimber before darting for the round-topped door the men had obligingly unlocked.

With nowhere else to go and no time to think, Emma grabbed Ambril by the wrist and dragged her along. Kimber yanked the door open, waited for them to pass by, then jumped in and pulled it shut. The men outside didn't say or do much. They might've even been laughing under their breath.

Their lack of urgency made frightening sense when Emma realized they'd gone into a relatively small room with no way out. The men must know the girls only trapped themselves even worse. Out in the treasure room, they had some chance, however small, of dodging around the men and running for the double doors. In here, they'd never make it back out the door without being caught.

"Oops," said Kimber. "I'm sorry."

"No, no, no, no," whispered Ambril. "Not again. Please, not again."

Emma spun to face the door. *If we're stuck in here, we're not leaving until it's safe.* She thrust both hands forward, concentrating on the dead wood. *Linganthas, please hear my voice. Grant this old tree new life.*

Dark green energy welled up around her hands before leaping into the door and spreading over it until the whole thing glowed. Wood creaked as the door came to life, growing and swelling as much as the doorframe allowed. A few small cracks appeared in the wall.

"Thank you," whispered Emma.

"What did you do?" Ambril stepped up behind her.

"Made the door grow bigger so they can't open it." Emma exhaled in relief. "We only need to wait for help."

A dull thud came from the door, along with a man groaning. More thumping and grunting followed. It sounded as if the men attempted to batter their way in without making too much noise. Emma hurried to the room's single tiny window, hoping to get the attention of a bird she could ask to go get Mama. She climbed up onto a table, standing on tiptoe to reach. Unfortunately, the window couldn't be opened. A single pane of glass had been mortared in a hole so small even she couldn't have squeezed through it.

"Inconsiderate cretins!" Ambril fumed, pacing in a circle. "I don't want to be kidnapped yet again!"

"Again?" asked Kimber.

"Yes! Again!" Ambril flailed her arms. "I've been grabbed at least eight times that I can remember. It's why Father moved us out here to the country instead of staying in Cimril City." She slouched into a sigh. "It seems we'll need to move again."

"No." Emma twisted to look down from the table at her. "Mama and me will keep you safe."

"I," said Ambril.

"What?" Emma blinked.

"Mama and I will keep you safe." Ambril raked both hands through her hair.

"Are yas doin' the teachin' fing when ya got men tryin' ta kidnap yas?" Kimber tilted her head.

"I'm scared." Ambril resumed pacing.

Kimber hugged her. "Don' be scared. We got kidnapped once. Some thieves wanted tae 'ave alla magic spider silk. They got me an' Em, and tied us up real tight in a cellar to a post. We could nae even move. I was scared. Real scared. Emma asked a nice rat ta chew us free, an' he did."

"A rat?" Ambril swooned, almost fainting. "You had a rat crawling on you when you couldn't move?"

Kimber nodded.

"Rats are nice." Emma sighed at the window, wondering if she should smash it open so a bird outside could hear her. "They're not bad. All they want is to be able to live and have food. People don't understand them, so they're afraid."

A heavy thud came from the door. Plaster flaked off the wall.

Emma peered out the window at the town, unable to see any birds. *Maybe one will be able to hear me and come looking.* She climbed down from the table and looked around for something she could use to break the window, certain she wouldn't get in trouble for it, considering three men tried to kidnap them.

"What are we going to do?" whimpered Ambril.

Emma gazed around the small storage room. Shelves on two sides held numerous small boxes and bins. A bunch of jewelry making tools and some scrap cloth sat on a worktable on the opposite end of the room from the window. "They won't be able to get the door open without making so much noise that someone catches them. We should be safe in here until your father comes home from his shop. But..." She hurried over to the table. "I'm going to break the window so I can call a bird to go get Mama."

"Okay." Ambril covered her mouth and nose in both hands, trying to slow her breathing.

All the tools in sight looked far too small to break a window. A hammer the size of a dinner fork wouldn't do the trick. Emma grasped a big piece of burlap draped over the desk and lifted it in hopes of finding a larger, heavier mallet.

When she flung the burlap to the side, she, Kimber, and Ambril all gasped at the same time.

There, on the little worktable, sat a solid gold box studded with rubies, emeralds, and sapphires. It looked huge for a music box, small for a jewelry box. The band of gems around the side glowed, projecting spots of blue, green, and red on the walls. Near the bottom, a strip of much smaller diamonds glittered and sparkled in the sunlight from the small window.

A stack of six old, dusty books stood beside the box.

Emma gawked, having forgotten entirely about breaking the glass.

"Ooh…" Kimber leaned closer. "What is it?"

"Must be something Father brought back from Sondaren." Ambril lightly brushed her fingers over the lid. "I've never seen it before." She picked up a scrap of paper tucked under one corner. "It says 'the box of wonder.' Father must have been trying to research it. These books look to be about magic and enchanting."

"Box of wonder," whispered Emma, still in awe of the riches sitting there.

Finding a treasure like that here certainly explained why men snuck into the house to rob it. She peered back at the door. Outside, the men argued in whispers, frustrated that their plans to rob the hidden workshop as well as hold Ambril for ransom appeared to be foiled by something as stupid as a stuck door. It sounded more and more likely they'd stop caring about making noise and do whatever they could to break in, hoping to outrun Mr. Starling's hired guards instead of relying on stealth. They'd already been exposed and wouldn't have another chance.

Emma stopped ogling the fancy, useless box for rich people. She had to break that window fast and call Mama before those men got into the room.

"Yeah, box o' wonder." Kimber lifted the lid about an inch. "I wonder wot's in it."

"Stop!" Emma grabbed her wrist. "We promised not to touch anything."

"Sorry. I fought 'at was jus' fer ta other room." Kimber smiled apologetically.

Intense light shone from the gap under the lid, so bright Emma had to squint.

"Whoa," whispered Ambril.

Kimber and Emma both 'oohed' at the pretty golden glow.

Behind her, the stuck door popped open in a spray of plaster flakes and wood splinters. Two of the three men, who'd evidently run shoulder-first into the door, crashed to the floor and went sliding.

Emma tried to scream, but no sound came out of her. The room blurred into a spiral of colors as the floor beneath her feet seemed to disappear. Emma fell straight down into a swirl blue, red, and green light.

4

A FINE MESS

*C*haos ceased a few seconds later.

Emma found herself standing on a cold stone floor. Ambril and Kimber stood on either side, both clinging to her. They appeared to be in a small alcove with grey brick walls, the only way out an archway in front of them. Shimmering sapphire blue light shone from a carved circle in the floor around them, decorated with bafflingly complex patterns and runic markings.

She stared at the pretty light until motion nearby distracted her from the glow.

Kimber, up on tiptoe, pulled a silver lever that stuck out of the wall, moving it from an upward position to a downward position. The girl seemed to want a closer look at a ruby the size of a rose at the end of the lever.

"Kimber!" Emma grabbed her shoulders. "Please stop touching things. You don't know what that does."

"Sorry." Kimber stepped back. "Should I put it back up?"

"Umm." Emma fidgeted. Nothing appeared to have happened in response to the lever moving downward. She didn't want to take the chance it would do something bad if touched again. "Not yet. Just... please leave it alone."

"Okay." Kimber bowed her head. "I'm sorry."

"It's all right. You're just curious and it *is* pretty." Emma hugged her. "But we don't know where we are or what happened."

Ambril wandered out of the magic circle, through the arch into the room beyond. "It's someone's bedroom, I think."

"A bedroom?" Emma tugged Kimber with her and followed.

The rectangular room appeared to be a combination of bedroom, dining room, and library, with several other pieces of furniture the likes of which she'd never seen before. A long, fancy table took up the middle of the chamber. Royal blue curtains hung from the four posts of a huge bed against the left wall between a pair of wardrobe cabinets. In the near right corner, a table with a four-inch-tall glass partition around the top contained a beautiful diorama map of land and oceans.

Most of the wall straight ahead on the opposite side of the room from the alcove with the magic circle consisted of bookshelves, so many it had to count as a library. At the center of the bookshelves, a square table held a huge crystal ball easily three feet in diameter. Two much smaller orbs stood atop golden settings on either side of the big orb, one blue and one red. Both small orbs glowed like lamps. The big crystal ball contained an image of the workshop room the girls had been trapped in a moment earlier.

Emma walked straight across the chamber, drawn to the scene playing out in the big orb. Kimber and Ambril followed. She stopped at the edge of the table, resting her fingers on the wood, nose inches from the crystal ball. Emma gazed at the three men converging on the fancy box sitting on the worktable.

"What was that flash?" asked the shorter man with the scratchy voice.

"How should I know?" replied Minstrel.

The short man nudged him. "You're the smart one."

"I'm the charmer." Minstrel pointed at the third man, the one who'd kept his distance in the treasure room. "Odelin's the brains of the outfit."

"That ain't saying much about our outfit." The short guy grumbled. "How in the depths of the pit did we lose three kids stuck in a room with no way out?"

Minstrel rolled his eyes. "If I could answer that question, we'd have our little princess and those two ragamuffins."

Kimber peered around the crystal ball at them. "Wha's a ragamuffin?"

"It's a not-nice word for children who aren't wealthy." Ambril frowned.

"I think we should forget about the girl." Minstrel reached for the jeweled box. "Your man at the docks came through with the tip, all right. This thing right here is worth more than all the gems in Starling's shop."

The room shook like a mild earthquake when the man picked the box up.

Emma gazed around. *Oh, wow. Are we inside the box?*

"Aye, probably yes." Odelin approached and looked the box over. "But if we can take it as well as the gems, why would we leave all that money sitting there?"

"Because all that money don't do us no good if we're in prison." The scratchy-voiced man exhaled hard. "Let's get out of here while we still can."

"Calm yourself, Rolfe." Minstrel lifted the box up higher to look at it. Again, the room wobbled.

"We're inside the box," whispered Ambril. "Somehow."

"Ooo." Kimber went wide-eyed. "Is magic."

Odelin swiped the box away from Minstrel, making everything shake again. He grasped the lid.

"Hide!" yelled Ambril. "They're gonna find us!"

Kimber sprinted across the room and dove under the bed.

"That's the first place they'll look!" yelled Ambril.

Odelin struggled at the box, unable to budge the lid. He grunted and strained so much his face reddened.

Emma stared into the huge crystal ball, watching the man

unsuccessfully attempt to open the lid. Unsure how long the box would resist, she glanced back at the alcove, waiting for the thieves to appear. These three men wanted to kidnap Ambril to make Mr. Starling give over his wealth. They probably wouldn't hurt her right away. It didn't mean they wouldn't hurt her after they got the money. They may or may not hurt Emma and Kimber. Emma watched the empty alcove, preparing to fight. Even if she couldn't stop them from being kidnapped, as soon as the men took them somewhere outside, she could start screaming for a bird to go fetch Mama. Hopefully, the men wouldn't care about her making whistling sounds.

Pulsing red light drew Emma's attention to the lever Kimber pulled on. The huge ruby at the end flickered. After a few seconds, Emma noticed the light matched up with the room shaking. Every time the men attempted to pull the lid open, the ruby lit up.

"Look at that." Emma pointed.

Ambril stepped closer, shaking in fear. "It's flashing."

"Yes. Every time they pull on the lid."

"A lock." Ambril slouched. "I think it's a lock. It didn't do anything we noticed when she pulled on it. It must have done something we couldn't see."

"What did I do?" Kimber scampered over. "I cannae find a better 'idin' spot."

Emma squish-hugged her. "You did great."

"I did?" Kimber went wide-eyed, mouth slightly open.

"You did, even if you didn't know it." Emma hugged her again.

Odelin swatted at Minstrel. "Forget opening it for now. We can't stay here."

The room bounced and wobbled when the thieves dropped the bejeweled box into a cloth sack and hurried out of the storage room. Via the giant crystal ball, Emma, Ambril, and Kimber watched the men walk through the house like they hadn't done anything wrong, even pausing to talk to other servants who believed the men worked there as part of the staff.

"Grr." Ambril stomped one foot. "Those two"—she pointed at

Odelin and Rolfe—"they've been working here for months, pretending to be servants."

"How do you pretend to be a servant?" Emma scratched her head.

"I mean..." Ambril huffed. "Well, they *were* servants, but the whole time they worked for my father, they'd been plotting to steal from him."

The view in the giant crystal ball remained centered on the box, looking down on it as if from an eye fifty feet or so in the air above. Emma stood, arms folded, tapping her foot, watching the thieves leave the house and go down the street. Motion made the room vibrate and sway about the same as riding on a horse-drawn coach going a little too fast.

"How can you be so calm?" Ambril glanced at her. "We're being kidnapped."

"I don't think we are." Emma let her arms fall slack at her sides. "They don't know we're in here. Those men are stealing the box, not us. We only have to wait for them to hide it somewhere and leave. As soon as there isn't anyone watching, we can go out and run for help."

Kimber scrunched up her nose, seeming confused. "Umm. 'Ow kin we git out? We go' in when I open'd the lid. There ain' no lid now. Is a ceilin'."

Emma peered up at a fancy decorated ceiling like the ones at Da's parents' manor house, certainly not a lid that could be opened from the inside.

"Are we tiny again?" whispered Ambril. "How can we fit inside a little box?"

"Magic!" Kimber thrust her arms out to either side, fingers spread wide.

Emma pondered.

The girls stood in silence, watching the crystal ball. The men walked out of town, off down the road to the southwest. Seeing them go into Widowswood forest made Emma smile. Not only did her magic grow stronger within the woods, Greyfang and the other wolves would be closer. Also, the woods teemed with birds. She'd have no trouble finding one to send off in search of Mama. Even better, in the forest, Nan would likely sense Emma needed help and come to her.

It took a little more than two hours before the men stopped walking at a cave hidden behind a bunch of leafy branches cut from nearby trees. The underground passage limited the crystal ball's view to a much shorter distance above the box, showing a view only inside the cave tunnel. At the end of the passage, the room opened into a wider chamber containing some tables and chairs, even a crude bar counter on the right side. It looked as though the thieves attempted to make a basic tavern. The men stashed the bejeweled box against the wall under a pile of burlap sacks behind the bar. Evidently satisfied no one would find the expensive trinket, the men left.

"They're gone." Kimber tilted her head. "Kin we go now?"

"Not yet." Emma tapped a finger to her chin. "They still might be outside. Probably arguing."

"Aye." Kimber nodded. "One of 'em's gonna try ta cheat 'em and run off wi' the box by hisself. They donnae trust each ovvah."

Ambril bounced nervously. "How are we going to get out of here?"

"Lever?" asked Kimber.

"That only locked the lid." Ambril sighed. "It didn't send us back outside. If you move it up, I bet it only unlocks the lid."

"Oh." Kimber shrugged.

Emma looked down at the two smaller orbs, red and blue. "I think it's one of these."

"Why?" Ambril peered at her.

"They're the only other things in here that look magic except for the glowing circle and the big orb." Emma gestured at the giant crystal ball. "We know the big orb is for looking to see what's going on outside. Whoever made this didn't want to leave the box and not know what might be waiting for them."

Ambril rubbed her chin. "That makes sense. I mean about wanting to know what's around the box before leaving it. What if those men are waiting right outside the cave?"

"We can get away." Emma smiled. "Linganthas will let us move easily in the forest. All we have to do is run into the thickest, thorniest, tangliest underbrush. It will move out of our way and close in behind us. They'll never catch us."

"Tangliest isn't a word," muttered Ambril.

"It is now." Kimber grinned. "Em said it, so it's a word."

Emma pointed at the blue and red crystal balls. "I think one of these will bring us outside. It's probably safe to try now. Just be ready to run."

"Okay." Ambril clenched her hands into fists. "Running, I can do."

"Which one?" Emma looked back and forth between the red and blue orbs.

"Blue." Kimber grinned. "Ey all say 'm trouble on account me hair is red."

Emma patted her. "You aren't trouble. A handful, yes, but not trouble."

Kimber laughed.

"I think blue, too." Ambril bit her lip.

"Okay." Emma rested her hand on the blue crystal ball. Nothing happened.

An obvious presence of magic tingled under her hand. She tried pushing it and wanting it to do something.

The room vibrated.

Emma's stomach did a flip. Her gut wrenched around as if the floor opened out from under them, despite nothing changing or moving. Ambril grabbed her stomach as well. Kimber briefly went cross-eyed. The three of them stood there staring at each other, on the verge of throwing up. After half a minute, the sensation of being sick faded.

"Well, that didn't work." Ambril gurgled.

"Loooooook," whispered Kimber, pointing at the big crystal ball.

Rather than a dark cave, the image now showed the bejeweled box sitting outside on a road of hardened sand in the moon-cast shadow of a plain rectangular building apparently made from solidified mud. Even more shocking, it appeared to be the middle of the night. Many such buildings stretched out around them. In the distance, the rolling dunes of a vast desert formed an endless ocean of rippling pale blue to the horizon.

The small crystal ball Emma touched no longer glowed, instead resembling a hollow sphere of ordinary glass, devoid of color.

Emma lifted her hand off it. "Uh oh."

5

SOMEWHERE THEY SHOULD NOT BE

*U*nsure what to do, Emma decided not to make their situation any worse by touching things.

Especially glowing things.

Kimber explored the room, hands clasped behind her back as she weaved around the bookshelves. Every few minutes, she called out, "I no' touchin' a fing."

Ambril sat on the edge of the large bed. She went back and forth between fretting and making faces as though she tried to think of what to do. Emma couldn't blame her for the fretting. Her friend might be smart, but she also happened to be rich, which meant she often got whatever she wanted with minimal fuss and always had people around to do things for her. Being stuck inside a strange magical box, which somehow took them to another place far from home, created a problem she couldn't simply solve by asking her parents or the nearest servant for help.

Emma didn't quite trust the big crystal. It certainly looked as though they'd been transported somewhere quite strange and different from the forest of Widowswood. However, an image inside a crystal ball did not necessarily prove anything. She wanted to believe it tried to trick them. Alas, she suspected it did not. For one thing, the large crystal ball obviously showed them the workshop around the box in Ambril's house. The motion inside the magical room matched the thieves carrying the box, and the images in the crystal ball appeared to show only the immediate surroundings outside.

For another thing, when she touched the smaller blue orb, everyone got a bit sick, as if they'd been on an out-of-control speeding carriage bouncing over a hill and careening down the other side. It also didn't make any sense for the magical box to try and fool someone inside it.

A whole room inside a jewelry box doesn't make sense either. She frowned to herself.

Another worry nagged at her. If they'd gone too far away from Widowswood, Kimber would be in trouble. Nan's ritual only happened a few days ago, so she didn't worry *too* much. It's not as if Kimber broke the rules of time just yet. In a few years, when she still looked like an eight-year-old, then it might make her sick to go away from the forest. For now, not enough time passed to worry her.

Still, Emma focused on one main goal: going home.

She no longer found the box fascinating. It scared her and she wanted nothing whatsoever to do with it other than to escape and return to her family. They had one more thing to try: touching the red orb. Emma paced by the crystal orb table, staring down at her feet as she walked in circles. Something about the red orb worried her. Bright red often meant danger, so she argued with herself whether or not to risk touching it.

"It's a map," said Ambril.

Emma looked up. Kimber and Ambril stood together on the side of the room by the long table with the glass wall around it. Her little sister still kept her hands behind her back, overacting how seriously she *wasn't* touching anything.

"Yes. A map of the world." Ambril looked back and forth. "It must have taken someone a very long time to make this."

"What?" Emma padded over to them.

The rectangular table had to be almost twice the size of the one at home where Emma and her family had meals. Gold fittings held glass barriers at the edges all the way around, making the table more of a shallow box with legs. It looked like someone poured colored sand into the shapes of six continents, oceans, and islands, creating a diorama of incredible detail. Two large continents sat to the left of the center, two other big ones on the right, with a small continent far to the north in the middle and another medium-sized one at the exact center of the map. Thin strips of white 'land' ran across the top and bottom made to look like ice and snow.

Each part of the map seemed to be alive. Miniature trees in forested regions appeared to sway in a wind that didn't exist. Rivers and lakes flowed. Sunlight from nowhere gleamed off the shiny sands of deserts or snowy places. The little snow-capped mountain ranges looked so real, Emma expected they'd feel like stone—even cold—if she touched them. Even the ocean space between the lands moved with rippling waves, the water so realistic it seemed possible to swim in. Every so often, a miniature sea dragon far off in one of the corners of the ocean surfaced, looked around, and dove under.

A silver needle stood on its point at the bottommost part of the northwestern continent. The pointer resembled one of Nan's knitting needles, only about half the length. Four small silver arms stuck out of a ring at the top end, each tipped with sapphire gemstones the size of cherries. Emma couldn't figure out how the needle remained upright. It should have fallen over. Some invisible force must be holding it. The four small sapphire-tipped arms at the top end rotated clockwise in a lazy drift.

"It's showing us where we are, I think." Ambril pointed at the needle.

A large mountain range separated the nearly empty, beige area the needle touched from a lush, green jungle. Emma leaned closer. The land under the needle looked the same as what they saw in the big crystal ball: sand dunes.

"Where are we?" whispered Emma.

"There." Ambril pointed at the desert region by the needle. "I don't remember what this kingdom is. This continent is called Endoriel. If this map is truly showing us where we are, that's a big problem."

"Why?" Kimber tilted her head.

"Because we don't live on this continent." Ambril pointed at the northeastern continent, slightly larger than Endoriel. "That's Loth Moraine. We live there."

Kimber stood up on her toes to reach over the glass wall, pointing at the desert area under the needle, her fingertip half an inch from touching it. "What's that called?"

"I don't remember." Ambril huffed. "Learning about maps is a bit boring. I might not have paid the best of attention. This is a map, but there are no labels or borders or anything. Who would make a map like this? What good is it?"

Emma took a step back from the table and folded her arms. "It's obviously for someone who already knows maps. They can see where the needle is and then look at another map if they want to know the name of where they are."

"Did we really go away?" Kimber scurried over to wrap her arms around Emma. "We in trouble?"

"Yes and no." Emma hugged her back.

"How c'we be in trouble an' no' in trouble at the same toime?" Kimber shivered.

"We are not going to be in trouble like when Mama or Da get cross with us for doing something wrong." Emma exhaled. "We are probably in trouble, like being somewhere that isn't safe."

"Oh." Kimber swiped her hair out of her eyes.

Emma peered at Ambril. "Do you know where we should be?"

"Somewhat." Ambril pointed at a spot roughly in the middle of the largest continent. "The kingdom we live in is called Andorath. It's around here somewhere. Difficult to tell because this map has no borders."

"'Ow's it a *king*dom when we's go' a queen?" Kimber scrunched up her nose.

Emma sighed. "I don't know. It's stupid."

The room jostled.

"Eep," whispered Ambril.

Emma ran back to the orb table to look at the large crystal ball.

The image still showed the box sitting out in the open on a sandy street. Small tracks going past it made her think a fox-sized animal zoomed by and likely bumped them.

"What happened?" Ambril rushed over to stand next to her.

"A little animal ran by." Emma leaned on the table, gazing into the orb.

They appeared to have landed at the outskirts of a sprawling desert city. A cluster of large buildings formed something of a town center much closer to a river in the east. Every structure here appeared roughly the same: boxy, plain, relatively small, and made of earth or clay. The homes near the box stood as close together as the houses in the center of Widowswood Village. Closer to the water, the buildings became progressively tighter until they touched each other, forming giant structures made up of ten or more individual huts fused into one. Bright lantern and torch light glowed from the heart of the city; however, the everywhere else had only moonlight.

"A lot of people live here," whispered Emma. "Maybe more than Cimril."

They stood around the table gazing into the crystal ball for a while. Almost nothing moved outside in the dead of night, save for a few men who occasionally wandered by close enough to the box—one street over—to be seen in the orb's view from above.

The men wore robe-like garments in light colors as well as strange, puffy hats with cloths hanging off the back to cover their necks. Curved swords hung from their belts, making Emma think they must be like the guards back home. Except for their unusual clothing, they seemed to be ordinary humans. Emma relaxed somewhat. At least they hadn't appeared in a wild place full of monsters. The lack of trees, plants, and animals here worried her, but the people looked friendly enough.

"It's hot here." Ambril pointed at one man. "Those hats are for keeping the sun off your neck. I think this might be Drajmir."

"Wot's that?" Kimber tilted her head.

"It's the name of a desert kingdom. I mostly remember it being on this continent." Ambril bit her lip. "I don't remember if they have a king, a queen, or something else, like a council. There used to be a lot of really *bad* dragons here, but the humans rebelled and won their freedom." She cleared her throat. "Ahlan wasahla. Asmi 'Ambiriyil Starlinji. Ana saeid limuqabalatika."

Kimber blinked. "Are you okay?"

"Yes." Ambril smiled. "I just said 'Hello, I'm Ambril Starling. Nice to meet you' in Drajmiri."

"Can you ask them for directions on how we can go home?" Emma tilted her head.

"No. I don't know how to say anything else. My tutor only taught me how to introduce myself so I could do so if Father ever meets with important people from other places." Ambril shrugged. "They wouldn't really want to talk to me anyway because I'm a child. It's just being polite."

Emma bowed her head, trying not to let fear get the better of her. They didn't have a monster chasing them around the forest with a giant axe, nor spiders trying to wrap them up in silk, or even a whole guild of thieves trying to kidnap them. But... somehow... this scared her more than anything else she'd ever been through.

"Are we trapped?" whispered Emma.

Ambril spun half way around, gazing at the room. "I don't think so. If the box was a trap for people, it wouldn't be so nice in here. Some wizard probably made it as a portable bedroom."

"Yeah." Emma sighed in relief. "So, there must be a way to go out whenever we want. It's not a cage."

"It's doing something." Ambril pointed at the blue orb. "Looks like a wine glass with a few sips left."

A small quantity of glowing blue liquid gathered at the bottom of the sphere.

"Wasn't there a moment ago." Emma squatted down to eye-level with the smaller crystalline orb. It had no openings from which any sort of magical liquid might go in or out. Yet, somehow, a small quantity of dark blue light made its way into the crystal ball.

Emma and Ambril stood completely still, watching the orb for several minutes. The amount of fluid inside it didn't change fast enough to see. Eventually, Emma felt sure it had more liquid in it than it had before.

"It's filling up," she whispered. "Slow."

"Resting." Ambril gazed up at the ceiling. "When it's full all the way, I bet we can go home."

"Em! Ambril" yelled Kimber. "I foun' anovver one."

Emma looked back over her shoulder at the alcove. Kimber stood in the glowing rune circle, pointing to the side at something out of sight behind the archway. "Another what?"

"Big blue ball." Kimber bounced up and down.

"Another one?" Emma stood out of her squat and hurried to the alcove.

Ambril followed. Her mood seemed halfway between scared and awestruck.

Kimber pointed at another eight-inch blue crystal ball embedded in the wall at the back of the alcove. It would have been behind them when they first arrived. This one didn't look empty, but it also didn't glow, appearing as an ordinary sphere made of solid sapphire... or as ordinary as such a magnificently expensive thing might be.

Carved lines in the wall adorned with fancy swirling runes traced a path down from the orb to the magic circle on the floor they all stood in.

"I think that's how we get out." Ambril pointed at the dim sapphire orb.

"Umm." Emma fidgeted. "Maybe. I thought the other blue orb would let us out and it... *didn't*."

Ambril gestured at the carvings. "It's got writing connecting it to the circle on the floor. This big circle has to be magic."

"Aye. Is glowin'." Kimber traced her big toe along one of the bright blue curves on the floor.

Emma leaned her face close to the blue crystal ball. "How come this one isn't making light?"

"The lock." Ambril pointed at the lever. "We can't get out if the lid is locked. The blue orb over there made the whole box go somewhere.

Maybe this one makes people go outside. It looks like it's connected to the magic circle on the floor."

"We're safe in here." Emma backed away from the orb.

"Yes, perhaps we are." Ambril fidgeted her hands together. "Until someone finds the box. Do you not think someone will steal a gold and jeweled box?"

"Is it stealing if it's simply out in the open?" Emma peered up at the grey stone ceiling.

"That's not better. Someone is going to take it when we're inside it." Ambril reached for the locking lever, but hesitated. "We should at least go outside, pick up the box, and hide somewhere until it's rested."

Kimber blinked. "The box is tired?"

"In a manner of speaking." Ambril pointed at the orb table in the other room. "Father sometimes trades in enchanted items. They have magical power in them, and just like people, if they use it, they have to rest until they're no longer tired. Then it can work again. I think when the orb fills back up, we can go home."

Emma couldn't come up with any reason to doubt Ambril's idea. She could stay calm. No reason to be scared. All they had to do was wait and use the blue orb again, and they'd be home. "All right. It does seem kind of silly to leave it out on the street."

"Very silly." Ambril folded her arms. "I don't want to get stolen."

"Don't you mean, you don't want anyone to steal the box? *We* can't be stolen." Emma smiled.

Ambril sighed. "We can if we're inside it."

"'Ow long a'fore it's rested?" Kimber danced around in a pirouette.

"Hours probably. It's going quite slow." Ambril gave a sad sigh. "Our parents are going to be worried."

Emma grasped the lock lever. "If someone takes the box, they might do something that makes it take longer for us to go home. Ambril's right. We need to hide somewhere."

"Yes." Ambril smiled. "Please hurry."

As soon as Emma pushed the lever to the top position, the blue orb in the wall lit up. Ambril reached out and touched it. Two seconds later, the room around them disappeared. Ambril stood with her arm outstretched, hand against the wall of the nearby little house. The golden jewelry box sat on the hardpacked sand beside them. Off in the distance, someone played music on a strange sounding instrument. It reminded Emma of a mandolin with only one string and an awful lot of twanginess. In another direction, a lone dog barked. No sound came from anyone or anything near them. A steady but weak breeze carried a sweet-spicy aroma. From one moment to the next, the scent changed from pastry to chicken and back. Emma couldn't tell what manner of food she smelled, only that it made her hungry.

The dirt beneath her feet sent a chill up her legs. In seconds, she shivered.

"It's cold here," whispered Emma.

"Deserts are supposed to be hot." Ambril wrapped her arms around herself. "I don't understand why it's so cold."

Seemingly unconcerned with the temperature, Kimber scampered over to a pile of junk against the wall of the next house down the street, rummaging around until she pulled a dusty cloth sack free. Prize in hand, she scurried back over and collected the box into the bag she found.

"Good idea." Ambril smiled. "Hide it."

Kimber beamed.

"Let's find somewhere to hide ourselves." Emma took Kimber by the hand and started off down the street.

The ground here didn't feel alive. Even before she knew about magic, Emma always hated wearing shoes. She now understood why: they made it more difficult to feel the energy of the earth. Wherever she stepped back home, the ground tingled from the life force of the woods. This place, this Drajmir as Ambril called it, had no such life. What such a truth might mean for her, she didn't know, but it likely wouldn't be good.

They walked along the narrow street, peering into simple cutout windows without glass in the buildings on both sides. Most windows had thin linen curtains of white, pink, yellow, pale blue, or beige. The huts appeared to be made from dried mud, somehow hardened to almost stone. Considering the lack of trees here, it made sense the people would build their homes out of something other than wood.

Each dwelling Emma looked in contained people, sometimes single adults, sometimes entire families. She noticed everyone had brown skin that varied in shade from the color Da turned in the summer when he patrolled outside all day to much darker than Emma thought possible for a person to be. Aside from their robe-like clothing, homes made of 'not-wood,' the people didn't seem much different from the ones back home.

If she didn't know the people here wouldn't be able to understand them, she might've gone in search of a patrolling guard to ask for a safe place they could wait. As much as she reasoned most people here were nice and friendly, there had to be bad people, too. She wouldn't have felt safe sleeping outside even in Widowswood Village with such an expensive golden box. After all, they'd been inside one of the safest houses there and thieves still came after them.

Kimber managed to keep herself unusually quiet.

Emma worried, since she'd never seen her little sister do that. The girl always chattered away about anything on her mind. She peered over at her. Kimber's expression gave off a sense of wariness, not fear.

"Is everything okay?" asked Emma.

Kimber nodded.

"You're so quiet."

"We's sneakin'." Kimber smiled matter-of-factly. "S'pose ta be quiet."

"Are we sneaking?" Emma blinked. "I don't think the villagers will hurt us."

Ambril took Emma's other hand. "Most people are nice, yes. Even a nice person seeing three children carrying a fortune in gold and gems could easily become... not nice. They might not hurt us, but they'd try to take the box and then we'd be stuck here."

Emma decided to stay quiet.

They crept down the street for a while more, turning along another road when they ran out of homes to peer into. Eventually,

Emma peeked through a window into a hut that appeared to be abandoned. Nothing inside it, not even furniture.

"Here," she whispered.

A tattered cloth, a little darker brown than sand, hung from a rod in the only doorway. She held it aside as the others ducked in, then followed. Two simple windows, one to the left of the door, the other in the rear wall, let air flow through the single-room structure. A fireplace-and-oven made of stacked mud bricks took up most of the left rear corner. Unfortunately, they had no wood to burn.

"There's nothing here to hide in," said Ambril.

"It's still better than out in the road." Emma pulled Kimber to the corner by the fireplace. "We've got the sack to cover it. No one's going to bother going into a house where no one lives. We can stay here until it's ready to go home."

Kimber set the sack on the ground in the small space between the curve of the oven's bricks and the wall.

Emma squatted over the sack and reached inside, grasping the box. "Get close. I'm going to open the lid. We can sleep or wait inside where it's safer."

"Okay." Ambril edged closer.

Kimber leaned against her.

Emma tugged at the lid, which didn't budge. "Grr. It's stuck."

"Stuck?" Ambril pushed the burlap aside, exposing the box. Its gems caught the weak moonlight inside the hut, barely managing to glimmer. They looked quite a bit dimmer here than they had in Ambril's house, almost as if they'd been actually glowing before and now didn't. "What do you mean, stuck?"

"Stuck means stuck." Emma struggled to open the lid, starting to panic. "I think the lock turned on by itself. Oh no! Please open."

Ambril picked the box up and also tried to open it. She said nothing, but didn't have to use words. Her face said it all.

"Is sleepin'," whispered Kimber.

Emma and Ambril almost bonked heads when they twisted to stare at her.

"The box. It sleepin'." Kimber pointed. "Gems was all light up afore. Now dark. I fink we kinnae git inside 'til it all sleeped."

Ambril stared at her in disbelief for a few seconds, then sighed. "I suppose she could be right."

"Yes." Emma nodded once. The idea the box might not be 'awake' to let them back inside while it recovered from transporting them across the world offered more hope than thinking they'd messed up and locked themselves out of the only way they had to get home. "Let's wait."

"What else can we do?" Ambril rolled her eyes. "We're stuck here."

Kimber stuffed the box deeper in the sack and covered it before reclining on the floor.

Emma sat beside her.

Ambril remained on her feet.

A few minutes later, Emma peered up at her. "Aren't you going to sit?"

"The floor is all dirt."

"Yes." Emma traced her fingers over the floor. "There's nothing in here."

"My dress..." Ambril glanced at her fancy peach-colored gown with layered overskirt, frills, and ruffled sleeves. "If I sit on the dirt, it will be ruined."

Kimber yawned. "Your legs gonna git tired standin' all night. I fink ya should sit. If ya donnae wan' ta gi' the gown all dir'y, ya could take it off."

Ambril's cheeks turned scarlet.

"You've basically got two dresses and a skirt on," said Emma. "And hose. Take off the outer dress and skirt, so the dirt only gets on the inside dress."

"It's called an underdress." Ambril fanned herself. "And it's not proper to be outdoors in only that."

"Why no'?" asked Kimber.

"It just isn't." Ambril huffed.

Kimber leaned toward Emma and not-quite whispered, "I don' fink she gon' wanna swim wif us inna river."

Ambril raised an eyebrow. "Why wouldn't I want to learn how to swim? It sounds like it might be fun."

Kimber ground her toes into the dirt. "'Cause o' what we wear when we swim."

Ambril made a series of confused faces. "I've learned about all manner of fashion, but I cannot think of anything specifically made to swim in."

"Do rich people go swimming?" asked Emma.

"Not as far as I am aware." Ambril fidgeted. "What do you wear when you go swimming?"

Kimber made a face as though she'd heard the dumbest question ever. "Nuffin."

Ambril blinked once, then fainted.

"Well..." Kimber glanced at Emma. "'Er legs won' git tired now."

6

FAR, FAR AWAY

*E*mma crawled over to Ambril and patted her on the cheek until she opened her eyes.

"Are you all right?" whispered Emma.

"I've never been so embarrassed." Ambril sat up. "Are you serious? You swim with... like you're taking a bath?"

Emma and Kimber nodded.

"Outside?" Ambril blinked.

"Off in the woods, yes." Emma scratched her head. "How else would one go swimming? If you went in the water wearing all that, you'd drown."

Kimber gestured at Ambril. "She donnae go swimmin'."

"And I shall refrain from doing so if it requires I disrobe outside." Ambril blushed again.

"Is fun. You shoul' nae say ya not do it 'til ya try et once. Me bruvva Tam, we kinnae git him ou' the wa'er once he's in."

Emma chuckled. "The boy's practically a mermaid. Err, a merboy." She scrunched her nose. "Merlad?"

"The stories tell of mermaids and mermen." Ambril fussed at her hair. She sighed, fretting at the ground beneath her dress. After a few seconds pause, she seemed to decide against moving lest it make her garment dirtier.

"Tam's only six." Emma smiled. "He's not a man yet."

Emma and Ambril got into a somewhat heated discussion about if children would still be called mermaids and mermen or if some other word existed for them.

Kimber opened her mouth as if to say something, but froze.

"What?" whispered Emma.

Her little sister made a 'shh' gesture, then pointed at the doorway. Emma and Ambril turned to face the house's only entrance. A shadow darkened the cloth hanging there; a man lurked outside, listening.

Emma tensed up. Only a certain sort of man might be prowling around a city in the middle of the night, the type of man who liked to take things belonging to other people. Or, perhaps, a guard. If a robber found them, they might not have *too* much to worry about. Neither she nor Kimber had anything of value, merely their dresses. Ambril's earrings and necklace would definitely draw a thief's eye. Kimber did a good job making the sack with the jeweled box look like a lump of debris left behind in an abandoned home. It might escape notice, especially with the distraction of Ambril's jewelry.

The shadow on the cloth door grew larger, the man outside creeping closer.

Ambril drew in a breath and clung to Emma.

Kimber scooted a little bit to her left to block view of the sack behind her.

He's going to come inside. Emma squeezed her hands into fists, trying to figure out how she should react. With each passing second the man continued to wait outside, looming in the dark, she grew more and more anxious. He couldn't be up to any good. She peered up and back at the window in the rear wall. All three of them could climb through the hole, though Ambril might get stuck thanks to her fluffy gown.

Emma eased herself up onto her feet, hands shaking. The deadness in the earth on top of what Nan and Mama said about how their power came from Widowswood made her afraid she might not be able to call upon her magic here. She could be as helpless as an ordinary undersized ten-year-old. Running sounded like a great option.

The instant she gestured for Kimber and Ambril to get up so they could go out the window, the door curtain swung aside—revealing a boy much smaller than the shadow he'd cast. Relief drained the tension out of Emma so rapidly her legs buckled; she plopped back down to sit on the floor.

Smiling, the boy stepped into the room and let the curtain swish closed behind him. He looked a little older than them, perhaps twelve or thirteen, scrawny, with large brown eyes. Unkempt black hair hung to his shoulders, touching the fabric of a plain beige tunic. His pants ended in tatters at the knees. Numerous healed scrapes and scratches covered his bare lower legs. A simple black cord around his neck held a carved bit of stone in the shape of a crescent moon close to his throat, almost a choker.

He looked at the three of them, eyes widening, then said something in another language, too whispery and fast for any of it to make sense.

Ambril stood, dusted herself off, and repeated the introduction she'd practiced earlier.

The boy seemed to find it amusing. He stood straight, tucked his left arm behind his back, and bowed to her, before replying in an obviously fake aristocratic tone. Emma couldn't help but grin. It seemed as though he made fun of her properness, or at least found it funny.

Ambril looked at Emma. "I think he said his name is Akeem."

The boy said something else.

"Umm." Ambril grimaced. "I don't know how to speak Drajmiri, only introduce myself."

Kimber pointed at him. "Akeem?"

He nodded.

She patted herself on the chest. "Kimber."

Emma also patted herself on the chest. "Emma."

Ambril waved around in a grand sweeping gesture. "Drajmir?"

Akeem nodded, then said something no one understood.

"Eep." Ambril smoothed her hands down the sides of her skirt in a repetitive motion. "We are *really* far from home. The map was right."

"What do you know about this place?" asked Emma.

"Not too much. Father has traded with merchants from here sometimes. They're pretty much just like us, except it's really hot here."

Akeem held up a hand in a 'please wait' gesture, then darted outside.

"What's he doing?" whispered Emma.

"How should I know?" Ambril huffed. "The tutor only taught me how to introduce myself. I can't say anything useful."

"'E seems noice," said Kimber. "I don't fink 'e's gonna 'urt or steal from us."

Emma idly dusted her fingers over the top of her foot, then flicked at the dirt gathered against her big toe. "He had a little moon necklace on. Do you know what it means?"

"It means he likes little stone moons." Ambril shrugged.

Kimber got an 'uh oh' expression.

"What?" whispered Emma.

"Moight be 'es wif'a thief guild." Kimber held up her left arm. "I 'member 'avin' ta carry messages fer 'em an' they gave me a bracelet so's t'other thieves knew me was official like."

"Not *other* thieves. You're not a thief." Emma squish-hugged her.

Kimber grinned. "I learn some fings about teefin', but I no do the stealin'."

Akeem swooshed back into the hut, making all three girls jump. He crossed the room in two steps, then sat on the floor near them, holding out a round loaf of bread.

"'E stole it," whispered Kimber.

Emma nudged her. "You can't say that."

"'E got no coin pouches. An' it's dark. No shops be open now." Kimber reached for the bread, smiling at Akeem. "Fank ya!"

Akeem smiled back at her, then said something else no one understood.

Kimber tore the bread into three roughly-equal pieces, handed two to Emma, and attacked her piece. Emma gave one to Ambril, shrugged, and decided to eat. The Watch back home wouldn't punish a child for stealing bread, so she figured the guards here wouldn't be too upset. Also, no one could be accused of stealing anything if no evidence remained.

Akeem sat there watching them eat, occasionally speaking. His tone varied between asking questions and making statements. Once or twice, he took Emma's hand and held it up or brushed his fingers at Kimber or Ambril's hair. Emma figured he'd never seen blonde or red hair before, or anyone pale. He probably wanted to know where they came from. Akeem seemed curious and friendly, so she didn't mind.

Once they finished the bread, Akeem stood. He backed a step toward the door, waving as if he wanted the girls to follow him.

"What?" asked Emma. "You want us to go with you?"

"We should stay here." Ambril dusted crumbs off her skirt. "He doesn't know we can get home and thinks we're all alone."

Kimber turned her head to face Ambril. "We *are* all alone."

"Yes, but it's temporary. Once the box has its magical charge back, we can go home." Ambril neatened her hair.

Akeem looked at the doorway, then back at the girls. His expression went from smile, to urgency. He waved more emphatically for everyone to follow him.

"Umm. Maybe we should see what he wants." Emma pulled her feet in close, ready to stand.

Ambril bit her lip. "I don't think—"

A man burst in the cloth door, towering over the boy. Akeem whirled around and took a step back, looking quite a bit like a small fox putting himself between an angry bear and a trio of rabbits. Not that a fox would be inclined to protect rabbits, Emma didn't think her metaphor through all the way in the moment.

Two more men stepped in behind the first.

All wore long tunics of white and burgundy, decorated in gold brocade over loose-fitting pants. Their boots looked a bit strange, likely because the leather came from some other animal than what people at home used. Each man wore a curved sword, as well as multiple daggers on their belts. Their puffy hats consisted of bundles of fabric wrapped around a rigid helmet forming a wide brim to keep the sun at bay. The first man to enter wore several gold rings and bracelets.

Akeem pointed and said something at the men in the tone of telling a stray dog to go away.

The man with the bracelets ignored him to glance around the room before his gaze settled on Ambril.

"Oh, no..." Ambril whispered. "This doesn't make any sense. Why are they after *me?*"

"You look rich," whispered Emma. "You're wearing gems on your ears and a big star necklace. I don't think they're trying to kidnap you. These men couldn't know who you are. They want your jewelry."

Akeem waved at Emma, pointing at the window hole in the back wall while yelling in an urgent tone, evidently telling them to run.

The closest man started around the boy toward the girls.

Akeem jumped to stay in the man's way, yelling at him.

The man smacked Akeem in the face with enough force to fling the boy off his feet.

Ambril screamed.

Akeem landed on his back in front of the girls, bleeding from the nose and mouth. He didn't pass out, though he did seem too dazed to get back up any time soon.

Emma snarled. She dug her toes into the dirt and spread her fingers wide, picturing an army of grabbing, tangling thorn vines growing up from the ground to ensnare the men. *Linganthas, please lend me your power.* Something responded to her request, but the sensation came from seemingly miles below her. Emma strained to 'lift' the energy out of the earth.

The man didn't appear to realize she tried to do anything more than make strange faces at them. He barked a harsh command to the two other men, then reached for Ambril. She screamed again, too paralyzed in fear to move as he grabbed her left forearm. Sweat beaded on Emma's forehead despite the cold desert night. She pulled and pulled, trying to draw Linganthas' power up from the ground. It took much more effort; however, it did work... or *would* work, eventually.

One of the men grabbed Emma's right wrist. He pulled her toward the door, breaking her concentration before any trace of roots or vines broke the surface of the dirt. Kimber grabbed the sack with the box in it and tried to dart between the third man's legs and make a run for it. The man appeared to expect this, spinning fast enough to grab her by one leg. Kimber fell flat on her chest as he tugged her back to him by the ankle.

"Uh oh," whispered Kimber. "He got me."

Emma struggled to pull her arm out of the man's grip. She even grabbed his fingers with her free hand and tried to peel them open, to no avail. The man who caught Kimber scooped her up in one arm and threw Akeem over his left shoulder. Feet sliding on the dirt, Emma did her best to resist being taken as the man dragged her outside.

They ushered Emma and Ambril forward, forcing them to walk down the street. The third man continued to carry Kimber in one arm, pinned to his chest. She grasped grunted and struggled, trying to pull herself out of his grip.

Akeem, draped over the man's shoulder, muttered incoherently. Whatever he said amused the men into chuckling.

The way the men collected and dragged them along made Emma feel like a thief being arrested. Her initial fear at being kidnapped gave way to anger and a whole heap of embarrassment. She couldn't concentrate well on trying to make root magic work while a man physically tugged her around. They also hadn't been too mean or cruel about it—other than hitting Akeem so hard he nearly passed out. For that, Emma didn't trust them. She also knew not every guard was nice. Some could be quite mean, especially in big cities like Calebrin.

"Where are they taking us?" whimpered Ambril.

"I don't know." Emma tugged at her arm. "Let go of me!"

The man didn't react.

"They don' know wha' we sayin'," said Kimber. "I kinnae move. I's stuck. Shoul' I bonk him wif the box?"

Emma tried to set her heels and resist being pulled. The man simply kept dragging her. She relented after a few feet of sliding, reluctantly walking again. "No. Don't hit him. You'll only make him angry. I'm not sure we're being kidnapped."

Ambril stopped sniffle-crying. She gawked at Emma. "What? Of course we're being kidnapped. What else do you call it when strange people grab children and carry them away?"

"They might be guards. I think we're being arrested." Emma sighed.

"For what?" Ambril burst into tears again. "We didn't do anything wrong!"

"Stole a bread," whispered Kimber.

A wave of fear ran down Emma's back, but vanished as fast as it appeared. "How could they know about the bread and find us? That doesn't make sense. There has to be someone here who can speak to us."

They reached a wider street where a few people loaded up small merchant carts, taking wares from their homes they planned to sell in the heart of the city. That meant it had to be an hour or less to sunrise. Emma shivered, wondering how they'd lost half a day and all night. At most, two hours passed since they wound up inside the box. How could it possibly be almost morning already?

"Help!" shouted Ambril at the group of merchants.

Most of them looked up, glanced at the men, and hastily pretended like they didn't see anything.

The man holding Emma pulled his sword a few inches out of his scabbard, showing it to Ambril before sliding it back down.

"Yes, very nice," said Ambril. "You have a shiny sword."

Emma reached over to take her hand. "He's telling us to be quiet or he's going to hurt us. Maybe they aren't guards."

"Em." Ambril sighed. "He's not going to hit me with a *sword*. I'm a child. He's just trying to be scary." She glared up at the man hauling her along. "Stop pulling so hard. You're going to rip my sleeve. Don't you have any manners?"

It no longer seemed like these men worked for the city as guards.

At least, no guard Emma ever knew about threatened to kill people for not being quiet. She worried even more at the merchants' reaction. They seemed afraid of these men, didn't even want to look at them. Something seemed wrong about this. But... her magic didn't work. Well, it sort of did. If she had time to concentrate, Linganthas' power would eventually make it to her. Summoning living roots and vines in a place without any plant life took a lot of work. Even the brief attempt she'd made in the house caused her to feel tired despite nothing happening.

If the men locked them up somewhere, she'd have the time to work on contacting the spirits of nature. Assuming, of course, the men merely locked them up somewhere and didn't do anything worse.

I could try asking for Uruleth's gift. Making herself stronger didn't require plants nearby. At her size, the Bear Spirit's gift only gave her about the same physical strength as a grown man. When she grew up, she'd be even stronger than that. Nan told her stories about some druids, big strong men, who could call on the Bear Spirit to become so strong they lifted horses. Emma would never be *that* strong, but she could make herself powerful enough to yank her arm free—if her magic worked at all here.

She also had Kimber and Ambril to worry about, plus Akeem as well. Sure, Emma might be able to get away from the man holding her; however, could she fight off all three men before they had the chance to hurt one of them?

Crippled with fear, Emma shrank in on herself and spent all her energy trying not to cry out loud. The last time she'd been this terrified, she'd been glued to a giant spider web staring up at the most massive emerald creeper in the forest. At least the spider queen proved to be reasonable. Emma talked her way out of that one. Perhaps she could talk her way out of this problem, too... if only they could find someone who understood them.

Worse, she couldn't send a bird off to find Mama or Nan. No bird could fly across the whole world. She didn't know exactly how long it would take to travel from here to home without a magical box jumping from place to place in an instant. It seemed like way too much distance to ask from a bird. The world happened to be a big place. What little she'd learned of it from Nan's stories made her wonder if it might take a whole year or even longer to get home from this place without the box.

Stuck in a strange land where no one could understand her, cut off from her magic, and without any possibility her family could help her, Emma found herself in the icy grip of fear so powerful she could barely think. Never in her life had she felt so alone and vulnerable.

Defeated, she simply hoped the men wouldn't hurt children and offered no resistance.

Kimber continued grunting and wriggling despite having no success. Ambril grumbled occasionally about the man damaging her sleeve or making them walk too fast. The rich girl didn't seem to understand the danger they'd stumbled into. Or perhaps she did and only complained as a way to distract herself from thinking about their situation.

A long, dreadful trudge later, the sun rose around the time they reached the outer limits of the city center where the hardpacked sand roads met intricate octagonal paving stones. The buildings here appeared to be made from the same material as the small houses, only more of it. Many had fancy spires, trim in gold and red paint, or murals on their walls. A few even had solid doors instead of hanging cloths, though made from long strands of inch-wide dried grass woven together.

Like the merchants they'd passed earlier, citizens went out of their way not to look at any of them, especially the guards... except for a few children who appeared curious enough about Emma and the others to stare. Within five minutes of the sun coming up, both the air as well as the street stones had become intolerably hot.

The men led them deeper into the heart of the city. Emma looked around at the two-and-three-story high buildings, all made of the same stonelike dried mud. She kept trying to get someone to look at her so she could silently cry for help. Alas, everyone who lived here appeared frightened of the men. No matter how dense the crowd in the street became, no one but the smallest children looked at her. Emma gave up on trying to beg with her eyes and called out for help. The man dragging her along didn't seem to care—nor did anyone else. Feeling completely at the mercy of this place, she bowed her head and simply tried to put her feet in shadier places or on top of anything to keep them away from the hot stones.

Eventually, somewhere deep within the confusing, twisty streets of the city's heart, the men pulled them around a corner into a dead-end alley, littered with cloth junk, narrow poles, and numerous clay urns. At the far end, a green metal archway in the wall appeared to lead into darkness.

"Where are we going?" asked Ambril.

None of the men said a word as they kept dragging Emma and the others toward the archway. Despite the annoying heat, she did not want to go wherever the archway led. Emma resumed struggling, stretching to grab hold of any random junk she could reach. She pulled over a few bundles of fabric before getting her hand on a dusty wooden crate. The man gave her arm a sharp yank, tearing her grip loose. Emma stumbled after him, glaring.

The man pulling Ambril entered the archway first. Emma started to scream, until it became obvious her friend went down stairs inside a tunnel. Blinding sunlight outside made the passageway seem so dark it looked like a magical portal of infinite night. Emma still tried to resist, though it didn't do much good. The man pulled her into the staircase and down a flight of stone steps. At least they were nice and cool compared to the scorching pavers outside. She shivered, still too terrified to think, and kept quiet. At the bottom, they entered an underground passage of grey brick walls and stone floors. Moss grew on the curved ceiling. A short distance from the base of the steps, too far away for the hot, dry wind to reach, everything down here looked and felt wet. The echoing ploink of water droplets falling into puddles came from everywhere up ahead.

"I'm a bite 'im," whispered Kimber. "'e's squeezin' all me air out."

Emma shuddered. Her little sister was scared, too. She didn't have Mama, Nan, or Da to help her. Kimber and Ambril needed her to be brave. She couldn't give in to fear. Emma had to think. She couldn't let herself be a scared little child at the mercy of whatever these men planned to do to them.

It might be scarier than it is. Maybe they only think we're orphans who need help.

She didn't really believe her own thoughts. Guards helping orphans wouldn't threaten them with swords, or drag them off into a tunnel underground.

"No, don't bite him." Emma tightened her jaw, focusing on Kimber instead of her fear. "Let him put you down first."

"If he puts her down, she won't have to bite him," whispered Ambril.

"Even better." Emma balled her free right hand into a fist to keep it from shaking.

The men dragged them down a long passageway to a right turn. Every thirty feet or so, a decorative metal grate in the middle of the curved ceiling let a shaft of sunlight in. At some point Emma hadn't noticed before, the middle of the passage turned into a water-filled canal. The air smelled musty and unpleasant, a little short of foul.

Ambril abruptly screamed.

None of the men reacted, continuing along.

"What?" rasped Emma, startled by the sudden loud noise.

"This is a sewer!" She screamed again, standing on tiptoe like she didn't want to touch the floor.

Emma blinked in confusion. "What's a sewer?"

"How can you not know what a—" Ambril stared at her. "Oh. I forget you've rarely left Widowswood. They have them in Cimril. Not where we live. It's... like an outhouse. A really big outhouse that everyone in the entire city uses. All the holes go to tunnels underground and water carries the foulness away. It's quite nice to keep the city clean and the smells away... but people aren't supposed to go down here!"

Kimber didn't seem to mind being carried off the ground so much anymore.

Ambril fretted and squirmed. "I demand you ruffians let go of me right this instant. I will not be marched into a filthy sewer!"

The man ignored her, continuing to drag her along. They went left at the next intersection and followed a curving passage to the right. Rats as big as small dogs scurried away from them. Thankfully, the critters moved fast enough for Ambril not to notice them, as she remained too occupied with watching the floor where she stepped.

Mama would have heard her scream from home.

The passage came to an end at an archway into a large square chamber with a tall domed ceiling. A decorative metal grating at the top opened to the sky, allowing a shaft of sunlight to fall almost straight down on a tall figure in a dark green hooded robe, who stood with their head slightly bowed, arms folded across their chest, hands tucked into opposing sleeves. The hood concealed the person's entire face, offering a view of only darkness.

Emma's legs locked subconsciously, refusing to take another step. An immediate sense of fear gripped her about this man. It had to be a man since women didn't usually grow that tall. The 'guard' holding her by the arm was about the same height as Da, and the robed figure appeared significantly taller than him, at least a full head's worth. The bright shaft of sunlight turned him half into a shadow. She couldn't make out any details about him other than the voluminous green robe with gold-trimmed sleeves.

The guard pulled Emma forward, dragging her like a stick doll, her feet sliding across the moss-slimed stone. She stared transfixed at the foreboding man in the robe... until her left foot slipped down through a hole.

"Gah!" Emma flailed her free arm, grabbing the man to stop herself from taking a tumble.

Once she caught herself, she looked down.

They'd moved from stone floor onto metal grating. Her left leg sank calf-deep in a square space between crisscrossing metal bars. Metal grating covered three-fourths of the chamber floor. Solid stone walkways formed a square path around the outside edge by the wall. Beneath the grating, a deep pool of water swirled and churned, flowing in and out via canals in the four sewer tunnels connecting to this room.

Emma pulled her foot up and set it on a solid piece of metal. This didn't look like a magistrate or a priest who ran an orphanage. Being brought to meet a tall, hooded figure lurking in a sewer didn't seem like the sort of thing that would end well for anyone involved.

Uh oh. We're in big trouble.

7

MUCH WORSE

*T*he man holding Emma's arm urged her forward.

"Stop pulling." She tried to yank her arm out of his grip. "You're going to make me break my ankle."

He ignored her, staring fixedly at the tall figure.

Emma scowled at him, then demonstrated sticking her foot through a square hole in the grating as if to say 'see! I can slip and hurt myself.' She pulled her foot out again and placed it on one of the slats. As if understanding her meaning, the man stopped trying to shove her and let her navigate the treacherous grid at her own speed.

She crept closer to the hooded figure, stopping at a distance suitable for conversation, but not so close he could grab her. The other two men stepped up beside her. One pulled Akeem off his shoulder and set the boy on his feet. He continued holding Kimber.

The redhead leaned forward, peering down at the grating. "Tha's wa'ter. No' a great place fer swimmin'. Sewer water nae good tae touch."

A pained sigh came from the hood. He gestured at Akeem while speaking in Drajmiri, his tone conveying disbelief as well as annoyance. His voice held an unusual timbre, deep and silken smooth. Though she couldn't understand the words, Emma imagined a rich merchant talking to a child he'd caught sneaking into the back room of his store.

Akeem lost all the bravado he showed in the house with the guards. The boy went wide-eyed, clearly frightened. He shook his head rapidly, hands up, and rambled in Drajmiri for a moment before repeating the same short phrase three times.

The hooded figure turned his attention on the girls. "Young Akeem tells me he did not steal from me, which means one of you did." His voice seemed to reach out like a phantom ghostly hand, gently caressing Emma's face and neck. The sound of it sent tingles down her arms and back.

Ambril squeaked in fear.

He can understand us! "Umm. Hello. I'm Emma. We didn't steal anything. There must be a mistake."

"You are quite far from home, child." He gave a long sigh that ended with a hiss like air leaking past teeth. All the hairs on Emma's arms stood on end. "Why do you associate with this boy? What do you understand of the significance of the crescent moon?"

Emma went blank, not sure how to answer.

"The crescent is the first phase of a new moon," said Ambril.

Another pained sigh came from the tall figure. "Do not try my patience."

"You asked what we knew about the crescent moon." Ambril shivered. "I was trying to answer you."

"She has a tutor," chirped Kimber.

The tall man pointed at Akeem. "The crescent amulet. You intend to join them? Why do you associate with this boy?"

Emma fidgeted. "He just found us. We can't even talk to him."

"Hmm." The robed man stood completely still for a moment. "Remove the necklace from the boy and drop it through the grating."

Akeem's eyes widened. He shook his head rapidly at Emma, a little too frightened to simply care about losing a non-precious trinket.

"No." Emma furrowed her brows. "That would be stealing. We don't steal."

The tall figure gave an annoyed, throaty sigh. "One of you *did* steal from me."

"We di'n'," muttered Kimber.

Ambril squeaked.

As if grabbed by an invisible hand, the burlap sack flew out of Kimber's grip, floating over to the hooded figure, who hadn't moved at all. The fabric fell away, revealing the bedazzled jewelry box.

"If you did not sssteal from me," barked the figure, his voice louder and frayed with anger, "then why isss thisss here? I sensed it return to my city."

Uncomfortable tingles crawled down Emma's back. "We didn't steal it. We found it. Thieves were trying to kidnap us, so we hid in a storage room. When we touched the box, we somehow went inside it. I put my hand on a blue orb and it took us here."

"Interesssssting," said the cloaked figure.

Kimber shot Emma a strange look and whispered, "Why's 'e talkin' like 'at?"

Ambril squeaked. She looked like she'd have fainted already if not for the man holding her arm.

Emma found a bit more courage. "If that box really is yours and someone stole it from you, then you must know what it is and how it works. We don't even want it… we only want to go home."

"I'as sorry." Kimber braced her hands on the forearm across her chest, struggling to push herself up. She didn't go anywhere. "I'as told nae touch nuffin, but ae forgo' meself and touched it. Accident."

The cloaked figure remained silent for a long, awkward moment. Despite the hood holding no sign of a face, Emma squirmed as though the figure stared straight through her.

Akeem appeared to be trying to look around for a place to run. He also eyed the man nearest him, sizing up the dagger on his belt for a grab.

Don't do it. We might not be in trouble. Don't make it worse. Emma shivered.

"Ahh," said the cloaked figure at last. "Very well then. You ssseem sssincere. I believe you did not sssteal from me. I am no longer angry with you."

Emma exhaled in relief. "Can we please use the box to go home? Unless you can help us without it."

"Child, you do not need to worry about going home." The hooded figure drifted closer.

An odd dragging sound echoed in the sewer behind him.

"What?" Emma leaned back. "What do you mean? Why wouldn't we go home? You're not going to put us in jail? We didn't steal it. You believe us."

"I do believe you." The cloaked figure pulled his sleeves apart, exposing arms the color of dark green river weeds. A hint of serpent scales glimmered in the sunlight along the skin of his forearms. Long, claw-like black nails jutted from the tips of his fingers. He reached up to pull his hood back, revealing not the face of a man—but the head of a giant jade-scaled snake with glowing red eyes. The figure's robe split open down the middle. Four feet down his neck, his body widened into a shape similar to a human man's torso before tapering back down into a snake tail. Except for the chest and spindly arms, he appeared to be mostly snake, over twenty feet long from nose to the tip of his tail. "However, you smell delicious."

Emma, Ambril, Kimber, and Akeem all screamed.

The creature raised one hand. A flash of crimson light burst from his palm—and everything went black.

8

A CHOICE BETWEEN RECKLESS
AND NOTHING

Shaking jostled Emma awake.

She opened her eyes to damp grey stone stained in swaths of green and brown where moss mixed with rust. Emma found herself lying on her side, Ambril squeezing both hands into her shoulder. Confusion as to why she ended up on the floor lasted only a few seconds before she remembered the snake man, the flash of red light, screaming.

Emma sat up and screamed again.

Her voice echoed across a stone-walled room. When she ran out of air, she kept trying to scream for a little while longer. Ambril's sobbing came from behind her. Panic faded, allowing her surroundings to change from a chaos of blurry fear to an enclosure of iron bars. She, Ambril, Kimber, and Azeem shared a large a cage. Flat iron slats riveted together created a five-foot cube with one door. Nothing soft protected them from the metal bars and stone floor beneath them.

Emma whirled to face Kimber. Her younger sister lay on the ground much the same way she did in bed each morning, arms and legs splayed in all directions as if she'd taken a tumble off a moving horse cart. She appeared unhurt, merely sleeping. To be sure, Emma placed a hand on her sister's chest, feeling for a heartbeat—which she found.

"It's going to eat us," said Ambril in between sobs.

Azeem sat in a ball, mostly hiding his face behind his knees. Surprisingly, he didn't look frightened as much as resigned. His expression worried her more than fear. The boy appeared to understand they would all soon die.

"Not again," muttered Emma.

Ambril sniffled. "What do you mean 'not again'? Are you making fun of me?"

"No." Emma gathered her hair off her face and tossed it over her shoulder. "This is the second time I've been locked in a cage by a monster who wanted to eat me."

"You aren't serious." Ambril gawked.

"I am. The banderwigh wanted to drain my happiness and feed on it." Emma rattled the cage door. "He wasn't going to eat me an' Tam like food. Wouldn't have even killed us, but it would've been almost as bad. I think the snake monster intends to actually swallow us whole."

"Stop scaring me." Ambril shivered.

"I'm not trying to scare you. I'm trying to make you feel better." Emma smacked at the hinges.

"How... is that... possibly supposed to make me feel better?" Ambril pressed a hand to her forehead.

"I was in a cage once before and got away. I can do it again." Emma stood to examine the bars overhead. "This one's bigger. And it's not swinging on a chain."

Ambril pulled her knees against her chest. "How did you get out last time?"

"Tried not to be sad. Sang a happy song with Tam until the banderwigh got sick. They hate happiness." Emma knelt by the door.

Ambril sighed. "Did you see that creature? I don't think he cares if we're happy or not. Singing songs isn't going to help us now."

"No. You're probably right." Emma reached outside the door to grab the massive bronze padlock as big as her whole head.

"What is that thing?" whispered Ambril. "It's not a banderwigh."

Emma looked back over her shoulder at the boy. "I think he knows. As soon as we saw the snake man, he got really scared. Akeem? What is it?"

He didn't even look up from the floor.

"Umm." Ambril nudged the boy, then patted herself on the chest. "Ambril." She held her fingers up like snake fangs, then shrugged.

"Naga," said Akeem.

Ambril exhaled. "His name is Naga or he *is* a naga?"

"I think naga is the creature." Emma tugged at the giant padlock, barely able to move it. *Oof. This thing is heavy.* "It doesn't sound like a name."

"Oh, yes." Ambril shivered. "I believe I've read about them in one of my storybooks. They're greedy, crave power and riches, and try to enslave everyone weaker than them."

Emma kept pulling at the enormous padlock. "That doesn't sound much different than a king."

"Cruel." Ambril gasped. "Nagas are far more cruel than people. They use magic like wizards. In the book I read, the naga made people do whatever it wanted by taking over their minds. We are really lucky it didn't do that to us."

"We are locked in a cage so it can keep us as a snack for later." Emma grumbled. "I don't feel lucky."

Ambril whimpered.

Uruleth, please grant me your strength! Faint white light appeared over her body, soaking into her arms and chest. Emma blinked. *It worked!* The magic didn't even feel different or strained. *It's not all my magic, only... Linganthas is weak here because there are no plants.*

"What did you do?" Ambril leaned forward and clung to her.

"Made myself stronger." Emma tried to break the padlock open, straining until her knuckles turned white, her face turned red, and she started to see spots of light dancing in her vision.

The lock didn't break.

Emma gave up and sank into a slouch, trying to catch her breath.

"If your magic can't make you as strong as a giant, you'll not be breaking that lock, I'm afraid." Ambril sniffled. "It's no use squeezing out. The holes are too small. Not even Kimber can fit."

A few breaths later, Emma rolled around to sit, raised both legs, and mule-kicked the cage door as hard as she could. The big iron structure shook to no avail. The thick bars would easily contain a full-grown man, even a strong, angry one. She might have been able to summon a root powerful enough to tear the door off, except for two problems. One: the ground beneath her appeared to be solid stone. Roots couldn't grow there. Two: Linganthas seemed to be weak in this place.

She turned her attention to the gaps between the metal bands. The flat, rectangular iron strips looked as big as broadswords, about three inches wide, half an inch thick. Rivets joined the vertical ones to the horizontal ones wherever they crossed. The square openings between the bars did, indeed, look far too small for her to crawl out. She could just about fit her head through them, but her shoulders, and the rest of her, wouldn't make it.

Akeem held up a fragment of bone that seemed to have once been a person's leg. One end came to a sharp, broken point. The boy wielded it like a dagger while whispering in Drajmiri. At a guess, Emma figured he tried to tell them he'd fight as hard as he could to protect them. Maybe he wanted them to run as soon as one of the snake-man's guards opened the cage. Of course, the next time this cage opened, one or more of them would become dinner.

Emma didn't want to be here then.

"There has to be some way we can escape." Emma gazed up at the top of the cage, studying every rivet for signs of weakness.

Three similar cages sat around them in the room, all empty except for a scattering of bones.

Emma sat there, thinking and studying for a while.

Kimber yawned, sat up, and looked around, one eye open wider than the other. "Oy. This nae good. I fink we in big trouble."

"Yeah." Ambril wiped her eyes. "It's so cold and damp here. My dress is ruined and we're going to catch our death of cold."

Emma stared at her.

"I am not being serious." Ambril buried her face in her hands. "I don't care about the dress if we're going to die."

Kimber stuck her head out the front to examine the lock. "I kin open it if I 'ad propa lockpicks."

"What?" Ambril gawked at her as though she'd done something criminally horrible, like show up at the dinner table with muddy hands. "You can pick locks? Like a thief?"

"Aye, if they ain't tae 'ard. I grew up 'round teefs an' the loike." Kimber smiled innocently. "But I'm no' a teef 'cause I fink stealin' is bad."

Ambril scoffed. "You didn't grow up. You're what, eight?"

Kimber nodded, grinning wider.

Frustrated at the solidity of the cage, Emma sat back on her heels and grabbed two fistfuls of her hair. "Grr! I hate cages."

With no better ideas, Emma lay flat on her stomach and stuck her head out one of the square holes. She could almost get one shoulder through, so she backed up and tried extending an arm out in front of her first. She still got stuck at the other shoulder and armpit.

"As skinny as you are, you can't fit... we're doomed." Ambril buried her face in her hands and wept.

"I'm not *that* skinny." Emma, partially stuck in the opening, rolled her eyes.

"You're likely the smallest, well, smallest for our age, person in town." Ambril sniffled. "Your mother as well. The two of you look like elves."

"Astari elves are thinner than us." Emma grumbled, still trying to pull herself forward despite having her shoulder braced against an iron bar.

"I don't see how that's even possible." Ambril giggle-sobbed. "Those silly superficial girls I have to socialize with would quite honestly kill someone if they could be as thin as you."

Akeem waved the sharpened bone around while talking as if explaining some grand scheme.

Emma lay there, too angry and scared to care about squirming back into the cage. She couldn't give up. Kimber took advantage of her compromising position and started tickling her sides. That her little sister could still find the ability to play while they sat in a cage waiting to be eaten by a giant snake almost brought her to tears. She squirmed, unable to bring herself to yell at Kimber to stop tickling her.

"You's not laughin'," whispered Kimber. "What's wrong?"

Emma wriggled backward, pulling her head past the bars. She sat back on her heels and fumed. If she stayed angry, she wouldn't break down crying like Ambril. "There is a lot wrong, but not with me. I'm not hurt."

We're too far away from home for anyone to help us. I don't know how long we have before the snake man gets hungry. She knew a little about snakes, nothing about naga. Ambril had some ideas from a storybook, though those could've been all made up. Emma did know snakes ate huge meals every few days. Based on the size of the creature, she figured he'd eat one of them, then wait several days before coming back for someone else. The last two survivors might even starve to death before he got around to swallowing them whole. She didn't think the snake man would take care of them by offering food.

In her fear and grief, she fell down a distracting road of trying to decide if it would be better to be consumed first or last. Should she volunteer to go first to buy time for the others in hopes something else might save them? Or would it upset Kimber too much to watch her taken away?

Stop. Sad thoughts won't help us.

Emma grabbed the bars in front of her. No amount of rage she had in her small body could defeat the iron. Still, Uruleth heard her. The forest spirits weren't stuck all the way across the world. They existed everywhere. Of all the forest spirits, Emma felt the strongest connection with Ylithir, the Wolf Spirit. He embodied cunning and also loyalty to his pack. Strength might not be the best way to go about escaping the cage.

Eyes closed, Emma concentrated on her memory of the time she'd met the Wolf Spirit in a dream state. She imagined herself kneeling in the meadow behind her home at night under a clear, star-filled sky where the ghostly form of a large wolf watched her from the trees.

Great Ylithir, please hear me. I need your help. Emma clung to every ounce of her fear as well as the desire to protect her family and friend, her pack. Her need to do anything to keep Kimber safe burned so strong in her heart it brought tears to her eyes.

In her imagination, the ghostly wolf emerged from the forest, crossing the meadow like a breeze before circling close around her. A sense of real presence fell over her.

A monster is going to kill us.

"Naga," whispered an ephemeral voice. "They are dark beings, full of malice, trickery, and venom."

Sensing Ylithir so close to her in a time of need made tears roll down her cheeks. *How can I protect my pack? How can we survive this?*

"You can outwit the Naga," replied the voice of Ylithir.

A sense of vertigo came over Emma as if she'd fallen off the bed. Rather than crash to the stone floor, she landed on her hands and knees… only it didn't quite feel as though she knelt. Despite being pitched forward, the cold touch of stone met her hands as well as the forward parts of her feet, not her knees.

Encouragement and satisfaction radiated from the wolf spirit.

Ambril gasped.

Kimber made an, "ooooh" sound.

Akeem yelped and babbled something no one understood.

The smell of the sewer intensified almost to choking. New smells she'd never encountered before danced in her nostrils. Emma opened her eyes. The square opening between the bars right in front of her face seemed bigger. Beyond, the sewer didn't seem as dark as it had before. This confused her until she looked down at her hands—and instead saw black-furred paws. Not quite believing her eyes, she twisted to look back at a body covered in the same lustrous black fur. The others in the cage appeared to have grown larger. Kimber stared at her, making the same face she usually gave fuzzy rabbits when they strayed into the meadow behind the house.

"Puppy!" cooed Kimber, right before scooping Emma up and squeezing her.

"Ack," squeaked Emma, realizing one of the new smells came from her sister.

The other scents must belong to Ambril and Akeem, as well as the guards who put them in here.

"A talking puppy." Ambril leaned closer. "Em? Is that you?"

"Ov course it is! Ya jus' saw 'er change in'o a wolf." Kimber squeezed her. "She's dorble!"

Emma, head draped over Kimber's shoulder, stared at Akeem. The boy pressed himself into the back wall of the cage as if frightened of her. When the full realization came over her that she'd shapeshifted into a wolf, she almost burst into a fit of cheering. For what seemed like forever, she looked forward to the day one of the forest spirits gave her such a boon—and she'd been hoping with all her heart it would be Ylithir. Not that she would've been upset if Uruleth let her turn into a bear or Strixian gave her the form of an owl... or any of the others.

But the Wolf Spirit? Perfect. She couldn't have asked for better. Despite her dire situation, she nearly cried from pure elation. Alas, she did not have time for a proper celebration. Emma couldn't bask in the joy of what he'd given her.

"Kimber," chirped Emma in a high-pitched voice not quite hers. "Put me down. We have to get out of here."

"Okay." Kimber set her on her paws.

"This is remarkable." Ambril pet her. "But I don't know how this helps."

Emma sneezed at the overwhelming smells. "It helps. Kimber needs lockpicks. I can go get them now... or maybe find a key."

Without waiting for them to ask more questions, Emma stuck her head through the square hole in the bars and wriggled out of the cage.

"She squeezed!" Kimber clapped.

Emma peered back at the iron box trapping her sister, friend, and the mysterious boy. Ambril looked terrified. The girl said nothing out loud; her eyes begged Emma not to leave them there.

"Be back soon," said Emma.

"We no' goin' anywhere," Kimber grumbled, rolling her eyes.

Emma dashed out of the room of cages and raced down the sewer passage, her little claws clicking on the stone. Scent trails offered her only sense of direction as she hadn't been awake when the men brought them to the cage. Minutes later, she scurried past a man who didn't pay much attention to her, perhaps mistaking her for one of the huge rats. She didn't feel *that* small. Yes, the rats in this place looked huge—for rats—but she'd turned into a wolf pup.

It made sense, after all, for a ten-year-old child to transform into a baby wolf. The significance of being given such a gift at this age did not escape her. To hear Mama talk, druids had to reach at least adulthood before a spirit chose them for a form. Mama herself only gained Naraja's blessing to turn into a panther recently. Nan used to tease her for it taking so long. Mama's gift from Naraja had also come a time of need. Ylithir knew Emma was in danger and would certainly die without his help.

She would forever hold him sacred, even more than she already did.

Assuming, of course, she managed to live long enough to go home. Turning into a wolf puppy did not exactly transform her into an engine of war like Greyfang or Moonsong. Either of those great wolves could tear the naga to bits... probably. Emma didn't know much about naga, after all, other than she did *not* want to fight one. Or be seen by one again.

Sneakiness would be her only chance to get out of here and save everyone.

She followed the scent trail to an archway in the sewer passage that led to an underground hallway. This part didn't look like a sewer. All sorts of noises came from inside—voices, clinking of plates, scuffing of boots, sounds her human ears would've missed. A small, fast-moving wolf pup had a good chance of getting away if spotted. The men would be slow and clumsy compared to her.

The children had no other chance but her. Emma and Emma alone might be able to free her sister, her friend, and some strange boy who apparently tried to help them before the naga devoured them.

Emma trotted into the hallway. She sniffed around, finding a room full of beds—living quarters for twenty or more guards. She hurried away before any of them saw her. The next doorway led to a corridor without any other doors except for the very end. It appeared to be a temple arranged around a jade statue of a naga. She couldn't tell if the creature was arrogant enough to have built a shrine to itself or if the statue depicted some manner of naga god. Emma also didn't care.

Nope. Not going in there.

She skipped the temple corridor and raced to the next nearest doorway where a thick, purple curtain hung in place of a solid door. Emma nosed under the fabric and slipped past it into a huge, rectangular room. She'd entered from the narrower end of the rectangle. The opposite wall had to be at least eighty feet away. Several long tables stood beside an array of large shelves on the right side, all laden with an assortment of boxes, scrolls, jars, and shiny things she didn't recognize. She looked to the left and nearly yelped in fear.

In a small alcove recessed midway down the left wall, the naga lay curled up on top of a huge round lilac-colored cushion, evidently sleeping.

At the farthest end of the room, the Box of Wonder sat on a small table along with a number of glowing potions, a metal scroll case, a sword, a dagger, and some wands.

It wasn't his. He collects magic stuff. He stole it from us! She blinked in surprise upon noticing her tail wagged excitedly and she hadn't even thought about doing it. *The naga probably smells magic things somehow. That's how he sent his guards right to us. They hadn't been chasing Akeem for stealing bread. Or, maybe whoever sold it to Ambril's father stole it from this naga.*

Emma stared at the box. The gems on the outside glowed. In this dark room, no sunlight could be responsible for it, meaning they really did light up with magic, as Kimber said. Her heart leapt. It had to be done resting. They could go home!

She eyed the sleeping naga, tempted to sneak in and grab the box.

It wouldn't matter if they could open the cage or not. If she took the box back to everyone else, they could all go inside it. Problem being, her little wolf cub form had a mouth too small to get around and grip the box. The naga might also hear her trying to jump up onto the table. She could turn back to her human form and grab the box easily. If she did that, all the guards she snuck by as a wolf would see her.

They're going to see Kimber, Ambril, and Akeem running around if I find a way to open the cage.

She narrowed her eyes, thinking.

Being spotted and chased by guards might not matter if they could get to the box before the men caught them. All they needed to do would be to open the lid and *poof!* In the box. The guards might be confused when the children they chased disappeared. That should give them enough time to lock the lid. They'd be safe inside the box.

The best plan sounded like getting everyone out of the cage, then trying to sneak back here. Even if the naga woke up, the same plan still worked. As long as they could get to the box before the naga did anything, the magic would let them escape. A big chance, but she had no other ideas. As a wolf cub, she couldn't carry the box around. In her normal form, she couldn't get the box back to the cage without being caught. Their best option would be to get everyone out and make a run for the box.

It would have to work.

She backed out of the naga's bedchamber and kept going down the hall.

A wisp of smell stood out from the other scents, one she recognized. She'd picked it up right outside the cage.

The man who put us there.

Trying not to snarl, Emma held her nose low to the ground and followed the scent track down another hallway, past a few more doorways to a small room containing a table, one chair, one basic cot for a bed, and a single man. The table stood against the left wall, the man seated at it had his back to the room. He appeared to be in the midst of dinner, or perhaps lunch since she had no idea how long they'd been asleep. He didn't notice the black wolf pup standing with her head poked past the fabric door.

An iron keyring with four large keys sat on the table beside the bowl from which the man ate.

Giant keys for a giant padlock.

Emma slipped into the room. She slinked to the right, moving around behind the man in the chair and crawling under the bed to hide in case another guard walked by. Emma flattened herself out and stared at the man's back. Unfortunately, the keyring sat right in front of him next to his meal. Maybe an experienced pickpocket could snag it without being noticed. Emma, not being an experienced pickpocket, didn't see any possible way she could get the keyring without him catching her. She thought about jumping up on the table, grabbing the keyring in her teeth, and running as fast as she could back to the cage.

It might work if she surprised him too much to grab her before she could jump off the table.

The plan had three big problems: the other keys on the ring. Only one of them went to the padlock she needed to open. If the man chased her all the way back to the cage, she wouldn't have the time to find the right key. They'd never get out of the cage at all, much less manage to get to the naga's bedroom without being caught.

Emma sighed, dropping her gaze off the table to the floor—right onto a big crack in the stone.

All a root needs is a little crack and it can break the biggest rock.

Safe under the bed—for now—Emma closed her eyes. *Thank you, Ylithir for the gift of the wolf shape. I will adore it always.* She needed to use other magic now, which required returning to her normal self. Soon after she thought about shapeshifting back to her human form, her forearms became cold.

Emma opened her eyes to find herself back to normal, no warm fur between her arms and the floor. It occurred to her that her entire body didn't freeze. She looked down at herself, still wearing her favorite blue dress.

Ooh. No wonder I've always loved this dress so much! I must have sensed magic in it. She smiled, choked up at the thought of how much she loved Nan. *There's magic in it. It followed me into wolf shape.* Emma grinned. Why would Nan go to the trouble of putting magic like that in a child's dress? Did she suspect Emma might earn Ylithir's favor so early? Or did the magic she put in the dress do more than one thing? The fabric never stayed wet and never seemed to get dirty. She could ask Nan about it later. Right now, she had bigger problems. The naga could wake up and eat them at any time. They might have days, hours, or minutes left to live.

She stared at the crack in the floor, extended her hands forward, and focused on the man eating.

This is probably stupid... but I don't have time to think.

9

A STICKY CONUNDRUM

*C*alling to Linganthas, Emma tapped into every bit of emotion she had… mostly fear.

The roots she tried to summon meant her little sister would live. They meant Ambril would live. They even meant the strange boy would live. Empowering the roots to crawl all the way through the world to Drajmir would prove Ylithir hadn't given her a chance she'd waste.

Not through the whole world. There's a river next to the city. There's water in the sewers. There have to be plants somewhere nearby. Linganthas, please send me your fury.

After minutes of exhausting concentration, a thin sapling peeked up out of the crack in the floor. Emma focused on it, her hands glowing under a shroud of dark emerald green light. The rootling grew taller and thicker, breaking the crack in the floor open a little wider. Emma called more roots one by one until a tangle of them sprouted up, displacing a large slab of rock. As soon as she felt the mass of vines sufficient to the task, she swung them at the man.

Lashing roots wrapped around the guard's head, neck, chest, and arms. He gave an oddly quiet murmur of alarm as the viny mass dragged him off his chair, flipped him over, and slapped him into the floor, mushing his face against the stone, pointed away from her. She gathered more strands out of the increasingly large hole in the stone, which she wrapped around the man's legs, almost mummifying him in thorny strands. The relatively small thorns wouldn't cause serious damage, only hurt if he struggled too much.

The man squirmed, grunted, and—at least for now—decided it not worth the pain to fight, so he lay still.

Emma crawled out from under the bed. She sprang to her feet, ran to the table for the keys, then darted out of the room so fast the hanging cloth serving as a door whipped into the air behind her. Three steps from the room, she clamped the keyring between her teeth and dove forward, reaching her hands out to catch the floor as she called upon Ylithir.

She landed on wolf paws, smoothly breaking into a galloping run. The transition from human to animal shape came so instinctively, she may as well have been doing it her entire life. Murmuring from the guard she wrapped up in vines grew louder. It wouldn't take long before the man shouted for help. Emma didn't think he saw her under the bed. He probably didn't see her with his head wrapped in vines. No one here except for the naga seemed likely to understand where the roots came from. Once the guards realized the keyring walked away, they'd go straight to the cage room.

Emma had extremely limited time. She couldn't risk getting lost. The scent trail would lead her back to the cages and the form of a black wolf cub would keep her hidden in a dark, underground sewer. Without invoking Naraja's magic, the wolf also ran faster than she could as a human.

The keys jangled in her mouth in time with her stride. She tried to trot gently out of the underground corridors where the guards lived, so the keyring didn't make *too* much noise. Once she reached the sewer again, she stopped caring about metal rattling. The man she trapped in roots would no doubt be screaming by now... unless the roots smacked his face into the stone floor hard enough to knock him loopy.

Running through the sewer passed in a blur, feeling like it took mere seconds.

She skidded to a stop outside the cage.

Ambril lunged forward, sticking her arm out through the bars and grabbing the keyring. "You got them!"

Emma shapeshifted back to human form. "Yes. Here. Let me do it. I can see. You're reaching around blind."

Ambril practically threw the keys at her.

"Yay!" Kimber clapped.

Akeem stared in mute shock at Emma.

She tried the first key, which didn't turn. The second key also didn't turn. At what sounded like footsteps in the hallway behind her, she jumped and fumbled the keyring, dropping it at her knees.

"Hurry up!" whispered Ambril.

Emma grabbed the third key off the floor and stuffed it into the lock. That one worked. The enormous padlock popped open, dragged down by its own weight. She needed to use both hands—and most of her strength—to lift the solid metal thing out of the hoop on the cage wall and drop it aside.

Ambril shoved the cage door open. She waited for Kimber to crawl out, then followed. Akeem scurried out behind them, taking a few steps away, staring warily at Emma.

"All right." Emma stood. "We have two choices, and one of them isn't good."

"What are they?" whispered Ambril.

She explained the naga's bedroom and the box, as well as finding the corridor that would lead them out to the surface on the other end of the sewer. "If we run to the surface, we'd be going away from the naga and all his guards. But... the box is still here. We'd have to find another way back home."

"That's not the good choice, is it?" Ambril bit her lower lip.

"It is. Leaving is safer." Emma ground her toes into the stone floor, fidgeting from indecision. "The bad choice is trying to sneak past the naga and get the box. I'm pretty sure he's going to wake up and catch us if we try to cross his room. It won't matter if guards chase us. All we have to do is get to the box. Even if they corner us, as soon as we open the lid, we're safe inside."

Ambril nodded. "I don't want to be in this place. And those men will probably chase after us outside if we try to run away."

"Would they? He's got the box." Emma smoothed her hands down her dress. "I don't think we taste so good he'd chase us across the desert. He could eat anything... or anyone."

Kimber made a sick noise.

"Eww." Ambril grimaced. "I don't like that he eats people. What can we do? We're only kids. He's going to chase us. I say we try to get to the box. Emma's right. If we just touch it, we go inside and can lock the lid."

"Yeah." Kimber pointed at the boy. "We bring him wif' us. Don't want him to get ate."

Emma spun to face him. "Akeem." She waved at him to follow.

He took a cautious step closer, asking something.

"I don't know what you said." Emma sighed. She pointed at the open doorway, made a 'shh' gesture at him, then pantomimed sneaking around.

Akeem flashed a roguish smile, nodding.

Emma took Kimber's hand. "Follow me and stay quiet. If anyone sees us and starts to chase, we have to run. Don't stop for anything."

"What are we doing again?" Ambril shivered.

"Go to the box. Open the lid, appear inside the box, lock the lid." Emma looked at her, then Kimber, then Akeem. "If someone sees us and starts chasing, try not to panic. Keep running. They probably won't work too hard to catch us if they think we're running into a dead end."

Ambril exhaled. "Okay."

"You 'ave a loud dress." Kimber nudged Ambril. "Try no' tae rustle."

Emma headed for the door. Kimber took Ambril's hand. Akeem followed them. At least the boy looked like he knew how to move quietly. Not being able to smell her way along, Emma relied purely on memory: not too difficult, as it had only been a few minutes since she went back and forth. She couldn't believe the guards hadn't erupted in a frenzy of searching yet. Maybe they did think something peculiar burst up from the floor and didn't blame her or some other outsider sneaking around. That man couldn't simply still be laying on the floor not doing anything, could he?

As fast as she could go without her feet pattering too loud on the stone, Emma scurried down the sewer passage and went into the dry hallway. She avoided going near the door to the living quarters, squeezing against the opposite wall. Here, the muffled grunting and growling coming from the trapped guard filled the hallway ahead. He didn't make too much noise. Apparently, he *did* continue to lay on the floor and squirm in relative silence.

Strange. Why isn't he calling for help? Did he see me? Is he ashamed a little girl beat him?

She didn't care enough to wait around for the answer. Feeling like an idiot mouse charging straight to the cat's den, Emma approached the purple hanging cloth in the bedroom doorway. She paused there, looked back at the others, and made another 'shh' gesture. Everyone nodded. Emma took two deep breaths to find courage, then pulled the cloth aside.

A tiny squeak came from Ambril's nose as they entered and spotted the naga curled up asleep on the huge round cushion. Even though he slept, being in the presence of such a monster nearly paralyzed the rich girl with fear.

Akeem glared at the creature, almost as if he thought about trying to kill it with his sharp broken bone.

Emma crept forward, favoring quiet over speed. Her bare feet made no sound whatsoever on the stone floor. Ambril's fancy peach-colored slippers occasionally scuffed, though not louder than the constant rustling of her dress. Barely breathing, Emma proceeded to the right, as far away from the naga's bed as the room allowed. She turned her body sideways to get another inch further away from him, sliding along the edge of a table full of various relics, jars, and scrolls, not caring at all what any of them might be.

She mouthed 'do not touch anything' without giving it voice.

Ambril and Kimber nodded.

Though he continued to stare death at the naga, Akeem followed them.

Emma passed the far corner of a table at the center of the room. They'd made it slightly past the midway point between the door in and the box.

"Dinner time already?" asked the naga.

She didn't look back. "Run!"

Emma bolted into a sprint toward the box. A whooshing noise came from the direction of the naga. Kimber's full weight lurched into her from behind, her sister clinging to her like a backpack. An instant after the strange whoosh, a wet splattering noise surrounded them. The bare stone floor turned into a gummy, sticky mess, dragging her to a dead stop. Slimy white muck like a mixture of raw eggs and congealed spidersilk reached up her legs past her ankles, holding her as surely as a pair of strong hands.

Screaming, Emma flailed her arms for balance. Most of Kimber's weight dropped off her back, though her sister continued to cling.

Ambril shrieked.

Emma peered back over her shoulder.

Akeem squatted atop the table, having avoided a large, round patch of white stickiness that covered a more or less circular patch at least ten feet in every direction from Emma. Ambril struggled to pick her feet up off the floor, seemingly glued in place.

"I'as stuck! Cannae move!" yelled Kimber, also struggling.

No! No! No! Emma stared at the box, less than forty feet away in front of her at the back end of the huge room. She looked down. The sticky mass entirely covered her feet and went halfway up her shins. Kimber's feet, however, rested *atop* the white slime. Her little sister only pretended to be trapped. Ambril, alas, did not pretend.

Akeem avoided whatever magic the naga threw at them entirely by jumping onto the table before it hit the floor. Unlike Kimber, he *obviously* escaped the trapping spell.

The naga chuckled. "Silly children. I suppose the boy will do for now. You'll need to be washed first, and of course, thanks to that little bauble of yours, I'll need to rid you of your head first." A curved gold bladed scimitar appeared out of thin air amid a sparkling flash in the naga's right hand.

Akeem looked around, spotted something of interest on one of the smaller shelves at the wall, then jumped to the floor, running across to the shelf.

"Where do you think you're going, boy?" The naga slithered after him in no great hurry.

When Akeem reached the shelf, he grabbed a small red bottle, spun around, and hurled it at the naga.

Evidently surprised, the creature screamed, crossing his arms to shield his snake head from the tumbling potion. The bottle struck his left forearm, exploding into a blast of fire, heat, and light that charred half the snake's face and most of his chest black.

The blast of light faded to reveal Akeem dashing out of the room past the purple cloth.

Roaring in anger, the naga shot a glare at the girls for less than a second, then raced off after Akeem, tail whipping side to side in fury.

He thinks we're all stuck. Emma strained to pull her right foot out of the mess, but it wouldn't budge.

"Wait," whispered Kimber. She jumped onto the table, ran a few steps to the end, then leapt off it to clean floor past the edge of the sticky patch. "Grabbin' the box!"

Emma couldn't do much more than wait for the few seconds it took Kimber to retrieve the Box of Wonder and rush back over to her and Ambril. She just about reached Emma's side when a magical glow rippled across the white stickiness at her feet and the substance grabbed her.

"Oops." Kimber peered down. "I'as stuck fer true now." She looked up, smiling at them over the box. "No, we're not."

Emma reached one arm back to Ambril, who took her hand. Kimber grabbed her other hand and opened the box lid. A flash of bright light shone out from inside, fading in a second to reveal the little alcove with the glowing rune circle.

Freed from the sticky slime, Emma's feet appeared unhurt— merely clean.

Ambril swooned to sit on the floor. "We're alive!"

"That was amazing!" Emma hugged Kimber. "You jumped up onto my back when the magic went splat."

"Aye." Kimber giggled. "Saw one o' the teefs use a fingee he frew at someone did the same fing, almost." She pantomimed throwing something. "It made sticky stuff when it smacked the ground, just black and gooey, nae like a spoider."

Emma started to reach for the lock lever, but hesitated. "Kimber. You stay in here with Ambril."

"What?" Ambril looked up at her. "You aren't going outside."

"Akeem. I can't just leave him." Emma shooed the others out of the magic circle.

Ambril hurried out of the glowing runes, then tried to pull Emma with her. "What are you going to do?"

"I don't know." Emma pushed Ambril and Kimber away from the alcove, then grabbed the blue orb on the wall. "But I have to try!"

She appeared in the naga's bedroom, hastily jumping off the sticky patch before it could grab her again. Angry screaming and commotion echoed in the hallway outside. A sick weight formed in her stomach. Chances were, she'd only get there in time to watch the naga chop the head off the boy who tried to help them. What could she possibly do against a creature so powerful and evil?

Still, it wouldn't be right to run away and leave Akeem to his fate, especially after he basically saved their lives by distracting the monster and making it chase him.

Emma tucked the Box of Wonder under her left arm and ran toward the commotion.

10

DUST AND BONES

*E*mma zoomed past the doorway cloth into the corridor.

The patter of Akeem running on stone echoed to her left along with the tromp of boots and the naga's magically deep, unnatural voice shouting in Drajmiri. Emma ran toward the ruckus, which seemed to be coming from around a corner at least sixty feet away from her. Emma sprinted down the corridor, stopped at the corner, and peeked around.

The naga and two human guards chased Akeem down the next hallway. Thankfully, the enormous serpent did not move with great speed, somewhat slower than a normal human could run. His two guards appeared capable—but not willing—to go faster.

Still not sure what she intended to do, Emma resumed chasing them. If she could find a way to get past the naga and his guards, then crash into Akeem, she need only lift the lid and they'd be safe.

The boy darted left around another corner.

At this, the naga slowed even more, laughing. He lazily glided around the corner where the boy went. Emma stared in horror as his thick serpent body—almost as tall off the floor as her waist—slithered out of sight.

Uh oh. Not good. Why is he laughing? Emma slowed from sprinting to jogging, trying to be quiet. If the naga saw her coming, she'd have no choice but to jump back into the box before he could magic her to sleep a second time. As much as it would pain her to leave Akeem to the naga, she wouldn't have a choice. If he caught her again, Kimber and Ambril would be in serious trouble. Kimber would never use the box to teleport home and abandon Emma there. She'd certainly leave the safety of the enchanted room and try to save Emma. This, of course, would definitely lead to Kimber being captured.

Emma stopped at the corner, listening to soft bootsteps and the low scratching of serpent scales on stone. She peered around.

Akeem pressed himself up against a dead-end wall. The naga and his two guards sauntered closer, taking their sweet time. Emma eased herself past the corner, creeping up behind them. She couldn't take her eyes off the enormous snake, thinking she could slip down his throat as easily as a foot going into a shoe. The naga could devour her and not even get fatter. She'd seen a normal snake or two, bulged out after eating mice or rats. If this naga swallowed Emma, it wouldn't bulge much at all.

What am I doing? She shivered, trying not to think about moving *closer* to a giant snake man who used magic, had fangs, and wanted to eat her. Emma cringed in fear. It was beyond foolish to go anywhere near the creature. It cast a spell that put her to sleep before. If it saw her, she'd have mere seconds to yank open the box lid or she'd wake in the cage again... if she woke at all.

Emma hesitated... until she looked up from the snake tail and saw the fear in Akeem's eyes.

The naga stopped, leaving only about ten feet of distance between him and the wall trapping the boy. A guard stood on either side of the creature, blocking the hallway. In order to reach Azeem, Emma would have to ram herself into one of the men, hoping surprise knocked him off balance and he didn't have a chance to grab her. Emma didn't weigh much. She probably wouldn't move him at all... like a squirrel trying to tackle a tree. Not good odds.

The naga and said something in Drajmiri, his voice dripping with arrogance.

Akeem held his head high, trying to act unafraid. He replied in a casual tone.

An evil chuckle slipped from the naga as he drifted closer to the boy. The creature leaned back, rising on his tail until his head nearly touched the ceiling. He drew his golden sword up high, about to swing at the boy's neck.

Gripped by desperation and horror, Emma thrust her right hand forward, squeezing her fingers into a fist. *Linganthas, I call on your wrath!*

Cracks appeared in the walls, floor, and ceiling around the naga. The unexpected noise and rain of dust gave the creature pause. He glanced left and right.

Emma poured her magic into her desire. *I won't let you kill him!*

Five more guards appeared at the end of the hallway behind Emma. All drew curved swords and stalked toward her.

Dozens of roots and vines exploded out from the walls, floor, and ceiling amid a shower of rock fragments and dirt. Whipping strands wrapped around the naga's head, neck, arms, and body, pulling him in four different directions. A muffled cry of rage leaked from the creature's non-lips, his mouth held closed by the roots wrapped around his snakelike head. A black serpent's tongue stabbed feverishly at the air. In seconds, rage became fear. The creature couldn't move or speak. Taken by panic, the naga thrashed, swinging his huge serpent tail side to side, accidentally swatting one of the guards next to him into the wall so hard the man bounced away and hit the ground, unconscious.

The other guard simply stood there as though he didn't care he might be crushed by a thrashing snake tail.

Emma crept forward, trying to continue focusing magic into the roots while moving away from the men coming after her.

Akeem darted over to the remaining guard in front of him. He ducked under a grabbing hand, yanked a dagger from the man's belt, and scrambled backward, evading another attempted grab. The naga's terrified flailing swept the second guard's legs out from under him. He fell on his backside, winded but awake. The men behind Emma closed in, the nearest two raising their swords. She couldn't go any farther forward without risk of the naga's tail smashing her. All her magic went to immobilizing the creature. If she stopped concentrating on it, the naga would break free. It appeared to realize she was the source of the enchanted vines and struggled to smack her with his tail. Mere inches stood between her face and the tip of the flailing serpent.

Emma did the only thing she could: she stared up at the men with her best 'please don't hurt me' face.

The men's expressions remained blank and uncaring. They didn't stop.

Emma threw caution aside and spun to make a mad dash past the flailing serpent before the swords took her head off.

Sensing opportunity, the naga swung his tail up and to the right, about to smash it down at her.

"Yamut 'ayuha alshirir!" shouted Akeem; he raised the dagger over his head in both hands, then rammed it at the trapped naga's heart.

A muffled gargle of agony slipped from the snake's bound mouth. His tongue flailed in a final dying frenzy. The giant tail swinging for Emma went over her head, smacked the wall, and fell limp at her feet.

The five men behind her froze in place.

Emma gasped, wide-eyed in disbelief. Standing behind the creature, she couldn't see what happened, but a fleshy *squish* gave her enough of a clue. Akeem, also apparently shocked by what he'd done, stepped back from the naga, no longer holding the dagger.

All seven guards in the hallway disintegrated into a dull red mist. Their weapons, their armor, and their clothes disappeared into the same crimson vapor as their bodies.

An orange glow leaked out from between the serpent's scales. In seconds, the naga's fleshy parts disintegrated into a faintly glowing cloud of red vapor, leaving behind only clean white bones—a dagger stuck in the center of the not-quite-human ribcage.

Not real. Emma swallowed, staring at the dusty remains of the guards. *No wonder they acted so strange. He made them with magic.*

Akeem picked up the naga skull, then rushed over to take her hand.

"Are you okay?" Emma looked him over.

The boy paused briefly to ogle the gold box, dismissing it way too fast to seem normal. He chattered excitedly in Drajmiri while shaking the naga skull at her, as if he'd found all the gold of a king's treasure.

"Umm. I don't know what you're saying." Emma sighed.

He backed up toward the open end of the hallway, tugging her along.

"You want me to go somewhere with you?"

Akeem smiled.

Oh, this is so frustrating! Why do there have to be different languages? "All right. But... wait. I have to put this in something." She lifted the skirt of her dress, partially wrapping it around the Box of Wonder as if to demonstrate the need to conceal it.

He said more she didn't understand, hurriedly pulling her down the corridor to the guard's living quarters. Emma almost yelled at him not to go in there, then remembered watching the guards turn to red smoke. Sure enough, they found the room empty of people. Or empty of 'not people.' She didn't want to know what the men were or how the naga made them. It didn't take Akeem long to find some plain cloth sacks from the guards' belongings. He gave her one and put the naga skull in the other.

She barely had time to stuff the box into the sack before he again took her hand and raced off, towing her down the corridor toward the sewer exit.

11

VAGABONDS

*A*keem towed Emma down the hall, through the sewer, up the stairs, and out into the city.

The abrupt change from underground darkness to desert daylight hurt her eyes. She cringed, unable to shield herself from the glare. Her left arm clutched the box to her side, her right stretched out in front of her, trapped in the boy's excited grip. She felt like a little frog Tam found and desperately wanted to show off to Mama, Da, and Nan.

It surprised her somewhat to find the sun out. The heat remained oppressive, though it waned with early evening. Akeem, also barefoot, appeared to be quite skilled at navigating the city by means of shaded spots to avoid the hottest paving stones. Shadows ran long, stretched in the late-day glare of a sun close to the horizon. This told Emma two things: the direction of west and that they had about an hour, perhaps two, of daylight left. Since the false men brought them to the naga at sunrise, the sleep spell must have knocked her out for most of the day.

What happened in the sewers of this city in Drajmir baffled her. She had no business being anywhere near a monster as fearsome as a naga. Even Da would likely have been worried about fighting it. Emma had used all of her magic, near to the point of fainting from exhaustion, and only managed to hold it still for a little while. It nearly broke loose despite her best effort. Another minute or two, and she would have been too tired to keep holding it down. How could a monster so powerful and evil lose to a simple young boy with a dagger?

She thought of the bad wizard Mama choked with a root around the neck. He couldn't use magic when he lost the ability to speak. Her magic wrapped the naga up in so many roots they tied his snake mouth shut. Emma hadn't done it on purpose. Perhaps Linganthas did. Or, she simply got lucky thanks to covering him with as many vines as possible. Emma didn't want to think about what might have happened if the naga used magic.

Also unbelievable: Akeem stabbed it.

He looked back as they ran, all smiles, and said something else she didn't understand while pointing ahead. She assumed he tried to tell her they had almost gotten to where he wanted to show her.

They ran for a little while more before he went down a narrow alley, past five homes, and stopped at one on the right. Like most every other building she'd seen here, it had a hanging cloth instead of an actual door. Akeem brought her inside, went down a short hallway, then a set of stairs to a basement.

After going through another hanging cloth, they entered a room where a large group of young boys gathered. The youngest child looked about her age, the oldest maybe fourteen. Two adult men and a woman sat around a small table at the opposite side of the room. Numerous sleeping mats, chairs, and tiny tables littered the floor, along with sacks of various unknown goods.

Is this a den of pickpockets? Emma managed a weak smile.

The other boys and the adults looked at Akeem, but soon noticed Emma and stared at her. While she had black hair like every other person she'd seen here, her pale skin and sapphire blue eyes definitely marked her as a foreigner, as did the style of her dress. No one regarded her with hostility or even suspicion. A boy a little older than her offered a tin plate with some bits of bread and a brown gloopy substance full of little beige beads. It smelled relatively good, probably beans of some kind.

Despite feeling guilty for having food while Kimber and Ambril sat inside the box, Emma didn't want to be rude, so she took the plate. She could always summon a meatplant for the others to eat once they found a safe place.

"Thank you."

The boy smiled and said something she didn't follow.

Akeem pulled Emma over to the table where the adults sat, chattering at them in rapid, excited Drajmiri. One of the men bore enough of a resemblance to the boy that Emma figured it must be his father, or perhaps a much older brother.

He nodded to the boy, then looked at Emma. "Hello, child. I am Jabir, father of Akeem."

"Hello!" She exhaled. "Oh, thank Ylithir, you know my language."

"I have traveled some." He smiled. "I understand you do not speak Drajmiri."

"I don't. Sorry." She gazed around. "I don't mean to intrude. Your son brought me here. Does he think I'm an orphan?"

Jabir laughed. "He wonders, yes. Thought you might need a safe place to stay. We are unaware of any other foreigners in the city. Do you have a family?"

"Yes. They are back home."

Emma sat at the table, eating the meal of bread and strange beans seasoned with strong spices. She'd not yet ever had anything so powerfully flavored, but found it quite good, even if it did make her tongue feel strange from the potent spices.

"You are welcome to stay with us if you need." Jabir waved at one of the older boys, said something in Drajmiri, then smiled at her. "We will not ask you to ply the trade since you would not be able to blend in here."

"The trade?" She tilted her head. "Are all these boys pickpockets?"

Jabir chuckled. "You are wiser than your age would suggest. Yes, the boys we look after do make a living by borrowing things from those who have more than they need. We also fight a noble war."

"A war?" Emma looked up from the food at him. "They're just children."

"They don't fight in the traditional sense." Jabir reached over and gently grasped the stone crescent moon hanging on the cord around Akeem's neck. "There is an ancient evil in our city. It clouds the minds of everyone here who does not have one of these. When my boys are close to someone, their amulets help free the mind for a short time. We wage war from the shadows, not with blades, but our presence. All one of my boys has to do is hide nearby, and minds around him are momentarily free."

Akeem grasped his father's arm and shook it while speaking rapid Drajmiri.

Jabir rolled his eyes.

The boy said the same short phrase a few times insistently, then reached into his cloth sack and pulled the naga skull out, holding it up so everyone could see it.

His father made a face like the one Da made when Tam whacked him between the legs with his wooden sword by accident. The woman rushed around the table, grabbed Akeem, and began yelling and crying while shaking him.

Akeem leaned against her. Once the woman's emotions settled down, the boy spoke at length to a room hanging on his every word. Emma unobtrusively finished off her meal. She picked up the last bit of bread as the boy stopped talking. Emma looked up to find everyone staring at her again, this time in shocked disbelief.

Jabir rubbed his face, seemingly at the edge of laughing out loud or fainting. "Emma…"

"Yes?"

"My son tells me quite the story. Is it true?"

She fidgeted. "I don't know what he said, so I can't tell you if I think it's true or not."

"Akeem says the two of you not only came face to face with the naga, but you *killed* it." Jabir barked a small laugh. "You two. Children. Killed the naga?"

"Oh. Umm. Akeem killed it. I only held it still." Emma set the bit of bread down on the plate and told him what happened, starting with the three guards finding them in the abandoned house to them showing up here. She avoided mentioning Kimber, Ambril, or the Box of Wonder.

"This is difficult to believe." Jabir picked up the skull to examine. "I cannot imagine how my son would have gotten his hands on such a well-made fake."

"It's not fake." Emma winced. "It's the real skull. After it died, it turned to ashes and bone."

"My meaning is not what my words would imply. It's so unlikely anyone could have made this, it must be real. I am simply struggling to believe my eyes." Jabir set the skull on the table. "We shall know soon enough if the creature's vile curse on this city has faded away. I believe your story is true and thank you for saving my son's life."

"Umm…" Emma's cheeks warmed with blush.

"My son told me you could have escaped with a magic jewelry box, but you ran after him instead."

Emma glanced sideways at Akeem.

The boy smiled at her. "I am sorry for tricking you. I do understand what you say."

"Why?" Emma blinked.

"To hear you being honest. If you and your friends thought I didn't know what you said, you'd speak the truth freely. Also, the Naga can read people's thoughts. I did not want him to see our secrets through your mind. If you had done his bidding and removed my pendant, he would have taken over all our minds. The naga and his minions couldn't touch it. That's why he wanted to cut my head off before devouring me." Akeem rested his hand on her shoulder. "My father and I, and all my brothers, mean you no harm. We well neither steal from you nor leave you to the scorpions."

"These are all your brothers?" Emma's mouth hung open.

"Not by birth. I am my parents' only son." Akeem smiled around at everyone. "They are all orphans. We are brothers of the street. The naga's curse is much weaker on children, so they escaped his control and gathered with my father and I after he learned to make these pendants to protect us."

Jabir gestured at the burlap sack in Emma's lap. "We can fence that for you. If what my son says of it is true, you would be able to live well for the rest of your life on the coins it would bring."

A knowing smile spread across her face. *I don't think the money will last that long.* "I can't sell it. It's not mine."

"I know." Jabir winked.

"I mean, we didn't steal it. We found it."

Jabir laughed. "Right. Of course. How silly of me. You *found* it."

Emma stuck her hand in the bag. These people seemed nice, but desperate. Three adults with almost twenty children to feed would not be able to resist a treasure like the one she held. She didn't think they'd forcibly take it from her. Spending any amount of time in the company of pickpockets made it almost certain the box would 'disappear' soon.

The boy who gave her food also seemed to have given her *his* food and sat there not eating.

Guilty, Emma took her hand back out of the bag and gestured at the dirt floor, calling upon Mythandriel. Vines sprouted up in seconds, from which hung six huge squash-shaped masses.

The boys, Jabir, the other man, and Akeem's mother all leaned back in awe.

"What is that?" Akeem reached to touch the vine.

"I call them meatplants." Emma smiled. "It's food. They taste like meat but it's a plant. You can eat them raw, or cook them."

"An interesting bit of magic." Jabir scratched at his beard. "If you let me see this jewelry box, I can tell you about how much it may sell for to the right person."

Uh oh. Emma stuffed her hand into the bag again and grasped the lid. "Thank you for being nice. I really need to go home now."

She tugged the lid open an inch... and landed on her butt inside the alcove.

Ambril ran over and pulled the lock lever. "You are crazy."

Kimber crashed into her. "You beat the snake man!"

"I can't believe..." Ambril paced around her. "That thing... the roots. You... I'm going to faint from being scared."

"We're safe now." Emma stood.

Ambril ran into the room, over to the table of orbs. In the big crystal ball, the vision showed the boys, Jabir, and the adults all ogling the Box of Wonder, which they'd removed from the sack and set on the table.

Everyone but Akeem looked excited, as if they'd soon be rich. Akeem simply waved goodbye and smiled.

Ambril placed her hand on the blue orb. "I'm thinking really, really, really hard about home. Please take us home. My house. Widowswood Village."

A moment later, the room wobbled and lurched. Once again, Emma felt as if her stomach tried to fall straight out of her to the floor and snapped back up into place.

She fell over, too dizzy to stand.

"We went somewhere..." Ambril groaned in discomfort. "It definitely did something."

"Where did we go?" asked Kimber.

"I'm afraid to look," whispered Ambril.

Emma sighed. She hesitated picking herself up off the floor for fear she would *not* see home inside the big crystal ball. *We can't just lay here.* She closed her eyes and stood.

Going to look in three... two... one...

12

NOT QUITE HOME

*S*now filled the crystal ball, swirling about in a chaotic storm. Faint shadows hinted at trees behind the blizzard. The scene, while beautiful and mesmerizing, also filled Emma with sadness.

"It didn't work." Emma reached down to help Kimber up. "We're not home."

"Ooh. Pretty!" Kimber leaned so close to the big crystal orb her nose touched it and her breath fogged the surface around her face.

Ambril remained on the floor. She closed her eyes and seemed about to burst into tears. After a few seconds, she sighed long and loud, then stood without crying. The girl didn't look happy at all. Her gaze darted back and forth around the room as if she tried to come up with some way to fix everything. She eventually wandered over to the map table.

Emma watched the snow for a little while more.

"It's snowin'." Kimber bounced. "Can we go outside and play?"

"We'll freeze." Ambril shivered. "None of us are dressed for winter. No coats, no mittens, no scarves. You two don't even have any shoes or hose."

"It's all right." Emma walked over to the map table. The silver needle with the spinning sapphires had moved. It now balanced atop one of the two smaller continents near the center of the table, the one far in the north. "We don't really need them. If we have to go outside, the forest spirits will keep us warm."

Ambril pointed to the desert at the southern tip of the northwest continent, then swung her arm to the northeast until she pointed at the needle. "We went in the right direction at least, only we stopped halfway to where we wanted to go."

"Maybe this box can only travel so far at once?" asked Emma.

"No. We went all the way to the desert from home the first time." Ambril tapped her foot. "I thought about home and it moved us in the right direction. None of us are wizards, so we might not be able to make it do exactly what we want."

Kimber remained over by the orb table, fixated on the snowstorm in the giant ball.

"Well, I suppose it's good in that no one will be able to find the box in this snow." Emma raised her arms and let them fall against her sides. "We can wait for the magic to fill back up and try again."

Ambril nodded. "Yes."

Emma crossed the room to flop on the giant bed. Ambril perused the bookshelves. Kimber continued watching the snowstorm in the orb. With nothing else to do, Emma closed her eyes and simply thought about how grateful she was to Ylithir for granting her the ability to take on the shape of the wolf. As far as she believed, the Wolf Spirit deserved all the credit for them surviving the naga. Without his help, they'd still be sitting in a cage, if not already swallowed whole. Nan always told her druids did not worship the animal spirits the same way priests and priestesses worshipped the gods, so she tried not to do that, instead focusing on the same emotions she had whenever Mama, Dad, or Nan did something nice for her.

It occurred to Emma she must've fallen asleep when sudden warmth manifested in front of her face. Breath, not hers, puffed at her cheeks.

She opened her eyes to find Kimber on top of her, nose to nose, staring into her eyes.

"You sleepin'?" whispered Kimber.

"Not anymore." Emma smiled.

"I gotta pee, an' there noffin in here ta go in."

A growl came from Emma's stomach. She yawned. "Well..."

Kimber rolled off her to lay on her back beside her. "I's hungry as well. Yer tummy rumblin'."

After another yawn and a stretch, Emma sat up. She glanced at the orb table. The blue one held about an inch of 'liquid.' It seemed they still had quite some time to wait, probably too long to ask Kimber to hold it.

"Do you really have to pee?" asked Emma.

"Yeah." Kimber nodded.

"Grr." Ambril grumbled, then squirmed. "Why did you have to say that?"

"Because I go'a pee!" Kimber almost yelled.

Emma couldn't deny she, too, wouldn't mind a trip to a privy as well as a meal. They'd been away from home for over a day now, at least, if not more. Her family, as well as Ambril's, must be frantic. "If we go outside, we won't be able to get back into the box until the magic is done resting."

Ambril got up from the table where she'd been reading and walked over. The way she moved made it quite obvious she desperately needed to pee as well, perhaps worse than Kimber. "If we go outside, we'll freeze to death."

"You wanna wee on the floor?" Kimber sat up, nose scrunched. "Eww."

"No!" Ambril blushed. "There's got to be a chamber pot in here somewhere."

Emma scratched at her arm and yawned again. "We won't freeze. I have magic to keep us warm. You and Kimber will only need to keep holding my hands, or keep touching me, so the magic works. We'll only be stuck outside for as long as the box takes to sleep."

"Ugh!" Ambril paced, flailing her arms. "I can't go out in the snow. It's wet. My slippers will be ruined."

"Em?" Kimber scrunched her nose. "Is nae a lit'l bit silly fer shoes ta be so delicate tha' walkin' outside gonna ruin 'em?"

"I think so." Emma covered her mouth to hold in a laugh. "But Ambril's slippers are made to look pretty, not serve a purpose."

Ambril folded her arms. "Looking pretty *is* a purpose."

"They won't look pretty if they get all wet and muddy." Emma pointed at the big crystal ball.

Ambril whined, squirming.

"You have to go bad." Emma stood from the bed. "Okay. I suppose we should go outside. I can make some food, too. Can't grow anything in here."

"But my shoes!" Ambril bounced.

"Leave them in here." Emma held her arms out to either side.

"My hose will be ruined then."

"Leave it in 'ere," whispered Kimber.

Ambril stared at them, face reddening. "You want me to go outside without hose or shoes on?"

"Yes, like a peasant." Emma peered down at her feet, raised and lowered her toes, then laughed.

"You're not a peasant. Your father's family has money." Ambril squirmed. "You just dress like one."

Emma fussed at her friend's gown. "Your father has money, too. You can dress like a peasant for a little while. It's either that or you ruin your clothing. You keep squirming like you really need to have a wee."

A strangled groan of frustration came from Ambril. She looked down at her fancy silk slippers and (mostly) clean white hose. A few greenish-brown smudges marked the fabric from the mossy slime that coated the floor of the naga cage.

"All right. Fine. I can't bear the thought of these being ruined. Are you certain we won't freeze?"

Emma nodded. "Yes. I promise."

Ambril sat on the bed, removed her slippers, then wriggled out of her hose. Her puffy skirt stopped an inch or so above her knees. She sighed at her bare legs and feet. "The girls would mock me relentlessly if they saw me like this."

"Do you care what they think? You don't really like them." Emma offered a hand.

"I suppose not." Ambril took her hand. "It's more that I don't want to embarrass Father."

Emma pulled her up to stand. "Would a knight wear a fancy dress into battle?"

"Of course not."

"But if she went to a ball, a knight would wear a nice dress." Emma twirled Ambril around once, pretending to dance with her.

"If they had any respectability, they would." Ambril sighed. "All right. I understand. Wear clothes appropriate to what one does. But..." She wiggled her toes. "This is hardly appropriate for a snowstorm."

"Neither are your slippers or the hose. Too thin." Emma headed over to the crystal orb. "They won't keep you any warmer, only get wet and ruined. My magic won't stop the wet and ruin, only the cold."

The view within the big crystal ball revealed the storm calmed somewhat. The image showed a dense pine forest, more or less sheltered from the worst of the blizzard. Snow covered everything. Long ice crystals dangled from branches and coated the needles of every tree. Merely looking at the scene made her shiver.

"How are you going to keep us warm?" Ambril made faces, squirming.

"It's magic. Keep holding my hand or the magic will stop and you'll freeze."

Ambril's face went bright red. "How am I supposed to keep holding your hand while I..."

"Easy." Kimber shrugged. "Just donnae let go o' 'er 'and while yer 'avin a wee."

"Uhh..." Ambril looked close to fainting.

"We're in an unusual situation." Emma took them both by the hand and led them to the alcove with the magic circle. "When we're lost in the forest, no one cares if you use the right fork."

Ambril nodded. "Yes, all right. Very well. I'm about to burst. This is mortifying. Alas, it seems we have no choice."

"Wait. Let me use the magic before we go out there or we might freeze so fast I won't be able to do it." Emma closed her eyes. "Andreth, Spirit of Storms, wind, and rain, please grant me your embrace." A faint tingle ran down her body. Nothing too noticeable occurred as the room inside the box happened to be an ideal temperature. "All right. We can go out now."

Kimber pushed the lock lever up, then Ambril touched the blue orb in the wall.

In an instant, they appeared knee-deep in snow near a huge pine tree, the box nowhere in sight.

"Oh, no!" wailed Ambril. "It's gone!"

"It's buried under the snow somewhere." Emma kicked at the white stuff.

"Snow." Ambril blinked and looked down at where her legs sank into the icy crystals. "Wait. It isn't cold. This is so strange."

Kimber kicked puffs of snow into the air, giggling.

"Remember." Emma gave them each a pointed stare. "Do not let go of me or you'll freeze."

"Yes. All right." Ambril trudged partially around the tree, as far as she could go without releasing her hold on Emma's hand. "It looks much colder here than winters where we live."

Emma stood with her back turned to give Ambril some privacy. Kimber didn't have any concerns of that nature. Emma would have preferred a little privacy, but given their circumstances, set it aside. Once everyone took care of their needs and became comfortable, they rummaged around the snow in search of the box. Kimber did most of the digging as Emma's hands were occupied transferring the warmth magic, and Ambril worried about ruining her gown.

Kimber burrowed around in the snow like a frenzied squirrel desperate to find her last remaining acorn. Emma moved her grip to her sister's shoulder, so Kimber had both hands free to dig. It didn't take her too long to find the box as it had been buried right next to where they appeared, a spot easily discovered thanks to deep tracks in the snow.

As expected, the lid wouldn't open. None of the gems on the outside glowed.

"The rubies will light up when the box is done resting," said Emma.

"Just the rubies?" asked Ambril.

"All of them." Emma traced her hand over the lid.

"The green ones are emeralds and the blue ones are sapphires." Ambril pointed at the strip of tiny, clear gemstones around the bottom. "Those are diamonds."

"Okay," said Emma, not at all concerned with the names rich people gave colored rocks. It mattered to Ambril, so she at least pretended to pay attention.

She summoned a single meatplant up from the snow, which provided more than enough of a meal for the three of them. Due to an unfortunate lack of utensils, they had no choice but to share the large fruit by biting it directly. They sat on an old, dead tree to eat. Emma wrapped her arms around her sister and friend, hugging them close while Kimber and Ambril held the meatplant, each nibbling on one end while Emma bit it in the middle. At first, Ambril seemed horrified acting like a bunch of wild animals savaging a carcass. It didn't take long for 'eating without a fork' to become a matter worth laughing about. Emma thought it quite silly her friend behaved like they did something mildly bad that they'd get in trouble for simply for not having dinnerware. Ambril's laughter sounded genuine and pure, so she clearly found 'living wild' to be more fun than she expected.

Emma leaned forward and took another bite. The fruit had the consistency of biting into a baked squash, but a flavor similar to venison. She happened to peer over the top of the meatplant into the snowy distance, spotting a large furry brown lump. It almost looked as though Mawr, the giant bear, curled up for a nap and got covered with a dusting of snow. As far as she knew, bears didn't usually sleep out in the open.

"I think there's a hurt bear over there," said Emma.

"A bear?" Ambril squished herself closer. "Where? Is it going to attack us?"

Emma lifted her right foot out of the snow to point with her toe. "No. He looks hurt."

"How can you tell that from so far away?" Ambril stopped shivering. "I... can't even tell it's a bear. It might be another big log. It's merely a dark spot in the snow."

"I'd like to see if the bear needs help."

"Aww, poor bear." Kimber took a few rapid bites of the plant, then picked up the gold box. "Okay."

"What will we do if it tries to eat us?" whispered Ambril.

"I'll tell him to behave." Emma pulled her arms out from behind the others, taking care to keep touching them, sliding her hands over their shoulders and down their arms to grasp their hands. "Natural animals won't attack me unless I start the fight."

"What is an unnatural animal?" Ambril let out a half-laugh. "Aren't all animals natural?"

"I mean things like manticores or gryphons." Emma trudged forward. She took two steps into the knee-deep snow before feeling stupid. *Linganthas, please guide my step.* Tiny amber light swirls appeared around her for an instant and faded. The next time she took a step forward, her foot remained on top of the snow as if she weighed less than a songbird.

Ambril oohed and ahhed at the strange sensation of walking atop loose snow.

Emma led the way through the forest toward the suspicious brown-grey, furry lump. As they drew closer, she started to notice blood in the snow. This made her walk faster.

"We're not leaving footprints." Ambril twisted around to look behind them. "It feels like I'm walking on a cloud."

"Noice innit?" Kimber giggled for two seconds, then went silent. "Uh oh. Tha's blood. I don' fink the bear's sleepin'."

"Eep," whispered Ambril.

Emma rushed over to the wounded animal. Claw slashes in the fur oozed blood. It looked as though an even bigger bear mauled this one. She raced around the other side to see its face… and gasped.

She hadn't found a bear, rather an incredibly large man wearing lots of heavy furs. Ice caked his beard and shaggy eyebrows. His face had turned grey, lips blue. The handle of a greatsword protruded from the snow not far from his gloved fingers. He looked even bigger than Guard Kavan, the tallest person she'd ever met.

Ambril 'eeped' again. "It's a man."

"Is he dead?" Kimber poked her big toe into his forehead and gave a nudge.

The man emitted a soft groan.

"No. He's not dead." Emma dropped to kneel beside him. "Hold my arms or something. I need my hands."

Ambril gripped Emma's left shoulder. Kimber wrapped both arms around her middle, resting her chin on Emma's right shoulder.

"Uruleth, please let me restore this man's life." Emma held her hands over the man, concentrating on tapping into the Bear Spirit's healing magic.

Emerald light appeared beneath her fingers. The magic glowed bright for a few seconds before seeping into him. His face lost some of its unnatural whiteness. She cast the spell again. Within a minute or two, the man's lips didn't seem as blue anymore.

Kimber squirmed around to sit in Emma's lap, then reached forward and put a hand on his forehead.

"What are you doing?" whispered Ambril.

"Touchin' 'im. So's Em's magic keep 'im warm." Kimber smiled. "Is bad ta be cold when you're 'hurt."

Emma cast the healing spell a third time. The man's injuries seemed serious, but not so bad she couldn't help him. If she thought he would die otherwise, she'd risk asking Mythandriel for the more powerful healing magic, the spell Mama used when someone suffered a bad injury. Alas, Emma needed a lot more practice with magic before she could call upon such power readily. Doing it now would leave her so exhausted, she'd likely pass out. If she fell unconscious, her other magic would stop shielding Kimber and Ambril from the cold.

The man gave another groan. More color returned to his face.

"Is he going to be okay?" whispered Ambril.

"I think so." Emma looked around at the snowy forest. "But, not if we leave him out here."

"He's too big for us to carry." Ambril swiped at the man's reddish-brown beard, knocking away ice crystals.

Kimber shrugged. "Then we stay wif 'im 'til 'e wakes an' keep 'im warm."

"Umm." Ambril shivered. "He kind of looks like a giant. What if he eats children?"

"'E no' a giant." Kimber whistled. "'E big, but nae *that* big."

Since they had to wait for the box to rest anyway, Emma saw no harm in staying there. The only other thing they could do would be to wander off elsewhere... and wait. Doing that could hurt this man. He would probably die without help if left alone. She looked around at the forest again, hoping to find some clue about where he came from, tracks perhaps, that might offer a path back to whatever village or town the man lived in. The girls couldn't move such a large person. However, once the box had its energy back, they could bring him inside, then carry the box to his village and drop him off.

While searching unsuccessfully for tracks, she spotted a rather large, fluffy bird watching them. It resembled a hawk, only much larger, with mostly white feathers ending at black tips, giving it a speckled appearance similar to the tree bark.

Strixian, please grant me the Wildkin Whisper. "Hello?"

Ambril jumped, then gave her a weird look.

"Yes? What is it? One of your kind, speaking?" asked the bird in a male voice. His tone reminded her of a temple priest who wanted to spend all his time reading books and little patience for people interrupting him.

"Do you know where this man lives? Where are his people?"

The bird looked off to one side. "There are others that way. I believe they are searching for this one."

Emma almost smiled. Strange people may or may not be friendly. Even though she hadn't done anything wrong—as far as she knew—by coming to this place, some part of her wanted to stay hidden and not let anyone see her before they could leave. Yet, she couldn't let this man freeze to death. If the people here turned out to be dangerous, she, Kimber, and Ambril could run away over the snow much faster than big, heavy men who'd have to trudge in the snow. Also, Linganthas would hide their tracks. Eventually, anyone chasing them would get lost. Also, despite the snow and freezing cold, they'd ended up in a forest. All of her magic worked here. This place brimmed with natural life energy.

"Would you please find them and guide them here?" squawked Emma.

"Why is she making bird sounds?" whispered Ambril.

"She talkin' ta a bird," replied Kimber matter-of-factly.

"Why ever would I do such a thing?" The hawk cocked its head at her.

"I could give you a meatplant to eat. It's almost as big as you are."

The bird pondered this for a few seconds. "All right." He leapt off the branch, zoomed over the girls, then pulled up in a long sweeping turn before cruising off into the woods at treetop level.

"There are more people looking for this man," said Emma. "I asked the bird to bring them here."

Ambril sucked in a breath. "Eek. What if they're mean?"

"Then we run away. We won't sink in the snow, remember?" Emma pointed at the wounded man. "They'll be more concerned with him than us."

Kimber searched through the man's belongings.

"What are you doing?" Emma poked her.

"Lookin' fer somefin' ta hide the box." Kimber pulled an empty fur pouch away from the man, which he'd been wearing on a strap over his shoulder. She put the Box of Wonder into the pouch. "Donnae wan' anyone ta see it."

"Yes, good idea." Ambril exhaled, shivering.

"Are you cold?" Emma made sure she hadn't accidentally lost contact.

"No. Nervous."

Kimber pulled the satchel strap up over her head, let it sit across her shoulder, and clung to the bag.

Emma summoned a meatplant.

"Another one?" Ambril put a hand on her belly. "I'm too full to eat any more."

"It's for the bird."

A few minutes later, the speckled hawk reappeared in the distance. He glided closer, coming to land on a branch almost directly above them. He looked back in the direction he'd flown from and let out a screeching cry. Kimber and Ambril winced at the loudness.

Voices emerged from the woods over the soft crunching of large boots in the snow.

"They are almost here," said the bird. "I've done as you asked."

Emma pointed at the meatplant. "Thank you."

The hawk glided down from the branch, seized the large fruit in its talons as if plucking a great hare from the snow, and powered back into the air, lugging the ponderous burden off into the trees.

A deep male voice bellowed something indecipherable.

Soon, three people walked out of the snowy haze, two bearded men and a woman with long, braided hair the color of moonlit snow. They advanced at a cautious speed, gazing up into the trees as if searching for the hawk. All wore the same manner of clothing as the injured man, furs of black, brown, grey, and white along with many satchels and pouches. The woman and one man carried huge swords, the other man a war axe. Emma could have asked Kimber to stand on her shoulders and the two of them would *still* be shorter than one of the swords.

"Here," called Emma.

The people lowered their gazes to her. They seemed neutral at first, until they noticed the wounded man—and their expressions turned grim.

Uh oh. I hope they don't think we *hurt their friend.*

13

ELDER VALGRA

*E*mma pointed at the injured man, then waved to beckon the people closer.

The people continued to stare at them. She couldn't help but think they looked like the 'barbarians' Da talked about. The man with the axe had dark charcoal grey hair and unnaturally amber eyes that glinted like gemstones. While the second man's hair was a more natural shade of brown, his irises resembled faceted rubies. The woman's hair appeared to genuinely be pale blue, her eyes almost the same color.

Unlike most people from Calebrin City, Da didn't accuse the barbarians of being stupid and violent. They did not follow the same ways as so called 'civilized' society. Then again, neither did Emma, Mama, or Nan. She didn't believe being or not being civilized made someone good or bad. These three people still looked upset, gazing at the three girls much the same way people might watch a large, dangerous wolf waiting to see if it attacked them—or perhaps the way said large, dangerous wolf might look at a fat chicken it fancied eating.

Emma tightened her hold on Kimber and Ambril's hands, ready to run if need be.

The woman said a few words in a language Emma had never heard before. Both men answered, one sounding confused, the other alarmed.

Emma stood, tugging Ambril and Kimber to their feet as well. The men continued to stare at them. Grimness in their expressions gave way to disbelief, then suspicion, then concern. Emma moved to one side, pulling the others with her so they didn't stand between the people and their fallen friend. All three strangers widened their eyes, staring at the girls.

The charcoal-haired man whispered in his language while making an odd hand motion.

After another moment of staring, the other man straightened his shoulders and trudged over to them. The other two called after him as if telling him not to get any closer. Emma looked up at him as he approached, and kept looking up until she almost teetered over backward. If she hadn't been standing on the snow surface without sinking into it, the top of her head wouldn't have reached his belt line. This man had to be at least eight feet tall. She stared up into his gleaming ruby eyes, wondering what sort of place they'd gone to.

They're not barbarians. I don't think they're human.

He took a knee, removed one of his furry gloves, and gingerly reached out. Nothing about him gave off any sense of malice anymore, so Emma stood there, allowing him to palm the side of her face. The man jumped slightly, as if shocked to find her solid and real. He brushed his thumb over her eyebrow, then lowered his arm, hastily stuffing his hand back into his glove.

The man looked back at his companions, speaking in a stern, urgent tone. They hurried over to the injured man while the one in front of Emma removed his outermost fur cloak and wrapped the girls up in it, squishing them together like the filling in Nan's stuffed cabbage.

"Umm," whispered Ambril. "Are we being kidnapped again?"

"I don't think so. This is too gentle for kidnapping." Emma snuggled against them. "He's afraid we're going to freeze. I think he believed we're ghosts."

"We no' ghosts," muttered Kimber.

"Of course." Ambril exhaled. "No warm clothes and we didn't sink into the snow."

The man bundled them up in the fur cloak—as big as a blanket—then swung them up over his shoulder. Leather cording snugged the furs around them. He didn't make it so tight that Emma couldn't have wriggled out if she tried to escape. She didn't feel *taken* as much as this man wanted to protect them from the cold… much the way any reasonable adult might react to discovering three children alone in a snowy forest.

"Loike free weasels inna sack we are," said Kimber.

"I don't feel very free," muttered Ambril.

"Not free. *Free*," said Kimber. "One, two, free…"

"You need a tutor." Ambril chuckled.

Kimber stuck out her tongue.

Emma contented herself to be carried for now. The 'barbarians' hurriedly built a basic stretcher, loaded the wounded man onto it, and marched off into the forest, dragging him.

Ambril squirmed and fidgeted, making faces like a housecat held against her will, but one too lazy to do anything about it. Kimber rested her head against Emma's and fell asleep. In the soft, furry, warm snugness of the cloak bundle, Emma almost passed out as well. She drifted in and out of napping as the men walked.

Fast motion woke Emma up.

The man who'd been carrying them swung the bundle off his back and gently set it down on the ground. It took her a second or two to wake up enough to realize they'd been brought inside a giant single-room, round hut, its floor more than halfway dug down into the earth. Dirt walls reinforced with small, stacked logs rose to about eight feet off the floor. A domed tent made of thick furry hides supported on giant curved bones covered the pit, turning it into a big, sunken house. Three wooden poles near the middle held up the highest point of the roof, where a covered vent hole let the smoke from a central fire pit escape.

Furry mats covered most of the floor. Small tables, thick-bodied wooden chairs decorated in runic carving, and beds stood against the wall. A group of men, women, and elders, all in clothing made of animal hides and furs, gathered around the cloak bundle, peering down at Emma, Kimber, and Ambril. Some wore enormous fluffy boots, others walked around in simple hide shoes with the fur on the inside. The women decorated their hair, necks, and wrists with wooden beads as well as feathers. Men wore similar beads and feathers in their beards. Some had normal colored hair of black or brown or blonde. Everyone else, Emma found herself staring at: white, bluish-white, slate grey, charcoal, and even ice blue. The eyes of every person here shimmered like jewels, mostly red, some blue, some brown, green, amber, or icy silver.

She looked from face to face, sensing either confusion or concern. No one appeared to be angry, mean, or likely to present a danger. The eldest woman crouched and opened the fur bundle around them. The villagers reacted with surprise and began chattering amongst themselves. A few now seemed slightly angry, though not at the girls.

"What's wrong?" whispered Ambril.

"I don't know." Emma sat up.

The group of villagers ran around in a bit of a frenzy, racing to shelves and huge wooden trunks. Moments later, they swarmed all over the girls. Three women descended on them and dressed them as if taking care of two-year-olds who couldn't put their own clothing on. Emma and Ambril's protests that they could dress themselves went ignored. Kimber didn't complain, merely giggled and soaked up the attention. Fortunately, the women didn't try to steal the dress Nan made, putting everything on top of it. In minutes, Emma found herself in a fur-lined dress, fuzzy boots, and a cloak. One woman draped a pair of furry mittens around her neck on a narrow leather cord.

"Oh." Emma sighed. "They were angry with whoever let us go outside in the snow without all this fur."

The oldest woman attempted to ask a few questions.

"I don't know what you're saying." Emma slouched. "Does anyone understand me?"

Murmurs went among the villagers.

"Valgra," said the eldest, patting herself on the chest.

Emma pointed at her. "Valgra?"

The woman nodded.

"I'm Emma." She patted herself on the chest. "Emma." She pointed at the others and introduced them.

Valgra asked something.

"I don't know." Emma closed her eyes and sighed.

A young woman with snow-white hair and crystalline blue eyes approached, offering them cups made from hollowed out bone or horn with a steaming tea-like liquid that smelled of honey and spices. Three strands of beads, blue glass, green glass, and etched bone, hung in her hair by her right ear.

"Thank you." Emma took a cup, then found herself staring in confusion at the woman in front of her.

She stood as tall as Mama, yet did not really appear to be a grown woman. Her round, soft face looked childish, and she lacked the shape of an adult. Despite her size, the girl couldn't have been older than twelve, if even that. This girl's height, compared to Valgra, seemed only a little bit taller than Emma standing next to Mama.

She's a kid like us, but... wow. Emma blinked.

Ambril, as well, seemed to notice this 'woman' who gave them the sweetened spicy tea didn't look like a woman. "Are they giants?"

"I don't think so." Emma glanced around at the people. "Giants would be a lot bigger. I don't think they're humans, though."

"What are they?" whispered Ambril.

Emma shrugged and took a sip of the tea. "They're nice. I think they're worried about us."

The villagers left the girls to sit in the center of the hut and sip tea. Some made their way outside, others went around the beds checking on people sleeping in them. The white-haired girl sat with them, attempting to ask things. Except for introducing herself as Thyra, words meant little, even though she spoke as if trying to teach a three-year-old how to talk.

Kimber made the first success at communication when she held up eight fingers and pointed at herself. Thyra appeared surprised, responding by holding up three fingers. Kimber shook her head rapidly, insisting on holding up eight fingers, then pointed at her. Thyra held up all ten fingers, then one more.

Emma blinked. *Wow. She's eleven, and she's almost taller than Mama.*

Except for their eye color, the people here didn't stand out as being obviously inhuman. If she looked at them from a distance, she wouldn't be able to tell anything unusual about them—except for the ones who had non-human hair colors.

A pained moan came from one of the beds.

Curious and worried, Emma stood and headed toward the sounds of suffering.

Thyra caught her and pulled her back, shaking her head no, then making animal scratching gestures.

"Someone's hurt?" Emma tilted her head.

Thyra stared at her blankly.

Emma pretended to sit down. As soon as Thyra let go of her, she darted around the girl and raced across the hut to the bed. A man—not the one they'd found in the woods—lay under a fur blanket. Scabs in the shape of bear claw wounds ran across the part of his chest not covered. Emma knew the smell coming from him: infection. This man didn't get better; he got sicker.

Thyra ran up behind her.

Emma faced her. "No. Wait."

Evidently shocked by the stern tone in her voice, Thyra froze. She briefly made a face like she didn't know what to do, then called for Valgra.

Not waiting to be dragged away from 'things little girls shouldn't see,' Emma faced the injured man, rested both hands on his alarmingly hot shoulder, and whispered, "Mythandriel, please bring forth your cleansing light."

The hurried rush of the elder coming to collect Emma slowed to silence as bright white light welled up around her hands, then spread out along the man's body. His scabs changed color, brightening from almost black to red. In a moment, the sickly stink of infected wounds disappeared.

Valgra and Thyra gawked at her. Another woman, not an elder, also stared. Two men in the midst of a meal at one of the small tables seemed to have stopped moving in mid bite. Satisfied no one would grab her before she could finish helping, Emma turned back to face the injured man.

The bed consisted of a thick piece of animal hide suspended inside a wooden frame and covered in multiple furs. She lifted the top blanket so she could see him. More bear claw wounds crisscrossed his chest and stomach. Most had the drying residue of a greenish-white poultice caked on them. Emma didn't know enough about the local plants to tell how effective such a salve would be, though now cured of infection, he didn't seem to be in danger of dying, so the poultice must have done something.

Still, she called upon Uruleth and cast a healing spell, which caused most of his scabs to shrink by a little less than half their size.

Valgra whispered something.

Emma lowered the blanket over the man. She took a few steps back toward the middle of the hut, stopping when she noticed more injured men and women in the other beds around the wall. *They must bring people here for healing.* Since none of the villagers tried again to collect her, Emma proceeded to make her way around the outside of the large hut, visiting all the occupied beds. She cast healing spells on two women and another man, all of whom suffered attacks from a bear—or similar large animal. One of the women required Mythandriel's cleansing as well, though her infection had not yet gotten bad enough to stink.

Valgra, Thyra, and every other villager continued staring at Emma the whole time, no one moving or speaking.

Finally, after visiting every bed with someone in need of help, Emma returned to sit beside her sister and friend, quite ready to take a nap.

"Uh oh," whispered Ambril. "They're either going to start worshiping you... or kill us."

Kimber scrunched her nose. "Why would they worship Em?"

"Because they're primitives. They don't know what magic is." Ambril glanced around nervously. "Also why they might want to kill us."

"Livin' in the snow an' not 'avin' a big city donnae make 'em primi'ive." Kimber folded her arms.

Emma picked up her tea, still half full and no longer steaming. She smiled at everyone. "They don't seem dangerous."

Thyra crept back over to sit near them. She now seemed hesitant to be too close to Emma. It didn't feel like she feared or disliked her, more afraid of making her angry.

Valgra, another elder, the younger woman, and both men who'd been eating, clustered together in a whispered conversation.

A few minutes later, Valgra approached. "Emma?"

"Hmm?" She peered up.

Valgra beckoned her to follow and walked toward the hut's exit, an opening covered in multiple heavy hides.

"May as well see what she wants." Emma stood.

14

THE DAUGHTER OF GODS

*E*mma shoved at the hanging hides, fighting her way out of the hut.

Similar to the fabric drapes of Drajmir, the hanging hides served the purpose of doors. Unlike the simple cloth in the desert city, these furs didn't like to be moved, especially by a small human girl. Their ponderous weight likely helped keep the icy wind out.

She stumbled past the burdensome mass of fur into a small pit a little bit deeper than her height. Stairs made of squared-off logs led up to the ground surface. Valgra waited for her up top, not far from the entrance.

Climbing the too-large stairs made her feel like a toddler. The big, clunky furry boots she didn't really fit into only made it worse. Emma didn't mind it too much. These boots were more comfortable than any of the shoes Da ever tried to get her to wear. Also, for the time being, she didn't have to worry about keeping Kimber and Ambril warm.

Emma scampered up the stairs and approached Valgra, who stood a few paces away, gazing upward at a grey sky.

The elder glanced down at her, then back up, pointing at the air while asking a question.

"I'm not sure what you're saying." Emma sighed. "I know we are far away from home. There's a whole ocean between this place and where I came from. No one here will understand me."

Valgra said a few more things, then sighed in disappointment. She appeared to think a while, then made a face like something all of a sudden made sense. The old woman gestured at Emma in a 'wait here' manner, then re-entered the big hut.

"Okay… this is strange." Emma lifted her arms a little and let them flop against her sides.

She turned in place, looking around at the snowy settlement. Dome-shaped huts surrounded her in every direction. The one behind her was easily the biggest one in the whole village, more than triple the size of the next largest. Every dwelling here appeared to be quite small from the outside, as most of their height went underground. No attempt at streets or roads existed, merely worn trails in the snow where people walked all the time. She also didn't see horses or any large riding animals, only shaggy, fluffy beasts somewhere between rams and goats. Any one of the creatures looked as if it had enough hair all by itself to stuff an entire mattress. Shiny ram horns ranging from dark grey to indigo adorned the heads of about half of the animals. They behaved as if domesticated, standing around, wandering, or eating whatever had been placed in buckets nearby.

Valgra, the other elder, and one of the men emerged from the large hut carrying Kimber and Ambril.

Both girls yelped in shock and scrambled to pull furs over their faces.

The elder gestured at Emma as if asking her to follow, then walked off. Sensing nothing amiss, she complied, following the old woman into the village.

"Sae cold!" yelled Kimber. "E'en wif a furs!"

"Where are they taking us?" asked Ambril.

"Somewhere they think we're going to live." Emma reached up to hold their hands, sharing the warming spell again. "We were in their healers' hut. Or maybe the person who's in charge here. The healer and the person in charge might be the same person. Probably Valgra."

"We're not going to live here." Ambril stretched to peer over at Kimber, in the arms of the younger woman. "You still have the box?"

"Yeah." Kimber patted the furry satchel.

Valgra led their procession to a hut much smaller than the first one. It, too, had a rounded shape and had been dug mostly into the ground. After gesturing at Emma to wait, the old one went down the steps and past the furs covering the opening.

Emma tapped her foot inside her boot, which didn't move.

Voices murmured inside for a few minutes.

Valgra pushed the 'door' furs aside, waving everyone in.

The man and woman carrying Kimber and Ambril moved forward, heading for the steps. Rather than leap to the side or get trampled, Emma hurried down the stairs ahead of them and darted into the hut.

A small fire burned in a pit at the center, smoke trailing up to a vent in the fur-and-hide ceiling. Large furs, mostly white, covered the floor like carpet except for a ring of dirt around the fire pit. Three beds stood against the wall opposite from the entry. Various shelves held all manner of items from clothing to tools to weapons. Five people stared expectantly at Emma and the others making their way inside.

On the left, a young boy with charcoal grey hair sat on the edge of a bed. He looked about eleven or twelve by size, which likely meant he'd be six or seven. A young woman stood near him, arms folded. She almost had the shape of an adult, not quite all the way grown. Emma guessed her to be sixteen. A man with brown hair and beard seated in a chair by a table seemed a little nervous. His expression reminded Emma of the way Mayor Braddon acted whenever someone rich or important visited town. She guessed him to be a little older than Da. He appeared pretty much human except for size as well as his eyes. His ruby irises glimmered like gemstones in the firelight. It took her a second to recognize the man who'd carried them back to town without his face half covered by a fur scarf.

Opposite the table from him sat an older woman, even more aged than Valgra. The old woman's long grey hair contained countless bead strings and feathers. She regarded Emma with a note of mild amusement. Behind her stood a woman about the same age as the man. Her hair had the color of grey stone, lighter than the boy's and darker than the elder's. The woman's emerald eyes held awe as well as curiosity.

The people carrying Ambril and Kimber set them down on their feet.

Valgra pointed at the family one at a time, introducing the man as Arne, the woman likely his wife as Yrsa, the elder as Ulfhild, the teen daughter as Revna, and the boy as Ulf.

The family all smiled at them in a welcoming manner.

"Yeah… they are letting us live here." Emma bit her lip.

"Is that bad? Why do you look worried?" whispered Ambril.

"Because they seem so nice. I'm going to feel sad making them worry about what happened when we go home." Emma tapped the toe of her boot at the fur rug. "I wish we could talk to them."

Valgra spoke to the family for a brief moment before everyone bowed to each other. She and the other two who carried the girls here took their leave.

Revna approached them. She said something, bowed to Emma, then gently took Kimber and Ambril by the hand and led them over to a counter. She and her mother, Yrsa, then got to work preparing food. They appeared to want Kimber and Ambril to help with the chores, attempting to show them by demonstration. Kimber took to it without hesitation, helping mix something mushy in a bowl. Ambril simply stared in disbelief.

The boy, Ulf, ran outside for a moment, returning soon with a large slab of meat crusted in ice. He handed it to his father, who set it on the thick wooden table and proceeded to cut it into steaks. Revna continued attempting to show Ambril how to prepare some manner of green vegetable as if she thought the girl slow of mind.

Emma stood there doing nothing… and feeling strange. No one tried to give her a chore.

Seeming frustrated, Revna grasped Ambril's hand and helped her cut the vegetables.

"I can help, too." Emma walked over to the counter.

"What are they doing?" whispered Ambril, sounding panicked.

"They're adopting us. They think we're part of the family now, so we have to help with chores." Emma reached for another knife.

Revna swiped it before she could touch it, then bowed at her, saying something apologetic.

"Why aren't they making you do servant work?" asked Ambril.

"I don't know."

"Well, I can't..." Ambril huffed. "Don't they have servants to cook?"

"Yeah. Us." Kimber laughed.

Emma again tried to help, but got shooed away. She glanced around. Everyone except for her and the old woman appeared to be involved in the chore of cooking. "They're not treating us like servants."

"What do you call this, then?" Ambril spitefully sliced a vegetable in half. "I've never done this before. What if I cut myself?"

"It's only servant work if you're getting paid to cook or clean or work for someone else." Emma gestured at Arne. "Everyone is doing the chores. It's a family."

Ambril whined out her nose. The girl didn't come off as arrogant as much as simply terrified she'd hurt herself.

Revna and Yrsa tried to stop Emma from helping. After several minutes of constantly attempting to do anything more than simply stand there watching everyone else work, Emma zig-zagged a little too fast for them and got hold of the bowl of mush, helping Kimber stuff handfuls of it into dough to make a dumpling-like food. Ulfhild waved dismissively at her daughter and said something that got her and Revna to leave Emma be, letting her work.

Ambril tried to do as little as possible, handling everything she touched as if the slightest wrong move would instantly light the entire house on fire and kill them all.

Not quite a full hour later, all the preparation finished. Arne grilled the meat over the fire while Ulfhild took the dumplings to an oven. Little Ulf sat near the pit, stirring the pot of boiling root vegetables and greens.

Since no one gave them another chore to do, the girls sat together and watched the food cook.

"Is the box rested?" whispered Ambril.

"Why ya whisperin'?" Kimber smiled, then peeked into the fur satchel. "They donnae know what we say. No. It na' glowin' yet."

Ambril buried her face in both hands. "What are we going to do?"

"Have dinner." Emma chuckled. "Then wait. It won't be long. We're safe here. There's no need to be scared."

"I *am* scared." Ambril looked down at her shaking hands. "I've never had to do anything like this before. I'm afraid to do it wrong. I don't know how to do anything."

"You kin work a broom." Kimber pantomimed sweeping. "Tis easy as pie. You ever sweep?"

"No."

"Wash laundry?" asked Emma.

"No."

Kimber tilted her head. "Cook?"

Ambril rolled her eyes. "Obviously not."

"She has servants." Emma nudged Kimber. "Her father gives other people money to do all the chores."

"Oh." Kimber yawned.

"I still want to know why they didn't want Emma to help." Ambril stared into the fire. "Something's a little strange. I read a story once where a girl went to a foreign land and the villagers were all really sweet to her. Treated her like a queen."

"That sounds noice." Kimber grinned.

Ambril glanced sideways at her. "They thought the girl was a gift from their gods and tried to kill her as a sacrifice after a week."

"Eep." Emma blinked.

Kimber's jaw dropped open. "Did she die?"

"Of course not." Ambril shook her head. "Father wouldn't let me read a book where a girl my age is killed by foolish villagers who can't tell real gods apart from orphans."

Emma glanced over the family. No one in the hut gave off any bad feelings. She didn't worry... much.

"I don't think they're going to try to sacrifice me. They seem nice."

"So did the people in the story." Ambril twirled her hair around a finger. "We won't be here in a week, though."

"Maybe they don't know about magic." Emma examined her fingers. "If they don't understand it, they might think I'm one of their gods or something."

Ambril's eyes widened. "Oh, maybe. That could be true." She giggled, then rambled on about how the other rich girls she *had* to socialize with would have started screaming and yelling if asked to do chores.

Eventually, dinner made its way to the table.

Yrsa waved at Emma and the others, then asked something. The way she clasped her hands in front of herself after speaking and the expression she wore made her look like a child who just asked their mother if they could have a sweetbread and *really* wanted it.

"I don't know what you're saying." Emma stood.

Ulfhild gestured at Emma, then said something in a flat tone.

Yrsa glanced at her, back at Emma, shrugged, then asked a question of her mother.

The old one laughed, spoke a few short words, then looked at Emma and the others before beckoning them over to the table.

They obliged, joining the family to eat. During the meal, the family taught them some words using the same method by which they introduced themselves. Arne pointed at the meat and said, "Døl." The veggie-mush-stuffed baked breads were called 'pakke.' Some of the words came close to understandable, such as 'kopp' for cup or 'stol' for chair, which sounded a bit like stool.

After the meal, everyone sat around, continuing to attempt to teach—mostly Ambril and Kimber—the language. Emma thought it odd how the family kept sneaking looks at her as if they expected her to be teasing them the same way Akeem pretended not to understand what they said.

Kimber checked the box a few times after dinner, still finding it dark. A few hours after the meal, when the family seemed intent on going to bed, the box *still* hadn't lit up.

"Did we break it?" whispered Ambril.

"No. It's just really tired. We used it twice in a day or two so it's exhausted. Takes longer to rest if we use it a lot." Emma sounded way more confident than she was, considering she totally made that up.

Ambril blinked. "How do you know that?"

"I don't. Guessing." Emma yawned. "It's magic, right?"

"Yes. Obviously." Ambril shook her head. "Normal jewelry boxes don't leap halfway across the world with people inside them."

"If we broke it, wouldn't it do something... magic? Like blow up or catch fire?" Emma scratched her head.

Ambril sighed. "How should I know? I'm not a mage."

The family arranged themselves around the beds. Arne and Yrsa shared the one in the middle. Ulfhild and Revna shared the one on the right. Ulf had the last bed all to himself. Arne shuffled things around a bit, seemingly trying to put Kimber and Ambril in the bed with Revna and Ulfhild, the boy in the parents' bed, and giving Emma Ulf's bed.

Emma objected. Not only did it overcrowd the poor old grandmother, she did not feel at all worthy of having such an enormous bed all to herself. As politely as possible to do while not knowing how to speak to this family, she pulled Kimber and Ambril over to the bed on the left.

The family appeared to understand the word 'sister' when Emma pointed at Kimber, though they pronounced it oddly. After a bit of confusion, neither Arne nor Yrsa appeared to object to the three of them sharing the bed.

Emma, Kimber, and Ambril pulled their boots off and peeled themselves out of the heavy cloaks and fur dresses. Once again only wearing their normal dresses, they scrambled under the thick furs serving as blankets and snuggled together. After one last check to find the box still not ready, they resigned themselves to sleeping.

A delay in going home annoyed Emma, but much better they found a caring family than a naga.

Ylithir, please let my family know I'm safe and trying to get home.

15

HRUNOR

*a*ctivity in the hut gradually pulled Emma out of sleep.

She soon discovered the very worst part of life in this part of the world: going to the privy. When she expressed the need to Revna by a series of pantomime gestures, the older girl appeared oddly baffled, as if it shocked her for Emma to need an outhouse at all. Insistence paid off. The older girl pointed at her pile of furry clothing as if telling her to get dressed.

After Emma bundled up, Revna led her outside. By now, the spell keeping her warm had long since ended. The wind nearly froze her face in seconds, as though she'd been slapped with an icy board covered in sharp frozen spikes. The cold proved so intense that even wearing all the furs she'd wrapped herself in, she hastily invoked Andreth's magic to warm up, then kept touching her fingertips to her nose to make sure she still had one. A few times, she'd left the house during winter back home without warm clothes. It hadn't been pleasant, but it didn't *hurt* in two seconds. Wherever they'd gone, it was *much* colder than home.

A few villagers walked around, carrying sticks or leading the strange goat-sheep animals around. The people didn't seem to mind the severe cold. This didn't shock Emma, since she'd already figured out the people weren't exactly human. They also didn't appear *too* different from humans, merely larger. Perhaps they descended from frost giants or some similar beings and had a magical tolerance for cold. They'd have to in order to live here.

Revna walked with her most of the way across the village to a plain hut set at the edge by the forest. From the outside, it looked the same as any other dwelling. However, once they entered, she realized it contained an outhouse. Two long benches, each with four holes in them, spanned over a square pit. The hole in the ground had no fencing around it or anything else to stop a sleepy, drunken, or clumsy person from having a highly unfortunate accident. The oddest thing— other than the apparent intent for six people to use the benches at the same time—was the lack of smell. The only aroma in the room, woodsmoke, came from two fires, one on either side in small stone firepits. At first, Emma thought it strange to have hearth fires inside an outhouse, until she remembered what the wind did to her nose. The fires kept the interior warm enough for the villagers to do their business without sensitive parts freezing.

Emma couldn't decide what bothered her more. Having to get all dressed up and walk so far across the village each time she needed to go, or having to use a shared outhouse. Fortunately, no one else happened to be there at the moment. Revna approached the bench, her expression conveying a sense of 'I'm already here, might as well'.

After a small hesitation, Emma decided to get it over with before someone else showed up. They sat on the same bench, two open spaces between them. Emma braced her hands on the wood, afraid of slipping through the hole and falling in. Being human—and small for her age to begin with—she could easily lose her balance and fit through the opening made for the much larger natives.

Revna gave her an odd look and asked something.

Never once in Emma's life had she engaged in a conversation while using the outhouse, at least not without a closed door between her and the other person. It just didn't seem like a proper thing to do. However, here she sat beside her newest 'sister' as casually as if they shared a bench at a long table for a town feast. Nan and Da both told her that different kingdoms and cultures had different ideas of what was considered polite or acceptable.

"Umm." Emma took a deep breath. "I still don't know what you are saying. It sounds like you're asking me if I'm good."

"Gude." Revna pointed up. "Er du en gude?"

"Umm. Wait. Are you asking me if I'm a god?"

"Guddatter?"

Emma blinked. "You think I'm one of your gods' daughters? Umm. Gude datter?"

Revna nodded.

"Oh. No. I'm not." Emma shook her head.

A soft thumping came from the furs hanging over the entrance, followed by a man's voice asking a brief question.

Eep!

Revna called out a response, seeming unbothered.

A man replied.

Emma gripped the bench on either side of her legs, shaking. A moment later, when the man didn't walk in, she realized he must have asked if anyone was inside… and decided to wait. Perhaps the four-hole benches didn't mean total strangers normally sat together after all. It might have been intended for families to share rather than whoever walked in at any time.

She hurried to finish, then jumped up, tugging her cloth dress, her furry dress, and her fur cloak back into place.

Revna escorted her outside, where a man politely waited for them to pass before going into the hut. They trekked across the village back to the family's home. The sky to the east glowed like a magical sapphire. Icy mountains and thick crystalline fog caught the sun in a shimmering display of pretty azure light. She couldn't tell where, exactly, the sun was due to the haze. Bands of glowing bluish vapors appeared to dance across the treetops like ribbons fluttering in the wind. The howl of the frigid air in the trees made her shiver despite the magic keeping her comfortably warm. Here and there, she spotted villagers in relatively light furs—some with their whole faces or even arms exposed. They didn't appear bothered by the temperature.

They reached the family home after a few minutes of walking to find Arne and Ulf outside at work, splitting firewood. Despite the boy only being Tam's age—though much larger—he swung an axe like his father, cracking the smaller pieces of wood. Both waved at the girls. Emma followed Revna inside.

Kimber and Ambril sat on the edge of the bed, almost in hysterics.

"I'm okay." Emma rolled her eyes. "They didn't sacrifice me. I just had to wee."

"That's not why we're crying." Ambril rushed over and grabbed her arms. "The box is gone. We're stuck here. We'll never get home."

Emma hung her head and sighed. "Where was it?"

"Inna bag." Kimber held up the furry satchel, which flopped about, empty.

"Hmm." Emma looked around. A jewel-encrusted solid gold box would stand out here like a torch in the night. She didn't see it anywhere in the hut. Ulfhild, Yrsa, and Revna prepared a morning meal. No one in the family had vanished, so they couldn't have gone into the box and made it teleport away. "It must be here somewhere."

Emma calmed them down, promising them they'd be fine. They took another long walk to the outhouse hut for Kimber and Ambril's benefit. Emma went along to provide the warming spell, which required her to keep in contact. This place had such cold to it, even the furs didn't seem enough to protect normal humans from the freezing. Mama told her about a more powerful version of the spell she could put on someone else without having to stay touching them. Alas, it required some mud be painted on the face or arms of the person. Everything here froze solid, which made finding mud a bit difficult. That, and she'd never tried it before. However, if they *were* stuck in this place for any length of time, she'd bring some frozen dirt inside the hut and practice until she made it work. Constantly having to hold everyone's hand to keep them warm would not be practical.

Once they returned from the outhouse, Emma and the girls scurried around inside their 'new home,' searching.

Yrsa, Revna, and Ulfhild attempted to ask them questions, but the language barrier proved impossible to defeat more than conveying that they looked for a box. Emma picked up a small wooden chest and tapped it. At this, Yrsa said 'eske.' Emma pointed at it and repeated the word, to which the woman nodded. She pointed to her eyes, then pointed around the hut before saying 'eske'. Kimber held up the empty fur satchel.

Yrsa and Ulfhild exchanged a look of guilt.

Screaming arose outside. A child shrieked in terror. Adult voices shouted in the manner of guards calling an alarm. Revna and Yrsa raced over to the big shelf beside the parents' bed. They each grabbed one of the spears leaning against it, then rushed outside. Emma ran after them, not paying too much attention to Ulfhild yelling at her. She didn't need to understand the language to assume grandmother didn't want her going outside during a dangerous situation.

Emma lifted the heavy fur 'door' out of her way with a little grunt and slipped into the stair pit. She crawled to the top step, then peeked over the earth at the village. If they'd come under attack, she didn't want to stick her head up high and accidentally take an arrow to the face—or be seen by an invader.

Kids ran to the left. Adults and a few teens ran to the right.

Emma couldn't see much, so she risked standing up a little higher. The shouting came from the edge of the village, far past the hut with the town's only outhouse pit. She still couldn't see anything other than people running to or away from the source of the problem. The way everyone shouted didn't sound like they'd come under attack by an invading army. All the voices on the wind belonged to the people who lived here... until the roar happened.

A bellowing growl rang out, sounding unmistakably like a bear.

Oh. A bear. Emma lost all fear. She sprang up to her feet right as Ulfhild pulled the furry door aside and reached to grab her. Emma leapt up out of the stairway and took off running toward the chaos. Ulfhild shouted at her, likely telling her to get back there, maybe calling her a foolish child, or something of that nature.

Strixian, please grant me the Wildkin Whisper.

Tiny swirling orbs of light appeared around her, dancing fireflies spinning around her a few times before sinking back into her chest.

The bear's roaring took on a more human quality, though it didn't speak as much as groan and bellow like an enraged drunk stumbling out of the inn.

Emma ran across the village. As soon as she went up a shallow hill a little past the middle of the settlement, a great white bear came into view. If he stood up on his hind legs, he'd be twenty feet tall. His six-clawed paws looked as big or bigger than the entire chest of one of the village men. A few people had already suffered swatting strikes, still on the ground at the ends of the trails they made in the snow sliding away from the bear. Thirty or more villagers, including Arne, Yrsa, and Revna, surrounded the bear, seeming hesitant to get close enough to attack with their spears.

"Bear!" yelled Emma. "What's wrong?"

The animal pivoted, turning his massive head to look at her, then tilted it like a dog who'd just heard a strange sound.

Emma ran down the other side of the hill, straight at the enormous furry beast. "Please stop fighting."

A few villagers close to her made baffled faces. To them, she ran down the hill making bear noises.

"Stop! Stop! Stop!" shouted Emma at the villagers, waving her arms. She knew some words—like stop—sounded close enough to their language to get the meaning across.

She tried to stop too fast out of a full sprint. The snow took her boots out from under her. Emma landed on her back and went sliding feet first toward the bear. Villagers nearest her dove to catch her before she slid right under the beast. A man and a woman fell on top of her, squishing her into the snow. She flailed her arms at the bear.

"Why are you attacking the village? Please talk to me."

"I am hungry," replied the bear. "There is little food. These creatures are all I have to eat."

The two adults who caught her stood, lifting her into the air. The man collected her from the woman and began to hurry away from the bear with her in a protective embrace.

"Wait. Stop. Please." Emma patted him on the shoulder.

He looked at her. "Stoppe?"

Emma made a 'talking' gesture with her hand and pointed at the bear.

The man slowed to a walk but kept backing her away from the animal.

"Stop." She squirmed. "Put me down, please."

He didn't.

"Bear, if I make something for you to eat, will you stop trying to eat these people?"

The bear sat back on his haunches. "I only need food. It does not matter to me what it is. The food you offer, will it fight back?"

"No. It won't." *Uruleth, please grant me strength.* As soon as the spell empowered her, Emma squirmed free of the man's grip, fell to her feet, and ran back toward the bear.

The man spun, trying to grab her, and slipped in the snow.

More villagers moved in front of her.

Emma held her mittened hand up making 'talking' gestures while pointing her other hand at the bear. Perhaps confused by the animal's sudden calm and her complete lack of fear, the people stood still and let her pass.

The bear leaned down to sniff her when she got close enough. "You are tinier than most of these creatures."

"I'm not from this place. Here." Emma widened her stance and held her hands forward, aiming them at the earth. "I'm going to make you meatplants. You're really big, so I'll make a lot of them."

When the bear did not swallow her whole or even swat at her, the villagers fell silent. Vines erupting from the snow drew gasps of awe. One by one, the bulbous, elongated fruits appeared.

"I am..." The bear's eyes widened. "This is a strange berry, but it smells like meat."

She smiled, continuing to call upon Linganthas' favor to rapidly grow more of them. One plant provided more food than most men could eat alone. She figured one of the men from *this* village could probably finish two by themselves. A bear this size? No idea. She made twenty. The bear nipped one off the vine, took a test chew, then flopped on his belly emitting a low, satisfied moan.

"This is soooo good." The bear lazily stretched his neck out to eat another one. "I've never tasted anything so delicious."

The sight of a giant bear reclining and acting almost like a pet dog so dumbfounded the villagers that some let their weapons slip from their hands. Emma plucked a meatplant off the vine and fed it into the bear's open mouth as if she loaded a log into a furnace. She continued feeding him each time he signaled he wanted another by opening his mouth.

More villagers collected to watch. Though their words didn't mean much to Emma, expressions and body language told her they'd never seen anything like this before. Revna apparently thought Emma to be a godling, which explained the way the family had been treating her. If they believed her to be the child of one of their gods, it made sense why they'd not expect her to do any chores.

After twelve meatplants, the bear gave a groan of contentment. "I can eat no more. Thank you..."

"Emma."

"You can tell the other Emmas I won't eat them."

She laughed. "No. I'm not 'an' Emma. My name is Emma. I'm a human."

"I see. Well, tell the others we do not need to fight."

She glanced around. "I think they know."

"Will you make more of these beautiful plants?"

"If I'm still here, yes. The ones you didn't eat will last a few days... maybe longer here since it's so cold."

"Wonderful." The bear rubbed his head against her, knocking her on her seat.

The villagers gave a collective breath of alarm.

Emma laughed and skritched him under the chin.

After a few minutes of that, the bear bid his farewell and meandered off into the woods.

Silence.

Once the bear went so far into the trees she couldn't see him anymore, Emma stood, brushed snow off her fur dress, and walked toward the village. Revna emerged from the crowd, ran over to her, and spoke, fast and excited.

Emma merely stared at her, making an 'I don't know what you're saying' face until the girl caught on.

They returned to the family hut together.

Ulfhild sprang from her chair at the table. She started to scold Emma until Revna interrupted her, likely to explain everything that happened. Kimber and Ambril sat on the bed holding each other, looking sad and forlorn. Emma plopped herself down between them, plucked her mittens off, and explained what happened. They still hadn't found the box.

"I'll get all the animals I can find to help us." Emma swished her feet back and forth. "Don't cry. At least we're safe here. This family is nice."

They sat together, talking in whispers, trying to come up with any idea of what happened to the box. No one here saw it since it remained in the satchel the whole time. It didn't seem likely someone snuck into the house while everyone slept to steal it. Ambril suggested a rather scary idea: perhaps the box could only be used so many times before it either automatically returned somewhere else or simply disappeared into nothingness. Magic items, according to her, could be 'strange.'

Arne and Yrsa entered the hut.

"Emma?" Yrsa beckoned her. "Komme. Gå med meg."

The woman still gave off a sense of curiosity and a little worry. She obviously wanted Emma to go with her somewhere and didn't know what would happen. Yrsa's mood conveyed mild worry. Emma assumed the worst possible result of going with her would be someone important becoming disappointed, perhaps that she didn't happen to be a baby god. Better they figured that out sooner rather than later. She didn't want to be worshiped or treated like a queen.

She put her mittens back on.

Kimber and Ambril scrambled to put the rest of their furs on. Arne waved at them, then pointed at Emma as if to say 'only her.' She couldn't tell if he meant it in a 'you two don't have to bother' or 'you can't go, we must only take Emma' way. The idea of being separated from her sister and friend didn't scare her; however, it also felt like a mistake. Perhaps a mild one, but a mistake nonetheless. Emma took them each by the hand and pulled them close.

"We would like to stay together." Emma raised their joined hands. "All of us."

"Alle?" Yrsa glanced at Arne.

He shrugged, seeming not to care that much either way.

Yrsa nodded, then beckoned them all to follow her outside.

Emma called upon Andreth to keep them warm.

"Why are you using the magic? We have furs." Ambril peered down at herself. "I smell like a wet dog, but they're comfortable."

"Your face will freeze. Your nose will break off." Emma shivered. "It's *really* cold. Trust me. I don't think humans are supposed to live here."

"Eek." Ambril shivered. "We have to get out of here."

Emma led them out past the furs and up the stairs. "I know. Try to stay calm. I want to go home as bad as you do. We have time. The people here are trying to protect us."

"Unless they're taking you to the sacrifice now." Ambril twisted to look behind them.

Umm, no, it doesn't feel bad. Emma didn't really think the villagers would want to kill her as an offering to their gods. Even if they did, such an event would undoubtedly get the entire village all marching in a procession for a big celebration. Only Arne and Yrsa walked with them. No one else appeared to even care they went anywhere.

They traveled out of the village into the woods. Emma glanced back every so often. Eventually, they'd gone so far she couldn't see any of the huts. Another worry crept into the back of her mind. How superstitious were these villagers? Did they now fear her? Had her 'new parents' been ordered to take her into the woods and abandon her? Such a fate would be certain death for any human... who didn't happen to be a druid. Yrsa gave off no sense of sadness. Either they didn't mean to abandon them or she so feared the strange children being separated wouldn't bother her.

Certainly, Revna would have been upset if she knew of such a cruel plan. The older daughter didn't appear emotional at all when her mother and father came to collect Emma. Their procession carried the mood of her being taken to meet someone important. Though... why would someone important be way out in the forest and not the village?

Emma had too many questions and not enough words in their language to even begin to attempt asking them. She found herself hoping if things took a dark turn, they'd only abandon them in the forest and not try to murder them.

Fear grew and grew with each passing minute. Walking so far into the woods didn't seem like anything likely to end well.

After almost an hour of constant walking, two wooden poles came into view. They stood about twice as tall as any of the men, thin like quarterstaffs, on either side of a path that followed a winding route into a thicker section of trees. A collection of beads, knotted rope, furry tails, and small pouches hung from the top of each one. Emma sensed magical energy in them similar to what Nan put in the little dolls she asked the spiders to carry up into trees.

Her fear evaporated.

"They figured it out!" Emma smiled.

Kimber and Ambril looked at her.

"Figured what out?" asked Ambril.

"Those things." She tried to point without letting go of Kimber's hand. "They're full of druid magic. Someone must have realized how I spoke to the bear. Now I understand why we're walking so far away from the village. There must be a druid here, like how Nan used to live by herself in the middle of the forest."

Arne and Ysra walked between the poles, stepping onto the footpath. Emma continued holding hands with Kimber and Ambril as they followed the adults downhill into a small valley covered in snow and forest. The trail eventually led to the mouth of a cave set at the base of an enormous cliff at the valley's far end. Large baskets stood stacked on an array of enormous wooden trunks on either side near some benches. Someone definitely lived here.

After calling out a greeting, Arne entered the cave. Ysra looked back, waving for the children to follow her, then entered behind him. Emma paused to gaze around at the cliff face. No additional talismans hung anywhere in sight, nor did she see anything out of the ordinary. Satisfied she'd probably only meet a druid she couldn't speak to inside, she grumbled to herself and trudged forward.

The cave connected to a wide chamber full of furs and furniture quite similar to the inside of the huts at the village. Great wooden bowls big enough for her to bathe in held bluish-white orbs that gave off heat without being on fire. Near the back of the cave room, a man sat upon a throne made of animal skulls and wood. He, too, wore mostly furs as well as an ornate headdress from which an impressive set of antlers sprouted.

He looked older than Da, but not so much he could have been her grandfather. Despite his appearance of moderate age, he felt ancient in a way she couldn't explain. Nan gave off a similar feeling, perhaps why Emma spent so long worried her grandmother didn't have much time left.

A pair of animals slept on the floor on either side of the throne. They resembled stout deer or elk, significantly larger than ordinary, with pure white fur deer. The male's antlers appeared to be made of ice. Both animals had glowing blue eyes and peered at Emma as if they possessed intelligence close to human.

Ysra put a hand at Emma's back and urged her closer, right up to the throne.

"Hello." She peered up at the large man. Standing right in front of him, she noticed his headdress had cutouts allowing the antlers to pass through the hardened leather. The man didn't wear an antler headdress—he *had* antlers of his own. "Wow..."

The man on the throne regarded her with an expression part way between baffled and annoyed. It seemed he had no idea why the villagers brought her here.

"Hrunor," whispered Yrsa as she gently squeezed Emma's shoulder.

"Am I supposed to bow?" asked Emma.

Ambril curtsied to him.

"Hi!" chirped Kimber, grinning huge and waving.

Hrunor asked something.

Emma sighed out her nose. *This is not helping... Oh... wait a minute.* She glanced at the two animals, concentrating on the Wildkin Whisper. "Can you understand me?"

"We can, child," said the female. "I am known as Una. My mate is Onai."

"I sense Strixian's blessing upon you." Onai bowed his head slightly at her.

"Can you speak to Hrunor?"

Both deer nodded.

Emma raised her hands in triumph, squeezing Kimber and Ambril's hands as she whispered, "Yes!"

Onai turned his head to face Hrunor. "This child wishes to speak through us."

"Why?" asked Hunor

"I can understand him?" Emma stared.

"I speak to Onai." A bemused smile curled Hrunor's lip. "We both speak the language of the storhjort. You speak to me as you speak to them. You are quite young."

Blush warmed Emma's face. She felt a little stupid for not realizing two druids using the Wildkin Whisper speaking to the same type of animal would understand each other. It made sense now that she thought about it.

Still intent on speaking 'deer,' she addressed Hrunor. "I am not the daughter of a god. The people think I am. I'm just a human from far away."

"You are more than a human. Your spirit is strong. Dryad? No... not the same, more than a simple tree spirit. I sense your blood is mixed."

"Yes." Emma smiled. "Nan is... something. I don't know exactly what. A forest spirit."

"Why have you come here?" Hrunor ran his fingers down the length of his beard.

"Because Yrsa and Arne brought me to see you."

Hrunor spoke to the two adults in their language for a few minutes, then glanced at her again. "You made a storbjørn stop his attack and go in peace."

"He was hungry. The forest did not have enough food for him, so he attacked the village wanting to eat someone. I fed him." Emma explained how she'd summoned the meatplants.

"Curious. I did not know of this magic." Hrunor continued stroking his beard.

Emma smiled to herself. She didn't feel like such an idiot of an apprentice anymore. So, she didn't know Wildkin Whisper could let her talk to Hrunor directly, but she *did* know a spell he didn't.

Kimber and Ambril finally burst into giggles.

Emma turned to look at them. "What?"

"I'm sorry." Ambril wiped laugh tears away. "You and that man... you're just making these weird squeaking noises at each other. It's *so* silly."

"Oh. Deer don't really talk much. But he understands me. Try not to laugh. He's pretty old and important and probably doesn't like being laughed at." Emma exhaled, then looked back to Hrunor.

The druid tilted his head. "I asked why you are here. You did not answer."

"Umm. You mean why are we in... wherever this place is?"

He nodded. "Eldrheim."

"We didn't mean to be here." Emma explained about thieves trying to kidnap Ambril and how they found the magical box. "Someone took the box from us when we slept. Can you please ask them to give it back? We really need to go home to our families. We're not orphans."

Hrunor spoke to Arne and Ysra for a few minutes. They both winced apologetically.

"Oh no," muttered Emma.

"This enchanted coffer you speak of..." Hrunor gestured at the man and woman behind them. "The people of the village believed it belonged to the gods and it arrived here with you. They have put it in the ancestral tomb."

Emma fought the urge to sigh. "Can you please ask them to give it back so we can go home?"

"They will not. It is forbidden to enter the ancestral tomb unless one is bringing family to their eternal rest or bringing an offering to the gods."

"But it's not an offering to the gods. It belongs to Ambril's father." Emma thrust her mittened hands out to either side, pulling Ambril and Kimber's arms with her. "We need it to go home."

"I am sorry, child." Hrunor spoke for a little while to Arne and Ysra, then looked back at her. "They have already offered it to the gods and cannot take it back. They tell me that since you are not a godling, you and the other children with you shall stay at the village. I have explained to them you've come from a far-off land and already have families."

"They know we have families, but they're still going to keep us here?" Emma tried not to get angry. These people had to mean well. "Why?"

"There are cities far to the south by where the frozen land meets the great sea. Rarely, outsiders arrive in boats to trade." Hrunor lowered his hand from his beard. "Our village is too remote. Journeying such a distance through the forests and across the ice plains is far too perilous an undertaking for three children they are perfectly capable of looking after here. The journey would take weeks, and can be deadly. Some may die along the way. The three of you are too small to attempt the trek."

Emma shivered in frustration and barely contained anger. "I can teach you how to make meatplants to feed the bears so they stop attacking the village. A fair trade for ordering them to return the box."

Hrunor almost smiled. "An offering to the gods cannot be taken back. We do not need these plants to feed the bears. Killing them works just as well."

She gasped. "No. You can't kill them. They're only hungry. They're not attacking people because they're mean. And fighting them gets your people hurt, too."

"It is our way." Hrunor raised a hand. "Life becomes death to become life anew."

Emma hung her head. "If I show you how to make meatplants, will you please do it so the bears and your people don't have to die?"

"We cannot un-offer a gift to the gods."

"I'll teach you, anyway." She sighed. "I don't want the bears to die."

16

THE TOMB OF ANCESTORS

*D*isappointed but not defeated, Emma followed Ysra and Arne back to their home.

She guessed either Ysra or Ulfhild had been tidying up their belongings after the girls went to sleep and discovered the gold box. The villagers did not seem to have anything made out of gold, nor any real jewelry of precious stones. Perhaps they'd never seen such a treasure before and assumed it belonged to their gods. At the time, they also believed Emma to be one of their gods, or at least a being who came from the same place their gods lived after they watched her use magic to heal.

The villagers obviously knew about druids, which confused her at their shocked reaction to the use of healing magic. When she asked Hrunor about this, he explained he did know spells capable of healing... but rarely used them. In his opinion, death only led to rebirth. He did not want to interfere in the natural order. Only if someone suffered injury as the result of something clearly unnatural —like a demon—would he call upon his magic. Although, in some cases, he made exceptions for children. Emma tried to convince him he should heal everyone. Death might have been a natural part of life, but she didn't think any harm came in making it wait longer. Hrunor gave no indication either way whether or not her pleas worked.

After he explained to Arne and Yrsa that Emma happened to be a druid and not the offspring of one of the gods, they stopped treating her like royalty. It took her a while to convince Hrunor to step in and help with the bear problem. Evidently, these bears had been attacking the village regularly for weeks. The man she'd first found when the Box of Wonder brought them here had been dragged off by one such bear. She didn't understand how Hrunor could let both people and bears die to needless fighting, claiming it to be a 'natural process.'

Emma couldn't let anyone, bear or person, continue dying by trying to use teaching the meatplant spell as a bargaining token to get the box back. She taught him anyway, and he gave his word he would provide food for the bears in lean times so they didn't have to attack the village anymore.

Upon their return from the woods, Emma, Kimber, and Ambril fell into an ordinary day in the life of this frozen village. Ambril struggled to cope with basic chores. The girl didn't know how to do anything. While she did try her best, she complained the entire time, certain she did everything wrong. It would have been difficult for her to cope with the kinds of chores Emma routinely did at home. Here, in the icy forests of Eldrheim, their tasks seemed more a fight for survival than simple 'chores'. Due to their small size compared to the villagers, most treated them like four-year-olds. They helped with a few easy tasks: helping to cut meat from a recent hunt into smaller pieces to be frozen in a small pit outside the hut, sorting and folding furs, tidying up inside the home, and so on.

Being considered 'small children,' they didn't need to work all day long and had a few hours to play between midday and the evening meal. Given the cold, Emma kept using Andreth's magic to protect them, which also meant they had to keep holding hands. Other village children ran about playing games, either pretending to hunt or get into stick swordfights. Emma used their play time to explore the village in search of every animal she could possibly ask for help locating the Tomb of Ancestors. The shaggy goats seemed lazy and didn't want to say much more than telling her to go away or get them more food. She found some ferret-like creatures near the edge of the village. Far friendlier, they only wanted to play and chatter without knowing much about where she might find the tomb.

As the afternoon ran into evening, Ambril and Kimber started to give up hope they'd ever see home again. Even if they someday learned enough of the language to ask someone to take them to the tomb, no one here would. From what Hrunor said, the villagers refused to go near the place at all unless they brought a dead person to be buried or carried an offering considered worthy. Emma thought it silly for them to refuse to return the box purely for the sake of their traditions. They didn't have any right to take it from them and put it there, especially without even asking first. Sure, they might be children; however, that didn't make it right for adults to steal from them.

Around when daylight showed signs of weakening into night, Emma spotted an arctic wolf watching the village from the woods. She called out, beckoning the animal closer. The wolf abandoned its wariness and dashed across the snow toward them. Ambril scurried backward as far as she could without letting go of Kimber and breaking the warmth-sharing handhold chain.

The wolf bounded up to Emma and sniffed her before speaking in a female voice. "Greetings, child. What are you doing here? This is not a place for you."

"Hello." Emma offered her hand to be sniffed, then brushed her fingers through the wolf's incredibly thick, fluffy white fur. "We did something wrong with magic and need to go home."

"Oh, you poor dear." The wolf nuzzled her.

"I'm not a deer. I'm Emma." She grinned.

The wolf made a noise similar to a chuckle at her joke. "I am Maea. Sadly, I regret there is little I can do to help you go home."

"Do you know where the Tomb of the Ancestors is?" Emma continued stroking Maea's fur.

"I know nothing of such words."

Emma sighed. "Maybe you don't know the name they gave it? Do you see where the people who live here bring their dead?"

"Yes. I know the place. It is in the forest." Maea turned her head to look at the trees. "That way."

"How far?" asked Emma.

"Far enough to find the travel a burden. Close enough to travel more than once."

Emma furrowed her eyebrows. "How long would it take us to walk there?"

"It would take as much time as needed." The wolf tilted her head, seeming confused.

She doesn't understand hours. "If we started going there right now, would it be dark before we found it?"

"No, but almost."

Emma gazed up at the hazy sky sparkling from swirling ice crystals, snow the wind picked up from the ground to play with. *Two hours or less. It's far, but not too bad.* "Is it dangerous for us to go there?"

"For some, yes. For you, no." Maea nuzzled her again. "All dangers you may face, you can speak to."

She smiled. That meant animals posed the greatest threat in the woods after the extreme cold. Except for the emerald creepers, Emma never met an animal that still wanted to bite her after she started talking to it. At least, not one in its right mind. She doubted there'd be a conjurer out there making false animals.

"Will you guide us there later?"

"Later?" Maea licked her nose. "Did you not just say you wished to go right away?"

"If it won't be dark before we get there, the villagers will see us going and try to stop us. We need to wait for everyone to go to sleep first."

Maea sat, cocked her head, and stared at her. "If the villagers will try to stop you, perhaps you should not go."

Emma sighed. "They don't understand." She explained about the enchanted jewelry box and how Yrsa and Ulfhild mistook it for a relic of their gods. "We need to go home. This place is too cold for humans. And we have families. My Mama and Da miss their cubs."

"I see." Maea gave a low, mournful whine. "I would be most upset if my cubs disappeared and I did not know to where they'd gone. I will return here after dark and wait for you."

"Thank you!" Emma one-arm-hugged the wolf, burying her face in the deep, plush fur of the animal's neck.

The sound of Revna shouting their names echoed over the snow from the village.

"We have to go now." Emma bowed. "As soon as we can, we will be back."

Maea nodded.

Emma led the way toward the village, explaining her plan to sneak out of the hut once everyone fell asleep. Revna soon collected them and ushered the girls home. They spent the next few hours inside, having dinner and listening to Ulfhild tell stories they didn't understand. Revna and Ulf appeared frightened, much like how Kimber and Tam reacted to some of Nan's tales.

Eventually, it became time to sleep. Once again, Emma, Kimber, and Ambril removed their heavy fur garments and crawled into bed wearing the dresses they'd had before. They huddled together under the thick furry hide blankets, watching the family make ready for bed as well.

It soon became too dark inside the hut to see anything other than the faint glow of embers in the firepit.

"Don't sleep," whispered Emma.

"I'm exhausted." Ambril gave a soft groan. "All that work."

"You'as kin sleep inna magic room," whispered Kimber.

Ambril grumbled. "What are we going to do?"

"Wait for them to sleep, then sneak outside and follow the wolf to the tomb." Emma stared up at a ceiling she couldn't see in the dark. The urge to go home made it nearly impossible to lay still.

"Are we goin' wif ya or waitin' 'ere?" Kimber snuggled against her side.

"Hmm." Emma pondered.

If she went alone, she could shapeshift into a wolf and run faster—at least going there. As a wolf cub, she couldn't carry the box without a sack or something to put it in. Not too difficult to find. If nothing went wrong, she could collect the box and bring it back here while her sister and friend remained safe in bed. However, she might get lost on the way back. Also, the villagers seemed afraid of something worse than breaking tradition at the tomb. If some manner of curse really hung over the place, it might be better not to remove the box, which had become an offering. At least, not removing it the normal way. If they teleported, the box moved itself. No person carried it out of the tomb, stealing an offering.

The decision proved difficult, but Emma decided it less risky if all three of them stayed together.

"I think you should go with me."

"Good." Kimber squeezed her.

Ambril didn't reply, likely asleep already.

Emma waited.

As soon as the sound of Arne's breathing changed, suggesting he'd fallen asleep, Emma nudged Ambril until the girl woke up.

"Shh," she whispered. "It's time."

Andreth, please lend me your power to keep us warm.

Tingles washed over her. Emma slipped out of bed in the dark, careful to keep a good hold of their hands.

Ambril started to feel around in search of her furs. Emma pulled her away, not wanting to waste time or risk the noise of them rummaging waking anyone up. A few squeaks of protest came from Ambril, but she didn't say anything. Emma bumped into something wood, likely a chair.

Gradually, she felt her way across the hut, relying on memory and touch to find the furry hides over the opening. Once they stepped outside into the pit, the moonglow from the sky lit the world enough to see. Icy winds moaned in the distance, making the darkened trees sway back and forth. It didn't snow from the sky anymore, though enough loose snow blew around in the wind not to feel much different. Emma shivered from the idea of cold rather than the feeling of it. Her magic kept them comfortable, warming the sensation of the air to feel like a pleasant day in early summer, neither hot nor cold.

They made their way up the stairs into the breeze. Emma's first step sank up to her ankle in the snow. *Oops. Forgot.* She called upon Linganthas to invoke the Dryad's Step. As if weightless, the girls scampered across the snow surface without breaking it or leaving tracks. They dashed from hut to hut to avoid being seen by a few adults wandering around with spears or swords, no doubt on guard for possible threats. Silent, trackless, and fast, the girls soon left the village behind without being discovered.

Maea waited for them as promised, at a safe distance from the village edge. Emma raced across the snow and ice, her footing as sure as if she trod upon meadow grass. The wind in the open clearing between village and forest blew so hard their dresses flapped loud enough to hear fluttering. Ambril and Kimber remained quiet even though they'd gone so far from the hut the family couldn't possibly have heard them talking.

The wolf welcomed Emma with a nuzzle and a nose lick, then bounded off into the trees.

A strong desire to go home to her family pushed Emma into the dark, icy forest. She kept alert for bears, wolves, or other animals who might think of three small humans as dinner, confident they'd leave her alone if asked. At worst, she'd offer them meatplants instead. According to the bear she'd met, this season happened to be rather lean. That meant most animals she might run into would be hungry. Even without her druidic nature having a calming effect on animals, almost any beast—including humans—would choose an easy meal over one they had to work for.

While this forest might have been fascinating and beautiful, a wonderland of a thousand shades of blue, brown, and grey, Emma couldn't truly enjoy the majesty of the place past her great need to go home. If she'd been here with her family, she'd have been overjoyed at the grandeur. Now, she felt like Tam at a festival: 'that's nice, but where's the food?' Only, instead of food, she wanted to ignore everything else and go straight to her parents, grandmother, and brother.

Maea trotted through the woods for a long time.

"I can't keep walking." Ambril whined. "I'm going to fall over."

"I's no' tired an' I smaller an' ya." Kimber giggled. "Me legs gotta do more work."

Ambril staggered. "You are used to being outside all the time. I am not. All I do is sit on nice cushions and read or talk to stuffy, superficial people who only care about being richer than everyone around them."

"I'm glad you're not one of them." Emma smiled.

"Thank you." Ambril took a deep breath and tried to march onward. "I still would rather be comfortable at home reading a book than running around barefoot in the woods at night."

"So would I," said Emma.

"But you *adore* running around barefoot in the woods." Ambril glanced at her.

"Yes, but not at night." Emma smiled. "We're too little to be out in the forest after dark. I'd rather be home."

Ambril blinked. "Then why did you insist we sneak away?"

"Are we gon' get in trouble?" whispered Kimber.

"We're trying to go home." Emma waved her free hand around. "There's a good reason for us to be walking into the forest at night. We aren't doing it for fun or adventure."

A snap echoed in the distance.

"That sounds loike adventure," whispered Kimber.

Ambril jumped. "Is something going to eat us?"

"I'll tell them to leave us alone. Don't worry." Emma walked a little faster.

"Telling me not to worry doesn't mean I won't worry." Ambril shivered. "I know you can talk to them. I'm still frightened of large wild animals with huge teeth and sharp claws."

Emma slowed her stride to go easier on Ambril. "I understand. It's not wrong for you to be nervous. Most people can't talk to them."

"We are almost there, Emma," said Maea. "This place holds strange power. I do not like being here, but I will not leave you alone."

Before she could think of a response, Emma sensed it, too. The woods up ahead held a dark, foreboding energy. The hairs on her arms stood up. Neither Kimber nor Ambril reacted in any way obvious enough to notice.

Dark magic. They can't feel it. Emma tightened her jaw. *The villagers are afraid of something here. It's more than only tradition.*

She kept walking while thinking of possible alternatives. They could wait for someone to die and then insist on going along to this place when the family brought the body here. Not only did that sound like a bad idea because it could take years before someone died, it felt wrong to intrude on a family's grief. Another option would be to find something they could bring as an offering. The problem there... Emma didn't know anything about the gods the villagers worshiped, nor what they might consider a worthy offering. The darkness ahead didn't seem overwhelming. It gave off less a sense of immediate danger and more a feeling that people should not be here without a good reason.

Going home to our family is a good reason.

The darkness didn't scare Emma enough to want to wait years to get home. Her family, as well as Ambril's, would already be out of their minds with worry. She couldn't make it worse on them. Whatever this Tomb of the Ancestors had in store for them, she'd find a way to get past it.

A short distance up ahead, Maea stopped walking and sat by a hole in the ground.

Emma jogged to catch up, coming to a halt beside the wolf with her feet a few inches away from a stone block, the topmost step of a giant staircase leading down into the earth. At least thirty steps led to the bottom, where a wall of heavy furs hung in place of a door.

At least we don't have to worry about how to open it. Furry hides don't lock.

"This is the place the villagers bring the remains of their dead." Maea gazed around. "We should not remain here long."

Emma leaned against the fluffy wolf. "Thank you. When we find the box, we'll use it to get home. You don't need to wait. We won't be coming out."

"That is what I fear, child." Maea nuzzled her. "This place is not one with the forest."

"We have to go inside." Emma steeled herself, having spoken to herself as much as the wolf.

Maea stood. "Then I will help protect you."

"Thank you." Emma hugged her one more time, then let go and started climbing down the stairs. "Please be careful."

The size of the stone blocks forced them to sit down and slip from one to the next, being too tall to traverse the staircase in the normal way.

"My dress is getting filthy and wet," whispered Ambril.

"You 'ave a lot of dresses." Kimber squeaked a grunt as she hopped down to the next stair.

"Yes, but that's no reason to be careless with them." Ambril eased herself down another step. "Father gave them to me. If I don't take good care of them, it's the same as me not being grateful."

Emma smiled, thinking of how much she adored the dress Nan made. Her friend treasured *all* her dresses equally. Admittedly, Emma had been a little dismissive of the other clothes Da bought. Perhaps she should make more of an effort to show Da she appreciated things he got her.

When they reached the bottom of the stairs, they paused to rest from the climb. Emma peered back up at the rectangle of starlight at the top, then at the fur wall in front of them.

"Mythandriel, please send forth your light," whispered Emma.

A small orb of transparent white glow appeared in the air by her face, then lazily drifted around her head, leaving a faint trail of faerie sparkles. It gave off about the same amount of light as a big torch without the fluttering and flickering.

Maea nosed past the furs.

Emma grasped the hanging hides and held them aside, allowing the light to shine into a stone corridor. It looked like people long ago found a natural cave and carved it out wider, turning it into a proper hallway. Thin sheets of ice covered the stone floor. Thanks to the magic Andreth bestowed on her, the ice neither melted under her feet nor made her slip.

The sense of darkness remained the same, not getting stronger. She listened for a moment to silence. Feeling confident, she moved forward into the tomb. Plain stone walls decorated in swirls of ice passed by on both sides.

"Wait," said Kimber. "I see somefin' bad."

Emma stopped. "What? Where?"

Kimber crept forward, taking the lead. She advanced another six steps before squatting. "Cord. Need me hands."

Emma crouched next to her sister and grasped her ankle instead of her hand. Ambril let go of Kimber's other hand—yelped from the cold —and grabbed Emma's forearm. The girl's startled cry at the shocking blast of icy air echoed into the dark.

Kimber leaned forward, tracing her fingers across a thin cord suspended four inches above the floor across the hallway. On the left, it knotted to an iron loop hammered into the wall. She shimmied to the other side, peeking into a hole. After studying it for a moment, she stuck her hand in and fiddled with something Emma couldn't see.

"What are you doing?" asked Emma.

"Is a trap. If someone walks inta the cord, it pulls the fing, and somefin' bad 'appens." Kimber unhooked the cord from whatever it connected to inside the hole, let it fall slack on the floor, then stood. "Safe now."

Emma moved her grip from Kimber's left ankle to her shoulder. "Do you think there are any more?"

"Yes." Kimber nodded, making her wild red hair flop over her face. She gathered it back around behind her head. "Always. Where ya fin' one, ya fin' ten."

Ambril stepped out of two melted footprints. "Eek. I only broke the touch for half a breath, and it felt like my toes were going to fall off. And... why does Kimber know about things like this?"

"I'as tol' ya's already. I growed up 'roun' teefs." Kimber crept down the hallway, slightly crouched, arms raised like she expected to have to dive for cover at any second. Three minutes later, she stopped and took a knee. "I fink this be a push plate."

Emma crouched next to her. Ambril dropped to kneel, bowed forward as if afraid of the ceiling.

Kimber fiddled at a not-quite-round stone raised out of the floor, trying to pry it upward. Something in the wall made a thud... and a huge icy blade swung down from above with a heavy *whoosh*. It missed their heads by several feet before disappearing back into the dark ceiling. Ambril screamed a full second after it vanished.

"Yep. Is a push plate." Kimber nodded.

"Eek," whimpered Emma. "Sometimes, it's good to be small."

Kimber crawled forward. "Cannae break 'em. Look fer stones stickin' up an' donnae touch 'em."

Emma kept a hand on Kimber's leg as they crawled. Ambril trailed after them, gripping Emma's right ankle. Another ice blade swung overhead. Emma couldn't tell who touched the stone to set it off, but at least the magical weapon flew at a height aimed for an adult's neck. The sudden sound and light startled them from more than anything else about it.

After a few more minutes of crawling, Kimber stood. "We past 'em."

Emma and Ambril stood, rearranging themselves to hold hands in a row with Kimber in the middle.

"This place is dangerous," said Maea.

"Yes." Emma exhaled.

They continued walking for another few minutes in the icy stone corridor before reaching a four-way intersection.

"Which way?" asked Ambril.

"I don't know." Emma looked left, then right, then ahead. "If there's a shrine here, it's probably in the middle. I think we should keep going straight."

"Something is coming." Maea faced the corridor on the right, growling.

A scratch came from the left, then a hiss and a creaking of bones.

No sooner did Emma think the noises coming from the darkness on either side of them sounded like the undead she'd seen in Calebrin, a pair of huge skeletons ambled out of the darkness, still clad in the furs and leather armor they'd been buried in years and years ago. Bits of beard clung to their exposed skulls, though no flesh remained. The horrors dragged themselves a half-step into the middle hallway before stopping, raising their arms to shield their faces from the glowing sphere orbiting Emma.

Mythandriel's light seemed to repel them, or at least proved so uncomfortable it made them stop.

I think I figured out what the villagers are afraid of. Emma blinked.

Ambril screamed.

Maea leapt at the undead on the right, biting its leg and wrenching the skeleton off its feet. The hissing fiend clattered to the stone floor, sliding across the ice. The clang of its ancient sword bouncing off the wall as it toppled over rang out like a bell in the dark.

"Run!" shouted Emma. "Maea, don't fight it! You'll get hurt. They're slow."

She waited for the wolf to backpedal into view, then took off at a sprint, dragging Kimber, who in turn dragged Ambril. The rich girl didn't need much of a prod to get her moving. She continued screaming in a high, clear, glass-shattering note as they ran down the hall.

Mythandriel's light followed, allowing the skeletons to shamble into the passage behind them. Emma tried not to panic at feeling trapped. If they couldn't find the box in here and had to leave, she could intensify the light. The undead would hopefully retreat. These two didn't seem quite as evil as the last skeletons she'd seen... not that she wanted to sit and have tea with them; however, they definitely gave off more of a sense of being guardians rather than evil.

A moment later, the darkness ahead widened where the corridor connected to a large, round chamber. Emma skidded to a stop. Kimber and Ambril smushed into her from behind. She focused on the little light orb, adding magic to increase its power, illuminating the entire space around them.

At the center of the room, a great cube-shaped boulder sat atop a rounded platform much wider than it. Ancient carved writing adorned the stone's four faces, as well as on top. Hundreds of bowls, urns, twig bundles, and pouches—offerings brought to this place over many, many years—sat on the edges of the platform around the giant stone. Only one object in the entire shrine appeared to be made of gold: the Box of Wonder, nestled between a pair of urns against the big stone.

Clattering and scraping came from the passage behind them, the two skeletons ambling closer and closer.

"There it is!" Ambril pointed.

"I donnae loike it in 'ere," whispered Kimber. "They's got dead people inna walls."

Emma looked over. The entire outer wall of the chamber, as well as the walls of three other passageways leading out from it contained numerous long hollows similar to the honeycombs of bees, stacked six cubbies tall. Each space contained skeletal remains.

"Well." Emma gulped. "It *is* a tomb. This is where they bring their dead. The bodies are supposed to be there."

"Let's get out of here." Ambril approached the shrine.

Emma hurried after her. Yrsa and Arne placed the box so far back —right against the boulder—the girls would have to go up on their toes, leaning past the waist-high edge and stretch their arm out to get a hand on it.

"Wait," whispered Emma.

Ambril glared. "Why?"

"Because." Emma looked around at all the dead. "I don't know if you can understand me. We don't mean any disrespect. We aren't here to steal. We only want to go home." She looked at Maea. "We're going to be okay. Can you get out of here safely?"

"Yes, child." Maea nuzzled her.

"Will you please go to Hrunor and ask him to thank Yrsa and her family for taking care of us? I don't want them to be sad that we are going away or worried about us. We have families who miss us and must return to them."

Maea bowed her head. "I shall do this."

Ambril, being the tallest of the girls, went for the box. Stretching didn't quite do it. She had to climb up to kneel at the edge of the stone shelf to reach. As soon as she picked it up, rustling came from every burial cubby around the chamber.

Kimber clamped onto Emma, shivering. "I don' fink the spirits want us takin' the box back."

Close to a hundred skeletons dragged themselves out of their burial cubbies, hissing and growling as they clambered to their feet and shambled toward the girls from every side.

Emma held Kimber tight and pressed herself against Ambril. "Open it!"

A bright flash of magic turned everything blinding white.

When the light faded, Emma found herself standing in the alcove inside the box, surrounded by the glowing blue rune circle. Kimber jumped up to pull the lock lever down.

"Excuse me." Calm as can be, Ambril neatened her dress, brushed some dirt from her legs, then walked into the other room. She sat on the edge of the bed, screamed, then burst into tears.

Kimber shrugged at Emma. "Skeletons are scary. She ne'er saw 'em afore."

KNOCK KNOCK

*B*y the time Emma and Kimber walked from the alcove to the bed, Ambril quieted.

She delicately wiped tears from her face, then folded her hands in her lap. "I'm fine now. I simply needed to let that out."

Emma tilted her head. "Are you sure?"

"I think so." Ambril squirmed. "It's likely I will have nightmares about those horrible fiends. How can you be so... so... calm?"

"I've seen skeletons before." Emma shivered. "And I knew we could get away from them."

Ambril dabbed her skirt at her face again. "I'll thank you not to scare me with any frightful details." She paused, then peered over the peach-colored fabric at Emma. "Are those things still outside?"

"Probably." Emma spun around and walked over to the orb table.

The large crystal ball showed only darkness.

"Can't see in the tomb because there's no light." Emma pointed at the smaller blue sphere. It once again looked like a solid glowing sapphire instead of a hollow ball full of magical liquid. "It's full."

Ambril jumped from the bed and ran over. "All right. Let's all touch it together. Everyone think about home."

"Okay." Kimber scurried over and squeezed between them.

Emma held her hand over the blue orb. Ambril put her left hand next to Emma's, touching thumbs. Kimber added her hand sideways at their fingertips.

"Concentrate on wanting to go home." Ambril gradually lowered her hand.

Emma and Kimber did the same, all three girls touching the blue sphere at the same time.

Home. Home. Home. Emma thought as hard as she could make herself think.

A moment later, the room lurched sideways. Emma gurgled as if her stomach tried to climb up and out of her mouth. Too dizzy to stand, she collapsed to the floor, head spinning, at the verge of throwing up.

Ambril coughed a few times. Kimber retched, making vomit noises several times without producing any mess. After a minute or two, the intense sickness faded, leaving Emma only dizzy.

"Did we do something wrong?" whispered Emma.

"Why are you asking me?" Ambril clutched her stomach in both hands. "I don't know magic."

"It sure felt loike we did somefin' bad." Kimber moaned. "My tummy 'urts."

From the floor, the big crystal ball still looked black.

"Oh, no." Emma swallowed. "It didn't let us leave."

"It? What it?" Ambril grabbed her.

"I dunno. Whatever 'it' became angry with us and sent the skeletons." Emma twisted to look at the empty alcove. No monsters made it into the box after them. The room remained still and quiet, so nothing outside the box touched it. "Unless we went somewhere else that's also so dark we can't see."

Ambril sniffled. "I don't like this box anymore."

"Is better than' freezin' our noses off." Kimber flapped her arms. "I donnae fink it's so bad."

"Grr." Emma reached up to grab the edge of the table and pulled herself to her feet.

Darkness covered only the bottom of the orb, not the entire thing.

A curious mixture of forest and swamp surrounded the Box of Wonder. Undergrowth around them, as well as the wild grass and small plants all looked as black as the night sky. Trees had black trunks, while their leaves took on shades of violet or dark blue. Mushrooms dotted the ground, ranging from black and pointy to purple and round. Some even appeared to be pink with white or purple spots. Tall bushes in the distance, mostly black, had bright blue bell-shaped flowers hanging from their sides as big as a child's head.

"This is not home," said Emma in a blank tone.

"Oops." Kimber sighed. "I tried. Sorry."

Emma patted her. "It's not your fault. This box is… being stupid. Ambril? Do you know where this is?"

"I need a moment. My stomach is still spinning." Ambril breathed hard. "If I try to stand now, I'll fall over again."

Kimber got up and peered into the crystal ball, shaking. "Is this the place where dead people go?"

"The Netherworld?" Emma put an arm around her sister. "I don't think so. This box is magical, yes. I don't think it's got enough power to bring us to a whole other world."

"Eek." Ambril gripped the table to pull herself up onto her knees so she could see into the orb. She stared, taking in the scenery. Shades of violet and pink light from the crystal tinted her awestruck face. "So strange. How can a place be terrifying *and* beautiful at the same time?"

"The pink and purple fings are pretty." Kimber pointed.

Emma tapped her foot. "We can wait a few hours inside. I think we should stay in the box. We're out in the forest where no one's going to find it… if there are even any people here."

"Yes. Let's stay inside." Ambril covered her mouth and nose in both hands.

"Bedtime?" asked Kimber.

"My hands are still shaking from those skeletons. I don't think I'll be able to sleep for a while but… it was bedtime in the ice place." Ambril exhaled. "We can try."

The girls went over to the bed, climbed in, and snuggled together under soft, luxurious sheets and blankets. Emma thought it as nice as the beds at Da's manor house. It didn't take her long to fall asleep.

EMMA AWOKE TO THE WHOLE ROOM SHAKING.

"Gah!" she yelled, flailing her arms in fright. It took her a second or two to wake up enough to recall what happened and stop thinking an earthquake tried to fling her out of her bed at home. As soon as she remembered being inside the Box of Wonder, the shaking took on an entirely different meaning: danger. "Someone's found us!"

Ambril flung the blankets and sheets aside, then leapt out of bed. Emma scrambled after her. Kimber, still mostly asleep, babbled about Princess Isabelle.

Emma and Ambril rushed over to the orb table.

The big crystal ball showed a strange girl holding the golden box in both hands, examining it. She looked to be about the same physical size as Emma with several rather glaring differences. Most obviously, the child's skin was pure black, the color of a midnight sky. Long, straight hair of periwinkle blue draped around long, pointed ears to frame a face with fine, delicate features. She wore an airy semi-translucent purple dress that left her shoulders bare, the material shimmery as if made of faerie wings.

"Wha...?" Ambril stared. "Is that... is she...?"

Emma glanced sideways at her. "She's a kid. Like us. Why are you scared?"

Kimber stumbled over, rubbing her eyes and yawning. "Wake. Why? Time tae ge' sick again?"

"I think she's a dark elf," whispered Ambril. "I've read about them." She ran over to the map table, then gave a yelp of alarm. "Oh, no... we're *there*. This isn't the Netherworld, it's worse!"

Emma glanced once more at the dark elf child, sighed, then hurried over to the map. "What are you fretting about now?"

"Look." Ambril raised her arm to point at the silver needle.

It balanced on its point near the top of the northwestern

continent. An area of black forests, grey rivers, and scattered violet foliage stood apart from the remainder of the continent on the other side of a dark mountain range.

"We're getting closer." Emma smiled. "That's the right continent? Yes? We live on this one."

Ambril grabbed Emma like a smaller child clinging to her mother for protection. "Yes, but this is Nimaraenna!"

"I still don't understand why you're so scared." Emma squeezed her back, trying to be comforting. "How could this place be worse than the Netherworld?"

"Dark elves are evil," she whispered. "They kill humans for games. They associate with demons. They're fast and deadly and cruel and vicious."

Emma pointed at the orb. "Did you see the same girl I did? She looks adorable."

"Bear cubs look adorable, too. But they grow up and eat people!" Ambril fanned herself.

"She's our age and don' 'ave any weapons," said Kimber, still over at the orb table.

"That girl might be a demon in disguise. Or have a pet demon." Ambril breathed so fast she appeared close to fainting. "Demons can trick us. They can look harmless when they want to."

Emma clamped a hand over Ambril's mouth. "Shh. Calm. Stop breathing so fast. You're going to pass out. She might be dangerous, or she might not be. It doesn't matter. We're in the box and she can't get us."

Ambril nodded.

Emma uncovered her mouth.

"You're right. I'm scaring myself." Ambril ran over to the alcove. "Lock is still on."

"Demon..." Emma frowned. "I think that sounds like what dumb people say because they're afraid of new things they don't understand."

Ambril gasped. "Did you just call me dumb?"

"No." Emma sighed at the ceiling. "You heard dumb people saying things and believed them. Look at Mama. You've heard some people call her the Witch of the Woods, and they didn't say it in a nice way."

Head bowed, Ambril crept back over to the map. "Yes. True. Wait." She looked up. "Isn't your Nan the Witch of the Woods?"

"Both really." Emma shrugged. "I guess it's more Nan than Mama. People are stupid. They used to think Mama and Nan were the same person who could make themselves look like any age she wanted."

"Wow." Ambril whistled. "Really?"

"Yes." Emma ground her big toe into the carpet. "A merchant once even thought I was Mama pretending to be a child to trick him."

Ambril laughed. "You really do look so much like her it's almost strange."

"Yeah." Emma grinned. She *adored* looking like Mama. It made her feel close to her mother. "I don't know anything about dark elves." She set her hands on her hips. "Maybe they *are* mostly bad. But, it's also possible some humans met some bad dark elves and came back to tell everyone about it, so we think that *all* dark elves are bad."

Ambril wrung her hands together in thought. "I don't know. There are a lot of books that talk about them being cruel and dangerous."

The room wobbled.

"Oh, no. Is she taking the box?" Ambril spun to look at the orb table.

"No," chirped Kimber. "She put it onna groun'."

Emma jogged over to watch. Ambril hurried after her.

The dark elf child knelt in front of the Box of Wonder, sitting back on her heels. She leaned forward and waved at it as if greeting a person. Though difficult to tell from a view fifty feet in the air overhead, the girl appeared to be smiling.

"She's a real elf." Kimber pointed. "Donnae look mean. C'we talk ta her?"

Emma frowned. "She probably won't understand us. No one else does."

The dark elf girl patted the top of the box three times. A soft thumping noise reverberated in the ceiling.

Ambril squish-hugged Emma from behind. "I think she knows we're in here. How can she?"

"Elf?" asked Kimber.

"Or a demon," squeak-whispered Ambril.

The dark elf girl fussed at the box.

Emma couldn't help but think she seemed worried. "I think she knows we're inside... or that *someone* is inside. The way she's acting, it's like she believes we're trapped and can't get out. Maybe she's nice?"

"Or hungry," whispered Ambril.

Flickering trails of violet-blue light followed the dark elf girl's hand around in circles over the box lid.

"Hungry?" Emma stared at Ambril. "Really?"

"What?" Ambril attempted to scrape together some composure, neatening her hair. "Demons eat souls. That's what I meant."

"If she's scared for us, she cannae be bad." Kimber bounced. "Fink she wanna play?"

"Harmless or dangerous, I think we should probably just stay inside and wait for the blue orb to fill back up." Emma scratched her left shin with her right foot.

Ambril sighed in relief. "Yes. Let's stay insiiii—"

A brilliant flash of light filled the room.

Silence gave way to the chirping, buzzing, and trilling of an uncountable number of birds, bugs, and other unknown creatures. The air heated up and became damp, warm but not intolerably so. Emma's feet squished into soft earth. As the flash left her eyes, the details of a black-tinted forest filled in around her. Kimber and Ambril clung to her on either side.

And a little dark elf girl stood in front of them, smiling.

Emma, too stunned at being forcibly removed from the box, could only stare at her. The girl seemed slightly shorter than her with thin, delicate limbs. Her violet eyes gave off a faint magical glow—as well as a sense of happiness and relief. Thin silver bracelets decorated both of her wrists and one ankle. Like Emma, the girl wore no shoes. The narrow tips of her slender pointed ears stood almost as tall as the top of her head. Teeth showing through her big smile seemed quite normal—no fangs and the usual color teeth ought to be.

"Na'lir ul dora vas M'ur Niim?" asked the girl in a melodic voice a little higher in pitch than Emma's.

Darn. Emma sighed. "See? She's not going to understand us."

The dark elf girl blinked. "Oh. Hello. What are you doing in the Forest of Sorrow?"

PETS

*E*veryone stared at each other in silence for a while.

"Forest of Sorrow," whispered Ambril. "I don't think we should be here."

The dark elf girl looked at them, seeming confused. "Did your owner lose you or did you somehow escape? Or… are you recently taken? You are speaking Doric, so… you couldn't have been born here."

"Eek." Ambril trembled. "I told you! We're in danger."

"Owner?" Emma blinked. "What? You can't own people."

Ambril clutched the back of Emma's dress, face to her ear, and whispered, "I told you dark elves are dangerous."

"You aren't pets?" asked the dark elf girl.

"Most certainly not," snapped Ambril.

"No. We're just lost." Emma folded her arms.

Ambril scoffed. "Pets? What do you mean *pets*? My Father is…" She sighed, taken by sudden fear and sadness. "Very far away."

The dark elf child flashed a huge smile. "I am glad you are not pets. My name is Rin. What are you called?"

"I'm Emma. This is my sister, Kimber, and my friend Ambril."

"How can you call us pets?" Ambril continued shaking, though it might have been anger as much as fear.

Rin looked down. "Humans like you have pets, yes? Dogs? Chickens? Other animals?"

"Sometimes." Emma gazed around at the forest and all its strange new sounds. *At least it's warm here. We won't freeze.*

"My kind sometimes keeps humans as pets," said Rin.

"That's awful!" Ambril glared. "How can they do that?"

"Because to some of us, humans are... like cats or dogs." Rin let out a sad sigh. "How old do you think I am?"

"Nine," said Kimber. "You's a little taller an' me but not as big as Em. But... Em and Ambril are boaf ten an' Ambril's taller. So maybe you're ten but small."

Rin let out a bright, melodic laugh that made it difficult for Emma to think her evil. "I'm 188 years old."

Emma's jaw fell open.

"You're lying," said Ambril.

"I'm not. I'm a Niltharien. You're a human." Rin flicked her blue hair back over her shoulder. "In human terms, I would be about nine. One year to a human is twenty for us. A human can be born, grow old, and die before one of my kind even becomes halfway an adult. They think of humans as pets because they're mean and humans don't live long."

Ambril narrowed her eyes. "Why do you say 'they' when you're a dark elf, too?"

Rin peered down again, tracing her toes back and forth across the ground. "I don't like it. It's cruel. Humans aren't pets. Cats, dogs, and chickens don't talk. They're not smart like humans."

Emma held up a finger, about to correct her. Animals *did* talk. She stopped herself before saying a word.

Kimber noticed her expression and laughed.

"If you aren't pets, how did you get trapped in that box?" asked Rin.

"We weren't trapped." Emma picked the box up. "We found it and tried to open it to see what was inside and... ended up going in. It's got a blue magic ball inside that makes it go places. We've been to a desert and a land full of ice. Now... here. We're trying to get home but can't make it work right. I hope it's not broken."

Rin crouched down to eye level with the box in Emma's arms. "Why do you think it broke?"

"Because it kicked us out. It never did that before."

"Oh." Rin stood, flashing a contrite smile. "I apologize. I did that. I thought you were trapped and wanted to help you get free."

"*You* did it?" Ambril looked back and forth between Rin and the box. "How?"

"I am studying to become a mage." Rin reached for the box. "May I examine it? I promise not to steal it."

Emma stared into Rin's eyes for a long moment. She seemed so sweet and innocent. According to stories, elves were fast and graceful, even the dark ones. If this child wanted to run away with the box, they probably wouldn't be able to catch her. *Maybe* Emma could if she asked Naraja to make her faster. This elf girl didn't look much slimmer than her, not as much as she expected an elf to be, anyway. Of course, everyone thought Emma to be part elf, unnaturally thin. So... maybe she could keep up with her after all.

Also, the girl didn't look as though she lied. She'd managed to make the box kick them out, proving she had some magical ability.

"All right." Emma held the box out.

Rin grasped it in both hands. She didn't try to pull it away from her, only stared at it while also touching it. "*Ianor lim orinar.*"

Blue light shimmered over the box.

"Oooh," whispered Kimber.

"This is a powerful artifact." Rin's blue eyebrows went up. "A shelter."

"There's a room inside." Emma nodded.

"Can you tell how the magic works to move us around?" Ambril stopped trembling, hope replacing fear in her eyes.

Rin squinted at the box. "I might be able to. Not from outside. The lid won't open for a while."

"Why not? Can you tell us that?" Emma pointed at the big gems on the lid. "These will glow when it's ready."

"Magical items can only hold so much power at once." Rin let go of the box, leaving it in Emma's hands. "Think of a pitcher of water. When it's full, it's full. If you use the water for something, the pitcher becomes empty and there's no more water until you refill it."

"Yes." Emma tilted her head. "How do we put magic back into it?"

"Time." Rin gestured at the box. "It takes almost all of the magic it can store at once to teleport. Going in and out uses a little. If you didn't teleport, you could enter or leave the box over and over again and it would probably never run out of magic."

"Can you tell how long it takes to charge?"

"One day." Rin traced her fingers across the lid.

"I don't understand why the lid won't open now." Ambril frowned.

"Do you think it takes magic to bring people in and out of a small jewelry box?" asked Rin. "Or would you fit inside a normal box that small?"

Ambril sighed. "Of course it takes magic."

"It doesn't have any to use right now. It's empty." Rin knocked on the lid twice. "After it teleports, there is a tiny fraction of magic left. Enough for anyone inside to leave. Then, you have to wait a day."

"So'as we gonna be 'ere a day?" Kimber gazed around. "It's pretty."

"My uncle has some aether stones. One of them would help it recharge more quickly." Rin pointed off to one side. "I invite you to my home as guests. You can stay there until you are ready to go home."

"I am sorry if this offends you," said Ambril, "but you don't mean to make pets of us?"

"No." Rin shook her head. "I don't like that. It's wrong and mean."

"You don't sound like a dark elf." Ambril managed a weak smile.

Rin bowed her head, a small tear gathered in her eyes. "I know."

"Sorry." Emma cringed. "She doesn't intend to be cruel. Ambril reads a lot of books and some of them say mean things about your people."

"I imagine." Rin wiped her tears, then sighed. "Most of them are true."

Ambril and Emma leaned back together, shocked.

"What?" Emma blinked.

"Please. Follow." Rin walked in the same direction she pointed before.

Emma took Kimber's hand and followed. Ambril hurried to catch up, then walked in step on her left.

"I am surprised you didn't ask me why a girl who's only 188 years old is alone out in the middle of the Forest of Sorrow." Rin reached up to a caress a pink flower on a huge bush they passed.

"Honestly... I thought it, but there is so much going on..." Emma exhaled.

"Among my people, there are noble houses. Humans would call them royalty." Rin veered to the left. "Don't touch that bush. It's poisonous."

Emma, Kimber, and Ambril all 'eeped' simultaneously, hurrying away from the black thorns.

"Members of the houses are constantly at war with each other to try and take the throne. It's not always a war with swords and spells. Most of the time, it's words and manipulations of law. Less often, it's poison or daggers." Rin sighed. "And every now and then, it becomes literal war."

"Your parents are... dead?" whispered Ambril.

"No. Unfortunately." Rin let out an annoyed sigh.

Emma, Kimber, and Ambril stopped walking.

"W-what?" Emma gasped. "You *want* your parents to die?"

"Not both of them. Only my mother," said Rin. "I am a natural descendant of the House of Loreth, next in line after my parents to the throne."

"You want to be queen?" Ambril grimaced. "You'd wish death on your parents to take the crown?"

Rin laughed. "No. Most of my kind would. I don't want to be queen. It's awful, really. Constantly having to look over my shoulder for someone trying to kill me. Afraid to eat anything for fear of poison. Afraid to sleep. I don't want it. No amount of power in the world is worth living in constant dread."

Emma resumed walking. "You ran away to hide?"

"That is close to the truth." Rin smiled back at her. "In order for me to inherit the throne, a few specific individuals would have to die and House Loreth would need to gain prominence in the court. I'm one of many heirs with a potential claim on the throne. It depends on which House claims power."

A furry, black-and-violet insect as big as a housecat flew by. Emma turned her head at the buzzing, gawking at a spider with wings. Thankfully, it zipped by too fast for Ambril to notice.

"Someone doesn't want you to be queen, so they exiled you out here?" Ambril shied away from a creeper vine on the ground. "Oh, why is everywhere so dirty and wet? This place would ruin my slippers, too."

"They would want me to be queen only because it's easier to kill a child than an adult." Rin scowled. "The other houses would laugh as they arranged things for me to be crowned, intending to kill me and bring ruin to House Loreth. No, that's not why I'm here. I've been hidden away out here by my father and uncle because I lack the wickedness and cruelty of my mother. She, and most of our house, call me an embarrassment."

"You'as tae nice?" Kimber giggled.

"Essentially, yes." Rin glanced down.

"Too *nice?*" Emma scratched her head. "You seem quite normal to me."

"Normal for you is not normal to my kind." Rin bowed her head, again near to crying. "They are ashamed of me and try to pretend I was never born. Among commoners, having sensibilities like mine is not such a great embarrassment. A noble, though? Unacceptable. I could not even pretend to be cruel... even when my life was at risk for it."

"How awful," said Emma.

Ambril made a face as though she suspected this all might be a trick for sympathy.

"You know magic?" Emma smiled, trying to brighten the mood.

"Some, yes. I am only learning." Rin added a pirouette to her stride. Kimber spun around as well, laughing.

"Can you show us how to make the box take us home?" asked Ambril.

"I will try as soon as we are able to go inside." Rin leapt over a black fallen log. "Be careful. Do not touch this tree. The sap is poisonous to humans."

Emma might have jumped over it if alone. To be safe, she went around it and pulled Kimber with her.

"Perhaps my uncle can work the enchantment if I cannot," said Rin.

"Is your uncle nice, too?" Kimber grinned.

"Nicer than most of my kind. Unlike me, he can pretend to be cruel when necessary." Rin peered back at them. "Do not feel the need to hide from him. He will not harm you."

Ambril stopped walking and screamed.

Everyone else spun to stare at her.

"What?" blurted Emma.

"Are you hurt?" Rin zoomed over.

"No." Ambril blushed. "I just realized she said she's from a noble family."

"So?" Emma blinked.

Ambril closed her eyes, shaking. "We're meeting nobility and you've got me traipsing about half dressed."

"You are not half dressed." Emma sighed. "Your dress is five times the material of mine. It's all puffy and whatnot. You've got another dress on under that dress."

"No hose!" Ambril stomped. "And I'm without proper shoes! That's as embarrassing as being half dressed."

Emma gestured at the gossamer faerie dress Rin wore, the garment that left her shoulders bare and stopped not quite midway between her hips and knees, then pointed at the dark elf's bare feet. "I don't think she will consider you under-dressed."

Rin burst into giggles.

A MOST DEADLY, AWFUL PLACE

*R*in led them through the strange forest.

Even the soil looked black as coal dust. Whenever Emma spotted an animal, she tried to say hello. None of them spoke back, though the way they stopped to look at her proved they understood. Birds tended to give her the same sort of annoyed glances she usually got from rich merchants in Widowswood Village, mistaking her for a grubby peasant. A cat the size of a pony reacted to her 'hello' with a resigned feminine sigh and an expression that said 'all right, I won't eat you,' but said nothing. Small, spherical fuzzballs somewhere between boars and giant chipmunks ran away from her when she attempted to say hello. A great ebon-furred stag snorted in response to her greeting. She scurried along faster, worried he might come after her for daring to talk.

Even the animals here are mean.

A glint moved from a tree less than two feet away from her face. Emma realized too late that she'd come eye to eight-eyes with a fuzzy black spider as big as a dog. At least this one didn't have giant purple dragonfly wings. Working with the emerald creepers mostly cured her phobia of spiders, but hadn't eliminated it entirely. She squeaked. The spider tensed as if to pounce on her face, then relaxed.

"Hello?"

It scurried away around the tree, grumbling to itself about druids as if annoyed it felt obligated not to eat her.

He wanted to bite me. Emma let an uneasy whimper slip out of her nose. She decided to stop trying to talk to the animals here for now.

"Don't touch any plants," said Rin.

"Wasn't going to." Ambril hiked her dress up. "I don't want to get dirty."

"You are kinda dirty already," whispered Kimber.

"Ugh. Don't remind me."

Emma bit her lip, trying not to laugh.

"Why can't we touch flowers?" asked Kimber.

"Many things here are deadly to humans." Rin spun around, walking backward. "Some can make you sick if you only touch them. Others won't hurt you unless you happen to be foolish enough to eat them. A few plants here are so dangerous, if a human were to place a single hand on them, they would die."

Emma squeaked. If she hadn't been so small herself, she'd have scooped Kimber up to carry her.

They walked for another few minutes, eventually arriving at the edge of a clearing which contained a fancy house. It seemed far too nice to be out in the middle of nowhere. Not a cabin in the woods, but a proper house with two stories and an angled roof covered in violet shingles. The black and violet colors made it look like something out of a scary storybook. Decorative stone walkways weaved in an elaborate pattern throughout a garden beside the house.

Emma thought the home so bizarre, it had to have been taken from a big city and moved out here by magic.

"Your house is pretty." Kimber smiled. "Do you live here by yourself?"

"No," whispered Ambril. "She already said her uncle is here."

Rin slowed to a stop and looked down. She squeezed her hands into fists, giving off both anger and sorrow.

"Sorry," whispered Emma. She edged closer. "I don't mean to pry. Are you all right?"

"Not really." Rin fought off a sniffle. "I'm always scared."

"Why?" asked Kimber.

Rin faced the girls. "I told you a small lie before. I haven't been sent out here to hide."

Ambril's eyes widened in fear. She looked ready to either scream and run or faint where she stood.

"My mother," said Rin, "wanted my father to take me into the forest and kill me."

Emma clutched her chest. "That's awful!"

Ambril's building fear collapsed into an expression of pity.

"Yes. My mother is embarrassed of me. Thinks I'm a dishonor to her house and bloodline. I am too weak to lead. Too weak to even call myself a Niltharien."

"What's a Niltharien?" asked Emma.

"You are a human. I am a Niltharien." Rin kicked at the dirt. "Or at least I look like one. Mother says I don't have the heart of one. She wanted father to cut my heart out and burn it."

Emma covered her mouth, too horrified to think of anything to say.

"You got away?" whispered Ambril.

"My father pretended to do as she asked. He brought me to his brother, my uncle, to keep me hidden."

Ambril wiped a tear. "Your own mother? Barbaric."

Emma looked down at her toes sunken in the black earth. "It's this place. This whole forest."

"I'as fink it's a swamp," whispered Kimber.

"This place is too far north to be so warm and humid." Ambril fanned herself.

"It is unnatural." Rin exhaled. "Everything about Nimaraenna is a mockery of the forest it used to be."

Emma squeezed her sister's hand. "It's both, and it's full of bad energy. Even the animals here are kinda evil. The friendliest critter I saw was that giant spider."

"Wow." Kimber whistled. "Somefin' is really wrong when the spiders are the nicest animals."

Ambril gave a nervous laugh. "I didn't see any spiders."

"We know you dinnae see them." Kimber poked her. "You dinnae scream."

Ambril blushed.

Rin waved for them to follow and approached the house. "Yes. Nimaraenna is filled with corrupted energy. This land used to be green and full of life, home to Ilmari elves. Many thousands of years ago, a foul demon, Inoru, broke free of the Abyss and came here. His mere presence started to change the land. The Ilmari who lived here tried to fight him in defense of their home. His presence was too strong. The Ilmari changed, sometimes in the middle of battle. One by one, they succumbed to his power, becoming Niltharien or dying, until none remained as they had been."

Kimber clamped onto Emma, shaking in fear.

"I'm... sorry?" Ambril forced a polite smile.

Rin let out a somber sigh as she reached the door to the house. "It's all right. This happened so long ago, it's as if it always was. Would you care to have a tea party?"

"Okay." Kimber ceased trembling.

"That would be lovely," said Ambril.

"Is the demon still here?" whispered Emma.

"No." Rin opened the door and went inside. "He absorbed the life force from the Ilmari who died attempting to stop him. He's now a god, the Night Lord, creator of Niltharien and the patron of my kind... or most of us."

Emma followed her. The furniture—long cushioned divans, smaller chairs, tables, and even the shelves had an airy design, made of thin spars of wood, carved or bent into delicate-looking forms decorated with flower shapes. The most striking difference between this house and the ones back home came from the lack of interior walls. Simple columns or thin partitions of black vines dotted with tiny flowers of white or purple only hinted at separate rooms.

"Most of you?" Ambril edged in behind Emma, cautiously, as if still fearing a trap.

"My uncle says that those of us who are not wicked are vessels for restless Ilmari souls who could not find peace in death and somehow evaded Inoru's endless hunger." Rin crossed the front room, following a hint of a hallway to an area enclosed by a relatively thick vine lattice, perhaps the most private area in the home. "It might be true and would explain why my mother wished me dead. I think and feel in ways too much like the Ilmari. She sees me as a threat to the Night Lord."

"I'm so sorry." Ambril exhaled. "That's foolish. You? One child a threat to a god?"

Rin led them into the room, which contained a ring of violet cushions on the floor, several tall black wardrobe cabinets painted with white, pink, and purple flowers, and a small table with a tea set. "Not only me. I said before there are others of my kind who feel as I do. For those who have no social status, it is not a great concern. Those who have power cannot allow a member of a noble house to be seen as… weak. They fear if a noble openly showed 'weakness,' it would embolden others to rally under them and lead to a great war."

"Not weakness. You mean niceness. Friendly." Emma tilted her head. "You thought we were trapped in the box and wanted to help us."

"Please, sit." Rin clasped her hands in front of herself, smiling.

Emma sat on the floor cushion. Kimber plopped down beside her, Ambril beside her.

Rin glanced sideways, her smile faltering momentarily to an expression of worry. "Hmm. I wonder if we have any teas that won't kill you. Just a moment." She smiled at them, then darted out past the vine lattice and scurried across the house to an area similar to a pantry.

"Oy," whispered Kimber. "Ya fink she means ta 'ave a tea party wi' actual tea? Nae jes' p'tend?"

Ambril sat taller to watch Rin search the pantry. "Perhaps it might be safer to have a *pretend* tea party here."

LOST

*T*he girls sat on the cushion ring waiting while Rin checked the pantry, ran across the house to look through a book, then returned to the pantry before going to the book again. She ran back and forth several times. Each trip across the house, she paused to gaze around as if waiting for something to happen. Eventually, she selected a wide glass jar three-quarters full with lavender-colored dry leaves from the cabinet and hurried back to them.

She sat on the cushion ring across the table from the girls, holding the big jar in both hands. "This is either ravenweed—which you can't drink, or it's ouro leaf, which is safe for humans."

"How do you tell the difference?" asked Emma.

"Ouro leaf is purple when alive and this color when dried out." Rin held the jar up. "Ravenweed is black when alive, and... also this color when dried out."

"That doesn't help us." Ambril fanned herself. "It is kind of warm here."

"You 'ave tae much dress on." Kimber giggled.

Rin grasped the cork on the jar. She glanced left at the house, waited a moment, then let out a quiet sigh. "There's another way to tell, but it might be unpleasant."

"You're not going to say if we drink it and drop dead, then it's ravenweed, are you?" Emma scratched idly at her chest.

"No." Rin winced. "That *would* be one way to test it. A bad way. We're not going to do that. Will one of you smell these leaves? If they don't smell awful to you, then it's ouro leaf."

"How bad will it smell if it's ravenweed?" Emma leaned forward, volunteering to be the sniffer.

"I'm not sure. It smells the same to me because ravenweed isn't poisonous to Niltharien." Rin pulled the cork out.

Emma waved her hand over the top of the jar, pulling air toward her face and sniffing. She got a mild fruity-flowery smell. "This smells fine. Sweet even."

"Good. That means it's ouro leaf and won't kill you." Rin took the lid off the teapot in the middle of the table, which already had plain water in it. She added several pinches of the bluish leaves, re-corked the jar, then placed one hand on the side of the teapot. *"Pa'laur Vokath."*

Orange flames appeared around her hand, spreading out around the whole teapot.

Emma, Kimber, and Ambril leaned back from the heat.

Four seconds later, the fire stopped. Rin smiled. "We must let it brew for a few minutes."

"What was that?" asked Ambril.

"A fire spell. It's normally used to fight. This teapot is enchanted to focus such a spell inward to boil water." Rin selected cups and set one out in front of everyone. "Will you tell me of your adventure?"

"It's not really an adventure, more of an accident." Emma squeezed her knees in a repetitive, soothing manner. "All right. We have a day to wait. May as well talk."

Emma shared the story of what happened since the thieves attempted to kidnap Ambril. A few minutes into the tale, Rin poured purple tea into everyone's cups. She took the first sip.

"Yes, that's definitely ouro leaf. Ravenweed tingles on the tongue." She smacked her lips a few times. "Alas. I used a little too much. It's overly strong."

Emma gingerly took a sip of the steaming tea. The taste reminded her of a fruit Nan called plums mixed with blackberries.

Ambril seemed to find the tea overly sweet. Kimber kept trying to drink it too fast for the heat and whimpering, evidently loving the flavor.

Rin occasionally looked around as Emma continued explaining their bizarre journey. Perhaps an hour later, the story got to the part where the bear attacked the village in Eldrheim. In the middle of Emma telling everyone about how she fed him so he wouldn't hurt anyone, Rin jumped to her feet, seeming in a panic.

"Quiet. Hide." She pushed at the girls, shoving them across the small room toward one of the tall, shiny black wardrobe cabinets.

Without any hesitation or question, Kimber grabbed the Box of Wonder, darted to the cabinet, and jumped in, vanishing between dark silken garments. Emma stepped in after her. Ambril nearly tripped but made it inside without falling. Rin hopped in last and pulled the doors shut behind her. In the complete darkness, her eyes projected a faint violet glow on the inside of the doors.

"No sound," whispered Rin. "Try not to breathe."

The violet glow ceased, likely because the girl closed her eyes.

A narrow strip of daylight leaked past the tiny gap between the doors. Overwhelmed by curiosity, Emma leaned a little to the left and peeked through the space.

Three adult Niltharien strolled into the tea room, two women and a man. All had long, straight ghostly white hair, the same ink-black skin as Rin, and none of the warmth. Their dark leather armor and drawn swords said they'd not come here to enjoy a nice conversation over ouro leaf tea. A milky white liquid dripped from one woman's sword. The thin, wickedly sharp looking blade swept along in a gradual curve much shallower than the weapons she'd seen in Drajmir, a fast, light weapon made for an elf.

All three assassins glanced at the table, then back and forth at the two wardrobe cabinets in the room. Seconds later, they all burst out laughing.

The man said something in a flowing, melodic language that somehow sounded sinister.

In between chuckles, the woman whose swords remained clean pointed at the wardrobe cabinet where everyone hid and said a longer phrase.

"Humans?" asked the man. "I didn't think you cared to keep pets. You may as well come out, Rin'loreth. Your family wishes to see you."

Emma shook her head no, not that anyone could see.

"Where is Ta'al?" asked Rin.

The woman with the milky substance on her blade held the weapon up, smiling at the liquid dripping off the edge. The other two snickered. "He's waiting for us outside. You'll see him soon."

Dark elves have white blood... Emma shivered. *They're going to kill her.*

"Oh, show yourself already, you foolish little weakling." The man tapped his sword on the cabinet door.

"It certainly seems your mother was right in deciding you do not deserve to live." The woman holding the bloodied sword wiped it on the cushion where the girls sat a moment earlier. "So pitiful and cowardly."

"At least have the honor to step out of there on your own and face what you deserve," said the man.

Rin barked a strangled sob. "Ta'al..."

The second woman held a hand to her ear. "Oh, do you hear that? The little dear is *crying* over her poor uncle. Maybe we shouldn't have killed him."

Both other assassins laughed.

Rin grabbed Emma's hand as easily as if she could see in total darkness. "Ambril, hold on to me."

"Aww, the poor thing is scared," singsonged the first woman. She wiped the other side of the blade on the cushion. "Shall we let her finish playing with her pets or just get on with it?"

Rin whispered rapidly in another language.

The dark interior of the wardrobe cabinet changed in an instant to the black forest.

Emma looked down at the jet-black hand holding hers, then up at the girl's face. Tears wet her cheeks. She looked beyond terrified. Kimber stood on the other side, holding her left hand. Ambril, behind Rin, had both arms wrapped around the girl's chest.

"We…" Rin's eyes rolled up into their sockets and she passed out, slouching down in Ambril's grasp.

"Eep!" Ambril, despite not being ready to abruptly support Rin's entire weight, didn't have any trouble holding her up. "What happened?"

"She used magic to bring us here." Emma felt the side of Rin's neck. "I think she used a spell too big for her."

"What do you mean?" Ambril shifted her grip to carry the little dark elf sideways in her arms.

"Uruleth lets me use a spell to heal people when they get hurt." Emma concentrated on Rin. The girl didn't feel as though she needed magical healing, only rest. "There is another spell, from Mythandriel, that heals a lot more. I haven't been practicing magic long enough. If I asked Mythandriel for her healing magic, it would probably make me sleep, too. When I'm grown up and a proper druid, I will be able to cast those spells as easily as I use the small ones now."

"Oh." Ambril peered down at the unconscious dark elf child draped across her arms. "What just happened?"

"Assassins." Emma turned in place, studying the forest. This place they appeared in looked no different from where they first left the box. For all she knew, the house could be a five-minute walk away or hundreds of miles. "I think they killed her uncle and were going to kill her."

Kimber scowled. "You would'a thumped them."

"No." Emma shook her head. "Not them. They looked way too scary."

"Would they have hurt us?" whispered Ambril.

"If they didn't stab us," said Emma, "they would've taken us to be pets."

Ambril shivered. "I'm not sure which is worse."

"Let's not think about that?" Emma tapped her foot, thinking. The ground here felt squishier, swampier than where they'd been. They had to have covered a significant amount of land. She figured Rin tried to go as far away as she could manage.

"I'as go' a silly question." Kimber held up the box. "How's it we no' feel sick?"

"Why should we feel sick?" asked Ambril in a wavering voice full of fear.

"When the box goes places, we all go' sick. Rin did the same fing, an' we ain't sick." Kimber tucked the box under her arm. "Dinnae even feel loike anyfing 'appened."

"That's not a silly question." Emma scratched her head. "I can't answer it."

"We don't need to worry about it now." Ambril also looked around. "We're lost in a swampy forest where just about everything can kill us."

Emma looked down at her bare feet sinking into the dirt. *I hope the ground isn't poison, too.* She took Kimber's hand, rested her other hand on Ambril's arm, and cast the Dryad's Step.

Kimber oohed at the dancing lights from her magic.

"You did something." Ambril's shivering made Rin wobble in her arms.

"Yes. I'm hoping Linganthas' blessing will shield us from stepping on something deadly." Emma started walking in a random direction. "Come on. Don't let go of me, so the magic keeps protecting you."

Ambril whined. "Do you know where we are?"

"No." Emma shook her head.

"Are we lost?" asked Kimber.

"What we are…" Emma exhaled. "Is much worse than lost. We're… lost-er."

Kimber scurried along behind her, gazing around at the flowers and strange mushrooms. "Where are we going?"

"Somewhere we can hide until the box wakes up." Emma looked at Ambril. "Do you want me to carry her? I can make myself stronger."

"When I get tired. She doesn't weigh much." Ambril adjusted her hold. "She's as light as a cloth sack of four broom handles."

"Stay quiet and keep looking for somewhere we can hide," whispered Emma.

21

A BARGAIN OF FISH

*E*mma wandered for a while in search of somewhere to hide, not caring much about direction.

The more she thought about the three assassins, the more worried she became at *not* knowing how far away they might be. Rin's spell teleported them... somewhere. The assassins could be hiding behind any random tree nearby as likely as so far away it would take them weeks on a horse to get there. She started to worry about accidentally walking closer to them. Unfortunately, she knew nothing about this place or where they'd ended up.

Not too long ago, she asked Linganthas to help her find her way so she could walk in a circle around the edge of the emerald creeper's territory. Nan wanted her to place ritual talismans up in trees to help empower a magical ward to confuse silk hunters so they wouldn't be able to find the spiders.

She didn't know if trying to use the same spell here would help, because she had no specific place in mind to go. However, they found themselves in perhaps the most dangerous forest in the whole world —for humans—and also might have assassins tracking them. Even if the spell did nothing, trying it wasted only a little energy.

Linganthas, I call upon you to guide me. Please let me find a path to safety.

Nothing visibly magical happened. She may or may not have felt an enchanted tingle in her chest. As nervous and jumpy as she'd become here, even if the spell sent a dozen tiny spiders racing across her skin, she probably wouldn't have noticed.

Trusting the spirit of woodlands to lead her, Emma walked on for an hour or more, allowing whim to guide her in whatever direction seemed right. Eventually, they reached a brackish river awash in the foul stink of rotting vegetation. Dozens of small vee-shaped ripples zipped around in the grey water, signs of either fish or other creatures moving close beneath the surface.

"Can you take her, please? My arms are going to fall off," said Ambril.

"Okay." Emma lifted Rin away from Ambril, finding the Niltharien girl surprisingly light. She still proved a little too burdensome for Emma to carry with ease, so she called upon Uruleth for strength. The magic made the girl's weight so trivial it hardly seemed noticeable anymore.

Ambril let her arms hang limp and groaned in relief.

Emma walked faster, careful to avoid stepping near anything thorny, slimy, spiky... or moving. Some of the mushrooms pulsated. Every so often, they encountered small viny bushes waving their tendrils about like a blind person trying to find a nearby object. She suspected those plants probably ate small rodents or anything they could grab.

Probably has venom.

"Em," whispered Kimber. "We's bein' followed."

Ambril whimpered.

"Is no' a dark elf. I fink is a cat." Kimber nodded to the left.

Emma peered back over her shoulder. A modest distance behind them, the large shadowy form of a feline creature attempted—rather poorly—to hide. The animal tried to keep itself low in the undergrowth as it crept along behind them, but its sheer size left it obvious. At night, its black fur would make it invisible in the black forest. During the day, she had no trouble spotting it. The animal had the general shape of a panther with longer, tapered ears and fuzzier, wider cheeks. Its paws made no sound as it stepped, flowing between trees with the grace of a liquid. Luminous green-yellow eyes remained fixated on the girls.

She'd seen that same look on a cat's face before... a cat trying to sneak up on a mouse.

Uh oh. Strixian, please grant me the Wildkin Whisper. As soon as the dancing magical wisps faded, she turned to look at the cat. "Hello. Please don't eat us."

The big cat hung its head, then spoke in a male voice. "Naturally. The first prey I spot in hours and it's one of you..."

"One of me?"

"A spirit talker. You call yourself druids." He grumbled.

"I'm sorry. So, you're not going to eat us?"

He gave up trying to sneak, rose to his full height, and sauntered over. "I'm still tempted to. Though I am curious why you aren't invading my mind and forcing me not to."

"I'm trying to be nice." Emma smiled. True, a druid *could* use their magic to control animals. She thought it mean. Also, she hadn't really learned how to force her will over anything yet... another one of those 'advanced' spells she didn't know. If this cat *did* decide to attack them in defiance of her being a druid, she'd desperately try to figure out how to control him as fast as possible. "I don't want to *make* you, or any other animal do something you don't want. Please don't eat us."

"Hmm. Your offer is almost tempting." He licked his jowls. "Alas, I remain hungry and the four of you smell delightful. Do you have a better offer than please?"

Emma gently set Rin down to sit propped up against a tree, then, summoned a meatplant. "Here. Eat this."

The large cat slinked closer and sniffed the oblong, bulbous fruit pod. "You are a druid?"

"You know this already." Emma folded her arms.

He sat back on his haunches. "How can you not understand that cats—of which I am one—do not eat vegetation?"

"You can eat that plant. It's magic." She patted the purplish growth.

"It grows like a plant, but it's meat."

The cat made a distrusting, almost nauseated face. "You will need to do better than that, I'm afraid. Meat tastes much better when it dies in terror."

Emma cringed. "That is the entire point of this spell. An animal doesn't need to die for us to have meat."

The cat rolled his eyes. "Linganthas is too soft-hearted. It is the natural order." He stretched out flat, crossing his front paws. "I shall honor the ancient accords with the forest spirits and not consume you. If it's not too much trouble, would you mind asking the others to run? I do much prefer to chase my meals first. It's far less fun when they simply stand still. Oh, and ask the taller one to peel itself out of all that fabric. It will get stuck in my teeth. Why do the two-legs insist on wrapping themselves in such annoyances?"

Emma shrugged. "I don't know why she likes those gowns, either." She blinked. "Hey! No. You can't eat them."

"Well, if you keep insisting, then you will need to come up with something else for me to eat." The cat licked his right forepaw.

"I don't know this place. What do you want?" Emma set her hands on her hips.

The cat narrowed his eyes in thought. After a moment, his eyes shot open wide, as if an invisible faerie whispered an idea in his ear. "Fish. Collect me some fish from the river just over there. I detest the water."

Emma twisted around to look at the sickly grey muck. Calling it 'water' sounded like an overly generous use of the word. "I don't think eating any fish that lives in there would be good for you."

"It is perfectly fine for me." He leaned closer, sniffing at her stomach. "Not so for you. *You* should not eat the fish from that river. To me, they taste exquisite. Even more so than the two-legs."

She studied the river, thinking. Could Linganthas have brought her to this cat? They hadn't found any sort of hiding place or sanctuary, despite her feeling like she followed a magical guide.

Emma faced the cat again. "I will get you some fish in exchange for two promises."

He lazily crossed his paws the other way. "Do tell."

"One. You don't eat us."

"Already offered you that. What is the other condition?" He exhaled.

"Will you stay with us for a while and protect us from anything trying to hurt us?" Emma reached out and began to scratch him under the chin. She'd pet many cats in her lifetime, but none had fur as soft as this one.

His eyes half-closed. An odd half-growl slipped past his teeth. The cat seemed both irritated and quite pleased at the same time. After two minutes of continuous skritches, he sighed. "All right. I accept your request. Five fish."

"Agreed." Emma crouched and shook his paw. "Do you have a name?"

"I am Kahavani."

"Please watch over my sister and friends while I get your fish." Emma looked at the others. "He's going to protect us in exchange for some fish. You don't need to be afraid of him."

Ambril didn't stop trembling. "Umm. All right."

Kimber nodded.

Rin, being quite deeply asleep, said nothing.

"Wait here. I'll be back soon." Emma approached the river's edge.

The black dirt gradually became shinier the closer it got to the water. Within a foot or two of the river's edge, it looked more like glass than soil. She suspected it softened to gooey mud at that point. Numerous mushrooms in shades of purple, pink, and black dotted the coarse grass scattered along the riverbank. Plants similar to cattails— except ink black—stuck up out of the muddy goo, studded with unfamiliar spherical growths somewhat larger than Da's fist. They ranged from orange to pink, covered in three-inch-long black thorns. She couldn't tell by looking if they were a form of mushroom, a fruit, or a flower... and didn't want to touch them to figure it out.

Everything here is going to hurt me... except maybe Kahavani.

Her life, as well as the lives of Kimber, Ambril, and Rin depended on her ability to collect five fish from the scary river. Da often talked of taking Tam out to teach him how to fish when he got a little older. He'd never thought to include her in that, probably because he'd grown up in a wealthy family and didn't think a girl would be interested in getting all wet, muddy, and smelly.

Emma had no problem jumping into stinky, wet mud... at least *normal* mud. This black substance near the grey water frightened her. All this talk of everything here being poisonous to humans made her worry about even touching the water. She knew people used long poles with strings and hooks to catch fish. The fishermen who needed to catch a lot of fish so they could sell them used nets. She had no pole, no string, and no net.

She didn't even know what the fish in the water here looked like.

After a few minutes of thinking and watching, a bright blue bug as big as a hen's egg came flying across the water. One of the vees disturbing the surface exploded upward in a splash, revealing an ugly, spiny monstrosity of a fish. She only caught a brief glimpse of the creature as it jumped into the air and snatched the bug in its jaws. It looked too big for her to catch using a pole, or even a net. Attempting to pull such a huge fish out of the water would only end in her being dragged in. It probably weighed almost as much as she did.

While she considered this new problem—how to catch a fish so large—a moving trail in the water quite close to her burst up into a splash. Another fish launched itself out of the river, straight at her. A mouth big enough to fit over her head opened wide, exposing rows of needle-like teeth dripping with clear slime.

Emma yelped and reflexively ducked to the side. The fish sailed past her head, missing by only a few inches. Its flailing tail smacked her in the face so hard she landed on her back, seeing stars. It took her a second or two to recover from the dizziness enough to sit up. Stranded on the ground a fair distance from the river, the fish flopped back and forth, attempting to bounce itself toward *her*—not the water, snapping its jaws.

"Eek!" She scrambled to her feet, backed up, and thrust her right arm out at the fish. "Linganthas, I call upon your wrath!"

A narrow thorny vine sprang forth from her outstretched hand, slapping down on the fish like a spiked whip before coiling around and squeezing. The fish twitched once and went still, seeming dead.

Emma stood there, watching it to make sure it didn't try to trick her. Once certain she'd killed it, she let her arm drop to her side and gave a sigh of relief. As soon as she no longer had the fear of a fish trying to bite her to think about, the pain in her face took over.

"Ow." She pressed a hand to her cheek and pulled it away with blood on it. "Uh oh."

The three-foot-long fish didn't appear to have scales as much as rocky, spiky growths all over it. Getting smacked by its tail roughly equaled being slapped with a board covered in a hundred stubby nails. Emma pressed both hands into her face, cringing at the pain, and called upon Uruleth to heal her.

Stinging pain gave way to a cool sense of numbness.

"Mythandriel, please cleanse me of venom and sickness."

Nothing seemed to happen.

Whew. Just spikes. The fish isn't covered in poison.

"Well, that's one..." She exhaled, then got an idea. "Naraja, I call upon your grace to empower me."

A warm, comforting sensation washed over Emma's shoulders and back, filtering down into her legs. The forest spirit Naraja embodied all things feline: agility, grace, speed, stealth, and fierceness. As Uruleth could help her become stronger for a time, Naraja's blessing made her faster and more nimble.

Emma crept as close to the muddy part of the bank as she dared, using herself as bait. Since she now expected the horrible fish to try eating her *and* had the speed and grace of an elf—for as long as the spell lasted—she easily ducked out of the way whenever a stupid fish threw itself out of the water at her. She spent the next fifteen minutes walking around close to the water's edge until a fish leapt at her, then diving out of the way. It took only one root lash to kill each fish. Even though she still had the benefit of the Wildkin Whisper, the fish didn't appear able to speak. Then again, no fish ever spoke to her. Speaking required air, after all. Whether or not she killed animals who didn't deserve to die, at least not being able to hear them yell at her or beg for their lives made it easier to hunt. Also, that they tried to rather viciously eat her first helped eliminate guilt.

Though, she doubted these fish would beg for their lives. Too stupid and mean. How dumb did a fish have to be to throw itself out of the water where it would die, anyway? Worse, once they landed on dry ground, they didn't try to get back to the river... they kept coming after her.

Da once told her he often found it difficult to tell the difference between stupidity and evil.

Emma understood what he meant in these fish.

Not wanting to touch them, she summoned some thin vines, tied the five fish into a bundle, and dragged them to where the others waited. Kimber sat astride the huge cat's back as if riding a horse. She lay on her chest more than sat up, happily petting the animal behind the ears and along the cheeks while hugging him and squishing her face into his long, plush fur. Kahavani gave Emma a stare that said 'get this creature off me, please.' She suspected he didn't mind the attention anywhere near as much as his glare claimed.

"Are these the fish you wanted?" asked Emma.

"Magnificent." Kahavani rose to stand. "Yes. That will more than do."

Kimber slipped off his back and darted over to Emma. "Rin still sleepin.'"

Emma sat next to the dark elf girl, who remained exactly as she'd left her, propped up against a tree.

Kahavani clamped his teeth around the head of one fish, stepped on its tail, then pulled, tearing the fish out of its stony, spiky skin as if removing a foot from a boot. It seemed roughly half of each fish consisted of rubbery, spiked skin, blobby entrails, and other parts the cat didn't care to eat.

Ambril covered her mouth and looked away, gagging. She squirmed and winced at every squishing noise as the large cat ate. Emma merely covered her nose in an effort to reduce the smell. The aroma of normal fish didn't bother her. Unfortunately, these creatures smelled like fish left sitting dead in the sun for a few days. Watching

Kahavani react to the odor as if smelling a palace feast made her glad she hadn't eaten anything in a while.

One by one, the great cat peeled and ate the fish she caught for him in no great hurry. He appeared to be savoring every bite. To distract herself from the grisly spectacle, Emma checked on Rin the way Mama examined people who got sick or hurt. She felt the girl's forehead, checked the side of her neck for a heartbeat, smelled her breath, and tried to lightly jostle her awake. Sometimes, Mama would look under a person's clothing for injuries. Emma didn't need to do that. Rin's present state hadn't been the result of a mystery injury. No need to go hunting for a wound, a small mark where something stung her, or perhaps a tick or other parasite hiding somewhere. Emma already knew exactly what happened: Rin drained herself too much, using magic well beyond her training.

The dark elf girl appeared to be fine, merely in a deep sleep.

Emma held her hand, marveling at the stark difference in color between them. Rin looked like an obsidian statue brought to life—but much softer. Even if the birth of her kind came as the result of forest elves falling to demonic corruption, Emma thought her to be a beautiful creation deserving to live free of constant fear. Alas, after seeing those assassins, she no longer doubted the majority of Niltharien still held demonic corruption inside them.

She's basically an orphan. Her uncle is dead. Her father is probably dead. And her mother wants to kill her, so she's not really a mother. Emma growled. *We should take her with us. Leaving her here is as good as killing her.*

Kimber peered around Rin at Emma. "We'as gonnae bring her wif us? Kinnae leave 'er 'lone."

"Yeah," whispered Emma. "I was just thinking about that."

"Aye." Kimber smiled. "Saw ya lookin' at her like ya sad and angry at the same toime."

Ambril unburied her face from her skirt. She kept holding the fabric up to shield her eyes from the cat eating as she glanced sideways toward the other girls. "Are you serious? You want to bring her home?"

"We can't abandon her. She'll die." Emma scowled. "You aren't honestly still afraid of her because she's a dark elf, are you? She saved our lives."

"No." Ambril cringed at a rather loud squishing splatter coming from the cat. "I am worrying the people back home might be mean to her."

Emma folded her arms. "I can handle mean people."

"They'as no' gonna be a' bad a' them lot wot tried tae kill us." Kimber glared into the woods, looking like a tiny, fierce, red-maned lioness. "If someone be mean ta 'er, I'ma thump 'em."

"All right." Ambril sighed at her increasingly filthy dress. "I'll ask Father to talk to the mayor about her and convince him she's nice."

Kimber grinned. "If Nan says she noice, she noice. Then the people will 'ave to be noice ta 'er."

Kahavani rolled onto his side and gave a contented moan. "That was delightful. You have my thanks. Where is it you wanted me to take you?"

"If you know of a place where we can hide for a while and be safe, please bring us there." Emma pulled one leg up and brushed mud off her foot. "We don't need to go a set place, just stay out of trouble until the box is ready."

"Well then." The cat chuckled. "You may be in trouble. Nowhere is safe for your kind here."

"As safe as possible, then?" Emma kept swiping at the stubborn mud clinging to her foot.

"You are as safe here as you would be anywhere else." Kahavani stretched. "May as well rest."

"Wot 'e say?" whispered Kimber.

She set her foot back down. "We are probably as safe here as we would be anywhere else in this place. He thinks we should rest here and wait."

The girls snacked on a meatplant while talking about what to do with Rin. Initially, Ambril thought the dark elf child should probably come live with her since she'd been royalty here. Emma suggested the townspeople might be more comfortable having her live at the outskirts rather than the middle of town. Also, people might be less inclined to cause trouble if she lived with Nan. When Kimber asked if Ambril's mother would approve of or be terrified of Rin, another entire debate started.

Ambril thought her mother would care more about the girl being equivalent to royalty. "Which makes me wonder. Do you think she'll tolerate living like a commoner?"

"She already does…" Emma glanced up, distracted at the sight of furry, black critters zooming along the branches above them, chittering like insane squirrels enchanted to move at triple their usual speed. They shot by too fast to see anything more than smears of darkness. At least the tiny creatures didn't appear to be a threat. "Live in a house way off in the woods."

"Because if she didn't, they'd kill her," whispered Ambril. "That doesn't mean she likes it."

"I don't think she cares. She might even hate being noble. To her, it only means everyone wants to kill her to get more power." Emma reached over and pulled some of the girl's periwinkle blue hair off her face. "What if being called royal makes her think of her horrible mother?"

"I fink she's sweet." Kimber nodded. "She donnae git mad o'er not 'avin fancy things."

Emma smiled. Her little sister had an uncanny ability to sense when a person she saw meant harm. Anyone Kimber seemed frightened of always turned out to be either mean or dangerous. She could somehow tell this at first sight of a person.

She learned who to avoid, living among thieves and criminals.

Their conversation drifted away from Rin, the matter settled. For a while, they talked about the strange flowers and plants around them. Kimber insisted Emma try to tell a story like Nan, so she made one up about Princess Isabelle having a tea party with three talking rabbits.

After sitting around for hours, Ambril grumbled. She stood and walked a short distance away, hid behind a tree, and hiked her dress up to have a wee. Seconds later, she screamed and fell over backward to sit on the ground.

Emma jumped to her feet.

Kahavani flattened his ears against his head. "Oh, must the two-leg make such a painful noise?"

Ambril flailed her arms. "Help! It's got me!"

"What's got you?" Emma ran over and grabbed her friend's hands.

"I don't know!" shrieked Ambril. "Get me away from it!"

Emma pulled.

Amid the tearing of fabric, Ambril popped free from... something, and flew into her. They collided chest-to-chest. The rich girl's greater size and weight—plus the force with which she popped free—knocked Emma over. Ambril hurriedly rolled off her, jumped to her feet, then flailed at herself while spinning about as if covered with ants. Her big puffy outer skirt had disappeared, leaving her dress plain and flat. Emma sat up and looked at the spot behind the tree. A mass of two-foot-long thorny vines sprouted up from a lump of a plant body as big as a man's head. The writhing, black vines busily shredded the skirt it tore from Ambril's dress into small scraps. Like a creature with fifty tiny arms, it picked through the fabric in search of something to eat.

Emma glanced over at Ambril. Her once-beautiful gown now looked like a commoner's garment someone left out in the rain for a week.

Ambril stared at herself, whimpered, "I backed into it. I didn't even see it," then started crying.

"It's all right." Emma grasped both of Ambril's hands together. "Are you hurt? Did it sting you with a thorn anywhere?"

"I don't think so. I felt the points of thorns, but I don't think it got me too bad. Nothing hurts." Ambril sniffled and gestured at her gown. "That's not why I'm crying."

"It's only a dress. It's not destroyed, only... simpler."

It took the girl a few minutes to compose herself enough to speak. "You must think I'm silly and superficial like those other girls I so detest having to spend time with."

Kimber mouthed, "A little" without adding voice.

"You are awfully upset over a dress when you almost got hurt." Emma exhaled.

"It's not the dress itself. Father gave it to me. He told me to be careful and take care of it. It's expensive. I've disappointed him. He's going to be hurt that I was so careless with something he gave me."

"Ambril…" Emma stared into her eyes. "We have been missing for days. We're presently stranded in perhaps the most dangerous forest in the world. If we get out of here alive, I promise you he is going to be so happy to see you again he won't care at all about the dress. It's just a bit of fabric. A dress can be replaced. You can't."

"I know." She sniffled. "So foolish. I didn't even look. How can I be so clumsy?"

"Right." Emma nodded. "Silly you, not spending months studying how to survive in the dark elf forest that you've never seen before."

Ambril laughed past tears.

"Let me make sure you're okay." Emma grasped her friend's hand. "Mythandriel, please let your cleansing light shine on Ambril."

The blonde girl made an odd face.

"Are you all right?"

Ambril's eyes fluttered. "That felt so strange."

"Something happened?"

"Yes." Ambril rubbed her backside. "From here down to the backs of my knees became quite warm all of a sudden, then cool, then tingled."

Eep!

"What?" Ambril stared at her. "Why are you making that face? What did you just do?"

"I don't want to scare you," whispered Emma.

"Too late. You just did." Ambril grasped both of Emma's shoulders and gave her a light shake. "Tell me."

"If the spell I cast made you feel something, it means the plant stung you with poison and Mythandriel cleansed it," said Emma. "I don't know how bad it would have been. It might've been as mild as itching."

Ambril nearly fainted into her. "Or it could have killed me." She turned so Emma could see her backside. "Am I bleeding?"

"I don't see any blood on your dress."

"Umm." Ambril blushed, though fear proved stronger than embarrassment. She lifted her dress as well as underdress out of the way, exposing her bare bottom.

"Looks like you sat on a thorn bush and jumped up before any of them stabbed too deep," whispered Emma. "Not bleeding. Little red dots all over. I think your skirt was so puffy it protected you from most of the thorns."

Ambril let her dress drop back into place. "Am I going to get sick?"

"No. Mythandriel cleansed the poison."

"Right. Thank you." Ambril nodded once. "I am going to go sit down and cry for the next hour."

Emma walked with her back to where Kimber, Rin, and Kahavani waited. Kimber had the box set in her lap. She kept fussing at the gems.

"Staring at it won't make them glow any faster." Emma sighed.

Ambril sat. She squeezed her hands into fists, gazed around while making a face as if she prepared to commit to a nice good fit of sobbing, but only sighed and stared at the box. "Rin said she had something to make it go faster. She never got it for us."

Kimber yawned. "She kep' lookin' round. I fink she was waitin' fer 'er uncle ta come 'ome. Fought 'e takin' tae long to come back. Bet she 'ad ta ask 'im if she could take one o' them magic stones fer us. Em's gotta ask Nan if she can go in' the potion cabinet. Nae s'posed ta touch it wifout askin'."

"Ahh. Yes. I imagine you're right." Ambril peered down at herself, idly plucking at stray threads where her outer skirt used to be attached.

Motion in the woods some distance away drew Emma's attention. A pair of glowing, pale pink-violet ghosts glided through the forest. Their faces had no features, their bodies and arms possessing only the simplest hint of a person's form. Rather than legs, the apparitions floated on trails of vapor.

"Kahavani?" whispered Emma, pointing at the strange sight. "Are those dangerous?"

The cat turned his head to look. "You are being hunted."

"Uh oh. Are you sure?" Emma tucked her feet in, shifting her weight forward in preparation to leap upright.

"Yes." The big cat yawned. "Those are phantasmal seekers. Mages are searching for you."

Emma blinked at him. "How do you know that?"

Kahavani exhaled, sounding frustrated, and a touch insulted. "The two-legged ones are so arrogant to think we are ignorant of their ways purely because we resemble lesser animals they know as maika."

"I've never heard of a maika. What is that?"

"Hmm. You seem to be much more different from the other two-legs than simply being paler." He exhaled out his nose. "Perhaps you are familiar with the term 'cat'? Maika are a type of cat native to forests where the long-eared two-legs live. Maika are much smaller than me."

"Long-eared two-legs? You mean elves?"

"If that is what you call them." The big cat waved a paw dismissively. "It is hardly worth my time to worry about what name various lesser beings wish me to use for them."

Emma thought back to what Rin said about how the Niltharien elves came to be, wondering if Kahavani—and his kind—used to be much smaller (and much nicer) cats. This also got her thinking he might be smarter than most animals, especially if he understood magical things like those phantasmal seekers.

"You're smart."

"You have a habit of stating the obvious." He rose to his feet. "You should move yourselves before they find you."

Emma stood, re-cast Uruleth's gift of bear strength, and picked Rin up. "We have to go. Follow me and stay quiet."

Kimber and Ambril hurried along after her as she followed Kahavani into the trees, moving along the river's edge.

"Beware of spiny orbflowers," said Kahavani. "If you disturb them, they will burst and throw poisoned needles everywhere. Also, do not step in the water. It will numb you at first, then paralyze you, and you'll probably fall in and drown."

Emma passed along his warning to the others.

"Gah!" Ambril shuddered. "Who would live here?"

"Dark elves," whispered Kimber.

Kahavani moved among the trees at a speed challenging to keep up with. Ambril slipped in the mud every few minutes. Each time she fell, she scrambled back to her feet as rapidly as if a pack of angry dogs chased them. Kimber didn't seem to have trouble keeping pace with the cat. She avoided tripping or wiping out on slippery mud, though nearly stumbled into one of the grabbing plants like the one that ate Ambril's skirt. Emma did her best to manage carrying the unconscious dark elf girl, a person not much smaller than herself. Her effort to avoid running Rin's dangling head or feet into the sides of trees cost her some speed.

Kahavani continued pushing the girls at the arduous pace until Ambril tripped again and didn't get up. Kimber doubled over, out of breath. Emma, too, could barely stay on her feet after almost a straight hour of not-quite-running. The cat finally stopped and swung his head around to look at the girls. His ears twitched.

Ambril rolled over onto her back. "Can we please rest? I can't get up. My legs hurt."

Kimber gave Emma a look, begging for a rest. Without Uruleth's magic, Emma would've been ready to drop where she stood and go straight to sleep. If they had to keep going, she'd call upon him to give the others the endurance to do so.

"I believe we have lost the seekers for now." Kahavani swished his tail side to side. "We can rest here."

Emma flopped on the ground and pulled Rin halfway into her lap. She called upon Linganthas to grow a dome of roots and vines around everyone, weaving them into a little hiding place. It probably wouldn't fool an adult dark elf up close. At a distance, however, they might just blend into the forest around them.

Kahavani positioned himself near the opening she'd left in the dome 'hut.' Anything trying to get inside would have to move him first.

Emma cradled Rin in one arm, put her other around Kimber, and tried her very best not to be terrified.

22

NOT A MOMENT'S REST

A while later, Ambril finally had the strength to sit up. She sighed at her ruined dress, more of it now black than peach-colored. To Emma's surprise, she didn't cry, merely gave a sad sigh. Perhaps she'd accepted the garment couldn't be saved at this point.

Emma checked on Rin. She looked the same as she did hours ago, healthy but sleeping.

"Is this going to take much longer?" asked Kahavani.

"I'm not sure." Emma pointed at the box. "We have to wait until it's ready."

"A shiny trinket?" Kahavani ambled over to Kimber and sniffed the box.

Of course, no animal could come within arm's reach of the little redhead without being skritched.

Kahavani gave an annoyed grumble—however, he didn't move away from her. "I do not think it will be long."

"You know about magic?" Emma sat up.

"Some."

Emma bit her lip. "If you are smart enough to know magic, why did I need the Wildkin Whisper to talk to you? You're obviously much smarter than an ordinary cat."

"Why do the two-legs use long, sharp pieces of metal to kill each other instead of swiping them dead in one paw stroke?"

"We don't have big claws." Emma made a clawing gesture at him. "Just itty-bitty nails."

"Indeed. I do not have whatever it is you two-legs have in your throats to make those obnoxious noises." He flopped down to recline near Kimber—who obligingly continued to scratch him behind the ears. "If we are to sit here for an irritating amount of time, you can at least amuse me by explaining what happened."

Emma told him about the box, jumping across the world, meeting Rin, and her teleporting them out here as a desperate attempt to escape.

"I do not understand the two-legs." Kahavani shook his great head. "Always trying to kill each other. They do not even eat their kills. How ridiculous. If one is going to spend so much energy killing something, at least have the decency to eat it."

"Do you eat others like yourself?" asked Emma.

"No. I..." He swished his tail back and forth, then frowned. "My kind also do not kill each other."

She tried not to laugh.

They talked a little more about him, Emma trying to understand what life felt like for a cat as smart—or smarter—than some humans who couldn't speak. Kahavani explained his kind *could* talk, in a way. Only others of his kind could understand their language. To the two-legs, they sounded like big cats making purrs, growls, and other noises.

"Yes." Emma laughed. "When I speak to animals, other people think I'm silly because I sound like the animals."

Kahavani's ears perked up, then rotated backward one at a time. "I would tell you to climb a tree, but you shouldn't touch them. Do your best to stay alive."

"What?" Emma blinked. "Stay alive?"

The cat zoomed away from the root dome Emma grew. She set Rin down and hastily crawled to stick her head out of the opening to look. Kahavani, already thirty or so feet away, mauled a pudgy, short, purplish-grey skinned goblin. At least, it somewhat looked like a goblin—if one had been killed and left underwater for a few days. The bloated, sickly creature had a puffy, round face, black lips, and pale white eyes without pupils or irises. Thin webbing spanned between its three fingers and thumb. Even though the creature didn't have any clothing on, she couldn't tell if it was a boy or a girl. Nothing about its flabby body gave any indication. Not even its high-pitched voice, which it presently used to emit a wail of pain.

More creatures like it jumped out of the undergrowth and came running toward her, all brandishing crude spears tipped with shiny onyx-like points. Each one differed slightly in height and the roundness of their faces, otherwise appearing mostly identical. Some had longer ears, some fatter bellies. It took the strange goblins only a few seconds to rip and slash the root dome apart with their spears and surround the girls.

"Eek!" Emma leapt to stand defensively over the helpless dark elf. *Linganthas, send me your wrath!* A long, thorny whip-vine sprang up from the ground at her feet, swinging around in a wide circle.

Shrieking goblins scrambled to jump out of the way. The first two didn't have enough time to react and went flying into the trees from the force of the magical root smacking them. The third one suffered a grazing swipe and several cuts. It hit the ground, wailing in pain. The rest scattered out of the way as the whooshing spiked vine swung the rest of the way around the circle.

Ambril screamed and took off running, seemingly in a random direction. Kimber darted after her, likely to try and stop her. Four goblins rushed at them from the side. Ambril swerved left. Goblins zoomed between them, forcing Kimber to go the other way. Two of the four kept chasing Ambril, two went after Kimber, who sprinted around in a circle so she didn't get too far away from Emma while also able to stay away from the goblins. Ambril kept going in a straight line away from everyone, lost to panic. Three more goblins rushed at Kahavani, waving their spears, trying to help the one dangling from his teeth. The last two goblins charged at Emma.

She couldn't run, or they'd get Rin. If she tried to help Ambril or

Kimber, the creatures rushing at her would make it close enough to stab her—or force her to retreat, in which case they'd be free to kill or kidnap Rin, who couldn't defend herself at the moment.

Emma loved Kimber as much as if they'd been born sisters. Despite the girl being two years younger, Kimber also had a better chance of keeping herself alive than Ambril—if only because she'd grown up used to having to run away from danger. The rich girl didn't really run much at all.

However, Rin needed help more than either of them.

Emma directed her thorny root to wrap around the pair of goblins coming toward her and Rin. Fear piled on top of her desperation to protect her family and friends, lending strength to the magic. The root thickened, growing as big around as her arm. It whipped down and wrapped around both goblins, squishing them together and squeezing. One of their spears, trapped against its body under the coil of root, snapped from the pressure.

Ambril screamed, her voice sounding far away and echoing. Emma glanced toward the shriek, keeping her right arm pointed at the two goblins coiled in her vine. She continued to focus power into the spell, squeezing the life out of them. She no longer saw her friend anywhere. Both goblins responsible for chasing Ambril away into the forest had stopped running to stare at the ground. One poked his spear at the earth. It seemed in her panic, Ambril had fallen down a hole.

Closer, another pair of goblins chased Kimber around in circles. She didn't appear to be having to work too hard to stay away from them. The squat, puffy goblins squealed and grunted, trying to make their little stumpy legs move faster. They did not look well suited to running on dry land.

The goblins ensnared in her spell gurgled and stopped moving. Pale grey gunk leaked from everywhere the thorns poked them. Emma grimaced at the sight. She didn't like having to kill things, even tiny wicked monsters like this. However, she wouldn't hesitate to protect her sister and friends. The world contained many awful creatures—like these hideous goblins—that couldn't be talked to and would simply try to hurt everyone they could.

"Help!" shouted Ambril.

Kahavani rushed past Emma, pouncing one of the creatures chasing Kimber and tearing it apart, spraying the one next to it in pale grey gunk. The other one screamed in terror, forgot all about Kimber, and fled toward the river. Emma didn't waste time attacking one trying to run away. She turned her attention to the goblins hovering above the hole Ambril fell into. Alas, they'd gone too far off for her to reach with a vine spell. Running over there would leave Rin defenseless. With her friend stuck down a hole, and momentarily safe from goblin spears, she decided it not worth taking the chance more goblins lay in wait to attack Rin if she left her alone.

"Bad goblins!" shouted Kimber as she ran up to Emma.

A death wail came from the one Kahavani mauled. He tossed the carcass aside and trotted toward the remaining two. At the sight of him approaching, the goblins abandoned their trapped prey and ran, screaming, toward the river. Kahavani sprang into a dash, overtaking and savaging both goblins in the tall grass before they made it to the water.

"Stay right here and watch Rin." Emma gripped her sister's shoulder and looked her in the eye. "If you see a goblin, yell."

"Okay." Kimber nodded.

Emma made her way over to where the goblins had been poking at the ground, going slow enough to watch where she stepped. She soon discovered a round hole in the dirt, similar to a rabbit warren or gopher burrow, only many times bigger. It went down to the side at an angle, not a straight vertical drop. Ambril, some twenty feet below the surface, struggled to climb. She kept falling back down whenever the dirt crumbled out from under her. Rather than escape, she'd only succeeded in burying herself up to her knees.

"Stop digging," called Emma. "You're going to make it collapse."

Ambril yelled. "I don't wanna die! I just want to go home! I want my parents!"

"You're not going to die." Emma knelt at the edge of the burrow. "I'll get you out. Don't panic."

Linganthas please lend me your aid. She held her hands out over the hole. Green light danced between her fingers. A thick root—without thorns—emerged from the loose black dirt in front of her friend at the bottom of the burrow. She directed it to wrap around Ambril from knees to armpits, then grow taller, lifting the girl upward.

Ambril grabbed at the tunnel wall, flinging handfuls of dirt all over herself a few times before giving up and simply letting the root do all the work. Taking care not to crush or hurt her friend required gentleness, resulting in the spell moving far too slow for her liking, especially when goblins might attack them again at any second.

"Got one!" yelled Kimber.

Emma turned her head to look.

Kimber stood astride Rin, who lay flat on the ground, pointing at another goblin trying to sneak up on them.

Oh no! If I stop concentrating, Ambril's going to fall back down and this burrow will probably collapse.

Her only option would be to risk hurting Ambril. A bruise or broken rib, she could heal later. Emma threw a surge of power into the spell, making the root lurch upward like the tentacle of an angry squid. Ambril screamed as the magical growth swung her up and around, then slapped her into the squishy damp soil.

Emma dropped concentration on the root and spun to take on the goblin going for Kimber—right as Kahavani leapt from the shadows and tore it to pieces. At seeing small pieces of goblin go flying into the air, she cringed away.

"Eww." Kimber stuck out her tongue.

"Ow." Ambril grunted, pulling at the hard, inflexible root pinning her legs together. "Thank you for getting me out of there. Can you please take this off me? It's squeezing too much. I'm trapped and can't move."

Emma grasped the root. As soon as she desired it to, it became pliable as rope. She pulled it away from her friend.

"I hate this place," whimpered Ambril. She gasped at herself. "I couldn't be filthier if I jumped in a bucket of ink. If I live long enough to get home, I am going to spend three full hours soaking in a hot bath."

"Dirt is temporary." Emma took her hand. "Worry about it when you don't have bigger problems... like swamp goblins."

"These are swamp goblins?" Ambril tried to pull her wet, muddy hair off her face, but it kept flopping back down.

Emma kicked at one of the goblin's feet. Webbing stretched between their extremely long toes, which looked more like fingers. "They have flippers. I think they live in water, or maybe mud. Perhaps both."

Like a playful oversized kitten frolicking with wads of yarn, Kahavani zoomed back and forth in the tall grass, shredding one goblin after the next until he ran out of 'toys'. Once he had no more goblins to 'play' with, he stood in place, twitching, turning his head back and forth as though he *really* wanted to keep playing. A moment later, he appeared to recover his dignity. Evidently satisfied the threat passed, he sauntered up to Kimber and Rin.

Emma pulled Ambril over to them as well. She brushed a hand over the cat's cheek fur. "Thank you."

He glanced off to the side, trying to act imperious despite seeming relieved no one got hurt—and having fun. "We had a bargain. I am merely keeping up my end of the deal."

She wiped slimy residue out of his fur, slinging it to the ground handful by handful. "Eww. This is disgusting."

"Bog goblins generally are." He sat up tall, curling his tail around his feet.

"They were going to eat us, right?" Emma frowned.

"Doubtful. You are small. It is most likely they mistook you for another type of goblin attempting to invade their home." Kahavani started to lick his paw, but stopped, making a disgusted face at the flavor of bog goblin muck. Thinking better of it, he set his paw back on the ground. "They simply wanted to kill you."

"That's not really better." Emma shuddered. It felt a little wrong to dislike a forest, being a druid. However, she didn't really like this one at all.

They settled down to rest. Ambril sat there, looking as miserable as a stray cat stuck outside in the rain. Kimber helped Emma clean Kahavani's fur as much as they could with only their hands and no clean water. Though he attempted to look stoic and unimpressed, Emma caught him purring.

A soft crystalline *clink* broke the silence, like someone tapping wine glasses together.

"Yay!" cheered Kimber, pointing at the box. "Glowing!"

All the emeralds, rubies, and sapphires on the box gave off light.

Kahavani's ears went back. "Be ready, child. More goblins approach."

Emma peered over the cat toward the river. A small army of round-faced, pale, puffy goblinoids crept toward them. At least forty, maybe more. They looked rather upset and angry. "Uh oh. We have to go. Now. Thank you for helping us, but you can run away. Don't get hurt. We can escape."

Kahavani sprang to his feet, standing between the advancing goblins and the girls. "I will hold them as long as it takes for you to activate the magical device."

Emma scooped Rin up in her arms.

Ambril rested one hand on Emma's shoulder, the other on Kimber's. "Hurry! Open it!"

Kimber scooted a little closer to everyone, then lifted the lid. Golden light shone out from inside the Box of Wonder, rapidly brightening until Emma couldn't see anything other than the blinding glare.

A slight sense of falling straight down came and went. When the light faded enough to see again, Emma found herself looking at the grey stone alcove and the blue-glowing rune circle. The warmth and humidity of the dark elven swamp-forest gave way to the comfortable dryness of an early spring day.

"We're safe," chirped Kimber as she pulled the locking lever down.

Emma stared at her sister. Somehow, Rin kicked them out of here with magic while it had been locked. It hadn't even crossed her mind that they might have been shut out of the box until that moment. Emma nearly fainted in relief.

"Whew." She exhaled, then carried Rin into the room and set her on the bed.

Ambril paced in circles. "I wish this room had a bath. My dress is too filthy to wear."

"Take it off," said Kimber.

Ambril gasped, blushing.

"You 'ave anovva dress on under it." Kimber tugged the stained peach-colored fabric aside to reveal a mostly white underdress.

"I can't go outside in that. It's an *under*dress." Ambril's face reddened even more.

"Your underdress is longer than my dress." Emma looked down at her dress. The hem stopped a hand's width or so above her knees. Ambril's 'under dress' covered her knees.

Ambril huffed. "I'd prefer to be dirty. Bad enough you've already talked me into going outside without shoes or hose. I'll wear this until I can clean up and get something proper."

"Okay." Kimber shrugged. "Bein' dirty kin be fun, tae."

Emma hurried to the orb table. The large crystal ball showed the swampy forest. A huge crowd of bog goblins gathered around the box, seeming confused. One poked a spear at it. Kahavani appeared to have run off.

"Good. He's safe." Emma rested her hand on the blue orb. "Home. Widowswood. Please take us home! Get us out of this awful place."

She pushed on the ball, concentrating on her desire to activate the magic.

The room lurched sideways, then downward as if someone punted the box off the side of a cliff. Emma collapsed to the floor, holding her stomach and trying not to throw up.

I hate this part.

23

SOMEWHERE SAFE

*E*mma lay on the floor for a while, staring at the ceiling.
She knew she'd get up, look at the crystal ball, and see somewhere other than home. The Box of Wonder didn't seem to care what they wanted. It merely jumped around at random. Unless the randomness came from them doing something wrong—which she accepted could be quite possible—they could spend years teleporting over and over again and never land back near Widowswood. To hope the box had taken them home this time would only lead to disappointment. Rin said she might be able to figure out how to make the box work properly. Alas, with an army of goblins outside, Emma wanted to get out of there before they did something bad—like take the box with them to the bottom of the poisonous river, or worse, give it to dark elves who could force them all outside and turn them into pets.

At least don't be dangerous or scary. Be somewhere we won't have to run away from things trying to eat us.

Once she finished preparing herself for disappointment, Emma sat up.

As expected, the image in the large crystal ball did not look like home. Fortunately, it also did not look like a nightmarish forest where everything—even the trees—could kill them. The scene outside the box appeared to be a reasonably ordinary city, albeit a big one. A wet cobblestone street ran between two rows of close-packed houses. Not far to the right, a dingy grey fabric awning covered a small wooden merchant stand where a nervous, pudgy man sold wares out of numerous baskets. The high-up view made it impossible to tell exactly what the baskets contained. Most of his wares resembled fish, though at least one held some kind of huge bugs that appeared to still be alive.

The man looked human and ordinary in every way.

Fading late-day sunlight painted half of the street in shadow, the other half in dark orange. Emma figured it to be roughly two hours before night time.

Most of the people wandering back and forth outside wore common garb ranging from grungy to mildly filthy. Their fashion, such as it was, looked unfamiliar. These people did not seem to be high class enough to care about the prettiness of their attire. Other than the occasional stray dog and alley cat or two, this street contained few animals other than a shockingly large number of medium-sized grey-white gulls perched on rooftops and posts.

Ambril coughed. "Where are we this time?"

"I don't know. A city." Emma peered down at her. "Are you all right?"

"Yes. I'm not really sick. It's just from the magic." Ambril shifted around onto her knees, then stood. "Well, that's somewhat reassuring. Humans at least."

"Do you recognize their style of dress?" Emma pointed.

"Hmm. No. It is a large city, but not Calebrin or Andor." Ambril tapped a finger to her chin. "They seem to favor clothing in grey, turquoise, pale blue, or brown. The nicer garments have bronze buttons. I think this might be a port city."

They watched the street for a little while. Most of the townsfolk looked like them, relatively pale. A handful appeared to be from Drajmir. A group of six people with much darker skin than even the Drajmiri people walked by. Two of the men were bald and wore strange, multi-layered fancy beige robes. Their four companions, a woman and three men, carried themselves like guards. They wore armor made mostly of wood and decoratively etched rock plates. One of the men had long hair in thick ropey strands, while the other three guards wore their hair short, in tight braids forming patterned rows.

"I've met people like them before." Ambril leaned close. "They're Asante. Humans, like us... except they live in a vast desert that's even bigger than Drajmir. I'd love to visit there someday. The stories I've read are unbelievable."

"But you believe them?" Emma smiled.

"Yes. I don't mean genuinely unbelievable. Just amazing. They're incredibly friendly and nice. In their whole kingdom, there's little crime or violence. They treat everyone like friends or family."

Emma watched the group pass by. They appeared to be smiling at everyone. "If they don't have crime, why are there guards?"

Ambril sighed. "They are not in their kingdom right now. Perhaps the person who wrote about their travels might have been telling a tall tale. Father said it's largely true. The Asante people consider themselves one. It's impossible to steal when everything is shared among everyone."

"Oh." Emma glanced at the birds. "What kind of birds are those?"

"We are definitely in a port city." Ambril leaned closer to the orb. "I've only seen those type of birds near the ocean and there are Asante and Drajmiri people here. This must be a busy port to have guests from so far away, not a small city at all."

"Is that why everyfing looks wet?" asked Kimber, peering around the big orb from the other side.

"Maybe. Or it just rained." Emma scratched her head.

A few people finally took notice of the box and stared at it.

"Uh oh. They're going to steal it." Ambril pointed.

"All poor people aren't thieves." Emma folded her arms.

"Haven't I already explained it isn't stealing when something is just sitting in the street?" Ambril gestured at the orb. "If they are struggling to feed their families, they're absolutely going to take a solid gold box covered in gems. Oh, I hope they don't start fighting each other."

"Should we do something?" Emma tapped her big toe into the floor repetitively. "The lid is locked. No one can open it. Even if someone takes it, they won't be able to get us. If we go outside, we're stuck until the magic recharges. Does it really matter where the box is if we're safe in here?"

Kimber shrugged.

"Umm." Ambril wandered back and forth. "Rin somehow made us leave."

"Yeah. She kin do magic." Kimber wiggled her fingers. "These people donnae look loike they 'ave magic. They do kinda look loike they gonna start stabbin' each ovva to get the box."

"We should be safe inside." Ambril bit her lip. "Unless they try to sell the box to someone who has magic. Some mages are *not* nice people. If a bad one finds us, they could... I dunno. Throw us out a window or turn us into pigs."

Kimber blinked. "I donnae wan' ta be a pig."

"Nor I." Emma kept tapping her toe on the floor. "We don't know there's even a mage in this city."

"I donnae wan' ta get frown out a window." Kimber smiled. "Or be turned inna a pig and den frown out a window."

A pair of men in dark brown tunics, one in a maroon cloak, one in a brown cloak, emerged from an alley, seemingly attracted by the commotion. They paused, listening to the people outside talk and argue about the strange jeweled box. As soon as they saw it, they drew small swords off their belts and began waving the weapons at everyone while creeping toward the box.

"They be thieves," whispered Kimber. "They gonna steal us. No doubt. Thieves inna big city gonna 'ave a mage, or someone who knows 'bout magic stuffs."

"Are you sure?" Ambril bounced nervously. "Why would thieves have a mage?"

"So they know wot's wurf sellin' and wot's junk." Kimber stared at Emma. "They gonna find us."

Emma clenched her jaw. As much as she would rather stay safe inside the box, Kimber seemed convinced they'd be in big trouble if they did that. She looked at Ambril. "Take your earrings and necklace off. Leave them inside so no one sees and steals them."

"Okay." Ambril hurried over to a small end table beside the bed while pulling her earrings out.

"C'mon. They're almost to the box." Emma sprinted with Kimber across the room to the alcove.

As soon as Ambril caught up to them, Emma flicked the lock lever up and touched the blue orb.

The girls appeared standing on wet cobblestones beside the box. Both thieves, now only three steps away, jumped back.

"Blimey," muttered one. "A bunch'a sprogs, jes' popped outta nowhere."

Kimber picked the box up. "Sorry. Worst night, privs. We need it gnomes. Nae saw yas. Nae rattle."

The men paused, seeming shocked.

"Did that little girl just...?" The man on the left eyed the man on the right.

"I think she tried to. Kinda jumbled." He took a step closer. "C'mon luv. 'And it over an' we'll get ya yer fill o' sweet breads."

Kimber backed up, nodding at Ambril. "It's maid fancy. Her glad may fines."

The men stopped, again seeming slightly confused.

"I fink she said 'er old man bought it." The one in the brown cloak scratched his head, then whispered, "How's a kid that small speak Cant?"

"She *almost* speaks Cant." The other man chuckled.

Emma shifted to stand protectively in front of Kimber. "We're not from here. She learned thief talk in another city. I'm not exactly sure what she said. I know this box looks valuable, but it's really cursed. You don't want it. It's been dragging us all over the place. We're just trying to go home and need it to get back to our families."

"Where are we?" whispered Ambril. "What city is this?"

"You don't know?" asked the man in the maroon cloak. "'Ow can ya be here and not know?"

The other thief gestured at them. "The sprogs just appeared outta nowhere. Bet they ain't fibbin' about the box being magical. Look at the thing. Ain't seen that many gems in one place in a long time."

"Oh. Right. Magic, I suppose." He pursed his lips. "This be Calathir, the grand capital city of Greymarch."

"I've heard of it." Ambril faced Emma. "We went too far east. *Way* too far east."

Emma ground her toes into the cobblestones. "Can we maybe come to an arrangement?"

"What sort of an arrangement?" asked the man in brown.

"Can you help us get home to Widowswood, and you can have the box."

Ambril stared. "You can't give them the box. It belongs to my father!"

"Would you rather have the box or be home?" Emma set her hands on her hips.

"Home," whispered Ambril.

"Got another idea," said the man in the maroon cloak. "How about we take the box, give you three some sweet breads and a pat on the head, then we all forget we ever saw each other?"

"Sorry. Can't do that." Emma exhaled.

"We could just take the box then." The other man frowned. "Your choice. I suggest you take the sweet breads."

"Aye." The other thief smiled. "Little ones like you lot have no need of such a fancy bit of rare. Give it here."

Kimber squeaked.

Strixian, please grant me the Wildkin Whisper. Emma looked at the nearest, largest pack of gulls. "Help us! Please. These men are going to hurt us. Can you distract them?"

The men stared at her, certainly having no idea what to think of a girl making bird sounds.

Without warning, twenty or thirty seagulls launched themselves into a feather-flinging frenzy of squawking, screeching, and flapping, mobbing the two thieves.

"Run!" yelled Emma, before sprinting away from the chaos.

Ambril scrambled to follow. Kimber swiped an empty cloth sack from a pile beside the merchant stand of fish baskets and stuffed the Box of Wonder into it, then raced off after Emma. The thieves flailed and swatted at the disorienting gull swarm, momentarily blinded by feathers. Alas, it didn't take them anywhere near as long as she'd hoped to swat their way clear of birds.

Emma dashed along the street past countless numbers of tiny houses, piles of junk, beggars, and small merchant stands trying to sell everything from near-worthless trinkets to semi-rotten fruit. The townspeople in their way paid little attention to a group of children running by other than to step aside.

The patter of bare feet running on wet stones echoed down the alleys and into the gaps between buildings, some too narrow for even children to fit into. Stamping boots coming up behind her urged Emma faster, dashing along the gently curving cobblestone street until it ended at a much larger crossing.

She waved her arms for balance as she stopped short, pausing for a quick look left and right down the biggest road she'd ever seen. This had to be the city's main thoroughfare, as wide as the entire town square of Widowswood Village and stretching off more than a mile in either direction. To her right, the road went downhill to a massive arrangement of docks. Hundreds of sailing ships sat in the harbor, their shapes mostly silhouetted upon a darkening ocean. Orange-yellow lantern spots drifted back and forth along the piers like fireflies in the night. A pair of golden griffon statues stood on either end of the harbor, gazing out over the vast expanse of sea.

To her left, the enormous road led uphill into more city, noticeably brighter than the other direction. The buildings became progressively larger as far as she could see before the great road leveled off at the top of the hill. She recognized some as inns and shops. The stark difference in daylight between left and right told her uphill went west, downhill went east, and it would probably be dark soon.

For no reason other than it being less work to run down a hill rather than up one, she decided to go toward the docks.

The thieves scrambled out onto the huge road mere seconds after Emma resumed running, calling after the girls to give up, promising they wouldn't be hurt, and so on. She didn't worry the men would hurt them. They seemed reasonably nice for thieves. However, they absolutely would steal the Box of Wonder and leave the girls stranded here. Worse, Rin was still inside. Emma couldn't let them take her—so she ran as though her life depended on her speed.

Ambril started to gasp for breath, close to collapsing.

The thieves might not bother with Ambril if she couldn't keep going. Despite being the daughter of a wealthy family, she by no means looked it now without jewelry, in a ruined, filthy dress, barefoot, and covered in dirt. They knew Kimber had the golden box. Fortunately, her little sister also had a ton of energy and showed no signs of slowing down any time soon.

Clinging to Kimber's hand, Emma kept running toward the docks, which didn't seem to be getting any closer. The thieves' yelling tapered off to silence. Travelers and merchants continued to step out of their way, scarcely even bothering to look at them. Numerous horse-drawn wagons labored to haul cargo up the hill away from the docks. She had no idea where to go exactly, hoping the darker part of the city would at least offer them for more hiding places. Unfortunately, it could also mean more thieves.

A pair of men in chain mail armor and blue tabards adorned with an image of twin golden griffons walked out from a side street, seemingly headed directly across to a matching side street on the other side.

Guards! Emma veered left, drifting across the giant thoroughfare toward the two armored men.

The guards seemed to notice the girls and stopped walking to watch them. Emma ran up to the men, then ducked around behind them to hide from the thieves. Ambril and Kimber followed, both huddling close.

The guards turned to face them.

Ambril bent forward, hands on her knees, struggling to breathe.

"We need help," rasped Emma. "Thieves are chasing us."

"Thieves?" asked the taller man. He peered back up the road. "What thieves?"

Emma leaned to the side to look. The men who'd chased them from the dingy little market square had vanished. "They're gone."

"Uh huh." The other guard rubbed his short beard. "What are you three doing running about so close to dark? And what are ya runnin' from? Did someone catch you picking pockets?"

"No." Emma shook her head. "Thieves tried to rob us."

The guard chuckled. "Of what? You lot ain't got a thing to steal."

"Aw, Wenferd, kin ya not see they're playin' around. Just kids." The shorter man smiled. "Where'd you girls come from? Ya look like you've had the fright taken out of ya. We'll walk ya home."

"It would be quite a long walk." Emma looked down. "We don't live in this city."

She didn't see any purpose in continuing to talk about thieves. The guards didn't believe her and the thieves already disappeared. She only wanted to get away from them. Whether or not the men got in trouble for trying to take the box didn't matter. In order to prove thieves had any interest in a group of apparently poor peasant children, she'd have to show them the box. If she did that, the guards would almost certainly accuse them of stealing it.

"You'd not believe me if I told you the truth." Emma rubbed a hand up and down her left arm. "We're from Widowswood. It's far away."

"Oh, yes. Widowswood." Wenferd raised a finger. "Been there many times I have."

Emma raised both eyebrows. Hope bloomed.

The other guard glanced at him. "Really?"

"Aye, Hesken. But not since I was a wee lad with a good imagination."

Hope collapsed.

Emma exhaled. "It's a real place. In another kingdom."

"All right, girls. Be serious for a moment, what?" Wenferd smiled. "Where are your families?"

"Andorath," rasped Ambril, still out of breath. "We're from Andorath. My father is Charles Starling. He's a trader in gems and fine jewelry. He's even sold some pieces to Queen Isabella."

Guards Hesken and Wenferd pretended to be impressed.

Ugh. Everything we say is true but it makes us sound more like liars. Or just kids telling stories.

"I know you don't believe us. We're not making it up." Emma tried her best honest smile. "We only need a while to rest and we can try to go home again."

"A safe place we kin sleep wifout thieves." Kimber clung to the burlap-wrapped box, swaying side to side.

"What say you, Hesk? I am sure we can find a nice safe place for these little ones to sleep."

"Aye." The other guard nodded. "C'mon, then. You don't belong on the street this late at night. We'll get ya somewhere safe."

"Thank you." Emma curtseyed. "Be alert. The thieves are likely to follow us."

The guards still behaved as if they thought them children playing imaginary games. However, they obliged, acting as if they watched out for 'thieves' while escorting the girls back up the street.

24

TALL TALES

A long, nervous walk came to an end at a tall wrought iron gate with a curved top.

Emma lost track of all the streets, shops, small fountain squares, small bridges over canals, and corners they went by. Shiny brass decorations along the top of the gate formed the shape of three cresting ocean waves. Emma gazed through the bars at a cobblestone courtyard around a three-tiered fountain. Behind the courtyard stood a rectangular two-story brick and stone manor house. It appeared fairly plain and in reasonably good shape, though not pristine.

She looked to the side down the street they'd taken to get here. Even though she hadn't seen the thieves, Emma felt certain the men followed them here. This house seemed enough like a fortress to keep thieves out for a night or two. They'd certainly try at some point to break in and look for the box. Hopefully, they would take more than one day to plan things out first. By then, Emma and the others would be... somewhere else. Sadly, not home, unless Rin could figure out how to make the box go to specific places.

No matter where they landed next time, they wouldn't be in this city with thieves after them anymore.

Hesken opened the gate. The metal let out a long, high-pitched noise so similar to the sound of a crying ghost it made the hairs on the back of Emma's neck stand up.

"What is this place?" asked Ambril.

"A place where you'll be looked after. Fed, taken care of, 'til you're grown." Guard Wenferd nudged them forward. "Unless you fancy telling us the truth of where ya live. If you got a proper home round here, we'll bring you to it. If you've got nowhere to be, then this be your new home."

"Andorath," said Ambril in a defeated voice. "It's far to the west. Another kingdom."

Emma hesitated. *This is an orphanage.* She bowed her head, all of a sudden missing home ten times more than a second ago. The two guards didn't believe they'd come from far away, or that thieves wanted anything to do with three poor-looking children. She didn't want to be in an orphanage. She also didn't want to fight town guards or get in trouble for trying to run away from them.

They're only doing what they think is right, trying to protect us.

Tomorrow, late in the afternoon, they'd be able to leave. It wouldn't matter where they happened to be. Not like guards would pay for an inn room for three kids who made up stories about thieves and selling jewels to a queen.

Kimber shivered. "It's a orphan place. We'as nae orphans."

Emma took Kimber's hand. "We'll be okay. It's just for a little while."

The guards exchanged a sad look, as if thinking all the kids they brought here said that... and never left until they'd grown up.

Head bowed, Emma stepped past the gate into the courtyard.

The guards walked them around the fountain, to the porch, then knocked on the door.

After a few minutes, they knocked again.

"Hold yer horses. I'm comin!" yelled a woman with a full voice, somewhat out of breath.

Thudding approached. Heavy footsteps vibrated in the porch. A moment later, the door opened to reveal a heavyset woman in a neat, but plain maroon dress with a black apron and frills. She looked a little younger than Da but older than Mama. Her black hair had been pulled back into a bun. The woman had great, rounded cheeks, smallish eyes, and a warm smile.

Kimber returned the smile.

"Aww. Aren't you three the most adorable..." The woman looked them over, then turned her attention to the guards. "What's the story with these three, then?"

"Found 'em wandering around alone." Wenferd shifted his jaw side to side. "They got quite the story teller's minds. Never seen 'em before. Claim they got parents, but not in this kingdom."

Hesken and the woman exchanged a sad look, as if assuming the girls made up stories about far-away families as a way to cope with their parents being gone.

"Oh." The woman pursed her lips. "I see. Well, come on in then. Matron Wavecrest is still finishing up for the day in her office. You got here in the nick of time. Come on, girls. I'm Morwenna, assistant matron." She fidgeted, seeming generally nervous. "This way."

The big, somewhat short, woman backed away from the door. Emma relaxed somewhat. Morwenna seemed quite friendly and nice. Kimber appeared to trust her, which meant a great deal. The woman led them down a hardwood floored hall and around a corner to another hallway lined in dark red carpet. The guards accompanied them, walking behind the girls as they navigated a series of turns and corridors. Not even a full minute inside this giant house and already Emma found it confusing to navigate. They passed a few other children who looked to be within a year or two of Emma's age, up or down. Every girl wore an identical style of grey dress, boys in identical grey tunics and pants. None wore shoes. She couldn't call them dirty, though couldn't truly call them clean either. All kept their heads down, walking fast as if late for something.

Morwenna continued walking down a long hallway past multiple doors until they reached a wide wooden archway of dark wood that opened on the left into a small room with several soft chairs and a sofa. It looked like a place people were supposed to wait in. Large, square hardwood tiles, dark in the center with strips of lighter wood framing each tile, covered the entire back wall of the alcove around a single door. The decorative wall had been polished to a high shine, looked expensive, needlessly fancy, and likely the most well-maintained part of the entire building.

Morwenna approached a door at the back right corner of the room and knocked.

"Matron Wavecrest? The guards have brought some children to see you."

"Come in," replied another woman who sounded little older and a lot less happy than Morwenna.

The large woman pivoted to smile reassuringly at the girls, then opened the door and went in. Emma crept up to the doorway, cautiously peering through it at a large office decorated predominantly in polished hardwood or slate grey. A slim, dour-faced woman with greying hair sat behind a large wooden desk in the middle of the room. The woman didn't look *old*, but she definitely did not appear to be young, the passage of time etched into her face in the form of faint wrinkles. A massive collection of shelves and cabinets towered over the desk behind her, full of cubbies containing books, little statues of sailing ships, crystals, and other bric-a-brac. It appeared to be one massive piece of furniture. Two cushioned chairs sat upon a square grey rug in front of the desk.

Dark curtains shrouded two tall, narrow windows in the corners of the room on either side of the giant shelf. Smaller, more ordinary bookshelves took up most of the side walls except for another door on the left side leading to a small sitting room. If 'serious' had its own office, this would be it. Morwenna hovered by the door as if afraid to step any closer to the woman behind the desk. She didn't appear literally frightened of the older woman, more like a young girl who dreaded getting in trouble.

The instant Kimber stepped into the room, she stopped short, staring at the older woman seated at the desk. After a few seconds, she edged closer to Emma as if trying to hide from her.

"Good day, Hesken." The older woman nodded in greeting at the guards. "And Wenferd. What have you brought to me this eve?"

"Found them wandering," said Wenferd. "Don't seem to have homes. Got some crazy tale about being from a far-off land."

"Gotta admit, they've a bit of an odd accent." Hesken glanced at Kimber. "Especially the little redhead. Could be they aren't making it up."

Wenferd peered down at the girls. "Have you three been taken against your will?"

"Wo'ts 'at mean?" whispered Kimber.

"Kidnapped," whispered Ambril. "He's asking us if we've been kidnapped."

"Somewhat," said Emma in a flat tone. "We don't want to be in an orphanage because we aren't orphans."

Matron Wavecrest sat taller, rested her elbows on the desk, and interlaced her fingers. "How did you get here?"

"The guards made us walk wif 'em," muttered Kimber.

Emma squeezed her hand. "She means this city. Sorry. My sister is tired. We are from a kingdom called Andorath. A little accident with some magic we aren't really sure how to control brought us here. We only need a safe place to rest for a day and we can try again to go home."

The guards and the matron exchanged a glance like they thought Emma told a wild story... or maybe lost her family and couldn't talk about it.

"We'as in trouble," whispered Kimber.

Ambril trembled. Her eyes reddened. She tried to say something, only managing a tiny squeak.

"Your parents are in some far-off land you can return to with magic in a day?" asked the matron.

"Yes." Emma nodded. "I know it sounds fanciful. It's true."

Matron Wavecrest smiled at the guards. "Very well. I have plenty of room for these three little dears and would be happy to look after them. Even for a single day."

Guard Wenferd chuckled.

"Course ya have room for them," muttered Hesken. "Two coins per head per month. Stack 'em like cordwood."

Matron Wavecrest frowned at him.

"C'mon." Wenferd elbowed Hesken. "Enough of that. Thank ya, ma'am."

The guards tipped their helms to the women and walked out of the office. Morwenna looked at the girls much the same way Emma would make faces at a lost, hungry kitten. Matron Wavecrest studied them in a different way, more like Mr. Starling examining a gem.

Emma didn't like it.

HOUSE WAVECREST

*E*mma, Kimber, and Ambril huddled together in front of the orphan matron's desk.

After a few minutes of silence, Matron Wavecrest rose from her seat and walked around to stand in front of the girls. The woman's black dress clung tight to her body above the waist, the skirt puffy, rustling as she moved. Dark grey lacy frill ran down the front of her shirt from the neck to the belt. The collar of the woman's shirt seemed so tight, merely looking at made Emma feel as though she couldn't breathe.

One by one, the older woman looked over the girls.

Emma tried to keep a polite expression, despite feeling like a horse being sold at the market.

Matron Wavecrest traced a finger along Ambril's jaw. "You are a pretty little thing. Maybe pretty enough you'll manage to get out of here before you grow up and I have to throw you out."

Ambril sniffled.

The older woman took a step to her right, standing in front of Emma. She studied her for a moment before reaching out and brushing Emma's hair aside to feel one of her ears. "Hmm. You're too pale. I've never seen a child so devoid of color before. Have you ever even seen the sun, girl? And far too scrawny. The big blue eyes might help you get adopted. Open them wide if anyone comes looking. And keep your hair off your ears if you ever happen to be fortunate enough for a viewing. You look too much like an elf. No one will take you, even with those big, pleading eyes. We'll have to pull that hair of yours back into a ponytail if we show you to prospective parents. They'll need to see you don't have pointed ears."

Stuck between insulted, frightened, and heartbroken, Emma couldn't find her voice. Tears welled up in her eyes, not quite heavy enough to fall down her cheeks.

Kimber glared.

"And you..." Matron Wavecrest stepped in front of Kimber. "Wipe that scowl off your face." She tapped a finger to her chin in thought, studying her for a moment. "Ehh... I suppose you're cute enough, but don't get your hopes up. You are going to be here until you're too old for me to keep anymore. Can't even marry you off. No man in his right mind is going to take you for a wife. No one wants a red-haired bride, or a red-haired child."

"You're wrong." Emma hugged Kimber. "I want her. Our parents want her. She's my sister and we already have a family. We're just lost. We're not orphans."

"You are new here, child." Matron Wavecrest regarded Emma with a steely stare. "So, I will tolerate this outburst once. Do not take that tone with me again or you will regret it."

"They're scared and lost, Matron Wavecrest," whispered Morwenna. "Go easy on them, please?"

"M-matron W-wavecrest." Ambril sniffled. "We are not orphans, like Emma said. My father is a wealthy gem merchant. He has shops in Calebrin City and Widowswood. If you help us get home, he'll give you a lot of gold."

The older woman raised an eyebrow at Ambril's ruined dress. After all the damage it suffered thus far, the garment looked as common as anything. "Do you hear that, Morwenna? This dirt-covered urchin is the daughter of a wealthy gem merchant? Dare I say we should immediately rush to make contact with this man and claim our reward."

Ambril shuddered into a sob.

Morwenna looked down, kneading her hands together.

"This gown was expensive…" Ambril fought tears. "We've been trapped in the sewers under a desert city, lost in a swamp full of dark elves. I fell down a giant gopher hole. Thieves chased us through wretched alleys. My dress is ruined."

Matron Wavecrest frowned. "You have quite the imagination, child. As I told the other girl, I do not tolerate liars. Telling stories for amusement is fine and well in its place. Lying to me… is not."

"Don't argue with her," whispered Emma. "We can go home tomorrow when the magic recharges."

"All right, girls." Matron Wavecrest clapped once. "Enough story time. I expect you to behave yourselves while you are in my care. I am fair and reasonable, but I do not tolerate misbehavior. The three of you are highly fortunate. Unlike other orphanages, I do not believe striking children is appropriate for discipline. If you break the rules or misbehave, you will spend a night in the punishment room. The more grievous your misbehavior, the more nights you earn in the room. There are certain… *things* living in the dark down there. They hate noise, especially noise from misbehaving children. I do not personally believe in striking children. However, if those creatures happen to strike you while you are down there for making noise, well… that is not my fault. That would be your fault."

Emma, Kimber, and Ambril all gasped.

Kimber squeezed herself into Emma, shivering. "I wan' tae go 'ome."

"What do you have there, child?" Matron Wavecrest reached for the sack.

"It's ours." Kimber backed up. "You cannae 'ave it."

"You will show me what it is." The old woman lunged forward and grabbed the sack.

Kimber pulled away. "No."

"Oh, no." Morwenna took a hesitant step closer. "Child, please just let her see it. Don't fight. Behave."

Snarling, Kimber continued trying to wrench the burlap sack away from the orphan matron. The older woman's expression darkened from pleasant to angry. Emma didn't want Kimber going to any horrible 'punishment room' where monsters in the dark might hurt her, so she jumped into the fray, grabbing the bag and fighting even harder to pull the woman's attention off her sister. If any of them got punished, she'd demand to take all the blame herself.

The tug-of-war grew increasingly violent. Matron Wavecrest lifted the sack, dragging both girls off their feet. Morwenna crept closer and closer, like she wanted to help the girls but couldn't quite find the courage to do so.

"Moine," growled Kimber. "'Tis ours. We need it to go 'ome."

Just as Emma felt certain Matron Wavecrest would break her rule and slap both of them for insolence, the sack gave out amid a loud ripping. The Box of Wonder tumbled free and hit the floor with a heavy thud. Emma and Kimber dropped back to their feet, holding only a scrap of burlap each.

"My word," whispered Morwenna.

All the color drained from Matron Wavecrest's face. She froze stock still, staring down at the sparkling, jeweled box lying on the floor of her office. Ambril buried her face in both hands and sobbed. Emma had to hold Kimber back from flinging herself at the woman and thumping her.

"Well, well, well..." Matron Wavecrest's eyes widened so much they seemed likely to fall right out of her head. She snatched the box up from the floor before Kimber could pounce on it, raising it to eye level. No trace of anger remained in her, as if she'd entirely forgotten the girls even existed. "Who did you steal this from?"

Emma stared at her. "We didn't steal it. It belongs to Ambril's father. The box is magical. It's how we got here. We need it to go home. Can we please have it back?"

"Why would I give a trio of desperate little beggars an exquisite treasure like this? Consider yourself fortunate I am willing to overlook where you got it from." Matron Wavecrest strolled behind her desk with the Box of Wonder. She glanced around as if looking for the perfect spot to display it, then decided to put it in a cabinet at the top center of the giant shelf, so high up she had to stretch to reach it.

Emma jumped at the *thwack* of the little wooden doors slamming closed.

"If whoever you stole this from does not come looking for it..." Matron Wavecrest turned to look at the girls. "It is now mine."

"You'as stealin' from us!" yelled Kimber.

The woman smiled, gesturing at the cabinet. "The jeweled box has always been here. It has been in my family for generations. Who do you think would believe the three of you? Talk of magic and far-away lands, indeed. You are lucky I don't have you carted straight off to prison for stealing."

Ambril sobbed louder.

I wish Mama was here. Emma fumed, badly wanting her mother to swoop in the door and put this awful woman in her place. At the word 'prison,' all fight left Kimber. She, too, started trembling and crying.

"Now..." Matron Wavecrest sauntered around her desk to stand in front of the girls, glaring at Kimber. "If you do not wish to spend your first night here in the punishment room, you will apologize for having the temerity to disobey me. There have only been two other children in all my time here who earned a night in the punishment room their very first day. The boy could not learn to accept authority. He came to a rather unfortunate end, prison if I recall. The girl is now a perfect example of how the appropriate use of discipline can mold proper young adults. Tell me, girl. Do you wish to be the third?"

Kimber gazed down, kneading her hands together and grinding her toes into the rug. "Sorry."

"I am sorry, Matron Wavecrest," said the older woman. "Say it exactly like that."

More tears rolled down Kimber's cheeks. She sniveled and called for Mama.

Emma squeezed her hands into fists. Watching this woman make

Kimber cry poked the same nerve in Emma as it struck in Mama when she learned Kimber's horrible father hit Emma. She didn't want to kill the old woman, though... merely punch her in the nose.

"I'as sorry, Matron Wavecrest," said Kimber a little louder than a whisper.

"I suppose that will do for now." The older woman folded her arms. "I do so hate getting off on the wrong foot on a child's first day here. I realize it is an adjustment for both of us to make. Once you three get used to how things work here, you will be happy. First, we shall need to give you proper dresses."

"Nan made this for me," said Emma. "I won't let anyone take it."

The matron waved dismissively. "I'm not about to take your filthy rags or make you get rid of them. If you wish to collect trash, do so. Keep it out of the way. Each of you will have a small space to hold whatever belongings you care to. If some other child gets sticky fingers, they will be punished. The three of you will learn to follow the rules, eventually. Since you are new, I am being quite lax with you. From now on, when you speak to me, you are only to say 'yes, Matron Wavecrest,' or 'thank you, Matron Wavecrest,' unless I ask you a question that requires a more specific answer. Am I clear?"

Emma said, "Yes, Matron Wavecrest," in an icy tone.

Kimber whispered it.

Ambril tried to say 'Yes, Matron Wavecrest' past a blur of tears, her voice too distorted to understand.

"Oh, do stop blubbering, dear." The older woman patted Ambril on the head. "It is unbecoming a girl of your station, is it not? What *would* your wealthy father say?"

Morwenna sucked in a small breath. She almost found enough courage to the older woman a disapproving look.

Almost.

BLEAKER AND BLEAKER

*M*atron Wavecrest ushered the girls out of her office. Morwenna hurried after them.

"Follow me, girls." Matron Wavecrest paused to lock the door with a key she wore around her neck on a cord, then walked away down the hall.

Emma put an arm around Kimber, squeezing her as they trudged along the lifeless grey hallway. Her little sister kept looking down. Ambril managed to stop sobbing out loud, sniffling every so often.

The matron led them along through a series of turns and halls, finally reaching an even longer hall containing several widely spaced doors. She approached one on the left side, opened it, and went in. Emma followed, stepping into an enormous rectangular room full of small beds arranged in two rows with the headboards against the longer walls. The nearer row had two fewer beds due to the doorway. An open aisle ran across the middle of the room between the footboards, slightly more than the length of a whole bed. Almost twenty other girls ranging in age from six to fifteen sat on beds or clustered in small groups on the floor.

Matron Wavecrest faced Emma, Kimber, and Ambril. "Wake up is at sunrise, every day. Morning meal is right after. You will have school times, chore times, and service times. It will not take you long to adjust to the routine. Baths are once a month and you do not want to miss them."

"Or we get the punishment room," muttered Kimber.

Several other girls in the room squeaked in alarm.

"Very good, child." Matron Wavecrest patted her on the head. "You learn quickly. Well then, you may each choose an unused bed. It will be yours for the rest of the time you are here. You should endeavor to do everything possible to ensure you get to sleep in it each night. For now, be ready. Dinner is soon. I will send someone to bring you the usual things. Once you have been given proper clothing, do not let me see you out of uniform. Welcome home, girls." She flashed an overly sweet smile. "And don't forget to smile."

With that, the matron walked out, leaving the three of them standing there.

Emma looked around, finally noticing all the other girls in the room sat still as statues, gazes downcast, and had been that way ever since the matron entered. They all wore the same style of plain grey dress. Only the oldest had shoes.

Kimber wiped her eyes. "Em, we should find the bigges' meanes' girl 'ere an' thump 'er good."

"What?" Emma gasped. "Why would we do such an awful thing?"

"Is wot yer s'posed tae do in prison." Kimber shrugged. "If we donnae' thump someone mean, we gon' get thumped alla time."

Ambril sniffled. "This isn't prison."

Kimber looked right, then left, then at Ambril. "Is nae a roight bit o' different, innit?"

A few other girls near enough to hear her made warning faces at them.

"What are we going to do?" whispered Ambril.

"Find a bed for now." Emma walked back and forth in the aisle between the beds' footboards.

The orphans in the room remained quiet, watching them.

Bare mattresses without blankets or pillows made unclaimed beds obvious. She couldn't find three in a row anywhere. The best option appeared to be somewhat close to the door on the left, two available beds next to each other on the near side with another empty one across the room from them. A tiny end table stood next to each bed with a small drawer and a lower shelf between the legs a few inches above the floor.

She walked over to the pair of open beds. "Here."

Ambril glanced at the one on the other side. "I guess I'll go over there so you can be next to your sister."

"Na," Kimber squish-hugged Emma. "I'as sleepin' in a same bed wif Em. Donnae wan' be alone."

Emma sat on the edge of the mattress, away from the bedroom door, facing the adjacent unclaimed bed. Kimber climbed up behind her, arms wrapped around her middle. *We are on the same continent. Even if we can't get the box back from that awful woman, I can send a bird home to get Mama.*

Ambril sat on her bed, knees almost touching Emma's. Her expression of heartbroken sorrow said she expected to be stuck here forever. "What are we going to do? Rin is still in the box."

"Eep." Emma squirmed. She had no idea how long the dark elf girl would sleep. It depended on how powerful the teleportation spell had been. Hopefully, the girl *would* wake up on her own and not need healing magic.

"Mama," whimpered Kimber. "I want Mama. I don't wan' tae be 'ere."

Some whispering ran among the orphans nearby, wondering if their mother abandoned them.

Emma patted her sister's hands, clasped in front of her stomach. "We'll get home. I have ideas."

"What ideas?" whispered Ambril.

"This might be difficult, for me too." Emma exhaled. "We need to pretend to behave until it's time to go. The matron wants to keep the box. Did you see her face when it dropped? She almost forgot we were even standing there. That woman only cares about money."

"Yeah," mumbled Kimber. "Sorry I didn' hide it good enough."

"How are we going to get it back?" Ambril shuffled her feet back and forth across the hardwood floor.

"She's basically a naga." Emma narrowed her eyes. "We don't need to get away with it, only get *to* it. Even if she catches us, it won't matter. Open the lid and we're safe."

Ambril wiped tears. "All right. What will we do if we can't get to it?"

"We're on the same continent as home. I can ask a bird to go find Mama." Emma squeezed Kimber's hands. "It might take weeks, but it will definitely work. I don't want to be here that long, so we should try to get the box back. Besides, it belongs to your father. We need to return it to him."

"All right. I can't believe they think I'm a beggar orphan." Ambril shook her fists. "It's so embarrassing. If I had my jewelry, she'd have believed me."

"She'd have taken it away from you and said you stole it." Emma frowned.

"You're probably right." Ambril scowled.

"Tomorrow," said Emma. "I'm going to—"

The doorknob turned.

Emma clenched her jaw and twisted around to see who walked in. The other girls in the room all froze in place the instant the knob rattled. The door swung inward, revealing a girl about fifteen years old in a grey dress and plain shoes. She walked in carrying a bundle of grey fabric. Upon seeing her—and not the matron—the orphans resumed talking or playing with their threadbare ragdolls.

The teen looked around, spotted Emma, then hurried over to stand at the foot of the bed she sat on. She had a tired, yet friendly expression, not quite smiling. Her straw-blonde hair hung a little past her shoulders. Pretty cornflower-blue eyes gave off a haunted sense of melancholy, or pity, as if she felt bad for them.

"Hello," said the girl. "I'm Nerissa. This is for you." She set the bundle down on the bed. "Three blankets, three pillows. Three dresses. They should fit. If they're too small, let me know and I'll get a different one for you. If they're too big, let me know and I'll put a couple of stitches in it to keep it right on you."

"Thank you," said Emma, trying not to sound annoyed. She found this *place* intolerable, not this girl.

"You should put them on right away." Nerissa bit her lip. "If the matron sees you wearing anything else, you'll get punished."

Emma closed her eyes, half furious, half about to cry. The blue dress was all she had left of her family at the moment. Taking it off felt like betraying Nan or abandoning her family.

I'm just pretending to behave. If I lose it, Nan can make a new one. It's only a dress, even if it's got a little magic in it.

"All right." Emma stood and pulled her dress off.

Kimber rose up on her knees, still on the mattress, and also pulled her dress off.

Ambril blushed scarlet. "You're changing right here? In the room with everyone?"

Emma grabbed the nearest grey dress. It looked small for her, so she handed it to Kimber and took the next one, which seemed bigger. The third dress looked even larger, so she kept the second one and put it on. "Yes."

Kimber threw the third dress to Ambril.

"I… can't." Ambril shivered. "Everyone can see me."

"Do it or punish room," whispered Kimber.

"If you end up in the room, it's going to make it take longer." Emma stood near her and held up one of the blankets to make a wall. "Hide behind me if you want."

Crying softly to herself, Ambril reluctantly changed out of her ruined gown and underdress into the drab grey thing. Emma dropped the blanket on the bed for Ambril, then folded her blue dress before tucking it into the drawer of the little table beside her bed.

"Nerissa?" Emma turned to look at her. "What is the punishment room, exactly?"

The teen looked around, then sat on the bed near her, speaking in a whisper. "It's in the basement. A little room where the matron or Groundskeeper Terle chains your hands up over your head to the wall and you have to stand there in the dark, alone, all night long, hoping the monsters don't get you."

All the color drained out of Ambril's face.

Emma blinked. "You have to be making that up. Chains?"

Nerissa glanced down. "I wish it was only a story. It's true. You can't even cry in there or the monsters will get you if they hear it. They make you stay in there all night long. If you can't fall asleep like that, you don't get to sleep that night."

Kimber shivered. "I'as said. Prison."

"That's not right." Emma shook her head. "That's far more cruel than paddling us on the butt."

Nerissa leaned close, whispering again even more quietly. "She's wretched and evil. She acts nice but she's horrible. If you look at her the wrong way or don't smile when there are guests visiting, she'll put you in the room overnight. Never during the day, only when we would be sleeping. It's so difficult to sleep in there, standing up while the monsters whisper in the dark. Poor Isla's on punishment every night this week because she tried to run away again."

Emma shivered.

Ambril appeared ready to throw up.

"Do the guards know?" whispered Emma.

"I have no idea." Nerissa shrugged. "Doubt they'd care. We're paupers. Orphans. We don't matter. The matron doesn't even really try to get us adopted. She makes it too expensive to adopt us for good, because she makes more money with service time."

"What does that mean?" asked Ambril, past a sniffle.

Nerissa took a breath. "She sends us to work in rich people's homes and they pay her. The work isn't usually too bad. For us, it's cleaning, dusting, helping in the kitchen, sometimes serving tea. Boys have to do much harder work. She says it's teaching us how to get on in the world once we're too old to be orphans. Sometimes, the rich people lie and say we were rude or tried to steal from them... and we get punished. Some of them are nicer."

Ambril wept. Kimber trembled.

"It's all right, sweetie." Nerissa brushed her hand over Kimber's hair. "The three of you are too little for service time. None of you are thirteen yet, are you?"

Emma, Ambril, and Kimber shook their heads.

"Then you won't have to worry about service time for a few years." Nerissa glanced down.

"Why is Morwenna afraid of her?" asked Emma.

"Because she's the matron." Nerissa brushed lint off her dress. "She has money and knows people who have power. The Wavecrest family used to be important. They owned many ships and a whole trading company. I don't know how it happened, but it's mostly gone. Something went wrong and their family lost a great deal of money. They had to sell off all their ships. Some of the family died. Some left the city and never returned. Matron Wavecrest is the only one left. I wish Morwenna was in charge of this place. She's so much nicer."

Ambril leaned forward. "This is the city of Calithir in Greymarch?"

"Yes." Nerissa almost smiled. "How can you not know? Haven't you lived here your whole life? Or did you stow away on a ship?"

"Neither." Ambril folded her arms. "When we get home, I am going to demand my father get the matron dismissed and maybe even thrown in prison if what you say is true."

"That would be nice." Nerissa patted Ambril on the arm. "It's good to dream. I used to dream that a rich and handsome count would show up and see me in the group of girls waiting to have a father, and he'd choose me. And then, I'd tell him all about what that foul witch did to me and he'd drag her out into the street while everyone cheered."

Ambril sighed at the dirt on her arms. "How do they have us bathe once a month?"

"There's a washroom we all use at the same time." Nerissa paused, biting her lip. "Well... not *all* of us. The boys go on a different day. On bath day, we all go to the washroom where we line up and wait. Bath day is also laundry day since it saves a few coppers on firewood doing it at once. Our dirty dresses go in another basin to be washed while we're all in the bath. Only twenty or so of us can fit in the big tub at a time. Once we finish, we get out of the tub and stand in line on the other side until everyone is done. Then we have to clean the tub, clean the laundry vat, clean the room, scoop the ash from the fire, and so on."

"Everyone?" Ambril blinked, her cheeks reddening. "At the same time? In the *same* bathtub… as in together? Bathing… with no clothes on?"

"That is how most people wash themselves, yes? With no clothing in the way? It wouldn't be a very effective bath otherwise." Nerissa tilted her head.

Ambril fainted back onto her bed.

Emma winced. "I think she meant how can they be so uncivilized as to only let us take one bath a month… not how do they actually go about the bath."

"Oh." Nerissa stood, leaned forward, and patted Ambril on the cheek. "Is she all right?"

"Yes." Emma glanced at the end table holding her beloved dress. "She'll be fine."

"Once we get outta here," whispered Kimber.

Nerissa covered her mouth in shock. "Oh, no. Please, sweetie. Don't try to run away. Matron Wavecrest gets very angry."

Kimber clung to Emma. "Donnae let 'er get me."

"I won't." Emma put an arm around her. "I won't let her hurt you."

Nerissa looked them over, seeming satisfied that the grey dresses fit reasonably well. "If your friend wants to clean up before bath day, sometimes we use one of the water pumps in the back courtyard. You won't get in trouble for that, but the water is quite cold and you might have to wash yourself near boys or anyone else who happens to walk by. It sounds embarrassing at first. Trust me, though, it's preferable to being put in the punishment room for getting too dirty."

Emma scowled. "If she's going to punish us for being dirty, she should let us bathe more than once a month."

"Aye." Kimber shook her head. "Punishment fer bein' dirty should be 'avin' ta take a baf!"

"The wood and coal to heat the water and the soap costs money." Nerissa made a coin-pinching gesture. "Matron Wavecrest doesn't like to spend money on anyone but herself unless she absolutely has to. See how thin these pillows are? And we only get shoes once she thinks we're not going to outgrow them."

"How awful," whispered Emma.

Nerissa let out a somber sigh. "Really, this place is not as bad as it sounds. There are far worse places to end up in the city. It's better than the street. If you obey the rules, you'll be reasonably okay here."

"Don't you mean reasonably *happy*?" asked Ambril, without sitting up.

"No… I don't." Nerissa sighed, bowed her head, and walked away.

THE DINING HALL

*E*mma, Kimber, and Ambril huddled together, whispering about plans to get the box and escape the orphanage. Their biggest challenge would be the lock on the door to the matron's office. Kimber wanted to look at it to see if it might be simple enough for her to pick. She didn't think a door to an orphanage matron's office would demand a complicated key. Emma got distracted talking about wanting to find a rat so she could ask him to go get a few hundred friends and swarm the evil witch as revenge for making Kimber cry.

They giggled at the idea.

A girl with light brown hair walked up to them. "Shh."

Emma glanced at her. The orphan appeared to be a little older than her, perhaps eleven. She seemed reasonably clean and healthy, though had a lingering sadness about her.

"You shouldn't laugh," said the girl. "If the matron hears you, you could get in trouble."

"For laughing?" Ambril gawked. "How cruel."

"After dark. She likes it to be quiet." The girl gave a soft sigh. "I'm sorry you've ended up here with us. I'm Bree."

Emma, Kimber, and Ambril introduced themselves.

"You were talking to Nerissa before." Bree scratched at her arm. "She's nice. Most of the other assistants are not nice."

"Assistants?" asked Ambril.

"Sorry. You're new." Bree exhaled. "Matron Wavecrest chooses some of the older orphans who follow all the rules and do everything right to help her. All the assistants are at least sixteen. Girls work with girls, boys with the boys. Most of them act like her, bossing us around. Nerissa is okay. If no one is watching her, she's nice to us, but any of the other assistants, you should act like they're the matron. Don't let them catch you doing anything wrong. Don't say anything they can hear you wouldn't want the matron hearing. You won't have any trouble with the rest of us. It's us against the matron, mostly."

"Mostly?" Kimber scrunched up her nose.

"We only have each other. But… if it's a choice between ratting on someone and getting them in trouble, or *you* getting in trouble…" Bree shook her head. "Everyone will pretty much tattle. No one's going to steal from you, or pick fights, or even be nasty. This place is miserable enough without us being mean to each other. We're together. The matron and her assistants are not to be trusted."

"Is loike prison," whispered Kimber. "Ae tol' ya."

Bree leaned forward, seeming to study Emma. "Are you an elf? You have such pretty blue eyes."

"Thanks. No. I'm not an elf." Emma pulled her hair off her ear. "See?"

"Oh. Someone in your family must have been an elf a long time ago, then." Bree kneaded her hands. "Sorry if it bothers you. I just thought you looked pretty. I'm so plain no one ever chooses me."

"Chooses you?" whispered Ambril.

"To take home." Bree scratched at her arm. "Sometimes, people who want a son or daughter come here looking for an orphan to keep. They never choose me."

Emma saw nothing wrong with Bree. She didn't look any more or less pretty than the other girls in the room. Perhaps the people simply didn't want a girl who carried such a heavy burden of constant sadness in her eyes. "I'm sure the right family will find and love you someday."

"I hope so." Bree wiped a tear and took a seat on the bed beside Ambril.

Any discussion about going home or getting the box back would have to wait for them to have privacy. Emma didn't want Bree getting in trouble, or worse, being put in a position where she might have to tattle on them to avoid being punished. The girl spoke briefly of how both of her parents worked on a sailing ship that never came back, presumed sunk. She'd been staying with her grandparents, who died not quite a year ago. Bree told them many of the other orphans here had been abandoned by parents who didn't want them, mostly unmarried mothers who had babies with men from sailing ships. A few, like her, lost their parents.

"I still want to know what Kimber said," muttered Ambril.

"I say a lot o' fings." Kimber grinned.

Ambril smiled at her. "To those thieves. You said it was the worst night... and something about priv and gnomes?"

"Gnomes means to go home." Emma rubbed her chin. "She's said that before."

"Is thief talk," whispered Kimber. "Use rhymes so no one know wha' they sayin'."

"It worked. I had no idea what you said." Ambril wiped at dried mud on her forearm.

"Worst noight means first roights." Kimber held her hands out as if holding something. "First roight means who'er finds a fing first, owns the fing. Ovva thieves s'posed ta respect it an' not try stealin' it. Privs jes' mean like dibs. I foun' it, I got dibs on it. I's tryin' ta tell them t'was me box and they cannae 'ave it."

A loud hand-bell rang in the hallway outside. All the other girls in the room leapt to their feet and hastily formed a line at the door. They didn't quite get to the point of pushing and shoving each other out of the way, though there definitely appeared to be a competition to be closest to the door.

"Come on." Bree waved for them to follow her. "It's time for dinner. When we're in the dining hall, don't talk. Don't make any noise. If she catches us whispering, we get punished and not allowed to eat. Keep your head down, too. If you look around too much, they think you're up to something bad. Might get punished or maybe only extra chores."

Fear in Bree's voice and expression stopped Emma from asking if she teased her or meant that seriously.

I hate this place. No... I hate that woman.

Emma added herself to the back of the line behind Bree, Kimber behind her, Ambril at the end. The girls at the front soon walked out into the hallway in single file, following it to the right across the middle of the manor house and into another corridor. Boys streamed into the same corridor from another hall, forming a second line beside them. Six older teens, almost adults, stood like town guards directing the smaller children around by pointing or raising their hands.

Eventually, Emma followed her line through a set of double doors into a grand dining hall. Three giant chandeliers hung in a row along the ceiling, each one aglow with numerous small oil lamps. Two long tables stood on either side from the door, separated by a strip of dull red carpet leading to a head table at the far end of the room at which sat Matron Wavecrest, Morwenna, a somewhat young man, and a wild-haired, grizzled older man in a once-nice suit. Emma assumed the scarier looking man to be the Groundskeeper Terle Nerissa warned her about. He looked like someone who both worked outside all day long and would love making children cry.

Girls headed to the left long table, boys to the one on the right.

Emma kept following her line around the near corner of the girls' table and down the space between it and the wall. As soon as she noticed none of the adults looked in her direction, she scowled at the matron for half a second, earning a small sense of victory at her unnoticed defiance. She ended up taking a seat on a bench at the girl's table near the end by the head table. *This is why everyone ran so fast to get in line. The closer they are to the front, the farther they sit from the witch.* The thick wood table looked as if it had suffered through many years, many children, and many meals. She dreaded the kind of cruel slop this woman would feed them.

The grand hall hung in eerie silence. Only the scraping of forks from the head table, and occasional murmur of conversation among the adults interrupted the unearthly stillness. Emma did as most of the girls around her did and kept her gaze down, aimed at the table in front of her. Before long, the same older teens who directed the children around in lines returned pushing carts loaded with bowls. They made their way around the enormous long tables, handing out one bowl each to all the orphans.

Emma didn't look, afraid she'd get in trouble for being the only child obviously not keeping her head down. She prepared for the worst as the rattle of a pushcart came up behind her on the left. A grim faced seventeen-year-old girl set a bowl in front of her, unceremoniously plonked a spoon in it, and moved on, doing the same for everyone else down the row.

Much to Emma's surprise, the contents of the bowl did not make her recoil in horror. She'd been expecting some manner of awful porridge. Dinner appeared to be a stew of sorts in an orangey broth. A few bits of fish plus some other kind of whitish meat floated in the steaming liquid. She recognized hunks of potato as well as peas. It smelled fairly good. She risked a spoonful of broth, finding it salty and hot-spicy, like whoever made it put too much black pepper in.

Not intolerable. The more she ate, the more she decided it went past tolerable to enjoyable. The stew didn't contain too much fish. Most of the meat was the other, strange substance. She had no idea what to call it. Parts of the unknown meat seemed stringy, parts mushy. While mostly white, it also had red markings. She found it to have a mild flavor somewhat reminiscent of the ocean. The temptation to ask someone what she ate got into a fight with her fear over the punishment room.

There can't be monsters in the basement. She's only saying that to scare us.

Emma exhaled out her nose, hoping Nerissa did the same by making up stories about chains.

She risked a sideways peek at the head table out of the corner of her eye. Morwenna engaged in conversation with the cleaned-up man, who also appeared reasonably friendly and about the same age as her. Matron Wavecrest sat so stiffly in her chair that looking at her made Emma's back sore. The woman did not seem to be in a good mood, spoke to no one, and maintained an air around her like an ill-tempered queen who adored having power. To her left, the wild-haired man spent most of his time staring out at the orphans. Emma hastily shifted her gaze back down to her food before he made eye contact with her. The man looked so grubby and disheveled it shocked her Matron Wavecrest tolerated him at the table. During the day, the man likely worked outside around the manor. Now, he appeared highly keen on trying to catch any orphan misbehaving.

Once the fear of being noticed wore off, Emma subtly glanced around at the other children. As long as she didn't turn her head, the groundskeeper probably wouldn't catch her. The other girls at her table all seemed sad and miserable.

A small girl with dark brown hair five spaces to the right on the opposite side of the table from Emma slumped over forward. She caught herself before her face went into her dinner bowl, sat up straight, and rubbed her eyes with both hands. Red chafe marks and small cuts surrounded both of her wrists. The maybe seven- or eight-year-old seemed utterly exhausted, as if she hadn't slept in days. Within seconds of her trying to eat again, she almost passed out a second time.

The girls sitting on either side of her shifted, trying to help hold her upright without being obvious about it.

Emma stared at the red marks on the girl's wrists, a chill sliding down her back. *By Ylithir... Nerissa wasn't lying. That horrible woman* really *does use manacles on the orphans.* She lost her appetite. *I have to do something.* The same way she couldn't leave Rin behind in Nimaraenna to be killed by her rotten mother, she couldn't simply run away from this place and leave the children to be mistreated by such a cruel matron. Her first thought was to stuff all the kids into the Box of Wonder and bring them to Widowswood. Alas, that didn't sound reasonable. There had to be over 200 orphans here. Her family would most likely allow Rin to stay with them because no one else *could* look after an elf child. Nan and Mama would live long enough to care for her until she grew up. But... this many children from six to nearly adult? That would be too much for the entire village of Widowswood to accept.

Morwenna seems nice. Alas, she's a chicken. Emma stared at her half-finished dinner. *We are going home, but I have work to do first.* Promising herself she wouldn't leave until she made serious changes here let her finish eating. She'd need her strength... and the food wasn't bad. This baffled her since Matron Wavecrest appeared to be quite stingy about everything else: cheap clothes, no shoes for kids small enough to outgrow them, cheap blankets, cheaper pillows, making everyone bathe and do laundry at the same time to save a few copper coins, making the older kids go work for money and then keeping it all... why did she feed them well?

Emma frowned. *We can't work hard and make money for her if we're starving.*

"Almost time dears," said Matron Wavecrest. "Finish up your food. Don't waste any."

The scraping of spoons intensified. Another mild surprise: the amount of time given to eat didn't feel rushed. Children couldn't eat fast while sad. Kimber seemed slightly less fearful. She'd cleaned out her bowl. Ambril also finished her food, though kept fanning air into her open mouth.

A few minutes later, Morwenna stood. "All right, children. If you are finished eating, stand up."

Everyone but two boys and a girl got up. One boy rose to his feet four seconds later. The last two got up at the same time soon after.

"Proceed back to your bedrooms." Matron Wavecrest walked around the head table into the middle of the room, arms folded, watching over the children as they formed into lines and filed out.

A group of four boys between ten and twelve scurried around gathering up bowls and spoons into large wooden bins.

Emma kept her head down, following the girl in front of her.

"You two," said the matron. "New girl, and the one in front of you. Come here."

Bree squeaked. She darted out of the line and scurried over to the matron. "Yes, Matron Wavecrest", she half-whispered, her voice an urgent plea not to be angry.

Grr. Emma walked over to stand beside Bree.

The orphan matron looked the two of them over briefly, then nodded in a 'good enough' manner. "Go wait for me outside my office. I require the two of you for a short time."

"Yes, Matron Wavecrest." Bree curtsied and walked off.

Ooh. Into her office. I might be able to get to the box. Emma followed.

"Emma," said the matron. "Stop."

She halted where she stood, watching the last of the children file out the door into the hall.

"Come here."

Emma spun to face toward her and took three steps back to where she'd been.

Matron Wavecrest folded her arms. "What did you forget?"

She stared blankly at the older woman.

"Not an hour ago, you stood in my office as I explained the rules." The woman tapped her booted foot.

Emma blinked. *Drat!* She couldn't land herself in the punishment room. Spending a night locked up in the basement would get in the way of her plans. "Sorry, Matron Wavecrest. Yes, Matron Wavecrest. I thought we were not allowed to speak in the dining hall."

The woman apparently mistook her fear of being delayed as fear of her, personally... and smiled. "You have not yet been here for a full day and I find myself in an unusually good mood. This time, I will overlook your forgetfulness. There will be no next time."

Emma squeezed her hands into fists. "Thank you, Matron Wavecrest."

"Now go, wait for me outside the office." The woman pointed at the door.

"Yes, Matron Wavecrest." Emma's fingernails cut into her palms from anger at having to talk like that, though she somehow managed to keep her voice sounding neutral.

Before she could lose control and blurt something bad, Emma spun on her heel and fast-walked out of the dining hall.

28

TEA AND GOLD

*O*pportunity sometimes proved to be too good to be true.

Emma stood next to Bree by the wall on the side of the small sitting room adjacent to the matron's office. Vertical blue stripes in gold, white, and dark blue covered the walls above the solid white wainscoting, which came up to within a few inches of Emma's height. The matron told them to stand there, hands clasped in front of themselves, and not move or speak unless signaled. They were to serve tea to some guests the matron had a late meeting with. If one of the guests waved to them, they could move from their waiting spot to either pour tea, bring sugar and milk, or collect an empty cup and put it back on the serving tray beside where they stood. Matron Wavecrest ordered the girls to smile politely at all times, not speak a single word, and stand still by the wall unless serving tea.

The worst part of the chore was having to hold still like a piece of furniture.

After giving them brief instructions, the matron left the sitting room to wait in the main office.

"Please don't do anything wrong," whispered Bree. "She'll send us both to punishment if we make her look bad in front of guests."

"I'll do my best." Emma clasped her hands in front of herself.

A few minutes later, Bree whispered, "This is not good."

"Why?"

"If we get picked for a special chore, and do well, she'll give us more special chores. We could get extra privileges, even become assistants if we don't get adopted before we're older."

"That's bad?"

"Yes. We cannot refuse the chores, or we get punished. We couldn't refuse to become assistants, or we'd be punished. If we became assistants, everyone would fear and hate us." Bree bowed her head. "I'm almost tempted to spill something on purpose. Spending a night or three in the punishment room is better than becoming an assistant."

Emma furrowed her brows for a second, then chased the anger off her face.

They stood in silence for about twenty minutes before a knock came from the outer office.

"Matron Wavecrest, your guests are here." Morwenna's voice sounded muffled behind a closed door.

"Wonderful. Have Sela bring the boys." Boots clicked across the office, moving farther away. Seconds later, the door hinges squeaked. "Welcome. You must be Captain Daegren."

"Ma'am," said a thick-voiced man. "You've not met Cialen yet. M' first mate."

"Ma'am," replied a younger man who spoke in a lighter, more practiced tone. He seemed to work quite hard to pronounce every letter of every word, like the wealthy people who'd been at Jamie's wedding in Calebrin City.

"This way, please, gentlemen." Hard boot taps again crossed the office, growing louder until Matron Wavecrest entered the sitting room, hands folded in front of her chest, a fake smile flattening some of the wrinkles around her mouth.

Two men followed her in, both dressed in strange sleeved coats with long tails, three big brass buttons on each cuff. The coats hung open down the front to reveal shirts, blue on the larger, older man, burgundy on his younger associate. The older of the two, likely

Captain Daegren, had a shaggy beard, white pants a little too tight for his generous belly and thighs, and shiny knee-high boots. His clothes possessed a certain degree of shabbiness to them that suggested he spent most of his days on a boat and spared little time for pleasantries like washing laundry. Something about him felt rather pirate-like. He also did not seem to be impressed with Matron Wavecrest or this place, giving off a sense of 'let's be on with it and leave.'

The first mate appeared to be as near as opposite to the captain as possible. He smiled, gazed around admiring the décor, and looked as if he'd have been quite pleased to sit for hours sipping tea and talking about anything. He seemed half the age of the captain, perhaps not yet midway through his twenties, clean shaven. The man wore his long blond hair pulled back in a ponytail, secured by a loose-tied blackberry-colored silk ribbon dangerously close to being a bow. The man carried himself like someone important or wealthy.

Neither man paid more attention than a passing glance at Emma and Bree standing by the wall as they entered and sat in the cushioned teal chairs facing the small sofa upon which the matron perched.

Matron Wavecrest raised a hand and made a sharp two-fingered wave toward the girls.

Emma picked up the teapot from the serving tray next to her. Bree carried a serving tray with two empty cups on saucers, a small pitcher of milk, and a bowl of sugar with a tiny spoon. The girls approached the men at the same time. Bree handed them cups. Emma poured tea. Bree offered the men sugar or milk. The captain declined both. His first mate accepted both.

Emma and Bree returned to their spot by the wall, set their trays down, and clasped their hands in front of themselves.

The matron and the captain got into a casual discussion about merchant shipping. She had a deep familiarity with shipping and trade, which surprised him. To this, he warmed up and got into a pleasant conversation mostly about how he ran a ship, the *Siren's Folly*. Eventually, they got around to the reason he and his first mate stopped by. They needed a young lad to work for the duration of one voyage, approximately three months.

Captain Daegren took a swig of his tea, downing almost half the contents of the cup in one shot. "Just wantin' to make it clear, ma'am. We ain't lookin' to keep 'im. Just got word you hire your charges out for work."

"Yes. Some of my children work to learn how to better take care of themselves when they grow up." Matron Wavecrest smoothed her hands down the skirt of her dress. "My head assistant, Sela, is on her way here with the four most capable boys for the job."

First Mate Cialen lifted his teacup to his lips and sipped politely.

"All right then." The captain drained the last of his tea. He raised his arm as if about to slam the delicate cup down on the table, then caught himself. "Oh. Forgive me. Been a while since I drank from such delicate porcelain. Tis a fine enough little mug. Too small. Can't hardly hold enough drink to notice."

The first mate chuckled.

Captain Daegren glanced at Emma.

She hurried over with the teapot and refilled the man's cup, then scurried back to her waiting spot. Doing a chore like serving tables didn't bother her. Doing such a chore for a person like Matron Wavecrest while she effectively sold a child *did* bother her. Alas, she couldn't think of any way to interfere yet without ending up in the punishment room.

Doesn't believe in hitting us, but she'll lock us up in the dark all night.

The sitting room door opened. A black-haired girl slightly older than Nerissa walked in, carrying herself with a sense of haughtiness. She wore a grey dress quite similar to the orphan dresses, though seemingly made of nicer materials and a small bit fancier. The girl's black shoes seemed neither nice nor shabby, perhaps obtained second hand.

First Mate Cialen raised an eyebrow at her, making a face much the same as Da whenever he saw Mama. He didn't stare long. He likely thought her pretty, though too young for him to pursue. The teen stopped a step in from the door, glanced backward at the office, then pointed to the floor by the end of the sofa.

"Gentlemen," said Matron Wavecrest. "This is my assistant, Sela."

Sela curtsied to the men.

Four boys marched into the room in a single-file line. They stopped at the indicated spot, standing in a row. All had relatively long hair past their shoulders, the leftmost boy blond, the other three brown in different shades, medium, light, and dark as they stood in order. The smallest, who stood third from the left, looked about Emma's size and had soft features. The oldest boy stood at the right end of the row, taller and more muscular than common for someone his age. They all wore the same grey tunic and pants as every other boy in the orphanage. None had shoes. All were suspiciously clean, as if they'd recently taken an unscheduled bath.

Morwenna slipped in and closed the door behind her. She also clasped her hands in front of herself the same way Emma and Bree had been ordered to do. The woman appeared distressed about something and kept making sad faces at the floor while kneading her fingers together.

Sela stepped up next to the boys, indicating them from left to right along the row. "This is Fisher. He's twelve. Galiot. He's also twelve. Heron is only eleven, but a hard worker. And Ortun. He is thirteen."

None of the boys seemed able to decide if they should look at the men or stare down, hoping not to be chosen.

First Mate Cialen stood, set his teacup on the table beside the chair, and walked back and forth in front of the boys. "Well, lads. You've a chance to get out of this place for a few months. The job is to be part of the crew of the *Siren's Folly*. You'll be climbing the rigging, cleaning pots and pans, fetching things, helping out with whatever minor task anyone gives you. Essentially, your duties will cover everything that isn't quite worth the time of one of our men to do, or that they cannot do due to their size, weight, or drunkenness."

The captain grumbled something to himself.

"Some days will be long and boring." The first mate stopped pacing and pivoted to face the boys. "Other days will be such hard work you won't even notice the sun went down before it's dark."

All four boys stared at the carpet. None seemed too thrilled about the idea of spending three months working on a ship.

"What do you think, Cialen?" Captain Daegren knocked back his tea mug, swallowing the entire cupful in one gulp. "That Ortun looks like a strapping lad. He ought to be able to haul his weight around."

The first mate examined the four prospective boys again. "I like the look in young Heron's eye."

"The lad's barely a full stone's weight. Scrawny. A bit... delicate, perhaps? Tha' is a *lad*, right?" The captain leaned forward, narrowing his eyes. "I think that brown-haired lass with the teacups over there's bigger 'n him."

"We have men to do the hauling." First Mate Cialen patted Heron on the shoulder. "This boy looks like he can fly up the riggings with ease. We could use a nimble lad more than another lummox. We've got plenty of muscle already. This boy can get around the cargo hold where none of the men can squeeze in. Can you swim, boy?"

Heron hesitated for a few seconds, then nodded.

"Only asking in case you fall overboard. We won't be ordering you to jump in the water." The first mate chuckled. "Don't look so frightened."

The other three boys seemed to relax.

Morwenna opened and closed her hands. She made faces at Matron Wavecrest like she rather disapproved of this whole arrangement. At least twice, she appeared about to speak up... but didn't.

"Very well." The first mate looked at the matron and clapped Heron on the shoulder again. "We'll hire this one. We set sail at the end of the week. Will you be sending him to the docks, or shall I have some crewmen return to fetch him?"

Matron Wavecrest smiled. "It would be best for you to send some crew to fetch the boy so he doesn't get lost or end up on the wrong ship. The docks are vast."

And he's likely to run away if he's allowed to roam the city by himself. Emma stared at the smallest boy, her heart heavy with worry and sympathy. Heron did *not* seem excited about this job. Given how much most of the orphans she'd spoken to wanted to run away from this place, how bad could being on a ship be that the boy would rather be here?

Ortun, Galiot, and Fisher glanced at Heron like they never expected to see him again.

"With me, boys." Sela walked out.

The four boys trudged after her. Morwenna sighed, giving Heron an apologetic look as he went by, not that he noticed with his head bowed.

Emma stared at the empty teacup, unsure if she should run over to fill it or collect it. Neither man nor the matron signaled her to do anything, so she stood there, growing increasingly worried she might be making an error.

The captain and Matron Wavecrest haggled over money for a few minutes, settling on a deal for twenty-five golden gryphon coins to hire the boy for three months.

"Twelve of those coins are a security." The matron made a note in a leather-bound journal with gilt edges. "If you return Heron in good health, I will return the sum of twelve golden gryphons to you. Thirteen will stand as his employment fee."

If? Emma blinked. *She said if he returns in good health? She doesn't know for sure he'll be okay?*

"That is agreeable." First Mate Cialen nodded.

Matron Wavecrest snapped her book closed. "Do try to return him intact without any missing limbs or he won't be of any use to me."

"Calm your sails, ya old bat," grumbled Captain Daegren. "We ain't pirates. The lad'll be just fine. The *Siren's Folly* is a merchant ship. We haul grain, booze, and whatever else needs hauling. Nothin' too valuable to attract the likes o' pirates."

Morwenna bit her lip. The woman certainly seemed worried for Heron's safety. Emma made eye contact with her, leaning into the intensity of her stare as if to say 'do something.' Morwenna hastily waved, shooing her. Emma cast her gaze to the floor again before Matron Wavecrest noticed.

Emma and Bree stood like statues by the wall while the Matron made pleasant after-deal conversation with the men. A tedious fifteen minutes or so later, she walked the men out to the office door.

How long are we supposed to stand here? She didn't tell us to go anywhere yet. Will we get in trouble? Is she leaving?

After seeing the men out, the matron returned to the sitting room. She stopped barely a full step in the door to wave at them. "All right, girls. That is all. Collect the tea service, bring it to the kitchen, then go to bed."

"Yes, Matron Wavecrest," chorused Emma and Bree together.

"Oh, and Morwenna…" The matron looked over at her. "See to it Heron has a little more food these next few days. He's going to need it."

"Yes, Matron Wavecrest." Morwenna bowed her head.

29

A MICE BIT OF REVENGE

*B*ree led the way down the hall to the kitchen.

Emma carried one serving tray with the kettle and empty cups. Bree carried the unused portion of milk and sugar on her tray. As soon as they reached a point in the hallway where no adults could see them, she stopped, drank half the remaining milk, then offered the cup to Emma.

"My hands are full," whispered Emma.

"Balance it on one hand."

"I don't want to drop it."

"Here then." Bree raised the little pitcher. "Open your mouth. They'll just toss it on the ground outside. We shan't waste it."

Emma drank two mouthfuls of milk Bree poured for her.

Milk gone, they resumed walking the rest of the way down the hall to the kitchen. The huge room held multiple stoves as well as three long tables, more cabinets than had a right to be in one place, and a handful of mice scurrying around the brick floor. To the left, a wide wooden door appeared to lead to a great pantry.

No adults nor other orphans in sight, Bree and Emma had the kitchen to themselves.

"We just set this on the table and leave it for morning." Bree, seemingly unbothered by the mice, walked past three of them to put her tray on the nearest table.

"I've never seen a kitchen this large." Emma put her tray beside the other one. "There must be a large staff."

"Only four. They do the cooking. All the cleaning, peeling, and some of the cutting is a chore for us. Except for the groundskeeper and the cooks, orphans do every bit of work around here." Bree indicated dark marks on both knees. "I spent most o' this morning scrubbing the floor in here."

Something tickled Emma's left foot.

She peered down at a curious mouse.

"They don't bite." Bree smiled.

"I'm not afraid of mice." Emma crouched, gently petting the mouse with one finger. *Strixian, please grant me the Wildkin Whisper.* "Hello."

"Hi," chirped the mouse.

The other ten or so mice in sight stopped sniffing around to stare at her and soon darted over.

"Help us," squeaked one.

"We're hungry." Another sniffed at her hand. "This too clean. No food."

"All right. Follow me." Emma padded over to another door leading to the rear area behind the manor house.

Bree covered her mouth to hold in a laugh. "You're squeaking."

"I'm talking to the mice." Emma grasped the doorknob.

"Eep! Don't go outside. It's too late. We'll get in trouble."

Emma opened the door. "I'm not going outside. I'm merely going to look out the door." She pulled it open.

A path of irregular sized stones led a short distance from the door to a cobblestone area in front of a small stable. It didn't look as though any horses had lived there for years. A long-disused coach sat beside the building. Nearby on the right, a metal water pump stood at the center of a muddy puddle. Emma smiled at the copious amount of open dirt between the house and the cobblestoned area by the stable.

She squatted in the doorway, careful not to let her toes touch the ground outside—so she could honestly say she did not leave the house

—and summoned a meatplant. "There," she squeaked to the mice. "That should feed all of you with plenty left over."

The mice swarmed the meatplant, nibbling on it. Two ran off, yelling for their friends to come feast.

Bree stood behind Emma, jaw open.

"Will you do me a small favor?" squeaked Emma. "You don't have to, but it would be nice."

All the mice peered up at her.

"What?" chirped one.

"Do you know the mean old lady?"

The mice made noises of annoyance.

"Yes," said one. "She always tries to step on us."

Another stood up on his back legs. "Or hit us with brooms."

"Or smash us with books," chirped a third.

Emma narrowed her eyes. "That awful woman made my little sister cry. She hurts the children here. Can you gather up every other mouse you can find and invade her room? Crawl all over her. Go up under her dress. Run across her face. Get everywhere…. Then run away before she hurts any of you."

The mice chattered amongst themselves, eventually nodding to her.

"Will you give us another one of these?" A mouse nosed at the meatplant. "There are more of us. Too many for one to feed."

"Of course." Emma extended her hand and summoned a second meatplant. "There you are. Oh, after you scare her, please don't eat any food you might find sitting out in easy reach. The awful witch will likely try to poison you. If food is too easy to get, don't trust it."

The group of mice, now numbering near to thirty, gasped in shock as if they could never imagine food left sitting out might be a trap. They swarmed her in thanks, most rubbing their cheeks against her or licking affectionately before scampering back down to eat. Emma thanked them again, stood, and backed into the kitchen, closing the door.

"What is happening?" whispered Bree. "Did you just do magic?"

"Yes." Emma smiled... and explained what she'd asked the mice to do.

It honestly wouldn't solve anything, but Matron Wavecrest deserved *something* for what she did to Kimber... and what she did to the orphans here.

SELA

*E*mma almost remembered the way back to the bedroom.
Not only did the manor house seem like a maze, the girls'
corridor had at least six giant bedrooms. At least she walked with
Bree, who knew her way around. The girl's constant, heavy sadness
lightened as they whispered about the imminent mouse 'attack,'
though Bree didn't seem able to laugh, nor could she even manage a
proper smile.

Two turns and a hallway away from the matron's office, Bree
paused to point down another corridor. "You shouldn't go there
unless you're doing a chore and you have to. That's the boys' hall."

"Okay. We get in trouble for going near the boys?"

Bree nodded and kept walking.

"Why?" asked Emma.

"Because we do. I don't know. The matron doesn't want us there if
we don't have to be. The boys aren't allowed in our hallway either."

Emma sighed. "That sounds stupid. Does she just punish us for
anything she thinks of?"

"Yes." Bree scowled. "If she believes doing something will make us
miserable, she does it just for that. It doesn't matter how well you try

to follow the rules. Everyone *will* end up in the punishment room at least once. I swear the woman is only happy when she makes us cry."

"Or when she finds gold," muttered Emma.

"That, too." Bree choked up, placing a hand over her chest where a necklace might hang. "She took my mother's locket when we got here. Said 'peasants don't need gold.'"

"Cruel." Emma glared at nothing in particular.

"Wasn't even real gold. My parents didn't have a lot of money. It only looked like gold. It had a little painting of my mum and papa inside."

"Sorry." Emma looked down.

They turned a corner, following a dingy grey rug down a long hallway toward the bedroom.

"I've a question," whispered Emma.

"Hmm?" Bree peered over at her.

"What did we eat tonight? Some of it was fish. Some wasn't."

Bree squirmed. "It's a giant bug from the ocean with two huge pinchers and a fat curly tail. Fisherman catch them in nets by accident all the time. No one wants them because they're ugly bugs. We get them because it's so cheap. I think the bugs are called lobsters or something like that. You'll eventually get used to the taste. Just don't think about it being a bug."

"It didn't taste bad." Emma licked her teeth.

They entered the bedroom. The other orphans all froze and got quiet for a few seconds. Upon realizing only Emma and Bree walked in, they resumed talking in whispers.

Bree pointed to the right. "I'll be over at my bed if you have any more questions or need anything."

"All right. Thank you." Emma smiled at her.

Bree didn't smile back, though she appeared slightly less sad for a moment before heading off to her bed.

This place... Emma sighed out her nose and walked to her bed a few spaces to the left of the door.

Kimber and Ambril sat cross-legged on the beds, which now had blankets and pillows. Ambril appeared thoroughly miserable in the drab grey orphan dress. Kimber curled up with her chin on her knees, hiding her face behind her fluffy hair.

Emma sat on the edge of the bed and put an arm around her sister.

"What happened to you?" whispered Ambril.

"Tea." Emma explained having to serve tea to guests. "Nothing bad."

"I've been kidnapped eight times." Ambril scratched at the top of her foot. "This is by far the scariest, and one time they tied me up and put me inside a coffin."

Emma widened her eyes. "Really?"

"Really this is the scariest or really they put me in a coffin?" asked Ambril.

"Umm. Both?"

"Yes. The kidnappers hid out in an undertaker's parlor." Ambril frowned. "They had the undertaker and his family locked up in the basement."

"How awful." Emma shivered. "How did you get out?"

"Luck." Ambril exhaled hard. "Some of the Calebrin guard came in to purchase a casket for a dead guardsman who didn't have any family. They had no idea the people in the room weren't undertakers. The kidnappers pretended to sell them a casket. I heard them talking. As soon as I realized guards walked in, I screamed."

"That's scarier than this." Emma glared. "This place isn't scary. It's sad and cruel."

"I fink it's scary." Kimber hugged her. "I donnae wan' tae go real prison. This loike prison fer kids. Nae as bad."

Ambril winced. "The box has to be ready by now. Or soon. We have to get out of here before something happens to us."

"Nae yet." Kimber grumbled. "Takes ae 'ole day. We only been 'ere loike five hours."

"The matron is doing bad things." Emma rubbed Kimber's back. "I don't want to just leave. At dinner, I saw a girl with shackle burns on her wrists. She kept fainting at the table like she hasn't slept in days."

Ambril covered her mouth. "I saw that girl, too."

"The matron is basically selling a boy to a ship crew. They're gonna make him work on a boat for three months." Emma raised and lowered her toes. "It's too dangerous for a boy. Even the matron kept telling the men they better bring him back alive and without missing any parts."

"Eep." Ambril trembled. "How awful! Are you seriously thinking about sneaking away from here to get the boy off the ship?"

"No. He didn't go yet. A few days. I have time." Emma narrowed her eyes.

"Father can fix it once we get home." Ambril pounded her fist into the mattress. "I'll demand he buy this whole place and make it nice."

"Heron doesn't have time to wait for us to get home or for your father to travel here." Emma bit her lip. "And what if he doesn't care? We're in a whole other kingdom. Your father has a lot of money… but people here don't have to listen to him."

Kimber squeezed her. "What are you gon' do? Frow the ol' bat outta winda?"

The distant scream of an older woman broke the stillness of Wavecrest Manor. It sounded like the sort of cry the matron might have made if someone dropped her into a giant cauldron of boiling water. All the orphans gazed around in wonder at the echoing wail. The scream lasted a rather long time before stopping… then happened again. A *thud* followed the second scream, then a bunch of banging and clattering. The commotion sounded far away, on the other side of the manor and upstairs.

Emma burst out laughing. Bree managed a faint giggle.

"Why are you laughing?" whispered a girl across the room from Emma in the other bed row.

Ten or so beds to the right, Bree already explained to the girls near her what Emma did with the mice. *So much for secrets.* Emma shared the story with everyone close enough to hear. Kimber mushed her face into their pathetic little pillow, trying to keep her laughter quiet enough to avoid getting in trouble. Ambril appeared equally horrified and gratified. Some of the orphans didn't believe Emma could talk to mice. Bree kept insisting the story was true. She came off as earnest enough for the others to give up questioning it.

After all, the horrible matron *was* screaming like a banshee. She'd never done anything like it before, and no other explanation made sense unless a thief had broken into her room.

"If you really did that," said a smallish six-year-old from a bed near the leftmost end of the room. "You're gonna be in huge trouble."

"The matron won't even think I had anything to do with a bunch of mice crawling all over her, getting into her hair, all over her bed, up under her nightgown." Emma grinned. "Walking on her face."

Most of the orphan girls squirmed and gasped at the thought of being covered in mice.

Kimber finally managed to stop laughing. She rolled over onto her back. "I still fink ya should toss 'er out a winda."

"No." Emma still wanted to thump the woman for scaring her little sister so much she cried and called for Mama despite being so far away from home. Throwing the matron out a window might make her feel better… until it made her feel guilty. It also wouldn't do anything more than turn the woman meaner. For now, she'd have to settle for scaring the life out of her with a swarm of mice. "If the guards find out what she's doing, they'll throw her in prison."

"The guards might be bad," whispered Kimber. "They took us 'ere."

Emma tried to brush her sister's hair using her fingers since they didn't have anything else. *Her father was a thief and a criminal. He taught her not to trust guards.* "I should at least try first. Remember what Mama said. If something is wrong and it's too big for us, we tell her or Da. If we can't find them, we tell one of the Watch."

"The Watch nae 'ere." Kimber shifted around on the bed so Emma could get at all of her hair. The girl adored having her hair brushed. Already, she seemed much calmer. "Big city guards nae the Watch. They kin be bad as thieves. E'ryone home knows the Watch. Big city guard donnae know anyone."

"Maybe." Emma sighed. "It's wrong to hurt people, even mean old witches who are cruel to children."

The bedroom door opened. Again, every orphan in the room froze and got quiet.

Sela walked in. The maybe sixteen-year-old gazed around the room almost as if she pretended to be the matron, making the same dour face. The other girls all scrambled back to their beds in a panic, certain someone was about to get dragged off to punishment for the mouse invasion.

However, Sela appeared too calm to have been sent to collect a specific wrongdoer. Her visit to this room appeared to be a normal inspection of sorts.

She wants to make sure no one's having any fun... or smiling. Emma scowled.

The teen wandered to the right, looking back and forth at the bed rows. Upon reaching the end of the room, she turned around and made her way past the door at the middle, soon stopping near Emma's bed.

Sela glanced across the row at the unclaimed mattress, back at them, then frowned, plucking at the *two* blankets on Emma's bed.

As much as Emma wanted to glare defiantly back at her, if she ended up locked in a basement cell, she couldn't do anything to save Rin, stop the matron from selling Heron to a ship, or work on getting the box back. So, she forced herself to look down and act timid.

"One of you has to move over there." Sela pointed at the unclaimed mattress. "You both can't use one bed."

"No," whimpered Kimber, barely over a whisper. She twisted around and clamp-hugged Emma.

Grr. Emma looked up at the older girl. "Why?"

Sela leaned back, both eyebrows up. "What?"

"I said 'why.'" Emma fought really hard to keep her expression blank and not let her anger show. Sometimes, she definitely had a little too much of Mama in her. "Why can't we share a bed? She's my sister and she's only eight. Why would anyone care? We always share a bed at home. She doesn't like to sleep by herself."

"I said 'what' because I am shocked. You aren't supposed to challenge me." Sela folded her arms. "What I say goes in here."

Emma gingerly peeled Kimber's arms out from around her, then stood. "You're not in charge."

A few gasps came from the other girls.

Rage flared across the teen's eyes. "I am Matron Wavecrest's favorite. I am the head assistant. As far as you are concerned, I am in charge."

"'Cause you as mean as she is," muttered Kimber.

Soft gasps of shock came from the orphans. Bree clamped a hand over her mouth, staring across the room at Emma with an 'oh no!' expression.

Sela glowered at Kimber. It definitely looked as if her little sister would spend the rest of tonight in the punishment room... unless Emma got the girl's attention completely focused on her instead.

This place really is like prison. Maybe I should *thump the biggest, meanest girl here.* Emma made fists. *Uruleth, please grant me strength.* "I'm not afraid of you." She stepped around the end of the bed, putting herself between the older girl and Kimber. "Leave us alone. Go mind your business."

About a third of the other girls gave an, 'oooh!' in whispers.

"Listen here, new brat." Sela pointed at her. "I don't know where you came from or who you think you are, but you do *not* want to make an enemy of me. I can make your time here good or bad, and right now, I'm thinking it's going to be bad."

"You don't scare me." Emma leaned forward. "You're almost grown up and you're being mean to smaller kids? That's sad. You should be trying to protect the smaller ones."

Sela slapped Emma across the face, almost knocking her onto the bed.

The room fell deathly silent.

Cheek stinging, Emma straightened herself and narrowed her eyes.

"Don't glare at me, you scrawny little ragamuffin." Sela leaned down, almost nose to nose with her. "You're going to spend a week in the room for that mouth."

Emma kept glaring, way too furious to cry at the pain from being hit.

Sela grinned. "Aww, the tiny little thing is angry. You want another one? Maybe if you apologize properly, it'll only be you in punishment and not your pretend sister as well."

A little snarl slipped out of Emma's mouth.

"Ooh. She's growling at me now. What are you going to do, *baby?*"

Emma screamed in rage—and punched the older girl in the face.

The hit flung Sela off her feet. She landed flat on her back and slid over the hardwood floor, stopping three bed-lengths away, more or less by the door, nearly unconscious. Blood dribbled from the teen's nostrils. She babbled nonsense, reaching up to grab empty air above her.

Every girl in the room stared dumbfounded at Emma.

"Oh, no," whimpered Kimber. "You'as gonna be locked up inna cell tonight."

"*Tonight?* It's going to be a month at least," whispered the girl in the bed next to Ambril's on the left.

Still shaking from anger, Emma closed her eyes. *Not going to cry. It's not a big deal. I can handle being locked in a dark cell. It's not scarier than a banderwigh chasing me with an axe. I can't let them put Kimber in there.*

The bedroom hung in tense silence. Ambril covered her face in both hands, peering between her fingers, eyes wide as saucers. A few minutes later, Sela emerged from her daze, rolled over onto all fours, and crawled for the door. Other orphans in the room started laughing at her, though not too loud. Sela crawled faster, face red. She seemed to be crying... which made the girls laugh more.

"You may as well try to run away now," said a not-quite-thirteen-year-old in the bed to the right of Emma's. "It isn't like you'd get in any worse trouble."

"No. I'm not going to run away." Emma looked around at the others. "I'll be fine. The matron doesn't scare me, either. She's cruel, and I'm going to stop her from hurting everyone."

"What's that little thing going to do?" whispered a girl on the other side of the room.

"She walloped Sela good," replied another orphan nearby. "Unbelievable. Knocked her right over."

"And she made Matron Wavecrest scream," whispered another girl somewhere in the crowd. "If you believe she can talk to mice."

"Good for her." A seven-year-old made a spitting sound.

UNBELIEVABLE

*E*mma stood at the foot of her bed, waiting to be dragged off to the punishment room.

She worried about Rin, mostly what would happen if the girl left the box and the matron caught her. The older woman did *not* seem to like elves. She likely would not react too kindly to a *dark* elf. Perhaps they'd be lucky and Matron Wavecrest would run screaming rather than be nasty to her. Then again, the three of them used the last of the magic to leave the box. Rin might be trapped in there until the magic recharged. Perhaps the dark elf girl *couldn't* get out until the box was ready.

Emma also worried about Kimber. Having to sleep in this awful place would have been bad enough with each other to cling to. Now, she'd be alone in the bed while Emma stood in a dungeon cell with her arms chained up over her head.

No. I can get out. She smiled to herself. If she shapeshifted into a wolf pup, she'd slip free of any manacles. Depending on what happened in the next few minutes, she'd either pretend to tolerate the matron's punishment or she'd set off an all-out rebellion. Inside a house like this, she couldn't make use of Linganthas' power and summon roots from the ground. The thorn whip spell, the one she used to slay the hideous fish, would work because it flew from her hand... but only if she needed to fight for her life. That spell tried to kill whatever it hit. She could invoke the wrath of the elders, throwing yellowish lightning bolts like Mama. The spell would make her tired fairly fast, so she couldn't do it too many times. Also, it had the same problem as the thorn whip, being a deadly spell. She didn't want to kill or seriously hurt the matron. Not to mention, Emma could get in *serious* trouble with the guards for using magic like that unless she needed to defend herself from a real threat. No matter how cruel the matron was, unless she tried to take Emma's life, hurling an eldritch bolt at the old witch would only make things much worse for her.

Tears threatened to fall down her face as fear started to overtake anger. She wanted Mama, Nan, or Da to rush in and make everything better.

The door opened. Unfortunately, it wasn't Mama, Nan, or Da who entered... but Matron Wavecrest, Sela, and Morwenna. Sela had a dark bruise on her face to the left of her nose. Matron Wavecrest appeared moderately disheveled, her hair a bird's nest. Her black dress appeared to have been quite hastily put on, not fastened properly. Morwenna wore a long white nightdress that hung to the floor, with rumpled frills at the collar and cuffs. She continuously kneaded her hands together in front of her generous stomach, unable to look anyone in the eye.

Every orphan in the room stopped moving, bowed their heads... and probably held their breath. They'd all witnessed Emma punch Sela. There'd be no denying it. The only question would be how many weeks the punishment lasted.

Matron Wavecrest glanced around. The woman seemed furious and a little bit frightened. A lone mouse crawled out of her hair to perch atop her head, sniffing at the air. Some of the girls spotted it and clamped their hands over their mouths, desperate not to make a sound.

"Her." Sela pointed at Emma.

The matron's hard-heeled boots clacked on the floor as she walked closer. She seemed oblivious to the mouse sitting on her head. Sela didn't notice it either. Morwenna gawked. She reached out as if to tap the woman on the arm and tell her, but chickened out.

Emma widened her eyes, trying to look forlorn in hopes she might only get one week of punishment.

The mouse looked down at her.

Matron Wavecrest lifted Emma's chin by one finger, studying her face. "Sela, why is there a red hand mark on this child's face?"

Sela stammered. "I... she was insolent. Talked back to me. Refused to obey. What she said was beyond. I... lost control of myself."

"You slapped her." Matron Wavecrest lowered her hand and peered back at Sela.

"Down," squeaked Emma in mouse. "Get off her before she finds you."

The mouse jumped from the woman's head, landed on Emma's chest, and scampered around to hide under her hair behind her neck, then whisper-squeaked, "We did as you asked. We all got away. None are hurt."

Good. "Thank you."

Speaking to a mouse likely sounded as if she nervously sucked air through her teeth. No one appeared to notice.

"She said things on purpose." Sela swallowed. "She wanted me to hit her. Then she did this to me!" The teen pointed at the bruise. "Nearly killed me. The girl hit me so hard I half lost consciousness. Lucky to still be alive. She knocked me straight off my feet. I couldn't even stand back up for a while."

Matron Wavecrest continued staring at the sixteen-year-old for a few seconds, looked at Emma, then back at Sela. "You are trying to tell me that this tiny little elf of a thing did that to you?"

"She did." Sela pointed at her.

Emma squeezed Kimber's hand to say goodbye for the night... or the week. Perhaps the month. Any second now, the matron would ask what happened and she'd admit to thumping her.

"Girls." Matron Wavecrest turned in place, casting her gaze around the room. "All of you. Look at me."

Whatever mirth came from the errant mouse in the woman's hair died in an instant. Every girl in the room stood up straight, expressions grim enough for a funeral.

"Is what Sela says true?" asked Matron Wavecrest. "Did this little one here truly hit her so hard she fell over and nearly blacked out?"

Emma drew in a breath to say, 'yes Matron Wavecrest,' but before she could, Bree and three girls near her blurted, "No, Matron Wavecrest."

The rest of the orphans all chorused, "No Matron Wavecrest" at the same time.

Sela's cheeks turned as pale as death.

"I thought not." Matron Wavecrest folded her arms. "What I think, dear Sela, is that you lost control of your anger and struck one of my children. Then, in hopes of avoiding consequences, you threw yourself face-first into a bed post and made up a story no sane person could ever believe."

"No..." Sela shivered. "Please! I'm not lying. It's true. I don't know how she did it, but she did it. They are all lying to you."

Emma ground her toes into the floor, unable to believe that *all* the girls in the room lied to help her. Bree said every orphan here would immediately tattle to save themselves from the punishment room. However, she also said they rather hated the assistants, too. Clearly, every one of them disliked Sela almost as much as they hated the matron, enough to risk punishment to get the teen in trouble.

"All of them?" Matron Wavecrest raised an eyebrow. "I find that even more difficult to believe than your story of a tiny wisp like this girl knocking you over."

Sela pointed around at the girls. "They're lying. They're all lying. They hate me. You know they hate me."

Morwenna looked up from the floor, making eye contact with Emma.

Emma nodded once.

Morwenna raised both eyebrows and mouthed 'no...'

Emma mouthed, 'I did.'

"Do not take that tone with me, girl." Matron Wavecrest swooped over to Sela. "You have spent the past five years being an exemplary assistant. I do not know what has come over you to suddenly want to destroy everything you have worked for with such an unbelievable lie and *striking* one of the children. It pains me, but rules are rules. You will spend the next three nights in the punishment room for lying, for striking one of my children, and being disrespectful to me."

Emma gasped in shock. She clamped both hands over her mouth. If the older girl hadn't been so awful—and called Kimber her 'pretend sister,' she might have blurted the truth. However, the matron wouldn't believe her without a demonstration. Emma didn't want to hit anyone again—except maybe the matron—and if she could stay out of punishment, she could work on her plans.

Sela deserves a little punishment for being so mean to everyone.

"But..." Sela broke down in sobs, trembling. "Please, no. Please don't put me in the room. I'll do extra service time. I'll do extra chores. Anything you ask. Just not that. Please, not that."

Matron Wavecrest rested a hand on the teen's shoulder. "I am not unreasonable. Everyone has bad moments. I know how frustrating insolent children can be. You should have come to me straight away and admitted you lost control of yourself. Accept your punishment with dignity knowing you did wrong and I shall forget the entirety of this discretion. Whether you retain your status as my head assistant is entirely up to how you conduct yourself over the next three days."

Sela clasped her hands in front of herself and bowed her head, crying and shaking. "Yes, Matron Wavecrest."

Emma raised an eyebrow. The older girl acted far more frightened than seemed necessary for simply being locked in a dark room. Could a girl her age really believe monsters lurked in the dark?

"Now, go. You know where." The matron pointed at the door.

Sela, sniffling and sniveling, trudged out. The matron followed close behind.

Morwenna remained in the room for a few seconds, staring in confusion.

"Why are you afraid of her?" mouthed Emma.

Seeming overwhelmed, the woman grimaced and hurried out, pulling the door shut behind her.

The orphans all jumped around, trying to celebrate and cheer while making as little noise as possible. Emma plucked the mouse from behind her neck and set him gently on the floor. He scurried off into the shadows.

Kimber jumped on Emma's back, clinging with arms and legs. "I donnae believe wot 'appened."

"Nor do I." Emma exhaled out her nose. "Is it still lying if I said nothing?"

"I think so." Ambril shrugged. "Does it matter? She wouldn't have believed you, anyway. I think it's lucky she became so distracted being angry at that other girl she never thought to ask you directly if you did it."

"I'as kinda feel bad for 'er." Kimber rested her chin on Emma's shoulder.

"Yeah." Emma sighed. "I'm going to go tell the truth."

Before she could take two steps, Ambril grabbed her, holding her back. Kimber dropped down and also held her.

"No. She won't believe you." Ambril shook her head. "And if she finds out that all these other girls lied, everyone will get in trouble."

Emma cringed. "Oh. Yes. You're right. I won't say anything."

Giddy whispering continued among the other girls as they all scurried to their beds.

A thirteen-year-old with long, unkempt brown hair hurried over to the bed next to them on the right. "Get under your blanket. If you get caught out of bed after bedtime..."

"Punishment room," whispered Kimber.

"Yes." The girl shivered. "I guess we're neighbors. I'm Merela. Can't believe you walloped Sela like that. She deserved it."

"I'm Emma." She crawled under their double blanket.

Kimber curled up against her side.

Ambril got in her bed. "It's so stiff and uncomfortable." She squirmed. "How can anyone sleep on this?"

"After you spend a night in the punishment room," said the girl in the bed to Ambril's left, a nine-year-old named Pearl, "these beds start to feel like what a queen would sleep on."

"I'll not be punished." Ambril shook her head.

"Everyone says that," replied Pearl. "They'll make stuff up for you to get in trouble for. We've all been in there at least once. Matron wants us to know what it's like, so we're extra scared of being sent down there again. You have'ta stay quiet or the monsters will get you. Can't even cry, 'cause they'll hear."

"Em..." Ambril looked over at her. "I don't like this place. Please get us out of here."

"You two can't be in the same bed," whispered Merela. "You'll both get in trouble for it."

"Kimber is my sister. I'm not going to sleep away from her if she's too scared to have a bed to herself."

Merela sat up, half her face hidden behind a curtain of her messy hair. "One of you can have this bed, so you're next to each other. I can move across the way if you help me swap the tables."

"Thank you." Emma also sat up. "Maybe. It can wait for now. We're not going to stay here long."

Merela made an 'everyone says that' face at her. "Are you sure?"

"Yes. We can move tables around tomorrow." Emma slid out of bed and kissed Kimber atop the head. "I'm going to go find help. Stay here and be quiet. I'll be back soon."

"Eep!" Merela shook her head. "Don't leave the room after bedtime. You'll get in *so* much trouble."

Emma padded around her bed to stand beside the older girl. "We are *already* in a lot of trouble. The matron isn't taking care of us. She's using us to make money and she enjoys being cruel. Sela did everything perfect for five years and that woman *still* smiled, watching her beg for mercy. None of us are safe here. The matron is evil... and I'm going to stop her."

"Be careful," whispered Kimber.

"All right." Merela swept her hair off her face, tucking it behind her ears. "If you're going to be stupid and leave the room after bedtime, the least I can do is warn you. Look out for Groundskeeper Terle. He wanders the halls until midnight. Morwenna wakes up a lot at night and goes for walks in the halls. Also, be wary of assistants. Morwenna isn't too bad. She'll usually only drag a kid back to their bedroom and not report them for trouble. Anyone else, you'll get punished. Especially Groundskeeper Terle. I swear Matron Wavecrest pays that man a bounty every time he gets someone punished. He seems so happy to catch us."

"Assistants?" Emma tilted her head. "Aren't they in bed?"

Merela gestured at the door. "Not all of them. One of their chores is to check on us a few times a night to make sure everyone's here, look if anyone's sick, and make sure no one's still awake. In short, if there's anyone or anything moving in the halls after bedtime, don't let them see you."

"All right. Thanks." Emma exhaled. "I should be okay, but if I get caught, please watch out for Kimber until I'm back."

"I will." Merela lay back down.

Emma crept over to the door and listened to silence. Once confident she wouldn't get caught right away, she gingerly turned the knob and peeked out at an empty hall.

Ylithir watch over me. Here I go.

32

AN UNLIKELY FRIEND

*E*mma crept along in the dark, heading down the hallway.
A handful of oil lamps high up on wall mounts gave off enough light for her to avoid bumping into any doorknobs or walls. She wouldn't be able to see a person much farther than thirty feet away as anything more than a shadowy form. However, this also meant anyone else wouldn't be able to recognize her.

She set her feet down as carefully as if trying to walk across a frozen lake. Speed didn't matter as much as staying quiet. This manor house had many long corridors without branching passages. Such hallways offered nowhere to hide in a hurry. If someone appeared up ahead or behind her, she'd have no choice but to run to the nearest corner or risk going through a door. The few small tables and bench seats scattered around weren't big enough to hide under. She'd be spotted right away.

Her plan, at least for the moment, sounded simple enough. Find the front door—or perhaps kitchen door to the yard—get outside, and go find a city guard. They'd have to believe her. The other girls didn't seem to think the guards would care. One even said going for help had been tried before and the guards merely returned the runaway to the orphanage. She might be foolish for thinking guards would believe her and not the other kids who tried getting help. However, she grew up in Widowswood, where the town watch truly cared about everyone. She couldn't fully believe guards who swore to defend the city could ignore children being tormented and mistreated like this. She hoped the guards only happened to be lazy and didn't really believe the stories, thinking the kids made it up. Emma *had* to at least try doing things the proper way before taking matters into her own hands. If the guards wouldn't help her, then she'd have no choice but to seek help from the forest spirits.

Wrapping Matron Wavecrest up in thorny vines would certainly be one way to change the woman's attitude. Before she did anything like that, she needed to make sure she had no other possible choice.

Moving lantern light flickered from around a corner up ahead. Emma stopped, trying to hold as still as possible. She had less than a second to decide between dashing forward to the nearest corner or retreating back the way she came around a different corner. The corner ahead would be a shorter run, but also require her going *toward* the patrolling lantern. Back required covering three times the distance, though it kept her in the dark.

A shadowy figure stepped out from a corner at the end of the hall. His slightly forward-hunched posture, bushy, shaggy hair, and constant low muttering made no secret of his identity: Groundskeeper Terle.

Emma kept creeping backward.

The groundskeeper raised his lantern. "Who's that? I see ya, little one."

Eep! Emma dashed away from him, running as fast as she could go on her toes to make less noise. Groundskeeper Terle grumbled and came tromping after her.

As soon as Emma went around the corner, she jumped forward, stretching her hands out to catch the floor as she shapeshifted into a wolf pup. She landed on her paws and peered back at the approaching lamplight. The plain grey dress she'd been wearing lay empty on the floor behind her.

Uh oh. Emma nipped at the fabric, hastily bundling it up into a wad she could pick up in her teeth, then scurried under the bench. A child couldn't fit under it and stay hidden. As a little wolf, though, the hiding place worked—as long as no one took a knee and peeked under it.

Groundskeeper Terle stomped around the corner three seconds after she stopped moving.

He kept on going right past her without even hesitating. "Where'd ya go, ya little rascal? Come out and show yourself. Be a lot less bad for you if ya give up."

Whew. Emma rested her chin on her paws, waiting for her heart to stop racing.

The groundskeeper returned seconds later. He opened every door in the hallway around where Emma hid, peeking in to the rooms, muttering about 'ungrateful kids' and 'misbehaving brats' to himself the whole time. After a long several minutes, he wandered off muttering about seeing things, questioning if he really had seen a girl out after bedtime or only imagined it. He didn't think it possible an orphan could have escaped him, so it must have been his mind playing games.

Emma waited another minute, then scurried out from under the bench. She dragged the dress out flat, then nudged it with her nose to roll it up more neatly. Figuring she'd be much less likely to get caught if she stayed as a wolf, she picked the dress up in her teeth and trotted along.

The manor house seemed three times as massive and even more maze-like from the view of a wolf pup, lower to the ground. She wandered back and forth down the hallways in search of anything that looked like a way to an outside door. Too many 'person smells' saturated everything for her to pick up on any individual, not that she tried to follow people specifically. Twice more, she retreated from a moving lantern glow, disappearing around corners before whoever carried the light made it into view.

It started to feel like the patrolling groundskeeper and older teens somehow knew what she wanted to do and constantly showed up at the wrong time to chase her away from any hallway leading to an exit.

It occurred to her she'd mostly gotten herself lost in the complicated set of hallways. So, she decided to pick a direction and keep trying to go that way as much as possible.

Minutes later, she rounded a corner into a dead-end hallway with four doors. Two went left, one went right, and the last door sat at the end of the hall.

This isn't right.

She started to back up until noticing the sound of soft crying coming from the end door. Human ears wouldn't have noticed it. Concerned, she scurried to the end of the hall. The last person to go through the door hadn't closed it all the way. Emma pawed at the wood until she managed to get it open enough to slip her head in.

A stairwell behind the door led down.

Fear made the fur along her back stand on end. The need to help whoever cried chipped away at her dread until she found herself moving forward. Emma skittered down the stairs, wolf paws not having the easiest time on polished hardwood. She managed to avoid slipping or falling as she descended to a landing, then took a second set of steps down to a dirt-floored area bathed in total darkness.

The soft crying came from the dark straight ahead, along with faint metallic clinking and a small voice occasionally grunting or gasping as though they tried to lift something heavy.

Emma shapeshifted back to human form, on her hands and knees with the dress still in her mouth. She reached up, plucked the garment out of her teeth, then sat back on her heels, whispering, "Mythandriel, send me your light."

A small orb of glowing energy appeared floating in circles around her. It illuminated a stone-walled corridor going about twenty feet farther ahead to a wooden door. Six more wooden doors stood close together, three on each side.

Fearing she might need to jump back into wolf form at any second if someone came down there, Emma kept holding her rolled-up dress. She approached the first door on the left. It had a small, square window too high up for her to see into, so she instead peered through the large keyhole.

In a tiny closet-sized room with stone walls and a dirt floor, Sela stood shivering against the left wall. Her hands dangled above her head, locked in manacles affixed to a metal bolt embedded in the mortar. A thin trickle of blood ran down her right arm to the elbow. The teen sniffled and wept, looking nothing like the cruel junior matron she'd been earlier. Light from Mythandriel's orb leaking in the tiny window appeared to confuse and frighten her. She squirmed, struggling at the manacles, making the iron rattle.

"Shh," whispered Emma. "It's only me."

Sela gave a soft whimper, as if afraid to speak.

Emma glanced to her right at the corridor. The other five close-spaced doors had to be more punishment rooms. At the end, the last door might be another cell or perhaps lead to a normal basement. She sensed nothing worse in the air than the ordinary unease of being in a dark place. Certainly, if there truly had been monsters waiting in the dark to attack children trapped in these tiny rooms, they'd already be coming after her. She'd also likely sense them. As a wolf cub, she'd heard nothing to make her think any sort of creatures lived down here.

"Sela," whispered Emma, shifting her gaze back into the keyhole. "There are no monsters. The matron lied to you."

The older girl lapsed into a frantic struggle, trying to pull the chain out of the wall. For a few seconds, she appeared completely lost to panic before regaining enough sense of reason to understand she couldn't break the iron manacles. Sniffling, she went still.

"There are no monsters," said Emma at a normal volume.

"Shh!" rasped Sela. "They'll get you."

Emma dropped her rolled up dress, then reached up to grab the bottom of the window before pulling herself up high enough to peek through so Sela could see her face. "I'm sorry she put you in there. I wanted to tell the truth."

"Why didn't you?" whimpered Sela.

"She wouldn't have believed me. You know that. And if she did, all the other girls would've gotten punished for lying. You don't have to be scared. Nothing down here is going to hurt you."

"I'm afraid of the dark," whimpered Sela. "I've been terrified of the dark ever since I was little. It's so much worse when I'm helpless. I get so scared I can't even think anymore and just panic."

"How many other kids did you help her put down here?"

Sela sobbed. "I'm sorry. What was I supposed to do? She liked me for some reason. Gave me special chores. Put me in charge of other kids. I was always so scared of ending up in here again."

"Again?" Emma blinked. "Aren't you her favorite?"

"The day I arrived here, I couldn't stop crying. Both of my parents died in the same week. Matron Wavecrest told me to stop sobbing, but I couldn't, so she locked me up down here. I was only six and already dreadfully afraid of the dark. I remember being so scared the monsters would hear me." Sela started to breathe faster and faster, shaking.

She's the one Wavecrest told us about. One of two orphans who got punishment on their first day here. "It's okay. You're safe. No monsters." Emma grunted. "My arms are tired. I'm still here, just gotta go down." She lowered herself back to her feet. "Want me to break you out?"

Sela's ragged breathing slowed. "Matron Wavecrest would be so angry. Even if you *could* somehow get me out of here, what would I do? Run away? It's only three nights. Then I can be an assistant again. She'll forget."

"Do you think you'll be okay after three nights? You're already shaking." Emma bit her lip. She totally understood the kind of fear this girl had for the dark. Spiders used to do the same thing to her. Da called it a 'phobia.'

"I…" Sela broke down sobbing.

"Do you really want to be her assistant?"

"No. I just didn't want to get punished. You don't understand. We *have* to do what she says."

"Why?"

"Because she'll lock us up down here."

"The entire orphanage? What if everyone disobeyed her? Would she squish hundreds of orphans into these six tiny rooms at the same time? Why is Morwenna afraid of her? Why is anyone afraid of her? Is she a demon or a mage or something?" Emma peered through the keyhole again.

Chains rattled as Sela wiped her tears on her sleeve. "No. I don't think so anyway. She's never done anything strange. Only cruel. Her family used to have a lot of power and money. She has connections."

"What does that mean?" asked Emma. "Connections?"

"It means she's friends with people who have political power. She could ask a favor of someone and totally ruin your whole life." Sela pulled at the manacles.

"Why did you help her?"

"I already told you." Sela sighed. "Are you trying to make me feel like more of a fool? What was I supposed to do when she told me to be her assistant?"

"You could've not been so mean about it." Emma frowned. "You sounded as cruel as she does. Why did you pick on me tonight?"

"Wasn't picking on you. You were breaking the rules. Two in one bed. If you'd have only listened to me right away, I wasn't even nasty with you." Sela bowed her head. "Matron Wavecrest doesn't like it when we're happy or feel loved. We're not even allowed to hug friends."

Emma wiped a tear.

Sela looked up. "Are you a demon?"

"No."

"How did you hit me so hard? And what's that light? How did you manage to get down here without being caught?"

Emma smiled. "I'm a druid. Sorta. Still learning. Not a full druid yet."

"A druid? I don't know what that means." Sela sniffled.

A whimper came from the door behind her.

"Moment," whispered Emma. She turned and took one step across the hall to peek through the other keyhole.

The same exhausted girl she saw at the dinner table with the red marks on her wrists hung from shackles on the wall of another tiny stone-walled closet, her arms pin straight above her head, not slack like Sela's. The girl, only seven or eight years old, dangled entirely by the manacles, her feet not even reaching the floor. She bawled, crying so hard snot bubbled out of her nostrils, though she made almost no sound. Thin trickles of blood crept down her forearms. Her hands looked purple. She continually scraped her heels at the wall in a futile attempt to lift her weight off the chains.

Emma's blood boiled at the sight. *Linganthas, send me your power!*

At her behest, a thick root sprang up from the dirt floor of the cell.

The child whimpered and started kicking at it.

"It's okay," said Emma, not whispering. "I'm going to help you. Don't be scared."

Emma grumbled to herself. She extended the root longer, growing it upward to grasp the bolt securing the shackle chain to the wall. The root coiled through the ring at the end, wrapped tight, and pulled. Gradually, a long iron rod slid out of the stonework. After a few seconds, it broke loose, allowing the little girl to drop straight down. She landed briefly on her feet, then collapsed. Her wrists remained shackled together, but at least she no longer hung off the ground. The child curled up in a ball, shaking.

Thank you, Linganthas. Emma shrank the root back into the dirt out of sight.

The girl whimpered.

"Are you okay?" asked Emma.

Again, the girl only whimpered.

"Isla won't talk," said Sela. "She's too scared of the monsters. And she's probably too tired to talk, anyway. She's been in there every night for four days already. Her third attempt to run away. Matron Wavecrest is really angry with her."

"I'm getting you out." Emma raised her arms at the door.

"No," whimpered Isla. "I'll get in more trouble. I'll get punished worse."

"You won't." Emma scowled. "I won't let her."

"Please don't. I gotta stay in here or I'm gonna get worse," whimpered Isla. "I'm gonna get in trouble again for breaking off the wall."

Emma paused to have a little daydream about wrapping Matron

Wavecrest up in thorny vines. Every whimper and sniffle from Isla made the idea seem more and more appropriate. "You won't get in trouble."

"I will!" wailed Isla.

Defeated, Emma hung her head. No point arguing with a child so terrified she couldn't think right. "All right. Fine. I don't want to scare you more, so if you really want to stay in there, I won't break the door. If I don't fix this place tonight, tell the witch it just broke. She won't believe you ripped it out of the wall."

"Fix it?" asked Sela. "What are you going to do?"

"Get the guards." Emma stooped to grab her rolled-up dress.

"The guards don't care. They think we're lying." Sela sniffled. "Other children have tried that already. All they do is take them back here and they get punished for running away and wasting the guard's time."

Emma paced, not at all liking the idea her plan might be completely futile. "I'm still going to fix this. I just have to figure out how."

"Hey," whispered Sela. "Are you still there?"

"Yes." Emma peered through the keyhole into Sela's chamber. "I'm still here."

"If the guards think you're lying, they won't help. You have to prove it to them. Matron Wavecrest has a log book where she keeps track of all the money she makes selling us to work for people. She's not supposed to do that. The guards won't care about orphans saying she mistreats us. They think we're making up stories. They *will* care about her not paying taxes on any of that money."

"Taxes?" Emma gasped. "It's basically slavery. That's wrong. Is slavery against the law here?"

"Yes, of course." Sela sighed. "But it's not slavery because she's not really selling us. She's selling our time. It's like working a job for money, only she keeps it all."

Emma frowned. "Not slavery, just selling time? That's something tricky people say to barristers so they can break the law without getting in trouble for it."

"If you say so." Sela tried unsuccessfully to pull her right hand out of the shackle.

"I can get you out if you want."

Sela shivered. "No. It's better for me to stay right here. I don't want to get punished worse."

"Okay. If I find this book and bring it to the guards, you think they will help?"

"Maybe. It's much more likely they will do something if you have the book than if you just go in there crying about cruel treatment."

"Help," said a soft childish voice from the second door on the right.

Emma turned to look. *Oh no. Another one?* She padded over to the cell, bringing her light orb along, and peered into the keyhole.

A boy about the same size as Emma, in terms of height, hung from manacles. His arms stretched tight over his head; his toes barely reached the ground. The boy alternated between letting most of his weight hang on his wrists or stretching to push himself up enough to give his arms a break. Longish light brown hair covered his face.

"Emma?" asked the boy. "Your name is Emma?"

"Yes."

He shook his head, trying to get his hair out of his eyes. "Did you really break Isla off the wall?"

"I did."

"Please, can you get me down, too? My arms hurt and my nose itches."

"Yes. One moment."

Emma called upon Linganthas once more, summoning a strong thornless root to reach up and tear the bolt out of the wall. As soon as the iron post broke free from between the bricks, the boy teetered forward, dropping to his hands and knees before sitting back on his heels and rubbing his nose furiously. A dagger-sized iron rod dangled from the chain between his wrists, bits of mortar still stuck to it.

"Wow. That's amazing. Thank you." The boy wiped tears on the back of his arm. "Are you sure there aren't any monsters?"

"Yes. They would have attacked me by now." Emma folded her

arms. "Do you want me to break the door, or would you rather stay locked up like the others?"

"I should stay inside. I don't want to, but it's better than getting a whole month of punishment. No one's ever escaped from the punishment room before. I don't want to know what she'd do to us."

"She loves us and doesn't believe in hitting children," said Sela in a sarcastic tone. "She won't slap us. She's much nicer. She'll only lock us up down here every night for a whole year."

"Umm. I'll stay in the cell." The boy shivered. "Emma?"

"Still here."

"Can you please do me another favor since you're a girl?"

"What does being a girl have to do with it?"

The boy looked up at the door, smiling even though he couldn't see her through the keyhole. "You can go to the girls' hall and not get in trouble."

"Oh. Okay. Sure. What do you want?"

"Tell my sister that I'm okay, and I miss her a lot."

Emma bit her lip. "Oh, you're the boy who got in trouble for trying to go into the girls' hall?"

"Yeah. That's why I'm in here. Four nights for my fourth time getting caught."

"That witch." Emma scowled. "Who is your sister?"

"Her name is Bree. I'm Morgan."

Emma stared at the door. *No wonder Bree looked so sad. She misses her brother. That witch is keeping their family apart. They only have each other.* "Grr. Okay. If you are absolutely sure you don't want me to let you out, I have to go. I'm going to fix it, so you never have to be locked up in here ever again."

"You may be right that there aren't any monsters." Sela sniffled. "I'm still so scared of the dark I may faint again. It's... maybe you should let me out."

"It's going to cause a lot of trouble," said Morgan. "The others will all tell on us because they'd get punished if they don't. We'll definitely get caught."

Emma stomped, leaving a small footprint in the dirt. "I hate this place. I will figure out a way to get you out of there before morning. Can you wait a little while more?"

"Yes." Sela exhaled.

"Uh huh," said Morgan.

Isla didn't respond.

Worried, Emma rushed to look in the keyhole. The little girl curled up on the dirt floor, sound asleep.

33

MORWENNA

*F*urious, Emma glared at the sleeping child, trying to melt the manacles off her by sheer anger.

After four nights of being hung on a wall, unable to sleep, the poor girl passed out within seconds. If she spent any more time looking at Isla, Emma wouldn't be able to stop herself from tearing the door off its hinges with a huge root. Children would certainly get caught sneaking around the halls of Wavecrest Manor at night. She'd be trying to help them but only get them all in worse trouble.

She couldn't allow the matron to know her days running this place had numbers on them until it became too late for her to stop Emma.

Children couldn't get through the corridors undetected, but a small wolf cub could.

Emma dropped to kneel on the floor. She placed her rolled-up dress in her teeth, leaned forward, and shapeshifted. She dismissed the light orb, which would definitely get her caught, and scurried up the steps. As soon as it became completely dark, Sela succumbed to another panic fit, fighting the shackles binding her to the wall.

Grr. I want to let her out. She's right. They'll get caught and the matron will know something is going on. It's already going to be suspicious two sets of chains fell off the wall. She's not going to believe Isla and Morgan broke themselves loose. They're too little. Not even Emma, with Uruleth's strength, could've done that.

Seeing the punishment rooms up close made Emma angrier than she'd ever been. Lucky for Matron Wavecrest, it hadn't been Kimber dangling off her feet in there. Isla looked pathetic enough to infuriate her, though family crossed another line entirely.

She trotted around the manor house, less and less concerned with getting caught. Even if someone did see her, they'd mistake her for a wolf and either shoo her out of the house or run away screaming. Shooing would be preferable than a lot of noise, so she decided to act like a friendly dog and start wagging her tail in the event someone caught her.

After a while of roaming around making random turns, she managed to find her way to the main foyer. Two large windows flanked the front door of the manor house. She trotted over to the door, wolf-claws clicking on the hard floor. Alas, the front door had not been left open like the one leading to the basement. She couldn't paw it out of her way. A wolf cub couldn't open doors or unlatch deadbolts. Emma would need to briefly resume her human shape for that part.

Someone might see her trying to leave.

The matron obviously knew the children here hated her and wanted to escape. Her excessive punishment for running away proved it. She probably had someone watching the courtyard out front all night long. She'd have to make herself human only long enough to open the door, then turn into a wolf again before running outside. If a teenage assistant saw a small black wolf zoom across the courtyard, they wouldn't care. Of course, if someone walked into the foyer at the exact moment she opened the door, she'd have a difficult time explaining why she ran around after bedtime with nothing on.

It won't even take a whole minute. She listened to silence. Looked around. Listened more, then stared up at the deadbolt and doorknob.

Okay. No one is here. Time to—

Thudding footsteps came down the hall at an unhurried pace.

Drat.

Emma tucked herself against the wall and waited, hoping her black fur would keep her hidden in the shadows.

Morwenna walked in from the left, still in her long nightdress. She carried an oil lamp in one hand, a thick book tucked under her other arm. The woman appeared sleepy and not on alert for wayward orphans.

Emma stared at her, watching her cross the foyer.

A little short of halfway across, Morwenna stopped—and looked right at her.

Uh oh. Emma rose to stand and wagged her tail. *I'm not a vicious wolf. Just a dog. Please don't scream.*

Morwenna blinked. "Aww. Aren't you just the most *adorable* little furball!" She set her book on a nearby table and hurried over, scooping Emma up in one hand. "What's in your mouth, little one? Did you swipe someone's shirt?"

"Mrrf," said Emma, past the dress in her teeth.

"Ooh. Someone's so cute!" Morwenna squish-hugged her. "Aww, you poor little pup. You're too small to be on your own? How did you get in here? Oh, it doesn't matter." She touched noses with Emma, waving her head side to side and making cutesy noises.

Someone... help... me...

"Come on then, love. I'll take care of you. It'll be all right." The woman cradled Emma to her shoulder, retrieved her book, and hurried off into the hall. "You can stay here. I'll feed you and protect you and keep you warm."

Emma stared over the woman's shoulder at the front door getting farther and farther away. *Well, that didn't work. Yes, they'll either shoo me outside or scream. I was not expecting this.*

Morwenna carried her down the hall, around a left turn, then a right, then to almost the last door on the right, which led into a moderately large bedroom. Paintings of dogs and cats decorated the walls around six bookshelves full to the point of sagging. An overwhelming fragrance of floral potpourri made the air thick to her canine nose.

Emma glanced around at the bookshelves, the animal paintings, a giant four-poster bed with canopy, at least eight pillows, three lit oil lamps on a desk, a wall shelf, and a little table by the door. One well-used wingback chair stood against the wall opposite the bed, nestled between two more small tables stacked high with books the room had no more shelf space for.

"Here we are, sweetie. This is going to be your home." Morwenna set the oil lamp she carried down on the desk.

Too many lamps for this many books. I hope she's really careful with the flame.

Morwenna grasped Emma in both hands and held her up, nose to nose again, making cute noises. "You're such a pretty fuzzball. Hmm. I've never seen a little doggie with blue eyes before."

She seems really sweet and nice. Maybe I should try talking to her now that we're away from the witch.

Emma shapeshifted back to human form, still hanging in the woman's grasp with the rolled-up dress in her teeth.

Morwenna stood there in shock, holding her off the floor, one hand under each of Emma's arms. She blinked. The woman appeared an inch or two away from fainting. She didn't. After a moment of baffled staring, she lowered Emma to her feet.

Emma plucked the dress out of her mouth, unrolled it, and pulled it on. "Can we please talk?"

"You were a dog." Morwenna pointed at her.

"Wolf. Pup, but still a wolf." Emma smiled. "Don't be scared."

"I am not scared. I'm confused. I've never had an orphan turn into a wolf before."

Emma clasped her hands in front of herself. "I'm not an orphan."

"Are you a real child?"

"Yes. I'm a person. Just not an orphan. I have parents, and they very much want me."

Morwenna glanced behind her, then backed up a few steps to sit on the edge of the bed. She patted the spot next to her. "We can talk."

Smiling, Emma darted over to sit beside her. Given the difference in their size, she couldn't help but feel like a cub next to a bear. If only she could find the 'mama bear' in this woman and wake her up. "Why are you scared of Matron Wavecrest?"

"Scared? I…" Morwenna looked down.

"You are. I've watched you. I can tell you're nice. You care about the orphans. Every time Wavecrest does something cruel, you look like you're about to tell her to stop… and you never do."

Morwenna opened her mouth, closed it. Opened it again, closed it. Sighed. Then looked down. "I suppose you're right. I am afraid. Not so much of her. She has political power. Family influence. I have nothing. If she says the wrong thing to the wrong people, I could be run out of town. Left in the street. I do what I can to make life more bearable for the children. Without me here, I fear it would be worse."

"Do you know about the punishment rooms?"

Morwenna swiped a handkerchief off the table and dabbed a tear. "Yes. I feel horrible about how that woman mistreats the children."

"Why don't you do something about it?"

"I don't know." Morwenna dabbed her other eye. "I keep meaning to. Then she glares at me and all my indignant rage simply dries up and runs away. That woman has a way… a few words and she can make you feel worthless. Small. Powerless. Stupid. Pathetic. Rubb—"

Emma reached up and put a hand over Morwenna's mouth, stopping her from saying more bad words. "You're none of those things. Wavecrest lied about the monsters in the dark. She lied about that. She loves making people feel awful. She loves making children cry." She lowered her hand.

"Yes." Morwenna dabbed another tear. "Sometimes, she goes down there. Stands still in the dark just listening to them whimper. She'll scratch on the doors to make them think the monsters are close."

"The monster *is* close." Emma folded her arms.

Morwenna sighed. "Yes, I suppose it is. I don't know what's wrong with her."

"We have to stop her."

"She needs to be stopped."

"No. *We* need to stop her." Emma stared at her. "You would make a much better matron. You care about the orphans. It's silly that you're afraid of her."

The assistant matron gazed down.

"Morwenna," said Emma in the same tone Mama tended to use when Tam wouldn't listen. "Look at me."

She lifted her gaze to make eye contact.

"Go let Sela, Morgan, and Isla out of the punishment cells. Bring them here and hide them in your room for now. Can you do that? Do you have the keys or know where to find them?"

Morwenna nodded.

The woman's rapid agreement somewhat surprised Emma. She didn't expect to be able to give orders to an adult woman, even one as timid as this one. Mama often gave people 'the look,' which could make grown men or even the Watch behave like small boys scrambling to do what their mother told them to do. Perhaps Emma had the same talent. She'd certainly become furious enough tonight.

"What are you going to do, child?" whispered Morwenna.

"I know Wavecrest keeps a book in which she writes down all the money she makes by selling children."

"She doesn't sell children," whispered Morwenna.

"Yes, she does. Even if she calls it 'hiring' them out."

Morwenna fidgeted. "Suppose… she does charge a rather high fee for adoption. She doesn't want the children going to homes. She can't send them to jobs if they leave. If people who want a son or daughter have to pay fifty or sixty gold gryphons as an adoption fee, that's rather not much different than selling the child, isn't it?"

"No." Emma shook her head. "It's not different at all."

"She says it's to help take care of the remaining orphans."

"It's to take care of her. She steals from the children, too. She took Bree's locket. She took our jewelry box… and it's not even ours. It belongs to Ambril's father. She won't even let Bree and her brother Morgan see each other."

"The woman is wicked. So wicked." Morwenna dabbed both eyes.

"I need your help." Emma took her hand in both of hers. "We can stop her. Just need you to turn into mama bear."

"Are you going to turn me into a bear?" Morwenna blinked.

"No. I can't do that. I mean, act like a mama bear." Emma slid off the bed to stand. "Go let them out of the punishment rooms. Bring them here to your room so they can hide for now. I want you to look at Isla. Look at what that woman did to her. I want you to look at what you could have stopped and didn't. And I want you to think about how much different these orphans' lives would be if you were in charge. Tell Isla she doesn't have to be scared anymore."

Morwenna nodded once, dabbing tears.

Emma set her fists against her hips. "One more thing."

"What, dear?"

"Do you have a key to the matron's office?"

"No. There is only one key and she wears it around her neck all the time."

"Thought so. How about some narrow pins or some such that might be used to pick open a lock?"

Morwenna tapped her fingers on her leg. "Well, that's a rather peculiar thing for a little girl to ask for. I believe we confiscated something like that from one of the boys some time ago. It's likely still in the storage room."

"Can you take me there?"

"It would arise suspicion for me to be escorting an orphan around the halls at night." Morwenna rose to her feet. "Can you turn into a wolf again?"

"Yes." Emma pulled her dress off over her head, rolled it up, and clamped it in her teeth. She crouched on all fours, then shapeshifted into wolf form.

"You really are quite adorable as a wolf pup." Morwenna picked her up.

"Mrrf."

Morwenna took the oil lamp in her other hand. She left the bedroom and hurried across the manor, passing Groundskeeper Terle and an older teen boy, neither of whom did more than nod in greeting as they went by.

A few minutes later, they reached a short hallway in the back corner of the manor. Morwenna opened a door and stepped into a storage closet. Five U-shaped shelves at different heights wrapped around the walls, leaving only a small channel in the middle. Morwenna shuffled sideways, having a minor bit of difficulty fitting into the room. She set Emma down and began to rifle through the numerous bins, baskets, and boxes.

"It's around here somewhere. The poor dear fell in with some thieves who were bringing him up to be a pickpocket." Morwenna sighed. "I'm not sure if he's better off here or with them."

Emma dropped the rolled-up dress out of her mouth. "Don't know."

"Aww. You can talk?"

"Yes."

"Your voice sounds so cute like that." Morwenna gushed. Seemingly unable to help herself, she scooped Emma back up and hugged her. "Oh. Dear. I'm sorry. You're irresistibly cute. You're not really a wolf, are you?"

"Not completely."

"Hang on..." Morwenna held her out to arm's length. "You're not a werewolf are you?"

"No. I'm a druid fortunate enough to earn Ylithir's favor. I have a kinship with wolves."

"Not a werewolf?" Morwenna tilted her head.

"No. Druid." Emma licked her nose.

"Not sure I've heard that before." Morwenna tilted her head.

"Druids are keepers of nature. We revere ancient animal spirits, protect the forest from bad things, and try to help people." Without even thinking, Emma scratched at her ear with her right foot. "Da says we're kind of like a combination of priests and wizards, but aren't really either one."

Morwenna exhaled in relief. "All right." She set Emma back down and resumed searching. A few minutes later, she held up a small, leather folding case. "Here they are."

Emma shapeshifted back to human form.

"Child, you really shouldn't run around with no clothes on. It's too cold."

"I have magic to stop the cold. And it's just for a moment. This stupid grey dress isn't magic. The one Nan made me stays with me when I change shape."

"Oh. That's why you asked Matron Wavecrest not to take it from you."

"Partly, yes. Mostly because Nan made it for me and having it makes me think about how much she loves me."

Morwenna dabbed a tear. "You really did come from far away? That's not a story?"

"We did. Thank you for helping me find these lockpicking tools. I'm going to get evidence and take it to the guards." Emma rose up on her toes and grasped the collar of Morwenna's nightdress in both hands, staring her in the eyes. "You need to stop being afraid of her. She's a skinny little mean old lady. The children will be safer and happier with you in charge. Go get Sela, Morgan, and Isla out of the dungeon. Isla was chained to the wall so high up her feet couldn't even touch the floor. She was so scared she cried snot bubbles out her nose. That woman is *awful*."

Morwenna broke down weeping.

Emma let go and dropped back onto her heels. "Please don't cry. Don't get sad. Get angry. You should be very angry. Help me fix this place. The orphans here have no one to protect them. They need someone who cares. They need you."

"All right." Morwenna wiped her tears, nodding. "I will."

Emma crouched, unrolled her dress, and wrapped the lockpicking tools inside it. She put the bundle in her mouth again, shapeshifted into wolf form, then darted out into the hallway as fast as her little wolf cub legs could go.

APPROVED MISBEHAVIOR

*T*hanks to Bree's scent on the floor, Emma found her way back to the correct bedroom.

Timing couldn't have been better. One of the older teen girl assistants arrived to check on the orphans at the same time Emma rounded the corner. After the girl went into the room, Emma scurried over and hid by the wall next to the door, waiting for the assistant to leave. A few minutes later, when the door opened, Emma slipped unnoticed past the teen into the room.

She went to the left, walking under three beds before reaching the space between her and Ambril's bed. She shapeshifted back to human form and spat the dress bundle to the floor.

Enough of this. She made a sour face at the dry fabric taste and reached for the little end table to grab *her* dress. Emma pulled it on over her head, wriggling into the wonderful, soft garment as if receiving a long-distance hug from Nan.

Kimber rolled to the side of the bed, staring at her. "Wot ya doin' that fer?"

"Tired of carrying that other dress in my mouth."

"No. I mean wearin' et. You'as gonnae git in trouble."

"I need you to misbehave, too." Emma smiled.

"Ooh. How?" Kimber's eyes gleamed in delight.

Emma held up the little wallet of lockpicking tools. "Can you really work these?"

"Aye. If the lock ain' too fussy."

"Good." She handed the wallet to her little sister.

"Uh oh," whispered Kimber. "We'as caught."

Emma looked up.

The other sixteen or so girls in the room surrounded them. Thankfully, none of them seemed angry, annoyed, or made faces like they planned to run off and get them in trouble. The orphans generally appeared curious... and quite conspiratorial.

"Bree," whispered Emma.

"Yes?" The eleven-year-old pushed to the front of the crowd.

"Morgan is okay. He wanted me to tell you he's fine, and he loves you and misses you."

Bree covered her mouth, tears welling up in her eyes. "He's in the..."

"Yes." Emma explained sneaking down to the punishment rooms, finding Sela, Isla, and Morgan... and breaking the manacles off the wall. "Morwenna is going to let them out. She's on her way down there right now."

Bree wept into her hands. "He's my brother. He just wanted to see me."

Emma patted the girl on the shoulder, then looked around at a sea of faces from age six to fifteen. "Morgan's fine. You'll be able to see him soon. Listen to me. We are getting rid of Wavecrest tonight. She better hope my plan works, because my secondary plan is going to end much, much worse for her."

"What's your secondary plan?" whispered the eldest girl.

"Sending a bird to find Nan and bring her here." Emma shook her head. "That would not be nice for Matron Wavecrest after I tell Nan what's going on here."

"Nan's gonna turn 'er inta a pig. Or a toad," whispered Kimber.

"Do that," whispered another girl.

Most of the orphans nodded.

"Too long. It would take days for her to get here." Emma bit her lip. "That boy's going to end up on a boat by the end of a week. I'm going to try to get rid of her tonight."

Kimber blinked in shock and made a throat-cutting gesture. "Get *rid* o' 'er?"

"No," whispered Emma. "I mean kick her out of the orphanage. Maybe arrested."

"What do you need us to do?" asked Bree.

"Anything," said another girl.

Merela nodded. "I'll even push her down the stairs."

"Two things." Emma held up a finger. "I know Sela has been awful to everyone."

The orphans grumbled and made noises of agreement.

"When I saw her in the punishment room, she looked like a scared little girl. I don't expect you all to forgive her right away, or maybe at all. What she did was wrong. She did it out of fear. If she stops being mean after Wavecrest is gone, please don't be mean back to her. You don't have to like her, just give her a chance to apologize."

The girls murmured, sounding neither opposed nor happy.

"Second thing." Emma held up two fingers. "Tonight, please stay here, in bed, be quiet, don't cause trouble. Everything has to look normal so they don't know something's happening. If what I'm going to do does not work, you *all* need to go tell the guards what's happening here. Wavecrest can't put everyone in the punishment room."

The girls nodded. While some looked frightened at the idea of group disobedience, none protested.

"All right. Time to go. Everyone, please just act normal for now." Emma tugged Kimber out of bed.

The girls scurried back to their beds. Everything fell quiet except for Bree sniffling into her pillow. Emma led Kimber to the door and pressed her ear to the wood. Once sure the hallway sounded empty, they slipped out into the corridor, pulled the door closed, and crept down the hall. Emma mostly remembered the way to the matron's office from the bedroom. She'd gone back and forth past it several times earlier as a wolf.

She didn't know what she'd do if anyone discovered them walking around—other than not being obedient. If they got caught now, the lockpicks would definitely be confiscated and the matron would know she wanted lockpicks, no doubt assuming Emma intended to use them to take the Box of Wonder. This meant the matron would certainly move the box somewhere else. Losing the box wouldn't be a huge tragedy at this point, at least as far as going home went. Emma could deal with waiting for Nan to fly here. Her bigger concern was Rin still being trapped in the box. She had to get her new friend out of there before the witch put it somewhere they'd never find it.

Thinking of Rin made her wonder if the girl had woken up yet. If she did, what would she think when she found herself alone in the box?

I can't worry about that right now. Need to stay alert. We cannot be caught.

Approaching lantern light warned of Groundskeeper Terle up ahead.

Emma tugged Kimber to the side, hurriedly going into the nearest door. Seeing beds, she got down on the floor and crawled under the first one, Kimber tucked tight against her side. Breathing from a bunch of sleeping orphans filled the silence. The slow, heavy footfalls of the groundskeeper went by in the corridor... and stopped right outside. Hinges squeaked. Lantern light stretched over the floor in front of Emma's face in the shape of an opening door.

Two large filthy boots stepped into view, close enough for Emma to touch. Groundskeeper Terle stood right beside the bed she and Kimber crawled under. The glow from his lantern crept back and forth.

He's searching... or looking for anyone who isn't asleep.

Moments later, the groundskeeper backed out of the room and shut the door.

Whew. Emma exhaled out her nose. She waited another two minutes, then crawled out from under the bed. When she turned to help Kimber up, she squeaked at the sight of a boy sleeping on the bed she'd been hiding under. They'd strayed into the boys' side of the house.

Getting caught in here would be extra bad.

Thankfully, none of the boys appeared to be awake. She took Kimber's hand and slipped out into the hall. They ran along as quiet as can be to the end of the hall where it connected to the foyer. Emma went left, hurrying across it to a corridor on the other side and down to the wooden archway by the waiting area in front of the matron's office.

Emma nodded at Kimber and pointed at the door.

Grinning, her little sister opened the leather folding case to reveal a whole mess of small rods, each with a slightly different shape at the end. Some looked like hooks, some like saws, and others had shapes she knew no names for.

Kimber put her face up against the door, peering into the keyhole. She studied the inside of the lock for only a few seconds before selecting a pair of rods from the case and sticking them both into the keyhole. One, she held relatively still, the other, she wiggled around and worked back and forth. Emma kept her eyes—and ears—on the hallway past the arch. At least here, the waiting area had enough chairs and a small sofa they could hide under relatively well.

A faint click broke the silence a moment later.

Emma blinked, as shocked at Kimber really being able to pick a lock open as Morwenna must have been watching a little wolf cub turn into a girl.

"Easy peasy lemon-squeezy," whispered Kimber while tucking the picks back into the leather case.

Emma pushed the door open, tugged her sister in, and eased the door closed. Being inside the office made her nervous—a severe punishment would follow if they got caught here. It also made her relax, since no one patrolling the hallways would even try to look in this room, assuming the door locked. Emma hurried around behind the desk and started searching for the logbook. Kimber went straight to the huge shelf along the back wall. She stuck the lockpick case in her teeth and climbed the shelves up to the top middle cabinet where Wavecrest put the Box of Wonder.

"Don't fall," whispered Emma.

"Mm mmnt," mumbled Kimber.

In the top right small drawer, Emma found a collection of jewelry. None of it appeared terribly extravagant, the sort of things children might wear. Everything there probably fooled the matron into thinking it would be worth something, only to turn out cheap. That they remained in the desk and hadn't been sold for coin proved the lack of value. Emma decided to check anything close in shape to a pendant to see if it opened. The third necklace she picked up did, indeed, open into a locket. Small paintings on each half depicted the faces of a man and woman, both of whom had the same light brown hair as Bree and Morgan.

Yes! This is it. Since she had no pockets, Emma put the locket on to carry it and kept searching for the log book going from drawer to drawer. A continuous, soft scratching sound came from above and behind her.

A moment—and two drawers searched—later, Kimber gave off a tiny squeak of victory.

Emma peered up. Her sister stood on a shelf, high up, feet as wide apart as the cubby allowed. She clung precariously to the shelf, head-level with the Box of Wonder, having successfully unlocked and opened the cabinet. Unfortunately, the gems on the lid and sides remained dark.

"Aww," whispered Kimber. "Nae lit yet."

"Of course not." Emma continued searching. "It takes a whole day. It won't be ready until tomorrow afternoon." She tapped her foot, staring up at the box, briefly considering using it to take all the orphans out of here.

Ugh. No. They'd still be orphans wherever the box took us... and this place really wouldn't be too bad if Morwenna ran it.

"She gonnae sell it. Or move it," whispered Kimber.

"No, she won't." Emma put a hand on the shelf. "Close the doors. I'll make sure she can't take it away from us."

"Aww. Okay." Kimber nudged the cabinet doors closed.

Emma concentrated on her connection to Linganthas, reaching out to whatever life essence remained in the wood under her hand. Faint green light shimmered over her fingers, trailed up the shelf, and circled the cabinet holding the box. The wood creaked and groaned. Gnarled roots grew out of the frame and doors, fusing into a tangled barrier that sealed the doors closed.

"She gonnae notice 'at," muttered Kimber, grinning.

"I don't care." Emma frowned. "She's going to notice the gems glowing if she looks at it late tomorrow afternoon. And she's probably going to try to open the lid... and then we're never going to get the box back."

"Yeah." Kimber climbed down. "I 'ope Rin is okay."

"Me too. We're almost done. Won't take long now." Emma spun around and continued rummaging the desk.

"I fink if she 'wake, she kin 'ear us inna crystal ball."

"Yes, probably."

Kimber whispered to the cabinet doors, telling Rin all about what happened with the thieves and the orphanage, warning her about Matron Wavecrest.

Emma found a drawer on the left in the middle that wouldn't open, seeming locked. "Can you unlock this?"

Kimber climbed down from the shelf, scampered over, and knelt in front of it. "Nope. Keyhole tae small. None'a these picks gonnae fit."

Grr. It's got to be in there. Maybe I can make the wood move. "Where is the latch?"

"'ere." Kimber pointed at the top center.

Emma crouched in front of the drawer and put her hand on its face. Again, she reached out to the wood. Green light danced across the back of her hand. In seconds, the wood around the latch shrank, receding away until the small metal tab no longer stopped the drawer from opening. Kimber eagerly yanked it open.

This drawer contained a few pouches, lots of folded papers... and the same leather-bound book Emma saw the matron writing in during her meeting with the sea captain.

"This is it," whispered Emma, grabbing the book in both hands. "Now, we get help."

She sprang to her feet, ready to run—and stared at Groundskeeper Terle standing in the doorway right in front of them. The man's confused expression, likely at finding the door unlocked, darkened to anger at the sight of Emma and Kimber behind the desk in the matron's office... after bedtime.

Uh oh.

BIG TROUBLE

a hint of delight showed within Groundskeeper Terle's angry expression.

Like a small boy receiving a surprise gift, the unkempt older man seemed to adore the opportunity to catch orphans misbehaving. Emma thought him a well-trained dog eager to please his master.

"You two are in big trouble." He jabbed a finger at them. "Ya like being outta yer beds past time? Well, I got a nice li'l treat for ya, then. Yer both gonna be spendin' a whole week out of yer beds at night. Bustin' inta the matron's office, indeed. Might even be two weeks fer that. Bet ya won't dislike those beds after ya try ta sleep standin' up. Then we'll see if you're ungrateful enough about havin' beds you get out of 'em when yer s'posed ta be in 'em. Now, get over here."

"No." Emma stepped out from behind the desk. "You aren't going to be cruel anymore. I will not let you put another orphan in manacles, especially Kimber. Lay a hand on my sister and you'll regret it."

The groundskeeper twitched, his right eye widening more than the left. "Shut your wretched mouth, ya grubby li'l orphan. Who do ya think you're talkin' to? That's gonna be another week in the basement."

"I'm not an orphan." Emma glared at him.

"Oh?" Groundskeeper Terle leaned back, faking surprise. "What are ya then if'n ya ain't an orphan?"

She held her chin high. "I am Emma Dalen, daughter of Watch Captain Liam Dalen and Bethany Dalen... who some people call the Witch of the Woods." She leaned forward, trying to make herself seem as scary as possible. "And you should consider yourself *quite* lucky Mama isn't here right now."

"Er Nan," added Kimber. "She'd tun ya inta a toad. Er a pig maybe."

He stared at her in silence for a few seconds. His eyes changed size, right getting small, left growing wide. "Right, then, ya insolent lass. You've got some imagination on ya. Witch of the woods... what's that supposed ta mean? Enough o' this nonsense. You do as you're told right this second. You can walk or I can drag ya."

Drat. Emma sighed out her nose.

"We'as a long way from 'ome," whispered Kimber. "He donnae know 'bout 'er."

"Ugh. All right." Emma glanced at her sister. "I'm going to go for help. Run. Follow me to Morwenna. She'll tell this guy to leave you alone."

Groundskeeper Terle widened his stance, raising his hands in preparation to grab the girls if they tried to run past him out the door.

Kimber nodded.

Emma stuck the logbook in her mouth and clamped her teeth around it.

The groundskeeper's eyes traded sizes again. "What the blazes is wrong with ya? Tis a book, not a hunk o' bread."

Emma dove forward, shapeshifting into a wolf cub before she hit the floor, the book still in her mouth. Her beloved blue dress seemed to disappear entirely. Bree's locket remained around her neck, though nearly touched the floor. She growled, deep and long, staring at him.

A strange gurgling noise came from the groundskeeper. Both of his eyes opened to the same width. She took a step toward him, still growling. Despite her being a small wolf cub, the man backed up another step, some color draining from his cheeks.

As soon as he backed away far enough from the door to leave enough room for Kimber to get past him, Emma charged. He gave a weak yelp, nearly falling over himself to get away from her. A second before attacking him, she ducked low and darted between his legs, scampering out into the hall amid the skittering of wolf claws on hardwood. Kimber ran out of the office before Groundskeeper Terle could recover his balance enough to grab for her.

Emma raced down the hall as fast as she could go without leaving Kimber behind, using a scent trail to find her way through the maze of corridors to Morwenna's bedroom. They rushed past an older teenage boy—one of the night watchers—who'd taken a seat on a bench in the hallway and fallen asleep. Still in the office, the groundskeeper shouted something she couldn't understand, then came crashing after them down the hall.

The man had to know exactly where they went, since Emma told Kimber to go to Morwenna's room. No point trying to lose the angry man in the hallways. She had to get to the bedroom before he caught them. Letting the man see her shapeshift gave up her ability to move around unnoticed. Now, he'd be looking for a small black wolf pup. However, the shock of doing it right in front of him allowed them to escape the office with the all-important logbook.

Hopefully, the trade would be worth it.

An older man like him had little hope of catching a small wolf and an eight-year-old who'd spent most of her life running... from her horrible father, from guards, from thieves, from bears in the woods, from goblins. Kimber didn't seem too afraid of the man, her expression mostly one of concentration.

Emma discovered an unfortunate truth of wolf paws and hardwood floors. When she tried to stop at Morwenna's bedroom door, she didn't—and crashed into it.

Oof.

"Who's there?" asked Morwenna, from inside.

"Let us in," called Emma, her voice high pitched and squeaky.

The door opened. Morwenna peered down at her. Emma darted

around her. The big woman nearly lost her balance, trying to turn fast enough to follow her. Kimber rushed in and pushed the door shut, then reached up to lock it.

Sela and Morgan sat on the edge of the giant bed. Isla curled up behind them, quite thoroughly asleep. All three orphans had been freed from manacles. Morwenna's eyes looked rather red, as though she'd been weeping.

The tromping footfalls of Groundskeeper Terle came down the hallway outside.

Emma shifted back to human form; her fur lightened from black to blue as her dress reappeared on her. She plucked the book out of her mouth.

Sela gasped. "Emma? You turned into a dog?"

Morgan grinned at her.

"Wolf," deadpanned Emma. "Yes. I can talk about it later. No time." She pulled the locket off and handed it to Morgan. "This is Bree's. I don't want to lose it."

"You found it!" Morgan teared up. "She's going to be so happy. We both thought that old witch sold it."

Emma faced Morwenna. "The groundskeeper is chasing us. Don't let him take Kimber. You can stand up to Wavecrest. You can stand up to that wretched old man, too."

Morwenna glanced at Isla, squeezed her hands into fists, then nodded once. "I can. I... didn't realize how bad..."

"I have to go find help." Emma ran to the window and opened it. "Please keep Kimber safe until I get back."

Terle banged on the door. "Miss Morwenna? I know yer in there. I can hear ya."

"I will." Morwenna moved to the door. "Be careful out there, child. I'll handle this lout."

Grinning, Emma hugged Kimber, then jumped up onto the windowsill and clamped the logbook in her teeth again. She jumped out the window, shapeshifting in midair.

As fast as a wolf could run, she zoomed from the rear yard, around the side of the manor house, and across the courtyard. At the gate, she tilted her head to fit the book between two bars, squeezed past them, and raced off down the street.

GREAT BIG CITY, TINY LITTLE WOLF

*W*et cobblestones soon soaked Emma's paws.

She zoomed down the street as best as she could remember the way the guards brought her to Wavecrest Manor. Though it had only been hours ago, it felt as if she'd been stuck in that awful place for weeks. It didn't help she'd stayed up far past her bedtime. She figured it to be less than an hour away from midnight.

Unfortunately, her memory of the route the guards took proved wrong.

Emma found herself on an unfamiliar street, staring around at unfamiliar buildings. She ran back the other way, took a different turn, and kept going. Every street looked the same as every other street. Not identical, rather equally wrong. So many scents covered everything, she couldn't even pick out the one she left behind. Wherever the streets became bridges over canals, she stopped to look around, certain it had to be the wrong way, even though they'd crossed at least six such small bridges on the way to the orphanage before.

Faster, and faster, she raced around searching for a guard, a guard's building, or anyone who looked like they might be able to help her find someone important to talk to. This late at night, the huge city appeared completely empty of people.

Out of breath, she trotted to a halt and rested. Looking around at the houses and cobblestones didn't help. She couldn't even tell which way to go to get back to the orphanage. This city made Calebrin seem smallish. The more she stared at her unfamiliar surroundings, the more convinced she became she'd spend the rest of her life hopelessly lost, never getting back to the orphanage, never getting back to Kimber, never going home.

A strong sea breeze ripped down the street, lifting a mist off the paving and scattering it around in a swirl. She cringed away from the pelting water and shivered. Despite her fur, the cold ocean wind seemed to blow right through her. She looked down, too scared, homesick, and sad to bother asking Andreth to keep her warm. Her mind tormented her with worry over Kimber. Emma had leapt out the window before Morwenna opened the door to speak with Groundskeeper Terle. Anything could have happened after she left. Sure, the woman found the courage to let the children out of the basement, but could she keep her nerve while the mean old man yelled at her?

Terle would adore dragging the children back to the punishment room.

Kimber's as small as Isla. Her feet wouldn't touch the floor in there.

A vision of her little sister hung by manacles on the wall, kicking, screaming, and crying lit Emma's sadness on fire, burning it off to rage.

Could she hope Morwenna managed to defy the groundskeeper? She supposedly had authority over him, being the second person in charge after Matron Wavecrest. The woman's mannerisms, so much like the orphan girls who'd been berated into meek, submissive servants made Emma think Morwenna had been an orphan herself, likely raised by Matron Wavecrest. Such a thing would certainly explain why the woman acted so afraid of her.

If I find my way back there and Kimber's in manacles... Emma fumed, daydreaming about throwing vines at the matron the same way she fought the bog goblins. *I'll drive her out of the manor with thorns and lightning!*

Determined to protect Kimber, Emma darted off again. She hurried from street to street, backtracking and going down different alleys in a seemingly endless routine of getting more and more lost.

The second time she ran out of breath, perhaps an hour later, her anger withered away to despondent sadness. Emma didn't feel like a hero anymore. She felt like a lost little girl who desperately wanted her parents. Overcome by worry for Kimber, Emma ran around, trying to get back to the orphanage. Alas, she'd gotten herself well and truly lost in the enormous city.

When ran herself to the point of collapsing for the third time, Emma flopped on the cobblestones under an empty merchant cart. Alone, frightened—without her sister, without her family, without any idea where to go, she tucked her wolf pup head against her belly, and cried.

RESTORING ORDER

ama... Da... Nan... where are you? Please help us.

Emma sniffled. Tiny wolf-like whimpers and mewls echoed off the uncaring cobblestones around her. Years of standing on wet ground left the wooden legs of the merchant cart above her saturated with ill-smelling mold. She glared at the logbook. How stupid had she been to think she'd take this evidence right to the guards and everything would be fine. She couldn't even abandon her mission and go back to the orphanage. She failed at failing.

At this very minute, Kimber might be locked up in a tiny cell—and Emma couldn't do anything to help her.

Another wave of hard crying came and went. She lay in silence for a while, having no idea what to do other than to wait for the sun to come up and hopefully find a guard when the city woke up. Sadness, fear, and dread that Groundskeeper Terle bullied his way past Morwenna kept her awake despite the late hour making her eyelids heavy. She lay there long enough to stop feeling tired from running around, though she couldn't find any reason to keep trying. She'd only get herself even more lost.

The echo of boots scuffing on the street startled her out of an almost-nap.

"Come on then," said a man at the other end of the street, his voice faint. "On yer feet."

Emma froze. The man obviously didn't speak to her from so far away. Her ears perked up.

"This one's fallen all the way inta the bottle," replied a second man. "Get up, you poor wretch. Can't leave ya out here like that."

"Night in a cell for you, friend." The first man chuckled. "Still more comfortable than the road."

A third man babbled incoherently.

Guards... they found a drunk.

Emma jumped to her feet, picked the logbook up in her mouth again, and trotted off toward the voices.

At the next corner, she tucked up against the wall of a hat shop and peeked around into the smaller crossing street. Two men wearing the same chain mail armor and gryphon tabards as Hesken and Wenferd stooped to grab the arms of a third man in drab commoner's clothing of olive and burgundy, who lay flat on the ground. The citizen appeared to have consumed so much booze he couldn't stand by himself.

Emma kept out of sight, watching the guards collect the man.

When they got him upright and started hauling him off, she followed.

"Don't worry, friend," said the guard on the left. "You'll get free room and board for the night. Finest in the city."

"Indeed. Soon as ya sober up... and take care of the fines, ya can be on yer way."

The guards continued to joke about jail as if it were an inn room, praising the niceties of their accommodations as they escorted—more carried—the drunk along. Emma followed them, keeping far enough back to avoid being seen.

They reached the giant road spanning from the massive docks at the east edge of the city all the way to the western side, or so Emma assumed. She couldn't see where the great road went past the top of the hill. She assumed it would proceed unobstructed to the city's western gate, thus allowing merchant cargo easy passage from inland areas to the harbor.

She followed the guards all the way to a large, three-story building on a street corner. From the outside, it more or less resembled an inn except for having small barred windows at street level on the side, no doubt prison cells in the basement. This didn't bother Emma. Prison cells belonged at the guardhouse—not in an orphanage.

The guards hauled the drunk man in the front door.

Emma sprinted ahead, dashing across the street, up the stairs, over the porch, and through the door before they could close it. She found herself in a wonderfully warm, plain room where another guard sat behind a desk. To the right, chairs surrounded a large, empty table— likely where the guards on shift ate meals. Two hallways led away from the foyer, a short one to the right, and a longer one straight ahead.

The guards took the drunk man to the right, so Emma went straight ahead. Neither the guards, the drunk, nor the man behind the desk noticed her. She trotted down the hall over a plain blue carpet with gold trim, peering into every doorway on either side. Barracks, storage rooms, small empty offices, and more storage rooms.

One door away from the end of the corridor, she peered into a larger office. A man somewhat older than the other guards sat behind a desk covered in books and stacks of paper, reading. His semi-curly brown hair hung down past his shoulders, and he wore an enormous mustache that ran around both sides of his mouth to his join his beard, though his chin had no hair on it. His armor seemed lighter compared to the other guards, as if intended for looks—or sitting at a desk all day—rather than fighting. He had to be someone important. A captain like Da, perhaps—exactly the sort of man she needed to see.

Emma approached the desk.

This man, unlike every other guard in the building, noticed her soon after she wandered into his office. He raised both bushy eyebrows. "What in the...? Well hello there, boy. Where'd you come from? What'cha got there? A book?"

Emma shapeshifted back to human form, rising up to her normal unimpressive height. She felt tall compared to a wolf pup, at least. She pulled the logbook out of her mouth. "Hello, sir. I'm not a boy. I need to talk to someone about a crime. You look like you're in charge. Can I talk to you, please?"

He leaned back in his chair. "Never a dull night. What manner of apparition are you?"

"My name is Emma Dalen. I'm ten years old. I'm a druid... apprentice."

"Ahh." The man's expression melted into a warm smile. "Been a while since I've met one of your ilk. Don't get many druids here in the city."

She walked up to the edge of the desk. "Will you please help me? I need to report a crime. Are you in charge?"

"I'm a shift commander, so I suppose that means I'm in charge... at least until morning." He chuckled. "Is that suitable, little Miss Wolf?"

"Yes, sir." She smiled. "It is."

"Name's Hurley. Emma, is it?"

"Yes, sir."

"All right then, young miss." He gestured at one of three plain wooden chairs facing the desk. "Take a seat and let's hear what you have to say."

Emma sat in the middle chair. "I'm not from this city. My sister, my friend Ambril, and I came here by accident. Some guards thought we were orphans and took us to the Wavecrest Orphanage. They were only doing what they thought was right. That's not the crime I want to report."

"Go on, child." Hurley rested his arms on the desk. "I am listening."

Emma told him about how Matron Wavecrest stole anything valuable from new children arriving, collected money from sending the children off to work, asked so much coin for adoptions that children rarely left the orphanage, arranged to sell Heron to a ship captain while not even being certain he'd come back alive... and worst of all, routinely placed children in manacles and left them locked in basement closets all night long after scaring them with stories about monsters.

Hurley's eyebrows crept like bushy caterpillars up his forehead with each new thing she said. They seemed likely to go all the way up into his hair.

"This is a logbook." Emma had to hop out of the chair to reach far enough to hand it to him. "She writes down all the money she takes, which child she sells, and who hired them. I don't think she's paying taxes."

"Taxes?" Hurley scoffed, taking the book. "If what you're telling me is true, taxes are the least thing I'm worried about." He leafed through the pages.

"It is, sir. I saw for myself tonight. Three orphans in irons. One's littler than me. They're free now."

Hurley glowered.

"You're angry?" asked Emma, somewhat surprised at his reaction, but also relieved.

"I am." He tilted his head. "You seem not to have expected this."

"The other children told me they've tried to ask the city guard for help before, but they didn't do anything."

Hurley sighed. "I wish I could say it surprises me to hear that. Good chance the patrolmen thought the kids were having a tantrum and making up stories. And, I suppose, the magistrates would likely not have been too inclined to set time aside to listen to orphans complain about their matron being overly strict. They are likely to pay attention to this labor-selling enterprise—"

"Overly strict?" Emma blinked. "Overly strict is making kids go to bed without dinner or paddling them for not saying, 'yes Matron Wavecrest' all the time. Overly strict is *not* chaining children to the wall so high up that their feet can't touch the floor... and telling them that there are scary monsters in the dark waiting to hurt them if they cry too loud. She kept Isla chained up down there every night this week. The girl couldn't sleep. She kept passing out at dinner."

Hurley's expression darkened in anger. "Are you certain this is all true?"

"Yes, sir. It's true. And probably worse. I've only been there for half a day. Come, look for yourself. Isla's wrists are all red and cut up. I broke her off the wall. I can show you the punishment rooms in the basement." Emma ground her toes into the rug. "I might need help finding my way back there. I got lost."

"What's that on your face, child." Hurley stood and walked out from behind his desk. "Someone hit ya?"

Emma sighed. "Yes. Another girl." She explained what happened with Sela, admitting to using magic to become strong enough to knock the girl out with one punch, then finding her in the punishment room later, terrified and sobbing.

"Bit late in the night for one your size to be out of bed, but... let's go then. If what you're telling me is true, it'll be the end of Wavecrest in this city. The whole family's rotten."

She blinked. "They are? I'm not from the city... I'm not even from this kingdom. I don't know anything about this place. What did the family do?"

He pulled a cloak from the wall, put it on, affixed a broadsword in a scabbard to his belt, then gently took her hand. "It is no story fit for the ears of a little one. Enough to say, they made their beds with dirty dealing. Killed whoever they felt like to expand their shipping company. Ruined families. Took whatever they wanted from whoever they wanted, leaving misery and poverty in their wake. Bad money, all of it. Every citizen of Greymarch cheered when that family came to ruin. What you're saying about Cordelia is not too out of character for them."

"Who's Cordelia?"

"The matron." Hurley grumbled. "Her name's Cordelia Wavecrest. She's been a dark cloud over us darn near sixty years. I wasn't around back when she was your size. Plenty o' stories about her, though."

"What was she like?"

"Pretty much the same as she is now, only shorter." He chuckled. "Thinks everyone else exists to serve her needs."

Emma frowned.

"Come on. Let's go 'ave a look." Hurley led her down the hall to the front room. Once there, he banged on the wall, summoning a few more men. "With me, lads. Got some serious accusations to investigate over at Wavecrest Manor."

MAMA BEAR

*U*pon returning to Wavecrest Manor, Emma marched in the front door.

Shift Commander Hurley and three guardsmen followed her. She headed straight toward Morwenna's room, trying to remember her way through the mazelike hallways. Racing around the third corner, Emma nearly crashed into a drowsy teen girl with a lantern.

"Hey," whispered the girl as she grabbed Emma's arm. "What are you doing out of bed this late?"

"Trying to fix things," said Emma. "Please let go of me."

"Are you out of your mind?" whispered the girl. "Hurry back to your room before anyone else sees you. I'm not going to—"

Hurley and the guards came around the corner behind Emma.

The teen's mouth fell open. She released her hold on Emma's wrist. "You… guards are here? What's going on?"

Emma smiled. "You'll see." She stepped past the older girl, who made no move to stop her.

"Sirs…" The teen scooted aside, out of the guards' way.

Distant shouting from up ahead grew louder as Emma hurried along. She rounded the last corner into the hallway leading to Morwenna's room to find the door open and Groundskeeper Terle in the midst of yelling at the woman, *still* trying to get past her to drag the 'miscreants' down to the punishment room. He'd advanced a few steps into the bedroom, though Morwenna physically blocked him from going any further. She might have been a head shorter than him, but had to weigh double or more, and was likely stronger than him as well. Morwenna held Isla in one arm, the girl's head resting on her shoulder.

Kimber and Morgan huddled together on the bed, watching the argument. They hid behind Sela, who sat on the edge, staring at the argument with almost no color in her face. The teen appeared simultaneously terrified and ready to throw herself at Terle to keep him away from the smaller children.

"... cannot believe you are making such an issue of it!" shouted Groundskeeper Terle. "In the matron's office! How kin ya make excuses for such misbehavior!?"

"I cannot believe I tolerated this awfulness for so long," roared Morwenna. She grasped Isla's arm and held it up to show off the bleeding red marks on the child's wrist. When she let go, Isla resumed clinging. "I'm a great puffed-up sea hen of a chicken is what I am. I couldn't say a word to that witch. No more. What's your excuse, Nicholas?"

"He loves making us cry," whispered Isla.

"What's gotten into you, Morwenna?" rasped the groundskeeper.

Hurley cleared his throat.

Morwenna leaned slightly to one side to peer over the groundskeeper's shoulder. As soon as she made eye contact with the guards, both her eyebrows went up.

Groundskeeper Terle twisted around, his expression lifting into a surprised sneer for a few seconds at the sight of the guards before he spotted Emma and frowned. "Apologies, gents. This little wretch is wasting your precious time... and at such a late hour."

Emma smiled at him. "I found the log book. The guards know about Wavecrest selling children." She walked past the groundskeeper, her stare practically daring him to touch her, and stopped beside Morwenna to point up at Isla's arm. "Shift Commander Hurley, look.

They hung her by her wrists in chains every night this week. Look at the blood. She's only seven."

"I'm eight," said Isla in a half-awake voice. "My birthday's two weeks ago."

"Em!" Kimber leapt off the bed and zoomed into a hug.

Hurley entered the room, forcing Groundskeeper Terle to back up by his sheer presence. The shift commander gingerly lifted Isla's arm for a closer look at her wrist. The other guards glared at the groundskeeper.

"Sela." Emma beckoned her over. "Show them your arms."

The sixteen-year-old hurried off the bed like a little child obeying her mother, scurrying over with her hands held out so the guards could see the damage she did to herself struggling so hard to escape.

Emma pointed at Isla's arm. "They hung her off her feet. All night long. From bedtime to breakfast. Every day this week." Despite having already said that several times, she repeated it in hopes Hurley and the guards he brought with him would become as angry as she was upon seeing her in the cell.

Hearing it again while having Isla right in front of them, the shift commander looked furious.

"I got a whole week of punishment," whispered Isla. "'Cause I tried to run away. It's dark in there. Bad things are hiding. They'll eat us if we make noise. I couldn't sleep." Her voice barely over a whisper, she described hanging by her wrists while she cried so hard her nose dribbled all down her face and she couldn't move to wipe it... or scratch wherever bugs crawled on her.

Hurley's knuckles creaked.

The guards all seemed angry as well.

Sensing the guards might not simply brush things off as a whiny child they could ignore this time, Groundskeeper Terle took a step back. He appeared quite interested in leaving the room as fast as possible; however, guards blocked the door.

Morwenna looked down, shame all over her face. "I'm sorry."

"Morgan?" asked Emma. "Please tell the guards why you got punished."

The boy slipped off the bed and walked over. "I got put here with my sister, Bree. Our parents died, so we had nowhere to go. Matron Wavecrest doesn't let us see each other. We can't talk in the dining hall, and we're always doing chores apart. I tried to visit her at night after chores, but got caught in the girls' hall." He showed his wrists, slightly red with only a few scratches. "I got put in the punishment room, too. I'm tall enough my toes touched the floor, at least. Wasn't hangin' like Isla. I'll do it again. The punishment room isn't so bad I won't try to see my sister."

"So sorry," muttered Morwenna, brushing a hand over the boy's hair. "You can see your sister as much as you like from now on."

Emma peered up at Hurley. "Please be lenient with Miss Morwenna. The orphans need her to take care of them. You've all seen this." She pointed at Isla's bleeding wrist. "Does she have to stay hurt so you can show a magistrate, or can I heal her?"

"Of course not, child. If you're able to, do so. No need for the child to suffer any more." Hurley shot a dark glare at Groundskeeper Terle.

Emma reached up to take Isla's hand. "Uruleth, please grant me the gift of life."

Emerald green glow welled up around her fingers. The children 'oohed' in awe. Morwenna pursed her lips. Groundskeeper Terle leaned back as if afraid of her. Neither Hurley nor the guards showed much reaction at all other than to nod, satisfied. They'd all apparently seen similar magic used before.

The cuts and bruises disappeared from Isla's arm. Emma faced Sela, grasped her wrist, and cast the healing spell again. Her manacle burns—and the bruise on her cheek—disappeared. Sela looked down in guilt.

Isla smiled at Emma, letting her head rest on Morwenna's shoulder again.

"Shh, dear." Morwenna patted the girl. "I won't let Wavecrest hurt you again. Or any of you."

The little one squeezed herself tighter to the woman's side, as if claiming her.

Emma smiled at the two of them. Morwenna now seemed more

like a mama bear than a big sea chicken. Being forced to confront what happened to Isla up close evidently lit a fire inside the woman. While Hurley and the guards spoke to Morwenna about the goings on at the orphanage—and kept Groundskeeper Terle from leaving—Emma contented herself to stand there hugging Kimber and trying not to fall asleep on her feet. Morgan and Isla told the guards all about how the groundskeeper loved chasing them around and dragging any orphans he could accuse of any wrongdoing downstairs to the punishment room. The older man claimed he merely enforced the rules as they existed and took no pleasure in his duties.

Emma didn't believe him. She also didn't think the guards believed him based on their expressions.

Hurley eventually turned his attention to Sela, asking her for her side of the story.

The teen confessed to helping Wavecrest be cruel to the children in her position as 'head assistant.' She told him of Wavecrest locking her up in the punishment room on her very first night here as a smaller child because she couldn't stop crying over the sudden deaths of both parents so close together. "I'd already been terrified of the dark before I came to live here. Ever since that night, being in dark places makes me lose my senses from fright. I'd been so dreadfully afraid of being locked up again, I did whatever she told me to do. I acted mean to hide how frightened I was of her. She made me her head assistant four years ago when I was twelve. I've no idea why she chose me."

"I know how you feel, dear," said Morwenna. "Couldn't tell you what about that woman was so frightening. I'll bet she chose you because she knew how scared you were and figured you'd do everything she told you to do without question."

Emma puffed a strand of Kimber's hair off her mouth, then peered up at Morwenna. "She's scary to kids, but you're not a kid. And Sela's almost not a kid anymore. You shouldn't be afraid of Wavecrest. She's just a bitter old woman."

"The witch isn't *that* old," said one of the guards, chuckling. "What's she, fifty-four or thereabouts?"

The other guards shrugged.

"That's old to me. I'm ten." Emma grumbled, then looked back up at Morwenna. "Please do *not* let those sailors take Heron. Give them back their coins. You saw the boys. As horrible as they were treated here, not one of them wanted to go."

"Oh, I can't imagine why a young lad wouldn't want to go to sea as a cabin boy," mumbled one of the guards.

"Because it's a lot of hard, dangerous work," said Emma. "And he might fall off the ship and drown, or the ship could sink. Or the ship could be attacked by pirates."

"Aye." The guard nodded. "Not a place for a lad."

Hurley patted Emma on the shoulder. "All right, child. You've done enough for a little one. You should go to bed now. We'll sort the rest of this out."

Morwenna nudged Morgan toward her bed. "You all can stay here tonight if you care to."

"Can I see my sister?" asked Morgan.

"It's late. First thing in the morning. I promise." Morwenna ushered him over to the bed. "Sleep now, dear. You look exhausted."

Sela stood still for a moment, as if expecting the guards to arrest her. She took a tentative step toward the bed. None of the guards reached for her, so she gradually eased her way over and lay down.

"Morwenna," said Hurley. "I'll need you to walk me around. Let us see these... punishment rooms straight away. Then I intend to have a word with Cordelia."

"Of course." Morwenna gave Isla a squeeze. "I need to help the guards, dear. Try to get some sleep. I'll be back as soon as I am able."

Isla let out a sleepy moan. She attempted to resist being separated from Morwenna, though in her exhausted state, couldn't effectively protest. Mere seconds after the woman set her down on the bed, the child fell asleep again.

Emma pulled Kimber close, not approaching the bed. She watched the guards, Morwenna, and Groundskeeper Terle walk out and close the door.

"You did magic," whispered Sela.

"Yes." Emma sighed silently out her nose.

"Why did you heal me?"

"Because you were hurt."

"But I was wretched to you."

"It doesn't matter." Emma tapped her foot on the soft rug. "I understand why you acted so mean. Fear. The other girls don't like you very much, you're right. I asked them to not be mean back to you. If you are nice to them, they might forgive you someday."

Sela sniffled. "Do you really think the guards are going to get rid of Matron Wavecrest?"

"Yes. My Da is a Watch captain. That's kinda like the same thing as the city guard. I know how it works." Emma smiled. "Sometimes, the normal guards are tired and try to make excuses not to have to do more work. If you go to someone in charge, stuff gets done."

"I'm sorry for slapping you and being so mean." Sela looked down.

"I forgive you."

The teen almost smiled. "Did you do magic on Morwenna? While you were gone... you should've seen her. She yelled right back at Groundskeeper Terle. I thought she was going to hit him."

Emma shook her head. "I didn't do any magic... but I think Isla might have."

"What? She's not a... whatever you are."

"Druid," said Kimber.

"Not that kind of magic." Emma grinned. "I think Isla found a mama."

"C'mon, go to sleep. There's plenty of room in this bed. It's huge." Sela patted the blankets.

"I'd rather not leave Ambril worrying what's happened to us." Emma glanced at the door. "It's all right. We'll go back to the big bedroom for now. We're going to leave tomorrow."

"Leave?" Sela sat up. "Where will you go? Why would you run away now that Morwenna might be in charge?"

"We'as gotta go 'ome." Kimber yawned. "We nae orphans."

Emma managed a sleepy smile. "Don't worry. It's magic. We'll be okay."

Sela blinked, seeming unsure what to say.

"I hope you'll help make this place better for everyone who has to live here."

"I will." Sela nodded. "Are we to see you again?"

Emma tapped her toe into the floor. "Perhaps a bit in the morning. We won't be able to leave until the magic is ready."

"All right." Sela lay back down. "Good night, Emma... and thank you."

"Noight," whispered Kimber.

"Night." Emma took Kimber by the hand and walked to the door. She peered back once at the bed, smiled at Isla who'd curled up around one of the pillows, and left the room.

Yes. She found a mama.

39

HALF AN INCH, A HUNDRED MILES

*Q*uiet as a mouse, Emma and Kimber ran to the large bedroom in the girls' hall.

The other girls all appeared to be sleeping. A few even decided to take a chance breaking the rules to share beds. Each orphan only got one blanket, so by sharing, they could use double blankets to ward off the chilly ocean night. Emma crept over to her temporary bed and got in, *quite* ready for sleep after spending hours running around. Kimber curled up beside her.

Emma thought about how sad she'd been after getting lost out in the city, when she thought for a while she'd never see her sister or family ever again. Overcome, she clung to Kimber and cried herself to sleep... though the tears came from happiness.

COMMOTION WOKE EMMA MUCH TOO EARLY.

It felt like she'd only *just* gone to sleep before someone started shaking her arm to wake her.

"Hurry up." Merela shook her again. "It's almost time to eat. You'll get in trouble if you're caught in bed when they come to lead us to the dining hall."

"I don't think we will." Emma yawned and forced herself to sit up.

The other orphans in the room scurried about, making their beds and rushing over to get in line by the door. None of them had to worry about getting dressed or changing since they all only owned one dress each, the garment also serving as their nightgowns.

"What happened?" asked Merela.

"Matron Wavecrest is gone." Emma yawned again. "At least, I'm pretty sure she is."

The orphans gasped in awed disbelief.

"Are you sure?" whispered one.

"I'll believe it when I see it. Sounds too good to be true," muttered an older girl.

Little Piper pointed at Emma. "She went outta the room at night and she's not in punishment."

"That only means she didn't get caught." A twelve-year-old folded her arms.

"Has anyone ever done that and not been caught before?" Merela raised an eyebrow. "No."

Emma smiled. "In fairness, I can be quite sneaky."

The girls whispered amongst themselves, discussing the chances Wavecrest might really be gone. Emma dragged herself over to the line, carrying a still-sleeping Kimber. Ambril, who'd managed a full night's sleep, looked wide awake.

Before long, Nerissa appeared at the door. Rather than ordering the girls to march around by pointing as the assistants had been required to do, she smiled and chirped, "C'mon. Follow me to the dining hall and try not to make *too* much noise."

The girls walked in silence, still used to the way things had been. Two or three did risk whispering. Upon reaching the dining hall, a gasp swept over the group of orphans. A few quite noticeable changes stood out as stark as anything. One: Matron Wavecrest was nowhere to be seen. Two: Morwenna sat in the middle chair where the awful witch usually perched. Three: Groundskeeper Terle had also vanished.

Four: little Isla sat beside Morwenna, between her and the younger man who'd been at the head table for dinner the previous night.

Five: some of the orphans already seated at the tables spoke to each other, though tried to keep it quiet.

And most shocking of all, many of the children appeared to be smiling.

Only the girls from the one bedroom had any clue Emma played some part in all of it. Those close enough to do so kept patting her as they filed around the table to take their seat. Alas, the horrible flavorless porridge she'd expected for dinner last night made an appearance as a breakfast meal. Some things might take longer to fix than others, after all.

In the midst of breakfast, Morwenna stood, walked around to stand in front of the head table, and made several announcements to the orphans. She told them she would be taking over as the head matron. Wavecrest would not be back. Morwenna went on to declare that punishment rooms would never be used again—this got all the orphans cheering.

"I do hope none of you misbehave, but you are children, so some degree of it is to be expected." Morwenna chuckled. "From now on, if any of you do something that requires punishment, your punishment will take the form of having to do extra chores."

The children quieted.

"And on the matter of chores." Morwenna tapped her foot. "I am making changes. There will be no more service time and much fewer chores."

The children cheered again.

"Instead, I am increasing the time you'll all spend with your teachers, learning."

Moans of—mostly playful—complaining came from the children.

Morwenna smiled. "Older children will be given some chores to help out and get used to growing up. You'll have more time to simply be children and play. There will be many more, smaller, changes I shan't pester you with right now. You will be seeing some new faces around here in the coming weeks. Much of the work around here you were all made to do will be taken over by proper staff. And lastly, before I let you all go about finishing your breakfast, I wanted to say how sorry I am that it took me *so* long to realize just how horrible a person she was and do something about how she treated you all. I hope you can forgive me."

The children fell quiet.

"Is okay," chirped a little boy at the other table. "She was scary!"

Snickering spread over the children, soon growing into laughter and more cheering.

Morwenna dabbed a happy tear as she started back to her seat.

The girls from Emma's room mobbed her, hugging, patting, and cheering. Even though they could scarcely believe she'd managed to get rid of Wavecrest, they couldn't deny it happened. Toward the end of breakfast, some rumors circulated among the children—started no doubt by the older teens who'd been out in the hallways last night—that guardsmen led Matron Wavecrest out of the building in manacles soon after sunrise.

FOLLOWING BREAKFAST, THE ORPHANS HEADED OFF TO THE CLASSROOMS.

They appeared confused at the idea of learning for more than two hours in a day before having to work. Emma, Kimber, and Ambril went along for now, since they still had a few hours to wait before the box finished charging. No one started screaming yet, so she figured Rin still hadn't been able to get out… or might still be stuck in her magically exhausted sleep.

Emma sat in a classroom with thirty or so other children. Her group ranged in age from eight to ten-year-olds, which allowed her, Kimber, and Ambril to stay together. A relatively friendly older woman taught them about everything from letters to numbers to animals to things about the ocean from breakfast straight until the middle of the day when the woman attempted to lead them to the dining hall. Apparently, she'd never had to do this before as the teenage assistants took care of it. The woman didn't seem to know the way there, but every orphan—except Emma, Ambril, and Kimber—knew the way.

After the mid-day meal, the orphans didn't know what to do with themselves. They weren't given any chores. None got sent off to work as servants in rich people's homes. Most ended up in the yard behind the manor house, playing. Emma caught sight of Heron, the boy who almost ended up on a ship. He looked thrilled, no doubt because he wouldn't be risking his life at sea any time soon.

Morgan and Bree sat together in the classroom and remained together outside while playing. The constant, heavy sorrow hanging over the girl seemed to have finally broken. She looked happy. Emma caught wind of some rumor whispering among the older girls about the man seated with Morwenna. The teens all thought the two of them might be engaged soon. Evidently, he had some job to do with money related to the former Wavecrest Shipping Company and with the outfit it became after the family collapsed.

Emma, Kimber, and Ambril sat in the shade of a tree, watching the other orphans play while talking about how much they hoped Rin could make the box go exactly where they needed it to in order to go home. It didn't seem right to run around playing. Not only did Emma feel far too homesick for it, she didn't want to make friends only to never see them again. Bad enough she'd kind of befriended Bree… and even Sela to a point, and wouldn't see them again in a few more hours.

A bit of commotion stirred up out front when a group of well-dressed people showed up to complain that the child they'd expected to spend the day working around their homes never arrived. Morwenna spent several hours meeting with head servants and even the occasional wealthy citizen. At times, she shouted so loudly her voice made it to the yard outside. The orphans could hardly believe the change in her.

Once it got toward late afternoon, Emma snuck back into the house, trying to avoid anyone seeing her. She felt it best if the three of them took their leave without making a big deal out of it. Ambril insisted on making a stop at the big bedroom so she could collect the remains of her gown and underdress from her drawer. Emma thought it a bit silly, but obliged her.

She hadn't quite come up with how to explain the Box of Wonder to Morwenna or talk her way past the woman to the cabinet. Even though it didn't seem likely the new head matron would try to steal the box from them, letting anyone see it made her nervous. Something so obviously valuable could easily cause problems.

Much to her surprise, she found the matron's office empty. Morwenna's voice carried down the hall from another room where she made it clear to some man who kept trying to overtalk her that he would no longer be able to hire orphans to work at his estate.

Smiling, Emma slipped into the office—which had been left unlocked.

The roots she'd grown over the cabinet remained intact, proving Matron Wavecrest never returned to take a hatchet to the doors.

"Oh, please be ready," whispered Ambril.

Emma reached both hands up at the root-locked cabinet, calling upon Linganthas. In seconds, the hardened roots softened and spread apart, pulling the doors open. The Box of Wonder gave off a brilliant glow of ruby, sapphire, and emerald light.

"Yay!" Kimber bounced around cheering, then climbed up the shelf to grab the box out of the top cubby.

"Be careful!" Emma moved closer, ready to catch her sister if she lost her hold on the shelves.

Kimber pulled the box out of the cabinet, then dropped it. Emma caught it and handed it to Ambril so she could still catch her sister if the girl slipped. Thankfully, she didn't fall. In her rush, Kimber jumped the last few feet to the floor and spun to grin at them.

"Ready?" whispered Ambril, her eyes gleaming with joy and hope.

"Do et!" rasped Kimber.

Emma pulled everyone closer to be sure the box got them all at once.

Ambril lifted the lid. A bright flash of light shone out from the box.

The girls reappeared in the alcove atop the glowing blue rune circle.

Emma dashed into the other room, heading for the bed... which had no one in it. She stopped, frozen in dread that the dark elf girl might have exited the box and gotten herself caught.

"Rin?" called Emma.

"Over here."

She turned.

The Niltharien child sat in a chair at one of the tables over by the library area. A dozen different books lay open in front of her or stacked on either side. It appeared she'd been reading for hours.

Relief almost made Emma fall over. She exhaled hard, then ran to her. "I'm sorry for leaving you in here alone. We had to move the box before thieves got it. Then this awful woman took it away from us..."

"I've figured out how to work it." Rin smiled. "The magic is powerful, but simple."

"Really?" Ambril bounced in place, spinning around in a circle. "We can go home?"

Rin stretched into a yawn. "It would be difficult to use the box to exactly reach your home."

"Oh no." Ambril stopped jumping. "Why can't we go home?"

"I don't mean that." Rin hopped off her chair and walked over to the map table. "Here. Look."

Emma, Kimber, and Ambril hurried after, grouping up around her.

Rin reached out and picked up the silver needle. The four small spherical sapphires at the top end stopped spinning around. "The teleportation goes to wherever this focusing device points. We can control where we go by putting the needle anywhere on the map... except for the oceans. If it's on water, it will move to the nearest land. The reason I said it would be difficult to go exactly home is the scale of the map. We'd have to be incredibly lucky to put the pointer down right on top of your home. Moving the tip of the needle even a little bit could make a difference in many miles."

"Umm." Ambril scratched her head. "Don't you mean the pointer moves to show where we are? We were using the blue orb to make the box go, and when we arrived, the needle moved to show us where we landed. None of us ever touched it before."

Rin glanced at the needle. "I am certain. The teleportation magic will move this box to wherever on the map this pointer is placed. The pointer cannot move itself. If you attempted to teleport without moving the pointer from where you already were, nothing would happen."

"I… it's been going all over." Ambril bit her lip. "How do you explain it taking us to absolutely random places when none of us have ever touched the needle."

"There is no doubt." Rin looked at the map again. "Something must be moving the pointer each time."

Emma shook her head. "We've not even been near the map. The blue crystal ball is all the way over there. All three of us were around it when we used the magic. None of us ever touched that needle until just now when you picked it up. I didn't even think it *could* be picked up."

"Hmm." Rin held the large needle up to examine it. "You must have been doing something wrong then. As far as I can tell, this enchanted device is only capable of translocating the box to wherever this pointer is placed on the map."

"I have a question." Emma glanced at the dark elf girl.

"Okay." Rin smiled. "Also, thank you for bringing me with you. I would surely be dead if you'd left me in Nimaraenna."

"You're welcome. I couldn't possibly leave you there to be hurt." Emma exhaled.

"She'as noice loike that." Kimber winked.

Emma chuckled. "My question is… when you teleported us, we appeared in the forest right away. We didn't have a blinding flash of light. We didn't feel like throwing up."

"Yes." Rin nodded. "That is normal."

"When we make the box teleport, we *all* get really sick." Emma rubbed her stomach.

"I frowed up," whispered Kimber. "Just noffin' come out. Still felt loike frowin' up."

Ambril made a sick face. "Yes. Last time was horrible. I thought my entire belly was going to come out of my mouth."

Rin made a face of deep thought, her violet eyes sparkling. "Strange. Teleportation should not make you feel sick unless…"

"What?" asked Ambril.

"Well." Rin set the needle back down on the map, balanced on its point near the east coast of the northeastern continent, about where it had been before. "I can only think of three reasons why translocation magic might make someone feel sick. This box is not powerful enough to jump across planes, so that's not why you felt sick. It's also not apportation. It's teleportation, so that's not why you felt sick, either."

"What's apportation?" Ambril yawned.

"Same as teleportation." Rin smiled. "Except someone else does it to you. Spells are considered apportation if I cast it on you and you go somewhere else while I remain where I am. If the person using the magic moves themselves or other people with them, it's teleportation. Same magic, slightly different. If you're apportated against your will and try to resist, it will make you feel sick."

Emma didn't really care about such small differences in words. "What's the other thing that could make us sick?"

"An outside force." Rin tapped her tiny ink-black foot on the stone floor. "If a teleportation spell starts and something outside happens that makes it to go somewhere else other than where you want to go, the rapid change will make you feel sick. It's like being in a carriage moving really fast and it takes a hard turn… only much worse."

"What would do that?" Emma scratched her head.

"I don't know." Rin shrugged. "Maybe a demon? Maybe something tremendously powerful and bored. Could be there is someone… or something out there who owns this box and is trying to get it back."

"You can activate the teleport and not 'do it wrong,' right?" asked Ambril.

"Yes." Rin smiled.

"Will you help us get home?" Ambril clasped her hands as if begging. "Please."

"Rin?" Emma bit her lip. "I'd like you to come with Kimber and me and live with us. You need somewhere to be safe."

The Niltharien girl lightly covered her mouth behind her fingers. She stared at Emma for a long moment, tears welling up in her eyes. "You... *want* me to stay with you?"

"Yes." Emma nodded.

"Yes." Kimber thrust her arms out to either side.

"But you're... human." Rin sniffled.

"Mostly." Emma winked. "Nan is a... forest spirit. We're not going to grow old as fast as you think we will. We'll probably grow up and become adults before you do, but we're not gonna die before you're an adult, too. We get to be friends for a long time."

"Is no' a 'ard choice," fake-whispered Kimber. "Live wif us an' be 'appy, or go 'ome an' git stabbed."

Rin blurted a short laugh. "I wouldn't call that place home, not really. All right. If your family will have me, I'd be honored."

"Yay!" Kimber cheered.

Emma clapped.

Rin faced the map. "Do you happen to know where you live?"

"Not exactly." Emma pointed at the big northeastern continent. "Somewhere here on this giant island. I'm not sure where home is. Do you know where the kingdom of Andorath is?"

"It's a continent, not an island," said Ambril. "Islands are much smaller."

"I don't know where Andorath is." Rin spun to face the library half of the room. "There must be maps in one of those books, though. We can find it."

"Why you'as 'ave the sleeps sae bad?" asked Kimber.

Rin shivered. "I am too inexperienced at magic to be safe controlling a teleportation spell. I shouldn't have even tried to cast one. It drained me, might have even killed me."

Emma, Kimber, and Ambril gasped simultaneously.

"However..." Rin shrugged. "Those three would have killed us anyway, so I had no reason not to take the chance."

"The bad lady was wrong." Kimber shook her head. "You'as nae a coward. You'as real brave, like Em."

Emma glared at the table, angry with it for being confusing. "We find a map book."

Kimber ran over to the alcove to lock the lid while Ambril unfurled her ruined dress and sighed at it.

"What happened to your dress?" asked Rin.

"Everything." Ambril exhaled. "Everything awful happened to it."

Rin waved her hand around in an intricate pattern. Thin strands of azure glow traced in the air, her fingertips acting like paintbrushes marking the air with light. "*Ama lior nas foran'a.*"

The peach-colored fabric twitched, then twitched again. As if watching a mushroom grow from nothing to full size in one minute, the gown burst outward, its fluffy skirt reappearing and stitching back together. All the rips, tears, and frays closed up. Soon, the garment once again looked perfect—albeit filthy.

Rin swiped her hand sideways in a dismissive wave. "*Nas veras.*"

Dirt and stains leapt out of the fabric, drifted a few feet to the side, then fell to the floor.

Ambril squealed in delight. She danced in circles, twirling with the beautiful gown like a dance partner. "Oh, thank you! That's incredible! How did you do that?"

"Wow." Kimber gawked.

Perhaps too thrilled to be embarrassed, Ambril changed out of the drab orphan dress into her restored gown. With only Emma, Kimber, and Rin there, it didn't seem to bother her. They had, after all, spent hours playing dress-up at her home. Also, having someone nearby to help her get into the garment made it easier.

"It's only a little cantrip spell." Rin shrugged. "Mending small broken things and getting rid of dirt are trivial. They're usually the first spells any mage learns as a child after how to make light."

Emma faced the bookshelves. "Okay. Everyone spread out. Look for any book about maps."

"Be right there." Ambril scurried over to the drawer to retrieve her earrings and necklace.

40

A FOND FAREWELL

*T*he room wobbled less than an hour into their search for a map book.

Emma and the others all ran to the orb table. Sela had found the box. The teen stood beside the matron's desk, gawking at it.

"Uh oh," whispered Kimber.

"She's going to steal it." Ambril narrowed her eyes.

Emma raised a hand. "Wait. She's never seen anything like it before. I don't think she's going to take it. She's just curious."

Nerissa, another teen girl, and Morwenna walked into the office.

Morwenna glanced around, and sighed. "This is going to be more work than I thought. You girls don't have to help if you don't want to."

"Happy to." Nerissa smiled. "It feels like we're cleaning her right out of the building."

"Yes," said the other girl Emma didn't recognize.

Sela stepped on a low shelf, stretching up to place the Box of Wonder back in the cubby at the top center. She seemed to think it fell. "Yes. Where shall we start?"

Late afternoon sunlight streamed in the windows of the matron's office, tinting the whole scene within the crystal ball faintly orange. Morwenna, Sela, the unknown girl, and Nerissa flitted about like birds building a nest. They appeared to be in the process of cleaning the room up—hopefully getting rid of all traces Cordelia Wavecrest had ever been there. The girls sounded happy, as did Morwenna, while she gleefully spoke of her plans to hire some proper staff and greatly reduce adoption fees so the children had a real chance at finding homes. She also mentioned word of what happened here made it around the city guard and one of the men who accompanied Hurley there the previous night would be stopping in soon with his wife to meet with Bree and Morgan. He'd been so infuriated at the cruelty of keeping the siblings from even talking to each other he wanted to adopt both of them to ensure they were never separated again.

"I'm rather worried about Emma and the other two, who just disappeared." Morwenna looked down. "I do hope that witch hasn't somehow hurt them."

"I haven't seen them since the dining hall at mid-day." Nerissa let out a somber sigh. "Poor children. Do you think they ran away? Is their story about being from a far-off land true?"

"Emma told me they'd be going home." Sela paused dusting a shelf. "Something about magic."

Morwenna approached the cabinet holding the Box of Wonder. "Cordelia took this from her. It's still here... Oh, no." She reached for it, but couldn't quite manage it, being a bit too short. "Sela, dear. Can you please fetch that jeweled box?"

The teen walked over, gawked at the box, then nodded. "Yes, Miss."

"Oh." Morwenna batted a wave at her. "There's no need to talk to me so formally. A simple 'all right' or 'okay' is fine. You aren't a *little* child and I'm not a puffed-up former noble who needs desperately to feel superior to everyone else. You have no idea how much I loathed that 'yes Matron Wavecrest' nonsense."

The three teen girls all laughed.

Sela stepped on the same shelf to reach the Box of Wonder, and took it down.

The room wobbled.

Sela placed the box atop the desk. "How do you think a girl like Emma found something this…"

"Expensive." Nerissa whistled in awe. "A king would have to count his coins to make sure he could afford that."

"It's not *that* expensive." Morwenna brushed her hand over the lid. "Either way. It's Emma's. We should keep it safe until she comes back."

"Will she come back?" asked Sela.

"I imagine." Morwenna bit her lip. "She said she needed this box to go home. It is still here, so she mustn't have gone home yet." The woman kneaded her hands. "I'm worrying."

Emma ran to the alcove. She lifted the lock and touched the blue orb on the wall. Amid a brief flash, she appeared standing in the matron's office.

Sela and Nerissa grabbed Morwenna from either side. All three of them yelped. The other girl squeaked.

"Emma!" Morwenna seemed to deflate with a relieved sigh. "What is going on?"

"I didn't want you to worry about us." Emma hugged her. "We are inside the box. There's a magic crystal ball in there that lets us see what's happening outside. You were worried about us, so I wanted to tell you we're okay, and say goodbye before we went home."

The teens stared in awe at the box.

"Inside?" Sela blinked.

Emma looked around. "It already feels so much brighter in here."

"Cordelia is gone." Morwenna gestured at the room. "It's as if a great dark cloud went with her."

"Gone?" Emma blinked. "The guards?"

"Yes. She's been arrested," whispered Sela. "They dragged her out at sunrise. They've spoken to every orphan here who told them about all the wicked things she did to them. I got in a little trouble, too… only scolded, really."

"You're a child, too. Only did what you did because that woman tortured you with fear." Morwenna patted her shoulder. "Cordelia is no longer the head matron. Even if her barrister manages to keep her out of prison, she won't be returning to this orphanage."

"I would not want to be that barrister." Nerissa cringed. "Almost 200 children, one at a time tellin' a judge about what she done to us... the woman will be in a punishment room for a long time."

"This really is a magical jewelry box." Morwenna poked it. "It's going to take you home?"

"Yes." *Or close to it.*

The office door opened. Isla ran in, scampering up to Morwenna. "Mama, there's a fancy dressed man at the front asking for you."

Morwenna picked her up into a hug. "All right, dear."

Emma grinned, thrilled her hunch about the two of them proved true. "I should go. My family misses me. We've been lost for too long."

"Lost?" Morwenna rested a hand on her head. "Do you need help, Emma?"

"We didn't really know how the box worked before. But now, we do."

"All right. Thank you for helping us and helping me stop being such a coward." Morwenna squeezed Isla and set her down on her feet. "I will run Wavecrest Manor with kindness and love... and probably change the name as soon as I think of something."

"Definitely change the name." Emma laughed.

The teens laughed, too.

Emma hugged them one after the next, saving Morwenna for last. "Goodbye, and I know you'll take good care of everyone here."

"Bye, dear. Do stop by if you're ever in the city again." Morwenna waved.

Emma grasped the box lid and lifted it an inch. She reappeared inside.

Ambril, Kimber, and Rin met her at the exit of the alcove.

"There is a small problem." Ambril set her hands on her hips. "None of the books have maps."

Rin held up a finger. "It's not *too* much of a problem. I know a little bit. Come. I'll show you."

They followed the dark elf child over to the map table.

"This map is quite detailed, even if it has no labels." Rin pointed at the large black-purplish-blue area near the top center of the continent. "That is obviously Nimaraenna. I recognize the flora. The Shadow Peaks"—she traced her finger along the mountain range separating her homeland from the rest of the continent—"define the southern border. Further south are the lands of Blackmar and Mordrehel. I *think* Andorath is right below them. This flat place in the middle is Vath Oruuk, the Orcish homeland."

"I've never seen an orc," said Emma.

"You don't want to." Ambril shivered.

Rin shrugged. "They are no worse than human barbarians. And I'm not calling all humans barbarians. I mean, humans who are barbarians."

Emma chuckled. "I know."

"I'm just not certain if it's Andorath then Sondaren… or the other way around." Rin tapped her foot. "Somewhere to the west is the Talethian Empire, but you aren't Imperials."

"No. Da doesn't like Imperials." Emma shook her head.

"So…" Rin circled her finger around the map a little left of the middle of the northeastern continent. "We're in Greymarch right now, which is quite far away from your home. Do you know if Andorath is north of Sondaren or if Sondaren is north of Andorath?"

"Sondaren is to the south." Ambril pointed at the map. "I'm sure of it. Father goes there to trade since it has a port city. So, yes, it must be south of Andorath. There are no port cities. Andorath doesn't touch the ocean."

"All right." Rin set the pointer down. "This spot should at least be in your kingdom. To get any closer to where you live, we'd need to find a good map… or someone who studies maps."

"What do we do now?" asked Emma.

Rin walked over to the orb table. "We activate the blue sphere."

"Do ya know wot tha' red one does?" Kimber smiled.

"Yes. Don't touch it." Rin stomped. The sharp clap of her bare foot on the stone floor made everyone jump. "It causes a fireball to explode outside the box."

"Eek!" Ambril shivered. "Why would anyone make that?"

"Uh oh." Kimber took a step back. "Tha's bad."

I almost touched that one the first time. Emma gulped. *It would've burned down Ambril's house.*

"To stop someone trying to steal the box when the owner is inside it." Rin folded her arms. "I can't tell how powerful the fireball is. It might do anything from lightly singe a person to burn them away to ashes. You don't need to be afraid of the red orb. The spell won't go off if you accidentally bump it. A person would have to think about wanting it to happen."

"Wanting a fireball? Or wanting 'something magical' to happen?" Emma tilted her head.

"The fireball. It won't work if you don't know exactly what it's going to do and want it to happen." Rin nodded.

Emma, Kimber, and Ambril sighed in relief.

"All right." Rin rested her hand on the blue orb. "Are you ready to go home?"

"Yes." Ambril grinned.

Kimber nodded rapidly, throwing her hair into a tangled red mess.

"Very." Emma squirmed from anxiety, still not quite able to really believe this time they teleported, they'd be home. She glanced over at the map table, not fully trusting it.

Rin focused her attention on the blue orb.

The pointer started to spin, the tiny sapphires at the top whirling into a blur. Magical lightning snapped intermittently from the top of the pointer to the map. A sense that a powerful spell built up energy about to release filled the room.

All of a sudden, a grey-and-black tabby cat sprang out from behind a bookshelf and leapt onto the map table, pouncing on the pointer.

"Wait! Stop!" shouted Emma. She grabbed Rin around the middle and lifted her away from the orb.

"Eeeeep!" screamed Rin.

Ambril and Kimber shrieked in unison.

The cat caught the spinning pointer in its mouth, tumbled over while rabbit-kicking its back paws at the device, then—seemingly terrified—scrambled off the table and darted behind another bookshelf. The pointer lifted itself up to stand on end once more, way out on the ocean. All by itself, it rapidly slid in a straight line to the nearest point of land, almost all the way to the southwest part of the same continent—an area that looked like an incredibly dense, lush forest.

"Cat!" shouted Emma.

"What?" stammered Ambril.

Rin wheezed like she couldn't breathe.

"Sorry." Emma set Rin back down on her feet and loosened her grip.

Rin spun to look at her, wide-eyed. "What do you mean, cat? And why do you want to wait? I thought you wanted to go home?"

"I do." Emma ran over to the map table. "When you touched the blue orb, the needle started spinning faster. A cat came out from behind the shelf and jumped on it."

The girls rushed over.

"Outside force." Rin laughed. "I know what happened."

Kimber and Ambril exchanged a baffled glance.

Rin pointed at the orb table. "You all were over there looking at the blue sphere each time you used the teleport."

The girls nodded.

"The cat must have attacked the pointer every time it started spinning, moving it while the teleportation spell worked. You started going to one place, then the cat dragged the pointer across the map while the box jumped... so you landed somewhere else. That's why you got so sick."

Emma furrowed her brows. "And why we kept going to random places."

"Yes." Rin stood tall, smiling with pride. "I told you I knew how this thing worked. If the needle stays in one place, you will go exactly where you put it... and you won't get sick."

"Strixian, please grant me the Wildkin Whisper," grumbled Emma before shouting, "Caaaaaat!"

41

ANDOR

*A*las, the kitty seemed too afraid to respond or show themselves.

Rin repositioned the pointer on the map, then hurried back to the orb table.

"Cat, please don't swat the spinning thing again," meowed Emma. "We won't hurt you."

Still, the animal didn't respond or appear. Emma decided to stay at the map table and defend the pointer needle from further feline interference.

Rin touched the blue sphere. A minute or so later, a faint flash filled the room and it vibrated slightly.

The most obvious sign anything happened came from the large crystal ball: the scene inside it changed. If not for the view switching in an instant to somewhere else, Emma might not have known the teleport went off.

"Hope we are close." Rin took her hand off the empty sphere. "Twenty-four hours before we can do it again."

"Wow. I don't feel sick." Ambril peered down at her stomach.

"Told you." Rin held her arms out to either side. "I might only be an apprentice, but I read everything at least twice."

Since it didn't matter now if the cat fussed with the pointer, Emma walked over to the orb table. The view in the crystal ball showed a rolling meadow outside a large city. It seemed to be only minutes after sunrise.

"Does teleporting take a long time?" Emma glanced at Rin.

"No. It's instant." The dark elf child shook her head.

"Do you know why it looks like the sun just came up? Is it tomorrow?"

"Because we traveled a really far distance." Rin dragged Emma back to the map and pointed to the east coast. "In Greymarch, it's still the same time, almost evening. Where we are now, it's early in the morning. Time isn't the same everywhere. Most people never notice because they can't travel far enough, fast enough without magic to become aware of the difference. When you're teleporting across the continent, you see it." Rin pointed at the far west side of the continent. "It's still dark there because it's too early for the sun to be up."

"That's crazy," whispered Ambril.

"So is teleporting." Emma shrugged. "Why is time so weird?"

"It's not time. It's daylight. Specifically, the sun." Rin held up a fist and traced a circle around it with her other hand. "The sun is a fireball way up in the sky. It goes around and around our world, which is a ball. The sun can't shine on the whole ball at the same time, so it's light in some places and dark in others."

Emma scratched her head. "How do you know that?"

"Mages like learning all kinds of things. Not just magic." Rin smiled, then bowed her head, seeming heartbroken. "My uncle loved to teach me things."

"I'm sorry." Emma hugged her.

"Thanks. I... expected it would happen someday, but I hoped it wouldn't be so soon." Rin wiped her eyes. "My kind can live for thousands of years, just like forest elves. Unfortunately, we rarely do because we keep killing each other."

"Is your mother going to come after you?" asked Ambril.

Rin bit her lip. "I don't *think* so. As long as I stay far away from Nimaraenna, I'm as good as dead and not a threat to her reputation or political ambitions. I don't want to go back. I don't care about being noble. I'd rather be alive."

"Me too." Emma exhaled. "I also need a privy. And I'm getting hungry. It feels like it should be time for dinner, even though it's early morning here."

"I think this is Andor." Ambril bounced and pointed at the big orb.

Emma had heard of the city named Andor, though never went there. She knew a great river ran southwest across the middle of the kingdom past Calebrin City—where Da's family lived. Going to Widowswood from Calebrin took a few days by coach to the southwest. One would need to travel much farther northeast along the river from Calebrin to reach Andor. Da sometimes mentioned they had problems with Orcish raiders there, since it sat so close to the border. Going home from here would probably take at least a week and a half by coach, if not longer.

"Almost." Emma scratched the back of her left leg with her right foot. "I think we should go into Andor and look for someone who knows maps. It's going to take us at least a week, maybe two to get home without teleporting again. Waiting one day for the box to be able to work again is much faster. If we can get the pointer in just the right place, we'll be home."

"Okay." Ambril nodded. "I'm hungry. I've some coin left. Let's find an inn and get something to eat."

"You have money?" Kimber blinked. "'ow'd ya keep it 'way from that bad ol' witch?"

"I left it in here." Ambril pointed at the drawer where she'd put her jewelry. "When Emma told me I could be robbed, I left everything valuable. Father gives me a few coins now and then to use on things I like. It's not that much, really. Plenty enough to buy something to eat."

Emma led the way to the alcove. Kimber snagged the grey orphan dress Ambril left on the floor, carrying it with her. Once everyone stood inside the magic circle, Rin touched the blue orb on the wall.

They appeared standing in waist-high meadow grass. The city of Andor sat off in the distance, not quite an hour's walk.

After everyone found a little privacy to water the grass, they regrouped. Kimber used the drab grey dress as an improvised sack to carry the Box of Wonder so no one could see it. The girls set off across the meadow toward the pale grey walls of Andor as the sun rose higher in the sky, soon spotting a well-worn road crossing the meadow. By the time they followed the road all the way to the city gates, dawn progressed to full morning. Farmers, villagers, travelers, and wanderers went back and forth under the great portcullis.

A few guards glanced at them, not seeming terribly concerned... until they spotted Rin. Their expressions conveyed a mix of fear and confusion. None did more than stare. Emma figured the people recognized a dark elf and considered them dangerously evil, but didn't know what to expect from a child.

Emma held her arm out. "Rin, hold my hand."

"Okay." The girl grasped her hand. "Do you think it will help, or are you trying to make me feel better?"

"Both."

Rin exhaled. "I expected as much. It's why I stayed in the box before. My people mostly deserve their reputation. Humans will not be nice to me. I am prepared for it."

More people took notice of them, especially Rin. As soon as each townsperson spotted the dark elf child, they stopped walking or setting wares out on display for sale and simply stared. Rin gazed around, trying to smile. Her apparent cheerfulness further confused the people. It pained Emma to watch the girl overact being happy when she still hadn't had time to mourn her uncle.

Ambril took lead, head held high like a princess returning to her castle city. Here, people would recognize her family name. With her dress restored to its former glory, no one would mistake her for an orphan without a copper coin to her name.

The whispering didn't take long to start. People wondered out loud if they'd just seen a dark elf. Some said stupid things like 'I thought they'd be larger.' Most people correctly recognized her as a child rather than thinking all elves only stood as tall as shorter-than-average nine-year-olds. No one approached the girls, got in their way, or tried to talk to them. Emma hoped no one would do anything meaner than stare.

"There." Ambril pointed. "The Gilded Fawn."

"'Oo chopped ae fawn's bits off?" whispered Kimber.

"You're thinking of *gelded*. Gilded means gold." Ambril blushed. "It's a nice inn."

"How do you know it's nice?" asked Emma.

"The ones that aren't nice have names like the 'drunken rat' or the 'blind-eye crow.'" She crossed the street toward a large, mostly white building with cris-crossed dark brown beams making X forms around the wall. "The nice inns usually have gold or fancy things in the name."

"I trust you." Emma gestured. "Lead the way."

The inn didn't have a porch, the front door—at the corner of the building—touched the street. Ambril opened the door and stepped into a small foyer. The interior, mostly dark brown wood and red velvet, appeared clean and cozy. Tables and chairs took up most of the room ahead and right. To the left, a man stood behind a bar counter in front of a row of empty stools. Sounds of activity in a kitchen came from a door next to the bar. The air smelled of baking bread and pies.

Emma's stomach growled.

Ambril looked around, appeared to frown slightly at not finding something, then walked into the room. She chose a table and sat in one of the chairs. Emma, Kimber, and Rin also took seats.

"Why did you look annoyed?" whispered Emma.

"There wasn't a host to seat us." Ambril drummed her fingers on the table. "This inn isn't as fancy as I thought. It's all right. Nothing to worry about. I just didn't want to be rude and not wait for a host if one happened to be here."

A scattering of other people, some merchants, some travelers, and a handful of men dressed in ordinary clothing that didn't make their status or occupation obvious, sat among the other tables. Most everyone in sight stopped talking and eating to stare at Rin.

Ambril tolerated this for a few minutes before standing out of her seat and facing the room. "This girl is my guest, and I expect her to be treated accordingly. I'll thank you all to compose yourself properly.

Our presence is no concern to anyone. We merely require something to eat and we shall be on our way."

Some of the inn patrons returned to their conversation and meals. A few kept staring, now more at Ambril than Rin. One by one—as she continued to glare at everyone—they appeared to lose interest in the girls.

Once no one obviously watched them anymore, Ambril took her seat.

The man from the bar approached the table. "Morning. You four are a bit young to be out on your own?"

"We are on the way home after an unexpected trip." Ambril held up a small silver-and-gold coin. "I found the look of your establishment quite appealing, so decided to stop here for a meal. Would you be so kind as to provide us whatever you have ready for a meal? As well as some water, please?"

The bartender raised an eyebrow at her. "All right, lass."

"Oll 'ave a basilisk bloinder," said Kimber. "Nae too 'eavy onna glowin' fog, please. The fizz makes me nose itch."

He stared at her, mouth agape.

After a moment, Kimber sighed. "Or yer foinest rum. Spiced."

The bartender continued staring at her, closing his mouth.

Kimber grumbled, set her elbows on the table, chin in her hands. "Or water is foine."

"Water it is, lass." He shook his head, then walked off to the kitchen.

"Where did that come from?" Emma blinked. "What is a 'basilisk blinder'?"

"Is a drink. The men at the teef guild in Calebrin used ta dare each other ta drink 'em." Kimber waved her hand about. "It's got a bunch o' glowin' foggy fizz comin' out of et. 'Alf the men wot drank 'em, dropped right tae sleep on the spot."

Emma leaned closer to her. "You are not going to drink a basilisk blinder."

"I donnae really want tae." Kimber grinned. "Jes wanted ta see 'is face."

"What would you have done if he gave you one?" She swiped at Kimber's hair.

"I'd *not* 'ave drunk et, thas fer right sure." Kimber gagged. "Jus 'avin a bit o' fun wif 'im."

Ambril covered her mouth to mute a laugh.

Rin appeared amused. "Why do humans drink things that make them pass out?"

"How should I know?" Emma shrugged.

"You're human?" Rin tilted her head.

"Yes, but I'm also not stupid." Emma rolled her eyes.

A few minutes later, the bartender returned. He set out a bunch of plates with bread, jam, apple slices, cheese, and four cups of water.

"Will that do, love?" He glanced at Ambril.

"Lovely. Thank you." She offered him the coin.

The man took it. "Back in a moment with the difference."

Ambril nodded. "No rush, good sir."

Emma grabbed bread, slathered jam on it, and ate. Seeing apple slices and cheese in the same meal made her intensely homesick as it reminded her of Da. She still couldn't bring herself to put both apple and cheese in her mouth at the same time like he did.

The barman returned, setting a small pile of all-silver coins on the table by Ambril. Mouth full, she nodded thanks to him, then pushed three coins out of the pile toward him.

"Kind of ya, lass." He scooped the tip into his hand and went back to the bar.

Emma furrowed her brow, not quite sure why the man acted as if one single gold-and-silver coin was worth so much. Then again, she didn't really understand money, nor did she care much about it. Despite being slightly thinner than Emma, Rin consumed a surprising amount of food, likely due to her having spent a whole day inside the box without having anything to eat. The girl didn't hesitate or appear to have any difficulty with 'normal' food, as opposed to the poisonous plants and teas common to her homeland.

While eating, the girls discussed whether they should be happy they made it to the right kingdom and take a coach home, or try to nudge the needle closer to Widowswood without going too far. Emma pointed out their biggest problem thus far had been an unknown cat moving the pointer. Now that they knew how to use the box, they didn't have to worry about ending up in a dangerous place much farther away. Ambril didn't think she had enough money with her to afford a coach ride for all four of them all the way to Widowswood. However, if the coach office recognized her father's name, they might be willing to take a chance he'd pay them extra upon arrival.

Kimber wanted to use the box since it would take one day instead of two weeks. Rin expressed confidence the box could take a small jump safely as long as someone guarded the pointer and kept the cat off it. After some back-and-forth, Ambril said she also thought the box would be a better idea since she feared an untrustworthy coach driver who recognized her family name might kidnap her for ransom once realizing they traveled without an adult.

Emma stuffed herself until she couldn't bear the thought of another apple slice.

Kimber had blueberry jam all over her face and hands. Somehow, she'd managed not to get it on the table and her dress. Ambril finished her meal without getting a speck of jam or single crumb on her dress or face.

"Two men are watching us," whispered Rin. "It's not because I'm Niltharien. They have taken note of Ambril's jewelry and coin. They're discussing following us and waiting for an opportunity to rob us."

"You can hear them?" whispered Ambril.

"She 'as long elf ears." Kimber gave a whispery giggle. "O'course she kin 'ear em."

Rin chuckled, then whispered, *"Nas veras"* while pointing at Kimber. The jam smeared on her face and hands peeled off, collected into a mass, and fell on her plate.

"We just need to be careful." Emma finished her water. "Stay away from dark places."

"Donnae loike bein' 'way from Mama, Da, an' Nan." Kimber frowned. "I'm scared."

Emma reached over and squeezed her sister's hand. She, too, felt the same way. A group of children their age so far away from home without an adult to look after them could easily find themselves in big trouble. Someone could try to trick, rob, or hurt them. "Hmm. Maybe one of the town guards would be willing to escort us home if I tell them who our da is."

"Are you royal?" Rin glanced at her, then ate another apple slice.

"No. Da is captain of the town watch where we live." Emma almost reached for a bit of cheese, until looking at it made her feel overly full. "We're close enough to home the guards here will probably know his name and be nice to us because he's a guard, too."

Kimber pointed at Ambril. "Her da has loads of... goats."

Ambril nearly choked on the water she sipped.

"Goats?" Rin's eyelids fluttered in confusion.

Ambril set her cup down, coughed once, then blinked at her. "Goats?"

Kimber leaned forward and whispered, "Was gonnae say gold but no' tae loud 'cause those men are watchin' us."

"Why don't we go talk to a guard and see how long it would take a coach to bring us to Widowswood?" Emma rubbed her full belly. "I might be wrong about it taking two whole weeks."

"If you're wrong, you aren't wrong by too much." Ambril dabbed her mouth with a napkin. "When my father visits Andor, he's usually gone for about four weeks, about two to go there and two more to return. He's also not in a hurry."

"Donnae 'urt tae talk ta one." Kimber hopped out of her chair. "An' guards gonnae keep the teefs away."

Emma stood. "All right. Let's go."

Everyone in the room stopped talking and eating to watch them as they got up. Most eyes followed Rin except for the two men she warned about, who didn't appear to be looking at the girls at all.

They're not good thieves. Every other person is staring at us except those two trying to act like we aren't even here. Obvious. Emma sighed. *Drat. They* are *going to come after us.*

THE SMALL PASSAGE

*A*fter thanking the bartender for the food, the girls went outside.

Concerned about the thieves, Emma didn't wait to look around. She hurried down the street in the direction she happened to already be facing, walking fast. It didn't matter which way she went as she wanted to get away from thieves rather than go somewhere specific. During the hour or so they'd been inside eating, more people filled into the streets, going about their day. Most who noticed the girls stopped to ogle Rin.

The sight of a dark elf would have been enough to make most humans pause. Spotting not only a child, but one wearing a gossamer pink-purple faerie dress seemed to so defy anyone's expectations, they didn't know what to do beyond staring in a most impolite way.

Sure enough, the two men who'd been watching Ambril followed them out of the inn and down the street. Emma picked up her pace, almost to jogging. The men did the same. Now scared, Emma searched around for anyone who looked like a guard. Seeing none, she tried to approach any reasonably tall, reasonably strong man who didn't look scary. Alas, everyone she intended to ask for help saw the dark elf coming and walked away in a hurry.

With nothing else to do, Emma grabbed Kimber's hand and broke into a run.

The men chased them, poorly attempting to be subtle about it. They didn't run as much as jogged fast, following the girls without trying to overtake and catch them.

I'm really getting tired of being chased by thieves. In a moment of childish fear, she almost screamed for Mama out loud. It wouldn't help. Mama couldn't hear her from so far away. However, the thought gave her hope. A bird could easily make it from here to Widowswood in a day or two. Maybe three. She could ask a bird to go get Nan, who could turn into a raven and fly here. While her grandmother would be weakened if she strayed too far from the woods, a quick trip up the river to collect Emma and go home shouldn't be bad. If she sent a bird for help, they'd only need to find somewhere safe to hide and wait. Not too difficult. The Box of Wonder made a perfectly safe shelter—if they could find somewhere to put it where no one would take it.

Whoever made it is an idiot. Emma fumed while running. *They should have made it look plain. Wood. Not solid gold with gems all over it. Everyone who sees it wants to steal it.*

Running along had the strange effect of causing *fewer* people to stare at them. They went by before anyone got a good enough look at them to recognize a dark elf. Also, they likely assumed children running around played or had fun, nothing they needed to concern themselves with.

"Em" Kimber tugged her to the side, pointing. "O'er there. Alley."

Emma reacted without thinking, following her sister's pull to the right. They ducked around the corner of a basket weaver's shop and came to a stop in an alley, the thieves maybe ten seconds behind. "What?"

"Little door." Kimber pointed again.

Thirty or so feet from the alley entrance, someone put a child-sized doorway on the wall. It looked even a bit small for Emma. An adult man would never fit through it. Mere seconds remained before the thieves came around the corner and caught them in an alley out of sight of any townspeople. Emma didn't have time to think. She dashed over to the tiny door, ducked, and shimmied in.

Five feet from the opening, the tiny corridor became a downward spiral ramp. Emma summoned Mythandriel's light and kept going. Ambril gathered her skirt and stuffed herself into the passage right as the echo of men's footsteps clapped upon the cobblestones in the alley. Head ducked away from the ceiling, Emma shimmied around several turns in the narrow passageway before it opened out to a miniature corridor with walls of crude bricks that went in two directions, left or right.

Kimber, Rin, and Ambril emerged behind her.

The hallway let her stand up straight, offering a tiny bit of clearance above her head. Ambril's hair touched the ceiling. Men's angry shouting came down the spiral.

"Come on out of there, kids," called a man. "It's dangerous. The rats will eat you."

Ambril let out a soft, 'eep.'

Emma shivered.

"'E's loyin'." Kimber shook her head. "'E's gotta be loyin' ta trick us."

"What is this place?" whispered Ambril.

Rin squinted, shielding her eyes from the glowing orb. "It's long. Probably goes across the entire city. Before you ask, yes, I can see in the dark."

Emma reached up to touch the dirt above her. *Is this how Guard Kavan feels when he goes into a house, head touching the ceiling?*

The thieves kept trying to coax them to come back up, their stories about rats wanting to eat or hurt them sounding increasingly unbelievable. A nimble enough thief might be able to squeeze himself down the passage, though he'd probably get stuck in the tight spiral. It didn't sound like the men were desperate enough to take the risk. Had they seen the Box of Wonder, they likely would have. Ambril's earrings and a few coins wouldn't be worth it.

If they recognized her and thought to kidnap her for ransom, they'd probably be trying to squeeze down the passageway, too.

Simple pickpockets.

"Em, look," called Kimber, from a little way down the corridor at the edge of the light.

"Don't run off." Emma hurried over to her.

Kimber pointed at a little door. Compared to the hallway, it appeared normal sized. As big to an eight-year-old as an ordinary door would be to an adult.

What... does Andor have a thieves' guild for children? Emma reached for the knob and found a simple lift latch instead. She opened the door and peeked into a small room with a table and chairs appropriately sized for this miniature world. Three battered tin plates on the table held a scattering of tiny bones. They looked as if they'd been there for some time.

Curious, Kimber darted in and sat. "Look Em! My feet are on the floor an' I'm settin' on a chair. I'as a grown up."

There didn't appear to be anyone down here. Thieves couldn't fit. This could be the perfect place to hide waiting for Nan. Or... at least waiting for the box to recharge. She still wanted to find a book of maps or someone who knew maps before teleporting again. If they relied on magic, she did not want to miss and waste another entire day waiting.

Emma entered the room and took a seat at the table, feeling like an adult. Rin and Ambril walked in as well. Ambril did not sit in one of the chairs, giving it a wary 'that's too dirty' frown.

"This is strange." Emma tapped her foot, not used to being able to sit in a chair without her feet dangling. "Who made this? Why?"

Kimber shrugged.

Ambril shifted around, trying not to touch anything. "The floor is dirt. The ceiling is dirt. If my dress gets ruined again, will you please fix it?"

"Sure." Rin smiled at her.

They sat there, waiting for the thieves to get bored and go away. To pass the time, they talked about what they thought might have made this odd miniature corridor and room. Kimber suspected 'large faeries.' Ambril brought up the idea a previous city existed here before Andor that shrank for unknown reasons.

Rin's laughter came to a sudden stop. She stared at the door. "Something's coming."

Ambril clasped her hands to her chest. "Is it going to eat us?" Kimber whined.

Emma sprang out of the chair to face the door, ready to call upon Linganthas' thorns.

The door flew open, revealing a crowd of strange creatures clustered out in the hall. They resembled enormous rats walking upright on two legs. Some wore vests made of leather armor, others only had belts on. All carried daggers or small swords. Four ratlings crept into the room, the nearest one locking stares with Emma. He drew a small dagger from a bandolier over his vest. Ones in the back whispered amongst themselves. The chattering made it sound like a great number of them lurked beyond the doorway.

Uh oh. We're in big trouble.

The lead ratling waved its knife at her. "No belong. You punish. Give life."

"No make bread," yelled Kimber. "We gnomes. Nae rattle. Dim time on step bruvva trip on us."

The ratlings all stopped chattering at once. Those with readied daggers put them away.

"Did she hit her head in that tunnel?" whispered Ambril.

"No, it's thief talk." Emma kept watching the ratlings, not trusting them at all. "What did you say to them?"

"Oi ask' 'em no' ta kill us. Bread means dead. Tol' 'em we want to go home and won't tell anyone we saw 'em."

"Did you say something about Tam?" Ambril raised an eyebrow. "Step brother?"

"'E nae ma step bruvva. 'E my bruvva." Kimber folded her arms. "Dim's mean hide. Step bruvva's 'ow ya talk 'bout teefs wot aren't in your guild. Rivals."

"They didn't trip over us." Ambril rubbed her head. "This is so confusing."

"Trip mean' search." Kimber rolled her eyes.

"Obviously." Ambril sighed at the ceiling.

"Search sound loike lurch. When ya trip, ya lurch." Kimber pantomimed starting to fall over. "Bad thieves' searchin' for us, so we dim—hide—in 'ere fer a time."

Rin gestured at the ratlings. "They don't look like they want to kill us anymore. That must be good."

"Why you here?" chirped the lead ratling.

"She told you." Emma kept her magic at the tip of her tongue, expecting this conversation to go bad at any second. "We're hiding from some thieves who tried to rob us. Saw the little door and had nowhere else to go."

"No why." Another ratling shook its head. "Mean *how* human and elf see door. Runes open only us."

"What?" Emma blinked.

"I think he's saying the little doorways are magical. Only they can see them because of the runes." Rin nodded to Kimber. "I think these creatures are confused. The runes probably work for thieves, not merely whatever sort of creature they are. Human thieves are usually too big to fit in the tiny doorways, so they must believe they can't find the openings. The runes must recognize Kimber as a thief."

"I'as nae a teef or a stealer." Kimber frowned.

"Not all thieves steal property." Rin crept sideways, putting herself behind Ember. "Some spy, or sneak around delivering messages without being seen. The runes could react to you knowing how to do that, or maybe because you understand that weird nonsense language. As soon as you pointed the door out to us, we could see it, too."

"I'as nae a stealer!" Kimber sniffled. "I'as only did the stealin' when Pa toss' me inna window o' places wot 'e coul' nae get inta an' make me open the door fer 'im. I donnae loike stealin'. Umm, but some rich people are mean, so I donnae much mind stealin' from them. I don't gotta steal now, 'cause I got a proper family."

"We're sorry for intruding on your home," said Emma. "We only wanted to hide from some bad people. I promise we won't tell anyone this is here. We'll go away if you let us."

The ratlings looked at each other, whispering as to whether or not they should trust the humans.

"You are clearly smart and wise people," said Ambril. "You know everything about this city and there's nowhere you can't go."

The ratlings murmured in approval.

"Certainly, beings as wise as you could tell us where we can find a human who is wise but not as wise as you, who knows about maps?" Ambril smiled.

A moment of whispered discussion went on among the ratlings in a series of squeaks and chattering noises—not normal speech.

Emma cast the Wildkin Whisper.

The ratlings spoke mostly of Ambril's jewelry and also wanted to know what Kimber had in the bundle of grey fabric. A few claimed to smell gold and gems.

"Will you help us find someone who knows about maps?" asked Emma through the spell.

The ratlings all shut up at the same time, gawking at her.

Once the shock of her seeming to speak their language faded, the lead rat pointed at her. "We will take you to a place where you can find such a human. We demand you hand over all your valuables in payment for this service."

Emma peered down at herself, then back up at the ratling. "All I have is my dress and it isn't worth anything."

The ratling pointed at Ambril. "Her earrings. Necklace. Coin purse."

Another ratling sniffed at Kimber. "Gold. Gems."

"Uhh..." Emma tensed. "Ambril, they want your jewelry and money."

She gasped. "You're really going to rob children?"

All the ratlings nodded with great enthusiasm.

"We prefer rob children," said one in human speech. "Children much easy to fight than big humans. No ratling gets hurt."

43

RATS

*T*wo ratlings moved toward Ambril.

She scooted around behind the table. Emma shifted left to get in their way. Three more scampered over to Kimber and grabbed the dress bundle. Kimber snarled, twisting and pulling away from them. Emma lunged at one, palming it on the chest and shoving it off her sister. The ratlings' claws sliced the grey fabric open, allowing the corner of the golden, bejeweled box to pop out into view.

Absolute chaos erupted.

As soon as the ratlings saw the box, they screeched and lost their minds. Apparently, since they had the children trapped in the room, they already considered the golden box theirs. Rather than attack Kimber, they went after each other, arguing over who saw it first and which ratling had proper claim on the box.

"Ow!" yelped Ambril. "It got my earring!"

Emma called on Uruleth for strength and threw the ratlings off Kimber whenever they tried to make a grab for the box. She stood at least as tall as most of them, taller than some, making it relatively easy —thanks to her magical strength—to throw them around. One ratling spun himself around so fast, his giant hairless tail swept Emma's feet out from under her. She crashed down flat on her back. The ratling stepped on her stomach and grabbed Kimber, who let out a war scream and two-hand walloped him across the face with the bundled-up golden box.

The ratling careened over the table, unconscious.

Ambril screamed, backing into the deepest corner of the room.

Emma rolled to her feet in time to grab another ratling attempting to climb over the table and pounce on Ambril. She dragged him off the table and threw him into the crowd fighting each other by the door, knocking three other ratlings over. They all scrambled to their feet, drew daggers, and glared at her.

Uh oh.

"*Nelvas kura ama dura vekh,*" chanted Rin, while making a series of complex hand motions.

A faint violet glow appeared around her for an instant before blasting outward in a circle. The magical burst of light startled Ambril enough to make her stop screaming. The ratlings' fight stalled. Rather than clawing, biting, and punching, they stood in place holding each other up like a bar brawl frozen in time. The four ratlings converging on Emma with daggers slouched forward, mouths agape to expose long, yellow teeth. Two seconds later, the ratlings all collapsed to the floor, unconscious.

Rin made a 'shh' gesture, then put her hands together beside her cheek, tilting her head in a sign of sleeping.

Kimber bundled the box back up in the grey fabric. Rin moved toward the door, carefully placing her feet between ratling bodies, limbs, and tails. Emma followed, sometimes having to hold her arms out for balance while taking a big step over a whole ratling without touching him. Kimber maneuvered gingerly through the ratlings out into the corridor. Outside in the corridor to the right, thirty sleeping ratlings lay between them and the doorway to the spiral.

Nope. I'm going to step on one or fall. And the thieves might still be up there.

Emma went to her left, which only required having to go past five ratlings. The creatures in that direction also fainted farther apart from each other making it easy to walk by and not step on them. Rin and Kimber followed her.

After gathering her fluffy skirt up, Ambril nervously attempted to navigate the sleeping ratlings without touching one. The girl whimpered and shivered as if she expected to die if she so much as brushed against one whisker. She stepped out the door into the hall, pivoted to face Emma and the others, took two more slow, careful steps, then stopped, staring at a ratling on the ground next to her.

"What are you doing?" mouthed Emma without adding voice.

Ambril crouched, reaching down at the creature beside her. Emma almost yelled at her, stuffing her right forearm in her mouth to keep quiet. Ambril grabbed something, trying to pull it out of the grasp of the sleeping ratling. The creature twitched.

"Eep!" Ambril jumped back, blindly stepping on the tail of another one behind her.

That one sat up, shrieking in pain. Its cry woke all the other ratlings.

Ambril screamed, yanked her hand up—with her missing emerald teardrop earring dangling from two fingers—and ran.

Emma thrust her hands forward. *Linganthas, lend me your aid!* A vast tangling swath of small vines burst up from the dirt floor, writhing around and grabbing at everything they could. Most of the ratlings got stuck, tiny thorns biting into their unprotected feet and tails. They hissed in anger, pulled daggers, and began slicing at the roots.

"Run!" shouted Emma.

She took Kimber by the hand and sprinted. Mythandriel's light chased her, weaving side to side above her shoulders. The glow from the spell only shone twenty or so feet into the distance, making it scary to run so fast... but not as scary as an army of ratlings with long daggers and even longer teeth. Ambril hurried after her, grunting and gasping from the effort to move so fast. Rin flew along behind her, not making a sound nor seeming to have to work very hard to keep up.

It didn't take the ratlings long to break loose and chase after them. At first, the creatures tried running upright. When that proved too slow, they dove down to all fours, scampering like actual rats. Doing that gained them a significant amount of speed.

"Look out!" called Rin. "There's a gap ahead."

At Emma's desire, Mythandriel's light orb floated out in front of her. Three strides later, the farthest edge of the area illuminated by the spell revealed a missing section of floor, ending at a jagged break. The hallway continued on the other side of a gap. Emma thought the opening looked possible to jump over—as long as she didn't slow down to look. She'd need to be going fast to clear the distance. If she stopped to check how deep the fall would be, she'd never be able to leap across from a standstill. Stopping at all meant they would have to fight ratlings.

They might be smaller than her—by a little bit—but there also happened to be thirty or forty ratlings to four children… and neither Ambril nor Kimber could really do anything in a serious fight, which turned it into a forty-on-two battle against an apprentice druid and an apprentice mage.

Bad odds.

"Jump across!" shouted Emma.

Kimber leaned into her stride, running faster.

Ambril made a strange, terrified noise that somehow translated to 'you can't be serious.'

Emma stared at the spot where the floor had fallen away. As she drew closer, the light went farther into the other part of corridor. Something, probably water, going by underground had eaten away the floor. The opposite face looked solid enough for her to commit to the jump. She sped up as much as she could. Uruleth's strength spell let her narrow legs fling her body forward in bounding leaps like a deer.

At the last possible second, she jumped.

Emma flew across the gap, swinging her arms. She landed clean on the far side, then toppled forward into a tumble, having too much momentum for her size and weight to contain. After somersaulting over twice, she slid on her back, feet in the air, staring between her knees at Rin and Kimber flying across. Rin alighted gracefully on the far side, landing a few steps past the edge. Kimber crashed into the earth, slamming chest first at the edge of the floor where it broke away. The Box of Wonder went bouncing into the hall toward Emma. Kimber dug her fingers at the ground, clinging.

Ambril stopped short at the edge, seeming too afraid to even try the jump.

Dozens of glowing red rat eyes appeared in the dark behind her.

"I got Ambril," whispered Rin. She raised one arm, reaching out as if to grab her. *"Vo nira sur!"*

"Linganthas, please send forth your aid!" Emma summoned a thornless root from the ground by Kimber. The snakelike tendril whipped around her chest, grabbing her before she slipped loose and fell into the darkness.

Ambril blurred forward as though she'd been fired out of a giant crossbow. The girl went from a standstill, to moving at the speed of an arrow, to a dead stop with Rin grasping the front of her dress in half a second.

Emma pulled Kimber up over the ledge. Unfazed by almost falling into a potentially bottomless pit, underground river, or some other unknown horror, Kimber scrambled to her feet and ran over to grab the box.

The first few rats flung themselves at the gap. One fell short, not even reaching the wall on the other side. One smacked into the dirt too far down to see. The third ratling landed like Kimber, its head and arms above the edge, frantically scrabbling at the floor to stop itself from falling. Two more jumped and also completely missed, falling without hitting the wall.

Emma cringed, horrified at watching creatures so greedy they leapt to their death.

Deep splashes came from the hole.

It sounded as if the ratlings landed in a small river or pool not *too* far down. They probably survived the drop.

They've got claws... they'll get out.

Another ratling leapt at them. He landed on the head of the one clinging to the edge, and stepped off into the hallway with the girls, pulling a dagger.

Rin pointed at him. *"Pa'laur Vokath!"*

A thin stream of fire shot forth from her pointing finger with a rushing woosh, striking the ratling in the chest. The creature howled in agony and jumped back, losing his balance and falling out of sight amid a haze of smoke and the horrible smell of burned hair. Seconds later, he hit the water with a kerplunk of a splash.

Other ratlings at the edge who saw this seemed to lose their excitement about chasing the girls.

"Go!" shouted Emma, not trusting they'd remain too scared to stop chasing them. She again took Kimber's hand and sprinted.

Shrieking ratling squeaks filled the hallway behind them. Thanks to the Wildkin Whisper, Emma understood all the vile names they called her, Rin, Kimber, and Ambril, accusing them of stealing the ratlings' treasure.

She didn't have too long to worry about what to do next. Two or three minutes after the jump, she spotted another doorway on the wall to the right similar to the one they came in through. Emma rushed over to it, elated to discover a spiral going upward. She moved aside and waved everyone else in first.

Kimber led the way up, Rin next, Ambril behind them. Emma backed into the doorway, raised her arms, and summoned a thick tangle of thorny roots to block off the passage. She backed up the spiral, filling in more roots until she'd created a plug filling at least six feet of tunnel. Even if the ratlings got over their fear of Rin's fire magic and chased them, it would take them a while to chew through the roots.

Confident she'd stopped the threat for now, Emma spun around and crawled up the spiral.

The opening at the top let them out into another alley. A woman sweeping a small stoop a short distance away jumped as if the girls simply appeared out of nowhere.

Emma looked around. No sign of thieves and no ratlings. She leaned against the wall beside the opening. "Whew. We made it."

"Nae stay here." Kimber pointed. "Alleys are dangerous. Go where people are so teefs won't do anyfing."

"Yes," said Ambril, nearly out of breath. "She's right."

Emma pushed off the wall. She hurried to the end of the alley and out onto a street full of townspeople.

44

THE TEMPLE

$\mathcal{E}$mma spent the next hour running around in search of town guards.

She found some. Alas, all seemed quite busy and didn't have the time to listen to her asking for protection from thieves, an escort all the way to Widowswood, or even where she might find a scholar who knew about maps. Some of the guards possessed more patience than others. A few played along, but Emma gave up once she realized they thought her a child playing pretend. One or two told them to stop horsing around and wasting guards' time.

The 'where are your parents / they're in Widowswood' exchange happened three times, each guard threatening to haul them off to the orphans' house if they didn't stop playing games. Ambril's fine dress and jewelry appeared to convince the guards the girls couldn't possibly be orphans—or here without their parents nearby. While it kept them from being taken to the orphan house, it also got them in more trouble as the guards accused them of telling stories.

"Ugh. This city is too big." Emma flailed her arms. "None of the guards know anyone. I don't like big cities. At home, everyone knows everyone."

They had about the same luck trying to ask for directions to a place where they could hire a coach. Every adult from guards, to merchants, to citizens, simply thought them children playing around... at least the ones who didn't run away when they saw Rin. Amazingly, no one turned mean or said nasty things about her.

Emma suspected they thought she might be a demon, so didn't want to make her angry.

She gave up on the coach idea or bothering the guards, instead going to shops, cart merchants or approaching anyone who made eye contact to ask them for directions to a scholar who knew about maps.

A little more than half the people she spoke to started to think of somewhere they could direct her, but once they spotted Rin, they came up with some excuse for having to go away fast... or shouted at the children to get out of there, or ran away screaming. One man even closed his entire store, claiming he'd come down with a sudden case of a highly contagious disease.

Two hours after leaving the ratling tunnel, Emma stopped in the shade of an awning hanging from the side of a pottery shop at a street corner, tired from all the running around. A bunch of pigeons collected on the orange fabric. Kimber sat on a bundle of burlap sacks and planted the box—safely wrapped in grey linen—in her lap. Rin and Ambril stood on either side of her. Emma cast the Wildkin Whisper.

"Excuse me," she cooed to the birds. "Would any of you be willing to fly to Widowswood and find 'The Raven?'" Most birds tended to know of Nan as 'The Raven.'

The pigeons muttered amongst themselves, then responded with loads of sympathy and a series of excuses. They wanted to help her but were too old, too fat, didn't know the way, feared getting eaten by hawks before they got halfway there, had a rather important engagement with a fountain in an hour, and so on.

Then they asked her for food.

Ugh. Not all birds are smart. Emma, being Emma, couldn't be mean to animals or even spitefully deny them food because they happened to be too cowardly or lazy help her. She summoned a meatplant and tossed it up to them.

"I did not think humans were so much like my kind." Rin frowned. "So many of you here, yet not one of them is willing to help lost children?" She scratched her head. "I suppose it is somewhat better. No one has thrown knives at us or tried to light us on fire yet."

"We're going to have to use the box again." Emma sighed.

"It shouldn't be too bad. You said the river runs southwest from this city?" Rin tilted her head.

"Yes."

"The map inside is detailed." Rin gestured as if placing the pointer on the map. "We can see the river. I'll just move the needle down a little bit. There are some little clusters of forest. One of them has to be Widowswood."

"That's them," said a man.

Emma twisted to look back.

The shopkeeper with the 'contagious disease' pointed at them, having brought a pair of town guards.

Ugh. He better not have lied and said we stole something.

Both guards approached. One unhooked a set of manacles from his belt.

"Right. You lot are coming with us," said the other.

"Wait." Emma raised her hands. "Simply being a dark elf isn't a crime. We're just children. What crime have we been accused of?"

The guard holding the manacles counted on his fingers. "Trafficking with demons. Planning to overthrow the queen. Spying… disturbing the peace."

Emma glared. "Someone lied to you. Overthrow the queen? Seriously? Four children?"

"Someone go' potatoes instead'a brains." Kimber rolled her eyes.

"Queen Isabella isn't even *in* Andor. She's in Calebrin." Ambril stomped. "If someone really was trying to plot against her, they wouldn't be doing it out here so close to Orcish territory."

"Why are you asking about maps, then?" asked the guard not holding manacles. "Planning an invasion?"

"We're asking for maps because we're trying to *go home*." Emma let out an exasperated sigh. "Do you not see that we're children?"

The guards narrowed their eyes.

The one holding manacles said, "You *appear* to be children."

"I'm ten years old," blurted Emma, almost shouting in frustration. "I don't even know how to get from here to Widowswood. Do you honestly think we're trying to plot against the queen? And why would we do that? Queen Isabella is wonderful."

"They're making things up." Rin looked downcast. "They're afraid of me and just saying anything as an excuse to arrest us because you are with me."

"You appear to be children," said the other guard. "Doesn't mean you are. How is it you're running around without your parents and no one recognizes you?"

"It's a really long story." She looked back and forth between the men. "My name is Emma Dalen. My Da is Watch Captain Liam Dalen in Widowswood. His family is from Calebrin City."

"That's a fair ways off," said the guard holding manacles.

"Witch of the Woods down that way," muttered the other.

Emma folded her arms. "That's my Nan."

The men exchanged a glance.

"Oh, you can put those away." Emma pointed at the manacles. "I know you're only trying to scare us. Those are way too big. They'd fall right off any one of us. Also, there's no need to arrest us because we haven't done anything wrong." She glared at the shopkeeper. "That man is lying because he's a coward who's afraid of a little girl who happens to have pointy ears."

"Pointed ears," said the shopkeeper in a nervous voice. "And she's black as barrister's ink, got glowin' purple eyes, and the blood of a *demon* in her."

Rin squeezed her hands into fists.

"She doesn't," yelled Emma, putting an arm around Rin. "Some of her kind do, but Rin is different. They were going to kill her because she's not like them. Look at her. Would an evil dark elf wear a pink faerie dress?"

"I fink it's koinda purple more'n pink," whispered Kimber past the back of her hand.

"It's called iridescence," said Ambril. "It's both pink *and* purple depending on how the light falls on it."

Kimber glanced up at the guards while nodding toward Ambril. "She 'as ae tutor."

"Whatever. It's faerie colored." Emma furrowed her brows at the guards. "Would a demon wear that?"

Both guards nodded.

"Aye. Ta confuse people." The left guard chuckled. "They don't all cover themselves in black armor with spikes everywhere."

"She's also nine," deadpanned Emma.

"188," whispered Rin.

"That's the same as nine to us." Emma patted her shoulder. "Humans are kinda dim sometimes. Use smaller numbers. Makes it easier for them to think."

"Well, then…" The guard re-hung the manacles on his belt. "If you're so sure she's not a demon, then you will have no trouble submitting to a small test."

"What kind of test?" asked Rin.

"Simple." The guard flashed a warm smile. "Come with us to the temple. A priest will be able to tell if you got any demon in you."

Rin looked up at the men. "I'm not a demon. I understand why you might think so. Most of my people *are* generally as bad as you say. Your caution is not without reason. I will talk to your priest."

Ambril blushed. "You're not… arresting us, are you? Mortifying."

"Not yet, love." The guard who brandished chains managed a pleasant smile. "Depends on what the priest has to say."

"Don't go running off." The other man reached toward Emma.

"We won't." She held out her left arm, allowing him to grasp her wrist. She took Kimber's hand.

Rin offered her arm to the other man, who seemed hesitant to touch her. After a few seconds, she widened her eyes, making a sad face at him. The guardsman gave a barely audible sigh, then gingerly grasped her wrist. The guards appeared to trust Ambril not to run away and didn't grab her arm.

The shopkeeper grumbled, seeming annoyed the guards treated the girls like children and not hardened criminals.

As the guards began to lead her down the street, Emma glanced up at the pigeons on the awning and cooed, "Will you please pelt that man over there with as much poo as you can make?"

All nine pigeons turned their heads to look at the shopkeeper, seeming as excited as Tam when Mama started baking sweetbreads.

"With pleasure!" chirped one. "Thank you for the food!"

Emma grinned as the birds leapt into the air. She turned away, not really wanting to watch the disgusting barrage. The man soon screamed.

She smiled all the way to the temple.

THE GUARDS BROUGHT THEM TO A HUGE BUILDING MADE OF GREY stone.

On the walk to the temple, the guard holding Emma's arm seemed to accept she had no intention of running off. Somewhere along the way, he'd shifted from holding her by the wrist to holding her hand.

A ten-foot statue of an armored man bearing a large shield and sword stood at the foot of a great stone staircase that led up to a row of tall columns supporting a stonemasonry roof above an open-air platform in front of the temple.

"This is a temple of Belephir," whispered Ambril. "He's the father of honor and patron of warriors… also one of the most common gods to have temples in big cities."

"Honor isn't only for warriors," said the man holding Emma's arm. "Belephir also watches when children lie or act in deceitful ways."

Emma shrugged. "It doesn't matter. We aren't lying."

They went up the stairs and past the columns to the platform. At its center, another, much smaller, statue of Belephir stood atop a fountain.

Da had been raised in Calebrin City, taught about various gods and goddesses. Emma heard of them only in passing. Neither Nan nor

Mama had any animosity toward the gods. They simply didn't feel any need to worship them when they already had the forest spirits to revere and seek wisdom from.

Emma looked up at the face of the stone man as they went around the fountain. If he could help her get home to her family, she'd be as respectful as she could be here. As they approached the temple doors at the back end of the platform, the guard who still held Rin's arm tensed. He cringed a little away from her, as if she might burst into flames as soon as they crossed the threshold.

Nothing happened when they entered the temple foyer. The two guards stood there for a minute or two, waiting to be noticed. Eventually, a muscular clean-shaven man in a brown tunic and grey tights walked up to them. A golden amulet as big as Emma's whole hand hung from a plain metal chain around his neck, depicting a sword across a tower shield.

"Good day." The man bowed. "Welcome. I am Taebras, priest of Belephir. How may I be of assistance?"

The guard holding Emma's hand gestured at Rin. "Is this child a demon? Is she a real child?"

Taebras raised both eyebrows when he noticed the Niltharien girl. "You've brought her into the building, so no. She is not a demon." He moved closer and took one knee in front of her. "What is your name, child?"

"Rin. I'm not a demon. I know most of my kind call on them for power. Not me. I'm scared of demons. They can't be trusted. They're wicked and evil and even worse than my mother. No matter how much you think you are controlling them and stealing power, it's the demons who win. They're bad."

The priest smiled. "You seem like an intelligent, cute little child. How is it you have come to be here? I've never seen one of your kind so young before."

"Emma, Kimber, and Ambril helped me get away from assassins trying to kill me. Most Niltharien would consider me a disgrace because I don't like hurting people or doing mean things. They call me names that mean 'weak forest elf.'"

"I see." Taebras held his amulet up. "Can you touch this holy symbol of Belephir?"

Rin raised her hand under the shield amulet. "Yes."

"Belephir, by your honor and wisdom, bless this child," said Taebras.

A faint light, like a pinhole in the ceiling let in a bit of sun, fell on the girl.

Taebras gently patted Rin on both shoulders. "This child is no demon, nor is she afflicted by their touch. I am truly sorry to hear you have had such a tragic life. May you find peace among us."

"Thank you." Rin curtsied.

Taebras stood. "What happened that you brought these children here on suspicion of demons?"

The guards explained having multiple people—especially one highly agitated shopkeeper—report them for asking about maps, snooping around acting suspicious, and having a suspected demon with them.

"Maps?" Taebras looked at the girls. "Why would children your size ask about maps?"

"To overthrow the queen, obviously." Ambril rolled her eyes. "Our plan is so sneaky, we're not even using it in the right city where the queen lives."

Kimber snickered.

The two guards smirked.

"We're trying to go home." Emma ground her toes into the marble floor. "I know it's bad to not tell the truth inside temples or to priests. I'm going to tell you the truth. Please don't steal from us."

Taebras coughed. He seemed caught part way between shock and anger. "Child, what would ever make you think a priest of Belephir would steal at all, much less from children?"

"The last adult who we tried to tell the truth to stole from us." Emma clasped her hands in front of herself. "I'm sorry. We were supposed to trust her, too, and she was bad. Maybe it's different because she wasn't a priest. When you see it, you will understand why I said that."

"See what?" asked Taebras.

"We found a magical jewelry box…" Emma told him about being at Ambril's house, the thieves chasing them, the box, going inside it, teleporting around, and pretty much everything exactly as it happened. She left out the part where she asked mice to scare Matron Wavecrest and pigeons to poo-bomb the merchant. "… and that's why we need to figure out how maps work so we can use the box to go home to Widowswood."

"That was… quite a story." Taebras exhaled.

Emma nudged Kimber. "It's okay. Let him see it. We're not that far away now."

"Okay." Kimber peeled back the grey dress.

Taebras and both guardsmen gawked.

"We didn't steal it." Emma pointed at Ambril. "Her father is a gem trader. He bought it somewhere. It belongs to Mr. Starling. We're trying to go home so we can give it back to him."

"Those men tried to abduct me… again." Ambril grumbled.

"It looks plain now." Emma patted the box.

"This is plain?" Taebras chuckled.

"No. I mean… it looks ordinary." Emma pointed at the rubies, sapphires, and emeralds. "These gems glow when the magic is done recharging. It takes a whole day. We won't be able to go inside until tomorrow morning. The box won't even open now."

Taebras glanced at the guards. "We can look after the children for a day. Tomorrow morning, we shall know the truth of their tale. I am familiar enough with maps to find Widowswood. Will you allow me to help you?"

Emma glanced at Kimber. Her little sister peered up at the priest for a moment, then smiled.

"Yes." Emma nodded.

"You are far from home and not orphans." Taebras took a step deeper into the temple, raising an arm in welcome. "You may stay here for the day. We will keep you safe."

"Thank Belephir," whispered Ambril.

"Very good." One guard bowed to the priest. "They're all yours."

EMMA, KIMBER, AMBRIL, AND RIN SPENT THE AFTERNOON AT THE temple, enjoying the garden in the central courtyard, listening to stories from books, and having good—albeit basic—meals. The priests and priestesses all ate the same food as they gave the girls, simple fare consisting of bread, vegetables, and inexpensive meat.

That night, they slept in an unused bedchamber, a smallish room only large enough to hold two simple beds, a little desk, and a tiny wardrobe cabinet. Emma and Kimber shared one bed. Rin and Ambril the other.

Much to her surprise, the priests of the temple let them keep the Box of Wonder, never once even asking them to part with it for 'safer keeping' or any other excuse.

When morning arrived, they joined the priests and priestesses for a simple meal of hard flatbread and jam. After eating, the girls sat in the garden talking for a little while until all the gems on the box lit up with a magical glow. At that, Emma ran off into the temple in search of Taebras. Asking after him to a few other priests and temple helpers led her to a room where Taebras and eleven other people in similar robes practice fought using wooden weapons.

Emma stood at the edge of the combat arena, staring at Taebras until he felt the weight of her eyes and glanced at her.

The priest signaled his sparring partner for a pause, then walked over. "Yes, child?"

"The box is ready. Can you look at the map now?"

"Of course." He turned back toward his sparring partner. "A few minutes. I will return soon."

The other man raised a hand in acknowledgement.

"Let us go then." Taebras set his wooden armaments down.

Emma rushed back to the garden with him.

Kimber sat on a small stone bench, the box in her lap, Rin and Ambril on either side, squished in close.

"We have to be together, close to the box." Emma looked up at Taebras. "When we open the lid, we appear inside."

Taebras pursed his lips. He didn't seem to fully believe her yet, though also did not make a face as if he thought she made up stories.

She led him over to the others, standing close enough for her legs to touch Kimber's knees.

Her little sister flashed the sweetest, biggest, smile, and opened the lid.

Everyone appeared in the alcove inside the glowing blue rune circle.

"By Belephir... An entire study inside a little jewelry box." Taebras stepped out of the alcove into the big room and looked around. "This is wondrous."

"Bet 'ats why they call it the Box o' Wonder," said Kimber.

Ambril covered a giggle.

"The map is over here." Emma walked over to the table.

Taebras followed. He gazed at the diorama of the world, eyes wide like a small boy getting a new toy sword. "This is... incredible. The level of detail is remarkable. I can see individual leaves on the trees moving in the breeze. The water is flowing."

"It's an illusion." Rin rested her hands on the glass partition around the table. "It's not showing us what each place is really doing. It's a moving painting."

"Can you tell us where Widowswood is on this map?" Emma picked up the silver needle. "We have to put this on the spot and the magic can take us there."

"Should not be terribly difficult..." Taebras leaned over the table, after a moment, he pointed at a spot. "This is Andor, where we are now. The river runs past Calebrin, which would be around here. The cluster of trees here is Widowswood." He tapped the spot.

Emma placed the needle as close to the edge of the miniature forest as she could get it. Her heart raced with hope. In mere minutes, they would be home, back with their families. "Thank you!"

"What happens now?" asked Taebras.

"We touch the magic orb and the box goes to Widowswood," said Rin. "If you don't want to come with us, you should probably go outside."

"Will you children be safe?" He looked at Emma, then Ambril, then Kimber, then Rin.

"Oh yes. Very safe." Emma smiled. "I'm not scared of anything when Nan, Mama, and Da are with me."

Taebras pursed his lips. "I've heard some stories about Widowswood. It may not be the safest place for small girls."

Emma gazed up at the ceiling. "The stories are wrong. Nan doesn't steal children."

"Your nan is the Witch of the Wood?" Tebras blinked.

"Yes. Sometimes people call Mama that, too." Emma scratched the side of her head. "Don't listen to the stories that say mean things. They're wrong. Nan and Mama don't talk to demons. We are druids. We ask nature sprits for wisdom and guidance."

"Ahh. Druids." Taebras laughed, so loud and sudden, Ambril jumped. "That explains the pigeons." He winked at Emma. "If you ask me, the fool deserved it."

Emma bit her lip. *Eep!*

"Very well then. I must admit, I am a bit uneasy leaving the four of you to this on your own." He glanced around. "This room is inside a box. So, I shall trust your story is true and it will take you home. May Belephir guide you."

"Thank you." Ambril curtseyed to him.

"Fanks for the food and lettin' us sleep inna temple." Kimber hugged him. "You'as much nicer 'an the bad orphan lady."

Emma also curtseyed. "Thank you and thank Belephir for his help."

Ambril offered him a few coins. "Thank you. To help you do Belephir's work."

He bowed to her. "Many thanks, child. Your generosity is appreciated." He took one last, long, look at the magical room, then returned to the alcove. "I imagine the way out is back through here?"

"Yes," called Rin. "Touch the blue orb on the wall."

A second later, Taebras disappeared.

Emma cast the Wildkin Whisper and meowed, "Cat. Please don't jump on the spinny shiny thing. We're trying to go home and you keep sending us all over the world. If you are tired of living in this room all alone, you can come with us."

"You aren't trying to trick me?" replied a soft, male voice from somewhere nearby. "The last mage kept trying to light me on fire."

Emma gasped in shock. "Certainly not. And I'm not a mage."

The grey tabby emerged from behind a bookshelf, eyeing her warily. "You are rather small for a mage."

"Why did you keep ruining the teleport?" Emma crouched low, waving him over.

"I didn't intend to..." The cat crept closer and sniffed at her hand. "The table barely interested me. However, once the shiny, spinny thing started shining and spinning..." His eyes glazed over. "Don't know what came over me. I couldn't resist. I *had* to destroy it."

Emma picked him up. "Oh, so you're simply a cat being a cat."

"You think so?" He tilted his head. "It's not a magical compulsion?"

"Nah." She pet him, carrying him away from the map table. "I need to ask you to resist this time. How have you lived in here by yourself with nothing to eat?"

"There's a small crystal. Every time I paw at it, food appears." He licked his paw. "I have not been in here *too* long. Had the misfortune of being too close to the last fool when he activated the lid and it pulled me in with him."

"Shouldn't there be...?" Emma lowered her voice to a whisper. "Poo somewhere?"

"What sort of uncivilized barbarian do you take me for?" He held his nose in the air. "I *do* know how to use the... the... thing the humans use."

Emma blinked. "There's an outhouse in here? Where? I don't see it."

"It's not an outhouse. It's an in-house." The cat pointed at the bookshelves. "Third shelf from the left. Pull on the green book sticking out from the others. There's a small room behind it with the seat."

Eep. Ambril is going to scream when I tell her we didn't have to go outside.

"Em! Get over here." Kimber bounced on her toes. "We'as goin' home!"

Cat in her arms, Emma rushed over to the orb table.

Rin put her hand on the blue orb and closed her eyes.

A faint flash filled the room for an instant.

The big crystal ball filled with trees... somewhere within Widowswood forest.

She'd know those trees with her eyes shut. Even if they had a few hours of walking ahead of them, they were home.

45

FALSE SERVANTS

*C*heering, Emma ran for the alcove. "Mama! Nan! Da! We're home!"

The room lurched and bounced, nearly making her fall over.

She wobbled to a stop, then spun to look back at the orb table. Kimber, Ambril, and Rin gripped the sides for balance, watching the orb intently. Emma set the cat down, then made her way across the swaying room to the big crystal ball.

Three men in leather armor and dark cloaks played tug-of-war with the bejeweled box. They didn't appear to be genuinely fighting like the ratlings, more like a group of brothers arguing over who got to play with the shiny toy first.

Kimber sprinted for the alcove. "Gonna lock!"

A fourth man in a hooded cloak hurried over to the others and yelled, "Knock it off. It doesn't matter who carries it. With what that thing's worth, we'll all be rolling in coin soon enough. An even split is still more gold than we'd ever expect to see."

"Oh, no." Ambril whined. "We're being stolen."

"Locked!" yelled Kimber from the alcove.

"What should we do?" Ambril stared over the big crystal orb at Emma.

"Fireball?" Rin pointed at the red ball.

Emma felt sick to her stomach. "No. Not yet. Those men aren't mean. They just found a gold box on the ground. We shouldn't kill them. Also, please don't make fireballs in Widowswood."

"They look like thieves," whispered Ambril.

"Lots of people wear light armor and cloaks." Emma gestured at the orb. "It doesn't mean they're thieves."

"That looks like the treasure box Odelin told us about, the one he saw in the Starling estate," said one of the men.

Emma sighed. "All right. Maybe they *are* thieves."

"I think it's the same thieves," whispered Ambril.

The view in the orb moved to follow the men as they jogged through the forest.

Kimber stumbled over to the table. "Room's shakin' bad."

"Yes, they're running with the box." Rin brushed her fingers across the red orb. "We can't really use the fireball now. There's not enough magic left after teleporting."

"Okay. I don't want to burn them anyway, thieves or not." Emma moved her feet wider apart for balance in the shaking room. "If we go outside now, they'll see us appear. They may or may not try to hurt us. We'd also have to run away and let them keep the box. If we have to choose between going home and losing the box, or not going home, I say we go home."

Kimber nodded.

Ambril grimaced. "Yes. It's only a gold box. Father would much rather have me home alive."

"Leaving the box now is not too smart." Rin shook her head, making her periwinkle blue hair dance back and forth. "It would force a conflict we might be able to avoid."

"She's right!" Ambril gasped. "The same thieves... they're going to want to kidnap me if they see me."

"What do you think we should do?" Emma stood up on her toes to peek over the ball at her.

"The men are moving fast. They are going somewhere specific, probably their hideout." Rin tapped a finger at her chin. She seemed to have no trouble at all keeping her balance without having to hold onto the table. "I think they're going to put the box in their hideout, then leave to find someone they can sell it to. Once they're all gone, we can go outside, collect the box, and run."

"That might work. Better than popping right out in front of them." Emma eyed the red orb. "I wish whoever made this put something less bad than a fireball in it. Like that sleep spell you cast on the rats."

Rin nodded. "That would have been nicer."

"Let's wait and see what they do," said Ambril. "At least a little while."

"Okay." Emma nodded at her.

The girls stood around the orb table watching the thieves run for about ten more minutes to the same cave they'd gone to days ago, the one concealed behind tree branches tied together. They hurried down the underground passage to their hideout in the improvised 'tavern.' A few oil lamps on the tables offered a feeble amount of light, mostly in the center of the room. The edges remained in shadow. One man stood by the bar, his back turned, sorting a stack of coins beside a fat, red candle.

"Odelin," called one of the thieves. "Look what we found."

The coin-counter muttered something too low to make out words, only annoyance.

"Not messing around," said another thief. "This is worth a fortune. Have you ever seen so many gems in one place before?"

Odelin sighed. "Ya darn fools made me lost count. Now I gotta start all over." He whirled to glare at them, then went slack-jawed.

"See?" The man holding the box held it up. "See? This is real."

"Where in the blazes did you find this?" Odelin rushed over. "Which one of you took it?"

They all denied touching it.

The men set the box on a table. All five of them pulled up chairs and sat around the table. One tried to open the lid. They broke into an argument about how the box disappeared from where they hid it only to end up outside several days later.

"You're telling me you just found it?" Odelin stared.

"I'm tellin' ya." The man who first picked it up slapped the table. "Was right there out in the woods. Lyin' in the dirt."

"It appeared in a flash," said another. "One minute, nothing. Next minute, flash. There it is. Like the gods themselves heard us and gave it back to us."

"This box isn't worth *that* much for the gods to get involved." Odelin grumbled. "It's for certain worth a great deal, but not as much as ya might think. Something like this, gonna be one of a kind. Hard to fence it."

Rolfe grabbed the box and attempted to pry the lid. When he had no luck getting it to open, the fourth man pulled it across the table toward himself, making the room shudder. Attempting to pry the lid open, he groaned loud and long, his face reddening. While he struggled at it, another thief went to the bar, grabbed a hammer and chisel, and came back. The men flipped the box on its side, put the chisel under the lid, and began pounding on it.

Emma felt like a mouse inside a drum while a three-year-old boy who ate *all* the sugar went to town on it.

After almost ten full minutes of non-stop banging, the noise changed. It no longer seemed to emanate from the ceiling, more like the man hammered directly on her skull.

"Set off the fireball," deadpanned Emma. "Make it stop."

Rin started to reach for the red orb.

Emma grabbed her hand. "I'm not serious."

The grey tabby cat sprang up onto the table and swatted at the red orb. He appeared to be sincerely trying to activate it. Emma didn't know whether to laugh or be frightened. Thankfully, the cat, being a cat, didn't appear capable of setting off the magic.

Two more minutes of horrible banging later, the man finally gave up.

"Not even a damn scratch," said one.

"This can't be real gold. It's too hard." Odelin grumbled.

"It appeared in a flash o' light." The man holding the chisel dropped the tools. "It's magic."

"Darn thing isn't a box at all. It's just a fancy block with gems on it." The third thief tilted the box to stand upright. "Whatever it is, we should just sell it and take the coin, split our gains."

"I found it. I should get at least half," said one. "You lot didn't even see it until I said something."

"Uh oh." Kimber winced. "They gonna start fightin'"

Sure enough, the thieves got into an argument over how much of a share each one should get. Two of the five shouted even shares for all. The other three went back and forth about one demanding a half share, another saying Odelin shouldn't get much because he sits in the hideout all the time while everyone else does all the work, and the last trying to assign different percentages to everyone based on how much he felt they contributed to this 'score.'

"This is going to take all day." Ambril squirmed. "I need to go."

"We *all* need tae go." Kimber shook her head.

"No, I mean I need to..." Ambril lowered her voice. "Have a wee."

Emma pointed back over her shoulder. "Third bookshelf. Pull on the green book that's sticking out. There's a privy in there."

"What!?" Ambril yelled. "You knew there's a garderobe inside and still told us to do it outdoors?"

"No. I just found out this morning."

"You haven't even been over there," rasped Ambril, red-faced.

"The cat told me."

Ambril stared at her for a moment. Her wicked blush subsided. "Oh. All right." She hurried over to the bookshelf. After a little poking around, she opened one of the shelves like a door, revealing a small outhouse-sized room with the usual seat. Ambril stepped in and pulled the shelf closed.

Emma continued to watch the thieves argue for several minutes until Ambril returned with a bizarre look on her face.

"What's wrong?" asked Emma.

She fussed at her gown. "The garderobe is enchanted. It... cleans you."

Emma grimaced.

"It's fine. Just... feels strange." Ambril examined her fingernails. "I wasn't expecting it is the problem. It's not bad. Just startled me. Flash of light. No more mess."

The thieves' arguing escalated to a fistfight. They traded punches for a little while before deciding to take the quarrel outside to avoid smashing up their hideout.

"Now's our chance," said Rin. "As soon as they leave, we can jump out, grab the box, and run. Go to the circle. I'll keep watching. We'll have to be fast."

"Okay." Emma called the cat over. "Come with us in case we lose the box."

The tabby zoomed over and jumped into her arms. "This place is nice, but dreadfully boring."

Kimber and Ambril rushed with her over to the alcove and stood inside the glowing runes. Emma held the cat. Kimber grasped the lock lever, ready to push it up and open the lid. Ambril rested her hand on the blue orb.

Across the room, Rin gazed into the large crystal ball, watching the thieves.

Minutes passed in anxious silence, the loudest sound came from the purring cat.

Rin abruptly bolted away from the orb table, racing in a straight line across the room to the magic circle. Rather than go around the big table, she effortlessly leapt up to run along the top as if flying on faerie wings she didn't have, then jumped to the floor and dashed into the alcove.

As soon as the little dark elf stopped in the center of the glowing rune circle, Ambril pushed the blue orb.

Stone walls disappeared in an instant. The room around Emma changed to the cave dressed up to look like a tavern. She scrunched her nose in response to an unpleasant smell: some manner of cheap booze, mildew, and the stink of unpainted wood left in a wet place too long.

Rin raised a hand toward the bar. *"Vo nira sur."*

A large burlap sack—big enough for any of the girls to have fit inside

—leapt up from the floor and flew across the chamber into her hand. She flipped it around, holding it open for Kimber to drop the Box of Wonder into. As the sack was many times larger than necessary to hold the relatively small box, Kimber bundled the fabric around it into a ball.

Shouts came from the men outside the cave. It sounded like a raging fistfight went on.

"Let's go," whispered Emma.

She padded across the chamber to the end of the cave tunnel leading to the surface, adoring the squish of chilly mud between her toes. The energy of Widowswood tingled in her legs, filling her with confidence.

"Ack. It's all muddy," whispered Ambril. "My slippers are going to be ruined."

"Why ya wear somfin' wot always get ruin?" Kimber started to laugh, but covered her mouth and made an 'oops' face.

"I'm not supposed to go gallivanting around woods, swamps, deserts, and sewers in them." Ambril sighed. "These slippers are for being inside, or in town. Civilized *clean* places."

Emma only made it four steps into the cave tunnel before Rin grabbed her and Kimber by the shoulders, pulling them back, whispering, "The thieves are coming! Hide!"

Somehow, Ambril managed not to scream.

They ran back into the cave chamber to the only possible hiding spot: behind the crude bar. Emma crawled in to sit on the lowest shelf. Kimber huddled against her. Ambril tucked into the same shelf at the opposite side, facing her, toes touching Kimber's. Rin squeezed herself into the much smaller upper shelf right under the bartop, lying flat on her stomach in a space only tall enough to hold drinking glasses.

The five thieves tromped in, grumbling at themselves for being fools. Somehow, after walloping on each other for a little while, they'd come around to agreeing on an even split of gold. Whatever the box sold for, they'd all take an even share.

Boys are weird. How does hitting each other solve anything? Men are just little boys with hair on their faces... except Da... sometimes.

"It's gone!" yelled one.

"Which one of you took it while we were distracted?" bellowed another.

The five men all began to accuse the others of stealing the box for themselves.

"I know you took it!" shouted a third man.

"To the Abyss with that, Rolfe!" yelled another. "You were kissing my fist the whole time we were out there. When the bloody heck would I have had time to swipe the box?"

"Must be Odelin," said another man.

"I'll slit the throat of the next one of you fools who accuses me of trying to cheat you." Odelin followed his threat with a growl.

Kimber gave Emma a wide-eyed 'we are in trouble' stare.

Another fight broke out inside the 'tavern.'

Emma cringed and winced at every thud of fist-on-face or smashing wood. It sounded as though the men tore the place apart.

Hold still. Don't make any noise. All we have to do—

A man came flying into the bar, knocking it over and smashing the poorly constructed thing apart into a loose affiliation of boards. Emma, Kimber, Ambril, and Rin—plus one grey tabby cat—landed in a heap of wood scrap, arms, and legs sticking out in a tangle.

Whoever got thrown into the bar didn't appear to notice he landed on four children and a cat. He leapt back into the fray, diving on another thief and punching him repeatedly in the stomach. For a moment, none of the girls moved, or even much breathed, exchanging baffled glances at how they hadn't been spotted.

"Wait, you fools!" roared Odelin. "What's that?"

"What's what?"

"There's a wee foot stickin' out o'er there."

Uh oh.

The brawl stopped.

"We got us a couple o' rats." A thief spat blood to the side.

"Maybe *they* stole the box," said Rolfe.

The five men approached the bar, standing in a curve.

"All right, you lot. On your feet," said Odelin. "This ain't a place for children."

Oddly, he sounded as though he only intended to shoo them out. Hopeful, Emma pushed a board off her chest, grunted, and got to her feet, still holding the cat.

The thieves' expressions softened as if to say 'aww, how adorable.'

Kimber scrambled out from under wooden boards. When the bar collapsed, she'd gone face-first into the earth. Her entire left cheek and half of her forehead had a coating of damp soil. She clung to the burlap bundle as if it were a doll. She got to her feet and stood close to Emma. Her glare said 'I'll thump anyone who tries to take this from me', while her posture and the way she half hid behind Emma gave off a sense of fear.

The thieves looked even more taken by cuteness.

Ambril flung a board draped over her head to the side, then stood. The rich girl had this look on her face like she'd reached a point of being absolutely *done* with it all. She glanced down at another plank as if contemplating picking it up and joining the brawl.

All the thieves went from making faces like they'd found some cute children who needed a little help to expressions of shock. Every one of them stared at Ambril.

When the girl looked back up from the board, she, too, went wide-eyed.

"Aww heck." Odelin scowled. "We're made."

Rolfe folded his arms, glaring at her. "Now what?"

"What does that mean?" whispered Emma.

"It means they know I recognize them." Ambril frowned. "At least two of them. Odelin and Rolfe are servants working for my father. Or... pretend servants working for my father so they can spy on us for the thieves."

"Oh dear," said the cat. "I am afraid this may soon lead to violence. Do what you can, girl. I shall most viciously shred the ankles of anyone who lays a finger on you."

"All right, you lot." A thief with a short beard took a step closer, pointing at them. "You'll be staying here with us for a little while until certain plans are finished. Can't go havin' the little princess ruin things by telling her parents half their house staff is with us."

Ambril pouted. "Hey... I'm not a princess. Do you really think I'm bratty and selfish?"

The man blinked. "Uhh... no, not really. Just said that because your family's got more gold than the queen."

"Oh." Ambril seemed relieved, then shocked. "What? *Half* of the servants? Not just two?"

Odelin swatted the man who said that over the head. "Fool."

"Relax." The man on the right end of the group patted Odelin on the arm. "This changes nothing. We just need to keep them quiet for a while, then it won't matter. Keep an eye on them, I'll go grab some rope from the horses."

Eep! Emma glared.

Kimber snarled.

Rin sprang out of the wood pile. In the dim cave chamber, her eyes glowed like violet fireflies. "You're not going to kidnap us. Don't force me to show you why it would be foolish to test my patience."

The men leaned back, surprised... though not quite afraid.

"What the blazes are we going to do with three little girls and a... whatever that is for two weeks?" asked Rolfe. "More trouble than it would be worth to keep them."

"That's one o' them dark elves," whispered the second man from the left. "She'll draw the souls right out of us with a look, she will."

"Rin is a person!" yelled Emma, pointing at Rolfe. "Not a thing. Apologize to her!"

The man next to Rolfe raised an eyebrow at him. "More trouble than it's worth? Are you sayin' what I think you're saying?"

Rolfe side-eyed the man at his left. "Do you fancy babysitting, feeding, and makin' sure a bunch of little ones don't run off for two bloody weeks?"

The other four men shifted their weight back and forth, seeming uncomfortable.

Realization hit Emma like a slap. *He wants to kill us!*

She eyed the burlap bundle, thinking their best chance to survive would be to go back into the box and lock the lid. Alas, wrapped up in so much fabric, they couldn't get to it fast. Worse, they'd recently teleported. It would be hours before they *could* even go inside. The girls had no easy way to escape. The box couldn't help them. Whatever happened in the next few minutes came down entirely on Emma and Rin's ability to survive a fight against five adult thieves.

Four of the men stared in shock at Rolfe. The one on the right end of the line made a face at Emma like 'sorry, kid. Business is business.' At least the other three appeared horrified at the suggestion of killing them. The odds of her and Rin being able to fight off five grown men trying to kill them didn't reassure her. However, she would not give up easy. Maybe if a huge thorny root crushed Rolfe, the others would change their minds and run away.

Emma *really* didn't want to use her magic to hurt a person. She also didn't want to be killed, nor let anyone hurt Kimber or her friends. Shaking from fear as well as the dread of what she thought about doing, she stretched her right hand out toward the floor, spreading her fingers to call upon Linganthas' power.

"Oh, dear," said the cat. "It gets worse."

"Worse?" whispered Emma, shivering. "How could it be worse?"

"Look in the tunnel." The cat squished himself tight against Emma's neck, trying to hide.

Emma peered between Rolfe and the man beside him at the cave exit. Two almond-shaped spots of pale blue light drifted silently down the passage in the dark. Eyes. Larger and wider-spaced than anything human. Something fairly large drifted closer. Emma's mouth opened slightly.

The eyes reached the end of the cave tunnel... and continued gliding forward into the chamber. The thieves stared at Rolfe in disbelief. Emma couldn't take her gaze off the strange entity stalking toward them.

As soon as the eyes neared the center of the tavern, the feeble oil lantern glow added the silhouette of a large panther behind them.

Emma's heart nearly exploded with joy. *Mama!* Tears rolled down her cheeks.

The panther gave a low growl.

All five thieves spun around, saw the great cat, and screamed.

Overcome with elation and relief, Emma sobbed despite grinning.

The panther rose upward as if to stand on its back legs. In a whirl of blue-black fur and unfurling cloak, the animal shapeshifted into Mama, in her green dress and dark cloak. She planted the end of her leaf-studded staff in the ground with a hard *thump*. The glare in her eyes could have stopped a man's heart.

"Why are you crying?" whispered Rin.

"I'm happy." Emma sniffled. "Really happy. That's Mama."

"Crying when you're happy?" Rin blinked. "Humans are strange."

Mama took a step forward. "I sincerely hope you men are not talking about what it seems you are talking about."

"Mama!" yelled Emma.

"Bloody hell," whispered the man on the left, sounding like a frightened boy. "It's the Witch of the Woods!"

"Can't be," grumbled Odelin. "That's an old one."

The man second from the right backed up toward the girls, shaking. "She looks as old as she cares to."

Rolfe raised a hand. "No. Swear by the gods, it's not what I meant. Sayin' we do the job tonight or tomorrow. Speed up the plan. Not gonna hurt 'em. They're just little kids. Just didn't want to be stuck with them for two weeks."

Emma darted around the man who backed up, racing through the hole he made in the thieves' line to scurry for cover behind Mama. Kimber rushed after her. Ambril took a step, seeming too afraid to go near the thieves to follow. Rin walked past the men, calm as anything.

Mama gave each man an equal share of scowl, then focused her attention on Rolfe. "I suggest you take whatever action you intend to take *without* involving my daughters and their friends. Ambril?"

The rich girl gathered herself and fast-walked past the thieves over to Mama.

None of the men moved.

"Good." Mama nodded once at Rolfe. "Do not let me see you following them... or see you anywhere near my girls, unless you fancy spending the next hundred years crawling around the forest digging burrows and looking for worms and beetles to eat."

The men backed up, two tripping over the ruined bar and landing on their backsides.

Emma had no idea if Mama could really curse people into small animals or only said it to be scary. The thieves' expressions almost made her laugh. She hugged Mama as tight as she could, shivering away the last of her fear as joy took over.

Mama turned away from the men, gathered the girls under her cloak, and walked with them up the cave to the forest outside.

46

FOREST SPIRITS

*M*ama carried herself with the commanding air of a furious queen.

As overjoyed as Emma was for being home, she couldn't help but start to dread how much trouble they'd be in. Mama didn't usually act like that. After they'd spent roughly twenty minutes walking through the woods away from the cave, Mama stopped, sank to her knees, grabbed Emma and Kimber together in an embrace, and cried.

It finally dawned on Emma her mother had only been acting that way to scare the men and hadn't been furious with *her*. She broke down and cried happily with Mama.

"I'm sorry, Mama..." sniffled Emma.

"I know, Em." Mama kissed her forehead. "Yilithir and Strixian told us what happened. Nan kept trying to go after you, but you were moving around so much, so fast, she couldn't catch up."

"Oops." Emma bit her lip. "We were trying to go home." She explained about the map table, the teleportation... and the cat.

Mama skritched the cat under the chin. "Who's this new friend of yours?"

"That's..." Emma couldn't help but think of the manic expression on the cat's face when he dove at the pointer needle. "Pouncer."

Pouncer flattened his ears. "Not exactly the most dignified of names. Ahh well. A name given me by humans could have been much, much worse than 'Pouncer'. It will do."

Mama brushed a hand over Emma's hair. "I also understand Ylithir has already given you his blessing!"

"Yes!" Emma couldn't contain herself. She jumped around, spinning and cheering, doing all the celebrating she couldn't when she'd first been able to take the form of the wolf. In the midst of her elation, she ended up turning into a wolf pup entirely by accident.

Mama scooped her up and cradled her like a baby. "The Wolf Spirit is wise. He sees greatness in you, Emma. We will need to thank him with a proper ceremony."

Emma nodded eagerly, unable to resist the urge to yip at the sky.

After holding her for a while, Mama set her on her feet again. Emma shapeshifted back to normal and danced around a little more.

"How far is 'ome?" asked Kimber, still clinging to Mama's side.

"Not terribly far." Mama resumed walking. "Ambril, we've told your parents what happened. They know you've been jumping around the world. As soon as I sensed your return to Widowswood, I sent Tam to bring word to them."

"You let the boy go alone to town?" Emma winced. "How much trouble did he get into after doing what you asked?"

Mama exhaled. "An emergency. I needed to come find you, and your father is off in town somewhere. I did tell him to stay with the Starlings until I arrived to collect him."

"Are my parents angry with me?" whispered Ambril.

"I don't believe so." Mama smiled at her. "They kept asking if you were all right. I don't even think he remembered the golden box at all. He said something about trying to determine what it did, but he hadn't been able to get the lid open."

"What are you going to do with it?" asked Rin.

"Father will likely sell it for a staggering amount of gold." Ambril swiped a strand of hair out of her eyes. "I'm so filthy. It's going to take two hours in the bath to recover."

"It'll nae ever make it to ae shop," said Kimber. "Someone gonnae filch it."

"It *is* nice. It's also more trouble than it's worth." Emma frowned. "People won't stop stealing it."

Rin nodded. "It should belong to a wizard. Someone who can hide it where no one can see it or is so powerful no one would dare steal from them."

Emma peered at her.

"Not me." Rin held her hands up. "I'm not powerful."

"Mama..." Emma pulled on her mother's hand. "This is Rin. We found her in—"

"I know, dear." Mama smiled. "I also know you offered to let her stay with us. The forest spirits share much knowledge."

Emma grimace-smiled. *Pleeeeease.*

Mama laughed at her expression. "Rin is welcome under our roof."

The dark elf girl clutched both hands over her mouth. Tears welled up in the corners of her eyes.

"You'as cryin' when 'appy." Kimber poked her. "Is nae jes' humans bein' weird."

Rin burst into giggles.

Emma raced around in circles, going around and around Mama and the others as they walked back toward home, burning off all the excess energy her happiness poured on her.

DA CAME RUNNING OUT OF THE HOUSE AS THEY APPROACHED.

He rushed over, scooping Emma and Kimber up in a spinning hug, holding them for several minutes without saying a word. At that, Emma squeezed him tight. Da didn't say much when he got emotional. Even if it hadn't been her fault, their unintended adventure across the world scared him.

Tam zoomed out of the house, yelling, "Em, Kimber!" over and over while adding himself to the hug. The boy couldn't stop bouncing around and cheering that his sisters returned okay.

Emma contented herself to be held and loved, not trying to say anything.

Eventually, he reached a point where he could make himself set the girls down on their feet. As soon as the boy could reach, Tam clamp-hugged her. The look Da gave Emma made her suspect he'd want her to tell him everything that happened. It would probably take several nights curled up in his lap by the fireplace to get through the whole tale. Tam let go of Emma and clamp-hugged Kimber.

"Who's this?" Da glanced at Rin.

Emma introduced her.

Rin curtseyed.

"Another addition to the family." Mama patted Rin on the head.

"Well then. Welcome, child." Da picked her up and perched her on his side. "By Belephir, she's tiny. Got to get some food in this one."

"Da, she's an elf." Emma nudged him. "She's s'posed to be small."

"An elf, you say?" He tilted his head. "I'd scarcely noticed."

Rin managed a bashful smile.

A great raven cruised out of the trees, swooping in to land nearby. Pouncer came out of nowhere, leaping on the bird, a manic glint in his eyes. The raven burst into a swirl of black feathers and fog that turned into Nan—with a cat atop her head. Pouncer's wild-eyed expression said 'I have committed a grave error.'

Nan rested her hands on her walking stick and smirked at no one in particular.

"Oh, terribly sorry about that," said the cat.

With a faint grunt, Nan plucked the cat off her head and set him on the ground.

Kimber and Emma ran into a hug and yelled, "Nan!"

"I'm sorry for making you go all over." Emma bowed her head.

"It's all right, dear." Nan squeezed the girls back. "None of that. I'm glad you are home and safe."

"I hope it's okay we invited Rin to live with us." Emma peered up at her.

Nan's grandmotherly smile created a bloom of warmth within Emma's chest. "We are stewards of the wood who look after all creatures. It is in your nature to want to help any who need. This little one is welcome among us."

Emma bounced on her toes. "Thank you, Nan."

Her grandmother patted Rin on the shoulder. "Most little ones bring home squirrels or rabbits. I think we can make room for a slightly larger critter."

"We'as go' a cat, tae," chirped Kimber.

Nan shifted her gaze to Pouncer. "I noticed."

Da let out a sigh. "As much as I do not want to go anywhere right now, I must escort Ambril back to her home."

Ambril bounced, smiling. "Yes, please. Oh! Captain Dalen! There are men pretending to be servants. One thief said that *half* of my father's workers are impostors. They mean to kidnap me and steal from him."

"Indeed." Da frowned. "All right. The Watch will handle it. Point out any you recognize. We'll need to make a stop on the way to your home to collect a few more men."

"Of course." Ambril hugged Emma, Kimber, then Rin. "I have to go home now. Hope we can play again soon—without teleporting across the world."

"Yes." Emma grinned.

"That would be fun." Rin gazed around at the trees. "This place is so different."

"Aye. Wan't ae play wif dolls." Kimber laughed. "Go take yer baf."

Da escorted Ambril off down the road toward Widowswood Town.

"Come on, I'll show you our room." Emma took Rin's hand and tugged her toward the house.

Pouncer trotted after them. "Hmm. Not quite as luxurious as the box. Rustic. Yes, this will do."

Emma thought about Mama being much older than she looked and how she and Tam would live for a long time, too, much more than normal people. Thanks to Nan's ritual, Kimber became a *real* part of the family and would also live just as long as her. It would take Rin even longer than them to grow into an adult. Emma didn't know exactly how long she'd live, but she *did* know that in this dark elf girl, she'd found a friend she would not lose to time, and a friend she didn't have to keep any secrets from.

She couldn't have been happier.

fin

ACKNOWLEDGMENTS

Thank you for reading Emma and the Box of Wonder!

I had been meaning to keep going with the series for some time. Alas, other projects always seemed to pop up and demand attention first. When readers are looking for more in other series, it's sometimes difficult to make time for the ones with a smaller following. I'd like to thank a reader, Cam, for emailing me to ask about the Tales of Widowswood series. Their email is why I bumped Emma up on the schedule to now.

Additional thanks to Ricky Gunawan for the artwork and Lee Hargrove for editing!

ABOUT THE AUTHOR

Originally from South Amboy NJ, Matthew has been creating science fiction and fantasy worlds for most of his reasoning life. Since 1996, he has developed the "Divergent Fates" world, in which *Division Zero, Virtual Immortality, The Awakened Series, The Harmony Paradox, and the Daughter of Mars series* take place. Along with being an editor at Curiosity Quills press, he has worked in IT and technical support.

Matthew is an avid gamer, a recovered WoW addict, Gamemaster for two custom RPG systems, and a fan of anime, British humour, and intellectual science fiction that questions the nature of reality, life, and what happens after it.

He is also fond of cats.

Visit me online at:
Facebook: https://www.facebook.com/MatthewSCoxAuthor
Pinterest: https://www.pinterest.com/matthewcox10420/
Goodreads: https://www.goodreads.com/author/show/7712730.Matthew_S_Cox
Email: mcox2112@gmail.com

OTHER BOOKS BY MATTHEW S. COX

Divergent Fates Universe Novels

Division Zero series

- Division Zero
- Lex De Mortuis
- Thrall
- Guardian
- Harbinger
- The Shadow Fixer
- Neuroshock

The Awakened series

- Prophet of the Badlands
- Archon's Queen
- Grey Ronin
- Daughter of Ash
- Zero Rogue
- Angel Descended

Daughter of Mars series

- The Hand of Raziel
- Araphel
- Ghost Black

Virtual Immortality series

- Virtual Immortality
- The Harmony Paradox

Prophet of the Badlands Series

- Prophet's Journey
- Prophet's Mercy

Divergent Fates Anthology

(Fiction Novels - Adult)

The Roadhouse Chronicles Series

- One More Run
- The Redeemed
- Dead Man's Number

Faded Skies series

- Heir Ascendant
- Ascendant Unrest
- Ascendant Revolution

Temporal Armistice Series

- Nascent Shadow
- The Shadow Collector
- The Gate to Oblivion
- The Queen of Discord
- The Burning Alchemist

Vampire Innocent series

- A Nighttime of Forever
- A Beginner's Guide to Fangs
- The Artist of Ruin

- The Last Family Road Trip
- The Phantom Oracle
- How Not to Summon Demons
- Ordinary Problems of a College Vampire
- A Vampire's Guide to Surviving Holidays
- An Introduction to Paranormal Diplomacy
- A Vampire's Guide to Adulting
- How to Stop a Vampire War in Six Easy Steps
- Ancient Vampire Death Cults and Other Annoyances
- Hunting Vampires for Fun and Profit
- A String of Seriously Unlucky Events
- The Summer of Completely Usual Strangeness
- Demonic Crisis Management for the Modern Vampire

Standalones

- Wayfarer: AV494
- Axillon99
- Chiaroscuro: The Mouse and the Candle
- The Spirits of Six Minstrel Run
- Sophie's Light
- The Far Side of Promise anthology
- Operation: Chimera (with Tony Healey)
- The Dysfunctional Conspiracy (with Christopher Veltmann)
- Of Myth and Shadow
- The Girl Who Found the Sun

Winter Solstice series (with J.R. Rain)

- Convergence
- Containment
- Catalyst
- Catacombs

Alexis Silver series (with J.R. Rain)

- Silver Light
- Deep Silver
- Silver Quarrel
- Silver Crucible
- Silver Heart

Samantha Moon Origins series (with J.R. Rain)

- New Moon Rising
- Moon Mourning
- Haunted Moon

Vampire For Hire series (with J.R. Rain)

- Moon Master
- Dead Moon
- Lost Moon
- Vampire Destiny
- Infinite Moon
- Vampire Empress
- Moon Elder
- Wicked Moon
- Moon Blade

Maddy Wimsey series (with J.R. Rain)

- The Devil's Eye
- The Drifting Gloom
- Dark Mercy
- Primal Wrath

Samantha Moon Case Files series (with J.R. Rain)

- Blood Moon

Immortal Operative (with J.R. Rain)

- Broken Ice
- Broken Wing

Four Elements series (with J.R. Rain)

- The Elementalist
- The Black Rose
- The Wakefield Curse

Witches series (with J.R. Rain)

- The Witch and the Hangman

Zeb Clemens series (with J.R. Rain)

- The Beast of Devil's Creek
- Wanted: Undead or Alive

Young Adult Novels

The Eldritch Heart Series

- The Eldritch Heart
- The Cursed Crown
- The Sapphire Soul

Evergreen Series

- Evergreen
- The World That Remains

- The Lucky Ones
- Nuclear Summer
- The Nuclear Frontier
- The World We Make
- The Threat Unseen

Progenitor Series

- Out of Sight
- Out of Mind

Diary of a Teenage Fey

(Short story series)

- Elder Horror
- The Hag of Barrow Falls
- Babysitter's Nightmare
- Lharakki
- Bauble for a Soul
- Simulacrum
- Amorphous
- Manticore

Standalones

- Caller 107
- The Summer the World Ended
- Nine Candles of Deepest Black
- The Forest Beyond the Earth

Middle Grade Novels

The Adventures of Ubergirl series

- My Dad is a Mad Scientist
- Aliens Ate My Homework
- The End of all Halloweens
- Dr. Infinity and the Soul Smasher

Tales of Widowswood series

- Emma and the Banderwigh
- Emma and the Silk Thieves
- Emma and the Silverbell Faeries
- Emma and the Elixir of Madness
- Emma and the Weeping Spirit

Standalones

- Citadel: The Concordant Sequence
- The Cursed Codex
- The Menagerie of Jenkins Bailey